PRELUDE

Eric gazed at the remarkably beautiful face so close to his. From the moment he had first seen her at her party, he had been inexplicably drawn to her, and now he longed to take her in his arms and make her want him as much as he wanted her. He looked into her eyes. "Don't underestimate my expertise," he warned. "My reputation speaks for itself."

Andy looked back at him. It was all she could do to keep from touching his curly blond hair. "Reputations can be created by publicity departments," she murmured. "I've always been more interested in action than reputation." She moved closer to him until their legs were touching.

They stared into each other's eyes for a few moments. Eric reached over and stroked her cheek gently, then drew her lips to his. Andy responded with overwhelming passion and then buried her face in his chest. "Come home with me," she whispered breathlessly. "I need you to come home with me."

(Cover photograph posed by professional models)

Also by Wendy Susans:

DUET

WENDY SUSANS
Promises To Keep

LEISURE BOOKS   NEW YORK CITY

A LEISURE BOOK

Published by

Dorchester Publishing Co., Inc.
6 East 39th Street
New York, NY 10016

Copyright©1987 by Wendy Susans

All rights reserved. No part of this book may be reproduced or transmitted in any form or by any electronic or mechanical means, including photocopying, recording, or by any information storage and retrieval systems, without the written permission of the Publisher, except where permitted by law.

Printed in the United States of America

Promises To Keep

May

The sun was just beginning to rise over the East River, bathing the 59th Street Bridge in a rosy glow. Light bounced off the towering skyscrapers, making the canyons beneath them seem even darker. An occasional taxi passed by, its headlights illuminating early morning joggers on their way to Central Park. New York City was on the brink of its daily rebirth—the cutting edge between the relative stillness of the night and the frenetic activity of the day.

Hidden behind the doors of their fashionable East Side brownstones, the rich and the famous were just waking up to begin their day. At 275 East 67th Street, however, the lights had been blazing for hours. An irate Andy Reuben paced back and forth in her living room, a cordless telephone clutched tightly in her hand.

"Look Ian, I don't care how many sell-outs

there are! I will not schedule any more concerts! One in each city, that's it! I'll be doing almost a concert a night and I *need* those few days off." Andy ran her hand through her curly blond hair. "Hey, I've just about had it with this tour already. Keep pushing me like this and I'll cancel the whole thing!" She listened for a moment, then snapped. "Well, Freddie may have told you that, but it doesn't mean I agree. That's right, it's my final word. Goodbye." She slammed the phone down on the table. "Damn Freddie! How dare he make decisions like that without consulting me!"

Emotionally drained, she curled up in the overstuffed wing chair by the fireplace. Tasha, her white angora cat, jumped into her lap and began to purr contentedly. Sometimes Andy felt as though Tasha was her only comfort. She leaned her head back, closed her eyes and thought back on the past ten years. Her rise to stardom had exacted more changes in her life than simply wealth and fame. Slowly but surely she had begun to have more confidence in her ability to make decisions. And that confidence was creating problems within her marriage. Her husband's imperious attitude towards her was getting on her nerves. It would be easier to deal with if she didn't care about Fred, but he was very dear to her. His love, his tempering influence and his unique understanding of what made her tick had sustained her through her most difficult times. The trouble was that she felt strong now, and she desperately wanted to take control of her own life. Freddie, however, refused to believe in her competence and continued to treat her as an errant child who needed his complete guidance. It was as if he felt that the busier he kept her, the more she would need him to manage her affairs. He didn't realize that all he was succeeding in doing was driving her away.

She smiled as her mind drifted to her identical twin whose life was nearly as complicated as hers, but who seemed to be able to balance it better. To her, Laurie was incredible—a superwoman. Her sister's ability to raise a child alone while maintaining a successful career as a physician constantly amazed Andy.

Snapping out of her reverie, Andy stood up and checked her watch. She looked down at her faded Calvin Klein jeans, old Radcliffe College sweatshirt and bare feet and realized that she had better start getting ready for the Rolling Stone interview scheduled for that morning. As she walked toward the stairs, a glance out the window revealed her husband coming up the front steps.

Fred was a walking ad for Brooks Brothers. His slim six foot frame perfectly carried the natural shoulder, three button, center vent gray chalk-striped flannel suits with cuffed trousers he invariably wore. His blue oxford button-down shirt was closed at the collar and he wore a blue and red diagonally striped silk tie. His short haircut hadn't changed since his undergraduate days at Harvard, and even then he had been out of step with the times. By anyone's standards Fred was considered handsome, although there was a remoteness about him that caused some people to label him as a snob. Those who knew him well were impressed with his business acumen—he was generally credited with building Andy's career and converting her into a multimillionaire. He was her manager and producer as well as the co-owner with Andy and several other rock stars of Nickelodean Records. To the outside world he was Andy's Rock of Gibraltar, her anchor. The problem was that she didn't see him as such. He had the distinct impression that she was ready to weigh anchor and take off without him.

Fred smiled sardonically as his wife opened the door. "My, what service! This must be a first! The great Andy Reuben deigns to come to the door herself."

Andy shook her head. "I don't need any of your sarcasm, Freddie. It's about time you showed up. Did you forget that we have an interview scheduled for this morning?"

"You know I never forget these things. After all, we must do whatever is good for the business, and certainly a spread in Rolling Stone is excellent for my dear wife's wonderful image." He started up the stairs. "I'm going to take a quick shower and change before breakfast." He hesitated and turned back to her. "Look, Andy, I'm sorry about last night. I shouldn't have walked out like that."

Andy walked over to the stairs and looked up at him. "No, you shouldn't have. I can't remember the last time we actually finished a discussion. One of us always walks out before we settle things. I told you last night that I didn't want any more concerts on this tour, and this morning I get a call from Ian confirming the extra dates. How dare you!"

"Andy," he said patiently, "I tried to explain it to you last night. Philadelphia, Atlanta, Chicago and Denver were sold out within hours and there's a stipulation in those contracts that if they sold out within a certain amount of time we were obligated to provide an extra date. I'm sorry, I know how much you wanted to go to Melissa's graduation. I just couldn't help it."

Andy sat down on the steps and put her head in her hands. "I had it all set up," she said wistfully. "I was going to fly to Boston the morning after the Atlanta concert, stay overnight and then go on to Chicago from there. She's my baby sister, Freddie, and I wanted to see her graduate from college so badly! It was going to be such a great surprise. . . ."

"I know. But it can't be helped."

"It could have been helped! You had no right to put that into the contract. You knew that I had this planned. I only like to do one concert per city anyway." She looked up and glared at him. "Why do you do this to me? I'm telling you once and for all, that was the last contract you draw up without my approval."

"Oh no you don't!" he said angrily. "I won't have you tying my hands like that!"

"That's exactly what I want to do. You're pushing me too hard and I won't stand for it any more. I want more control."

He pursed his lips and stared at her. "Mmm, we'll see. Right now we have that interview and I want to get ready." He turned and continued upstairs. "Why don't you do the same."

"I don't know why I bother talking to you," she muttered to his retreating back. "You never listen to me anyway."

Philip had barely thought about Andy in the ten years since he had last seen her. His visit to the doctor had changed all that. Originally, they had thought that his wife, Marilyn, had some sort of problem that prevented her from conceiving. It was obvious now that the mild case of mumps he had suffered from two years earlier had caused him to become sterile.

He'd had a chance to have a child, though, when he was in law school. He'd been in love with Andy Rabinowitz, and she had become pregnant and had an abortion without telling him. The pain of that loss, long forgotten, now returned to him so powerfully that he felt drowned in it. He'd wanted the child she had been carrying, and all she had wanted was her independence. She hadn't been concerned with anyone's needs but her own. He clenched his fists in anger and said aloud, "If only I hadn't told Marilyn about the abortion. Damn my pride, if only I hadn't told her about Andy. Now I'll never hear the end of it." He sat down at his desk, opened his briefcase and tried to do some work.

Joyce Jones climbed the steps of the 67th

Street brownstone and rang the doorbell. As she waited, she admired the stained glass windows that were framed in the heavy oak door. Within seconds, the door opened. "I'm Joyce Jones from Rolling Stone. Ms. Reuben is expecting me."

"Yes, come in," Andy's housekeeper, Alice, said. The plump, pleasant-faced woman ushered the reporter through a panelled foyer into a magnificent living room. "Please make yourself comfortable. Ms. Reuben will be down in a moment. There's coffee and tea on the table over there, please help yourself." She smiled and left the room.

Joyce walked over, poured herself a cup of coffee and took a small danish. She sat down on a straight-backed chair and looked around. The highly polished wood floor was covered with thick oriental rugs. Wine-colored velvet draperies framing the windows blended gracefully with the busy patterns of the obviously antique furniture. No two pieces matched, but the effect was charming. An unusual lamp caught her eye and she got up to look at it more closely.

"I thought so," Joyce murmured to herself, "Tiffany." The house was not what she had expected. It was very elegant and carefully planned. It didn't fit Andy Reuben's casual, impetuous image at all. Joyce turned around and looked at the paintings that hung on the pale pink walls. Picasso lithographs were grouped with Gropper drawings, and over the fireplace was a large Georgia O'Keefe canvas. A small Degas oil was placed just to the right of the entrance to the room. As Joyce moved over to study it, the doors slid open and Andy Reuben entered.

She stood framed in the doorway for a moment, her striking blue eyes staring through tinted oversized glasses. As was her custom, she was dressed fastidiously. The white cotton slacks she wore were tailored to accentuate her extreme thinness. In fact, she was so thin and her legs were so long that she appeared even taller than her 5-feet 8-inches. A two-inch braided brown leather belt encircled her tiny waist, and a thin black tie hung under the wing tip collar on her white blouse. Her permed blond hair was a study in controlled disarray and it surrounded an angular but delicate and appealing face. She exuded an aura of leashed energy, yet her appearance was as fragile as an eggshell.

Andy smiled when she saw Joyce standing in front of the Degas. "Like it? I acquired it about a month ago. Actually it was quite a find. I'd been looking for something like it for a long time." She stood next to Joyce, folded her arms and fondly gazed at the picture.

At that moment Fred walked in and held out his hand. "Ms. Jones? I'm Fred Arnold. Shall we start?" He steered Joyce to an easy chair and sat down on the couch. "Andy, come sit down."

Reluctantly, Andy left her painting and sat down on the edge of the couch next to Fred. She nervously clasped her hands together so tightly that her knuckles turned white. Interviews were very difficult for her, and she usually allowed Fred to do much of the initial talking. As he

PROMISES TO KEEP

explained about the coming tour and the new album, Andy thought of the long two months that lay ahead of her. She hated the thought of leaving New York. She would miss her sister Laurie and her niece, Bette, and she wished anew that she could be going to Melissa's graduation. She wouldn't be around for Melissa's move to New York, either. Andy sighed. It seemed as if she missed every important family occasion, and she resolved to do something special to try to make it up to her baby sister.

"Andy, aren't you listening?" Fred snapped, interrupting her daydreaming. "Joyce just asked you a question."

Andy blinked her eyes and apologized. "Excuse me, I was thinking of everything I have to do before I leave tomorrow. Could you please repeat the question?"

Joyce smiled stiffly. "I just said that this album of yours is radically different, and I was curious to know whether you were changing your style."

"Actually, as I'm sure you know by now, no two of my albums are ever the same. But yes, I think my style is changing somewhat. It's a natural evolution—something I think should happen to any good musician. I was not terribly pleased with my last album because I didn't think it was innovative enough—"

"But it still went platinum," Joyce cut in. "I assume it made you quite a bit of money—"

"Double platinum," Andy interrupted, sighing. "I don't really care about the money; my records always make plenty. I need to do interesting things, otherwise I get bored."

Joyce turned to Fred, who looked on with amusement. "Any comment?"

Fred shrugged his shoulders. "Andy is a genius, a musical genius. We try to keep her as happy as we can, then we're sure that the artistic juices will keep flowing." He looked at his wife and winked at her.

Shifting in her seat, Joyce glanced at her notes and asked, "Any plans for another movie? After all, you did win an Oscar for best song last year."

Andy shook her head and smiled. "Yeah, I know that 'Hot Moves' did well at the box office, but I personally didn't care for it. Actually, the money is pretty bad for the time you have to put in, and I really don't like making movies. All that waiting around and—"

"Andy is discussing another film deal now," Fred interrupted, "but we really don't want to talk about it until it's firmed up."

Andy looked sharply at her husband and narrowed her eyes. "I am *not* discussing another film deal," she said under her breath, "and you know it. I better not find out that you are."

Fred closed his eyes and ignored her. "The tour will be winding up on the West Coast and we'll see what happens out there." He put his hand on Andy's arm and squeezed it.

Missing none of this byplay, Joyce continued. "Speaking of the tour, is your health good enough for the strenuous activity?"

"I've had no problems lately. The transplanted

PROMISES TO KEEP

kidney is functioning well. You know that my twin sister, Laurie, donated it to me."

"That was seven years ago, right?" Andy nodded. "You were living on the West Coast while you were filming the movie. Any plans to leave New York and move there for good?"

Andy laughed. "No, New York is my home. I feel more comfortable here. I like the diversity of people and the excitement."

Joyce looked up. "Sometimes it gets a little too exciting. There's a lot of danger here, too. Especially for a famous, controversial figure."

Andy pursed her lips. "I know that for awhile many of my friends were hiring bodyguards, but I never thought it was necessary. Not that I think of myself as immortal, I know all too well how mortal I am. But I can't live in fear. I enjoy my life very much. *Que sera, sera.*"

Fred nodded in agreement. "There's no question that there's a lot of violence out there, not only against the famous but against everyone. We live our lives as best we can. We have more immediate problems anyway."

Joyce smiled and asked, "Does that mean that the rumors of discord between the two of you are true?"

Andy looked at Fred and answered, "There's no discord between us. We understand each other."

"But there are persistant rumors that the two of you are very close to separation—"

Andy interrupted sharply. "Separation is out of the question. What is between us privately is just that, absolutely nobody else's business.

There are definitely no plans at all to split."

"Andy and I have a relationship that some might find . . . different," Fred joined in. "We are two very opinionated people who want what's best for each other. Don't forget that besides being Andy's husband, I'm also her business manager and record producer. So of course it would be natural for us to disagree occasionally on what is best for her career. We do try to separate the business from the marriage, most of the time successfully."

"And the rest of the time?" Joyce asked.

Andy stood up abruptly and turned to Fred. "That's it. We have no more time for this. I have to go upstairs now." She walked towards the hallway and then turned back. "I hope you got what you wanted. Good-bye."

Joyce turned off the tape recorder, stood up and shrugged her shoulders. "Friendly, isn't she?"

"I would say that she was quite friendly," Fred said softly. "You people do so love to goad her, don't you?" He shook Joyce's hand and led her to the front door. "Thank you for coming. We look forward to seeing the article in print." He shut the door behind her and headed for the stairs. It wouldn't do to have Andy too overwrought before her tour.

Dr. Laurel Rabinowitz locked her apartment door and gently took her daughter's hand. "Come on, Bette, you don't want to be late for school, do you?"

Bette shook her head. "No, mommy, we're

making Mother's Day presents today and I want to surprise you."

Laurie smiled and said, "Guess what? I'll be picking you up from school today. We'll come home, change you into something really pretty, and then we're going to go over to Andy's for dinner. She's leaving tomorrow, and it would be nice for us to see her before she goes."

"Where is she going, mommy?"

"She's going on tour, honey. Remember, I told you that she travels to different cities to sing her songs?"

"I like her songs. Can we go to her concert?"

"Well, I think if you ask her nicely, she would sing some of her songs just for you. You know how much she enjoys doing that."

"I love her so much. I wish we could see her every day."

"That would be nice, but our schedules don't always coincide. Hey, let's move it. We've really got to hurry." Laurie pressed the elevator button and impatiently ran her hand through her short straight blond hair. Although she and Andy were indentical twins there would be no mistaking one for the other anymore. Laurie had none of Andy's ethereal look. Her 5-feet 8-inches was solidly built, and she was as no-nonsense as she appeared. Her tastes tended toward the functional rather than the artistic, and she felt most comfortable wearing tailored clothes such as the shirtwaist dress she was wearing on this day. Instead of glasses she wore contact lenses because they gave her better peripheral vision. If you asked anyone who knew her to describe Laurie, they would invariably say that she was a warm and loving person who would rather give than take. It was these qualities, in addition to her skills as a doctor, that had led her to being appointed head of New York Hospital's Neonatal Critical Care Unit at the age of 30.

The past five years, however, had not been easy for Laurie. Besides her demanding job, she'd had to raise her daughter alone. Her marriage to Dr. Edward Chancellor had been shaky from the start. She had always suspected that part of the reason he'd been initially interested in her was because Andy was her twin sister. She never pretended to be as exciting and sophisticated as Andy, she never even wanted to be. She was happy with her work and with her marriage, but Chance wanted something different. It became painfully clear to her one night when he called out Andy's name in the middle of their lovemaking.

After that, it had become increasingly difficult for her to have sex with him. Chance began staying out late and then not coming home at all until, for all intents and purposes, their marriage was over. It was ironic that amidst all this discord the best thing that ever happened to her was conceived. Late one night, Chance returned home drunk, came into her bed and they made love. When he found out that she was pregnant, he wanted her to have an abortion. "We don't have a marriage," he said. "Why should we have a child?"

Laurie had thought about having an abortion,

PROMISES TO KEEP

but ultimately decided against it, and instead divorced Chance. He moved to England, and was killed in a car accident some years later. He never saw Bette.

Laurie looked down at her daughter as they entered the elevator. How empty her life would have been without her daughter to come home to at night! She smiled and pulled Bette to her as the door closed.

It was cool for a May evening, and Laurie was glad she had insisted that Bette wear her winter jacket. Anxious to get to Andy's house, Bette excitedly skipped ahead of her mother. "Don't even think of crossing the street without me!" Laurie called as she hurried to catch up. Bette's independence was increasingly worrying her. Sometimes she despaired of ever being able to control the child again. She reminded Laurie so much of how Andy had been when they were children: curious, headstrong and stubborn. She took her daughter's hand as they crossed to the other side of 67th Street and didn't let go until they reached Andy's townhouse.

The minute the door opened, Bette ran past her aunt and uncle to the kitchen where Alice was busy preparing dinner.

"Where's Tasha?" she demanded, referring to Andy's cat. "I want to play with Tasha!"

Alice laughed. "I think she knew you were coming. We haven't seen her for hours."

Bette's face fell. "Doesn't she like me anymore?"

"She would like you better if you didn't dress her up in your doll's clothes and drag her all over the house!"

Bette hid the tiny dress she had brought from home behind her back and solemnly said, "I won't dress her up any more, I just want to see her. Can you help me find her?"

"Well, if you promise not to upset her, I think she might be sleeping on my bed."

"Oh, thank you, Alice! I'll be careful of her." Bette scampered into Alice's bedroom, which was off the kitchen.

Shaking her head, Alice picked up the dishes and went to set the dining room table for dinner.

In the living room, Fred offered Laurie a glass of wine. She took it and turned to Andy, realizing that something was most definitely bothering her. "What's wrong?" she asked.

"Why don't you ask my husband? He fancies himself my spokesperson anyway."

"But I'm asking you. Don't pull me into any of your arguments."

Andy shook her head and set her lips in a thin straight line.

Resigned, Laurie turned to Fred. "I give up. You tell me."

"I'm sorry, Laurie, but I don't think that Andy will be able to get up to Boston for Melissa's graduation. She's going to have to do an extra concert that night in Atlanta." He moved to put an arm around Andy, but she violently shrugged him off.

"But it was all set," Laurie protested. "What

happened?"

"I really don't want to talk about it." Andy walked across the room, her back to Laurie and Fred. Laurie opened her mouth to speak, but a glance from Fred made her think the better of it. At that moment, Alice called them all to dinner.

During the meal, Andy relaxed and began enjoying the company of her sister and niece. It was only when she was with them that she felt she could let down her guard and not live up to some nebulous image that had been fashioned for her. Sometimes the strain of projecting that image was too much for her and she longed for a simpler, more serene existence. It was not that she didn't revel in her fame, it was just that it exacted such a high price.

Alice cleared the dinner away and asked if Andy, Fred and Laurie would like some coffee. "Yes, thank you, Alice," Fred answered. "Oh, and I promised Bette some of your homemade ice cream. Would you bring some out for her?"

Laurie looked at Andy and asked, "So, exactly how long will this tour last?"

"Oh, almost two months. I'll be going to, I think, forty cities and I'll wind up in L.A. Fred's going to meet me there. Then we're going to head for Hawaii for some rest before the concert here in New York." She took a sip of her coffee, then brightened as a thought struck her. "Hey! I have an idea. Why don't you guys meet us in Hawaii? We'd have a great time. I'm renting a house right on the beach complete with staff, so Bette would be taken care of."

Wendy Susans

Laurie thought for a moment. "When will you end up there?"

"Probably around mid-July, give or take a few days," Fred answered. "I think it would be terrific if the two of you could join us."

Bette pulled on her mother's sleeve. "Can we mommy? Oh, please! I want to see hula girls."

Laurie looked down at her daughter and smiled. "Well, I am due for two weeks in July. I was going to postpone it, but I don't think I can pass this up."

"Fantastic! Then it's settled. Fred will make the reservations for you and arrange to have you picked up at the airport." Andy took her coffee cup and walked away from the table. "Come on, folks, let's go sit in the living room." The adults moved to the next room while Bette remained, eating her dessert.

Laurie sat down facing Andy. "I spoke to Ma yesterday. She said she hadn't spoken to you in quite a while. Apparently she's tried to get through to you, but she never catches you at home. She complained that you don't call her back. I really think you should let her know that you won't be up for the graduation."

Andy nodded her head ruefully. "I know, I know. Believe me, I'm not looking forward to talking to her. She's sure to blame me and say I did it on purpose—that I really don't want to be there. Little does she know. . . ."

"Why do you always create a scenario in your mind about what Ma's reaction will be? Maybe this time she'll surprise you. Anyway, it seems that Melissa has a steady guy now, and Mom thinks it might be serious. He's a professional squash player, of all things."

"A professional squash player? I never knew there was such a thing. What does he do for a living?"

"I'm not quite sure. It seems he started playing squash when he was at Dartmouth and is trying to make a career of it. I know, it sounds strange to me, too, but after all, you know what a jock Melissa is."

Andy thought of the ordeal that lay ahead of her. Calling her mother was one of her least favorite things to do. "I'll call Adrienne tonight," she said with a sigh. "I really have been swamped lately, and my hours have been crazy. First of all, the record industry is not what it used to be. Last quarter profits at Nickelodean were down twenty-two percent. We're experimenting with videos now—it seems to be the wave of the future. I've also had to get my band together for the tour, and the rehearsals have been going lousy, so they last into the wee hours. Then I've had to have fittings . . ." She put her hand to her forehead and closed her eyes. "Oh, I'm not going to bore you any more with my problems. I'm sure you aren't really interested."

Knowing the pressure that his wife was under, Fred intervened. Turning to Laurie, he said gently, "Perhaps we should call it a night. Look at Bette, she fell asleep in her ice cream." They looked toward the dining room and saw the little girl, head on the table and curly blond hair dipped in chocolate ice cream. Tasha stood on the table, busily lapping up the leftover melted dessert.

Laurie jumped up and quickly went to rescue her daughter. "I guess it's time to go home. I have an early call tomorrow, anyway. Fred, would you please call a cab for us?"

"It's okay, Laurie, I'll drive you home. I have to stop at Nickelodean." Fred took the sleeping child from his sister-in-law's arms and the group walked to the garage.

Andy and Laurie stood side by side, watching as Fred settled Bette in the car and strapped her in. "I'll see you in July, Laur," Andy said, hugging her sister. "Take care now."

"*You* take care. I still worry about you, you know."

Andy smiled and took Laurie's hand. "I know, big sister. Hey, don't, I'll be okay."

Laurie looked into her sister's eyes. "I mean it. I don't want to see a wreck when I get to Hawaii."

Andy shrugged her shoulders, and said mockingly, "Then don't come!"

"Oh no, you won't get me to cancel this vacation that easily. See you in Hawaii, kid. I'm going to miss you." Laurie kissed her sister on the cheek and slid into the car.

It was 2 A.M., and Fred had just returned from the Nickelodean offices. He took off his clothes and carefully hung them up, slipped into a robe and headed for the shower. Turning on the shower massage, he directed the pulsating spray toward

PROMISES TO KEEP

his back and luxuriated in the invigorating sting of the hot water on his skin.

Fred had first met Andy when she was a Harvard medical student singing at the coffee shop he managed. It had been his third time as a senior at Harvard, and he never did get his diploma. Instead, he followed Andy to New York when she asked him to manage her fledgling career. When she started making money in earnest, he was right there to advise and invest it for her. The deal for Nickelodean had been a coup, and after that there'd been no stopping them. Since then, it seemed that everything he touched turned to gold. Except, perhaps, his marriage, which was definitely deteriorating.

As he turned to adjust the spray, he felt a draft and saw Andy slip into the stall with him.

"Well, I had to take a shower anyway, and why waste water?"

Fred put his hands on his hips and smiled. "What's the use? I can't stay mad at you, no matter how hard I try. Anyway, I was just figuring out a way to sneak into your room." He pulled her all the way into the shower and hugged her tightly. "God, you feel so good," he whispered. "You're warm and soft—"

"—and wet," Andy finished for him. She laughed as she picked up the soap and started to slide the bar over his body.

"Stop it!" he yelled. "That tickles!" He grabbed her hands and pulled her toward him.

"I want you now," she said as she put her arms around his waist and lay her head on his chest.

Filled with desire, he lifted her, pushed open the shower door and carried her to his bed. Sopping wet, they clung to each other. Fred stroked Andy's hair as he gently kissed her neck, then ran his tongue down her body.

"Freddie," she moaned. "Come on, love me now." She shivered as she felt his familiar touch. The old comfortable feeling of security and warmth enveloped her as she gave into his passion and matched it with her own. His masculine scent overwhelmed her and she tenderly kissed the hollow of his throat, softly repeating his name over and over again. He looked deeply into her eyes and held her close to him as she traced the outline of his lips with her finger. "It's always best with you, Fred. You make me feel so comfortable. I love feeling comfortable...."

He kissed the tears on her cheeks and covered her body with his. Slowly, he made love with her. "Ahh, Andy, it's so good, you're so good," he murmured as he buried his head in her breasts.

She kissed his thick dark hair. "For me, too, Fred. Please, I don't want to leave you this time. I'm scared of what might happen. Maybe you should come on the tour with me. Please? I get so lonely. I need..."

He wrapped his arms around her and hugged her. "I know, baby. If I could drop everything and go with you I would. I have too many commitments here, though. Nickelodean needs me in New York. You know we're having problems."

PROMISES TO KEEP

"What about my problems?"

He closed his eyes and sighed. "I'm sorry."

Andy pulled away abruptly and reached for a cigarette. It was as if his words confirmed the growing distance between them. "It's too bad we can't spend our life in bed, we're so good there. No fights, no digs, nothing but loving." She turned to him. "Fred, I wish you'd help me. I feel so trapped."

"Oh, here we go again. I'm tired of hearing how trapped you are. You're only as trapped as you make yourself. Who the hell traps you? I don't. There's nobody on earth with a freer marriage. I tolerate everything and anything you do, and man, you can think up things that can boggle anyone's mind. Come on, you're a big girl now. Not only are you unbelievably famous, you're also fantastically rich. How in heaven's name can you feel trapped except in your own mind?" He got out of bed and put on his robe.

"Oh, yes you do trap me!" Andy flung back at him. "You know full well that I hate half the things that I do. Wait, strike that, I hate ninety percent of the things that I do. I hate tours, so you set up another tour. I hate movies, so you're working out a deal for me to go to Hollywood to make some pictures. I hate business and now I have to worry about Nickelodean going under. If that isn't being trapped, I don't know what is." She fell back on the pillow and closed her eyes. "All I want is to write and sing my songs. I don't want to do anything else."

"That's impossible! You're Andy Reuben! You

can do it all! You're the best in the business, you can do anything! I want to do so much more for you. Remember our dreams? Remember when we started? We were going to show them—"

"Fred, we have shown them! We've surpassed our wildest dreams, and I'm tired now. I want to sit back and enjoy what we've done."

"No! It's not the time to let up yet. Anyway, don't tell me that you don't want the power and the recognition and the money."

"That's not what I mean! I—Oh, Fred, you get me so confused. The only thing I do know is that I don't want what you're pushing me into right now."

He paced back and forth in front of the bed, nervously running his hands through his hair. "Andy, it's just that I love you so much. I'm trying so hard to do what is best for you. Please, babe, I only want to know that you still love me."

Andy got out of bed and walked towards her husband. "I do love you, Fred, and I do need you, in many ways. It's just, oh, I don't know. As trapped as I am now, maybe I'd be a damn sight more trapped without you."

Fred held her close. "I'd miss you and your temper tantrums. My life would be so strange without you." He put his hands on her shoulders and looked into her eyes. "Ah, Andy, I hate to see you so torn up."

She averted her face. "I'm going to go to sleep now. I'm really tired. I'll see you in the morning. Don't worry, I'll handle it somehow." She kissed him softly on the lips and went back to her own room.

PROMISES TO KEEP

Fred lit a cigarette and sat down in his reclining chair, unable to even think about going to sleep. It seemed Andy was as impossible to handle as ever. He despaired of her ever growing up, but then, most of the people he knew in the business were exactly the same: forever children, needing attention and reassurance, but not wanting the responsibility of growing up. Still, he loved her, and wished with all his heart that he could make her happy. The problem was, he simply did not know how. He took a puff of his cigarette, ground it out, then headed for bed. He knew that even if they stayed in bed forever, as Andy had said, they would still fight, and their marriage would wear thin. Andy didn't even suggest staying with him all night. "Shit," he said out loud. He didn't want to lose her, but he wasn't sure there was anything he could do to prevent it. Wearily he closed his eyes and fell into a troubled sleep.

He put the ticket to his lips and kissed it. He was lucky to have gotten such a great seat. Her Philadelphia concert had been sold out for weeks. The scalper had charged him one hundred bucks, but it was worth every penny. He had never missed an Andy Reuben concert. To him, she was an angel, an absolute angel. He had been following her career since it had started and, as far as he was concerned, she was getting better and better. He remembered when she'd been so sick with her kidney problem, and how he had written her note after note pleading with her to get well. Even though she had been unable to answer him, he knew she had gotten the notes and he was positive that he had helped her recover.

He'd been pleased when he'd read she had married her manager. Mr. Arnold was the only one who could keep her on the straight and narrow. Sometimes Andy got into trouble, and it was important that she remain an angel. He had even written to Mr. Arnold to tell him that marrying Andy was the best thing for him to do, and Mr. Arnold had written him back thanking him for his good wishes. The letter was safe in his desk drawer, and sometimes, when he was feeling depressed, he would read it and it would make him feel better. Perhaps he would write them another letter telling them that he still cared. They would be happy to hear that. Right now he had to get ready for the concert. He had to shower and shave and put on his new tie. He was sure that she would know he was there and that George Sloane still cared.

June

The Boston suburb of Brookline lay right on the edge of the city. A predominantly middle-class neighborhood, it was filled with substantial single family homes and attractive brick apartment buildings. Harvard's medical school was located there, as well as several world famous hospitals. The MTA, Boston's renowned transit system, cuts through Brookline's heart, down Commonwealth Avenue, making it a popular bedroom community for city commuters.

The Rabinowitz home on Longwood Avenue had been built in 1928. It was a three-bedroom brick colonial on a quarter acre plot, very well maintained and occupied now only by Adrienne Rabinowitz and her youngest daughter, Melissa. Ben, Adrienne's husband, had died six years earlier.

Adrienne, an attractive, slightly plump woman

with graying red hair, sprayed some wax on the baby grand piano and rubbed it vigorously with a chamois cloth. Melissa would be graduating from Boston University tomorrow, and by next week she would be in New York living with her boyfriend, Shep Greenberg. This was a source of great aggravation to Adrienne, but it was impossible for her to talk to her twenty-one year old daughter about it.

Frowning, she glanced up at the clock. Laurel and Bette were late and she was getting worried. She thought with irritation about Andrea and their last phone conversation. As usual, it was brief and Andrea wouldn't let her get a word in edgewise. Andrea had announced in her most royal voice that she would be unable to attend graduation because of prior commitments. Prior commitments! She knew about the graduation months ago, so why did she make any plans for that day? Adrienne knew why: it was because she didn't want to be there! Not that she was surprised Andrea wouldn't attend, it had been more of a surprise that she had even mentioned coming. She tried so hard to be patient with her famous daughter but she was fighting a losing battle. She might as well just give up attempting to understand Andrea, Adrienne thought, and accept the fact that her daughter wanted nothing to do with her. Laurel, though, was different. Even though it had been some time since Adrienne had seen her, Laurel kept her supplied with letters and photographs of her only grandchild. She smiled as she thought of Bette. The sound of a car pulling into the driveway roused

PROMISES TO KEEP

her out of her reverie. She glanced out of the window and was overjoyed to see that it was her daughter and granddaughter.

She turned to the stairs and yelled excitedly, "Melissa! Laurel and the baby are here!" Then she ran out, rushed over to the car and pulled open the door on the passenger side. Bette jumped out into her grandmother's arms and hugged her tightly.

Laurie turned off the ignition and got out of the car. "Hi, Ma," she said as she rubbed her back. "Thank God we're here. The drive took longer than I expected."

"Well, sweetheart, come in, sit down and have a cup of coffee." Adrienne kissed her granddaughter. "Bette, would you like some cookies and milk?"

"Hey, Laurel!" Laurie looked up and saw her younger sister hanging out of her bedroom window, her long straight hair framing her pixie-like face. "Boy, am I ever glad you could come. Can you believe it? I'm actually graduating! Bette! Come on up here! Let's see how big you've gotten!"

Bette scrambled down from her grandmother's arms and ran into the house. "I'm coming Aunt Melissa!"

Adrienne went over to her daughter and put her arms around her. "And how is my girl?" she asked. "You look a little thin. Are you eating properly?"

Laurie grinned. "Oh, Ma, you'll never change. Here I am, thirty years old and a doctor and you still think of me as your little girl. Yes, I'm eating properly." After extricating herself from her mother's embrace, she unlocked the trunk and took her suitcase out. "Would you take a look at this car?" she said, gesturing toward the large car she had just driven up from New York. "I asked for the smallest car the rental place had, and this is what they gave me. It felt as if I was driving a truck. Maybe I should have borrowed one of Andy's cars. After all, she only has five of them!"

Adrienne shook her head and curtly said, "She should have found some way to come. She hasn't been up here in such a long time. I know Melissa was hoping against hope that she would show up. After all, it's not often that your little sister graduates from college."

Laurie tried to explain, even though she knew that her mother would never understand. "Look, Ma, don't blame Andy, it's not her fault. Really, she absolutely planned to come but some sort of extra concert came up at the last minute." Laurie held out her free hand in a helpless gesture. "Let's face it, Andy's life is unfortunately not her own. I think she's under a tremendous amount of pressure right now. I don't like the way she looks at all. She's extremely pale and I know she isn't eating well. Bette and I were over for dinner right before she left and she just picked at her food. I don't know, ma, I can't explain why, but I get the feeling she's depressed."

Adrienne sighed. "There's no way we can help her if she doesn't let us. She's beyond me; I don't know what to do any more. I try to be nice, it doesn't work. She seems to resent me and I don't know why."

Laurie grimaced and changed the subject. "Well, we're joining Fred and her in Hawaii for a vacation. Maybe she'll be able to relax then."

Adrienne patted her daughter's shoulder. "That'll be nice, dear, I'm sure both of you can use the rest. But why are we standing out here? Let's go into the house. I made your favorite, my strudel."

Laurie laughed. "Still remember, huh? Thanks, ma, that would sure hit the spot." She put her arm through her mother's, and together they walked into the Rabinowitz home.

Laurie placed her suitcase on the desk and lay down on the narrow bed that once had been hers. Melissa had taken Bette over to the Five Corners and she was grateful for the time alone. She glanced around the room and thought about how little it had changed since she and Andy had shared it. There were two identical desks, dressers and beds.

As she lay on the bed, she let the familiar smells bring back memories of bygone days. She recalled her childhood and how alike she and Andy had seemed. She remembered their college days at Radcliffe, their acceptance to Harvard Medical School and Philip . . . oh yes, Philip. She had hated him and blamed him for all of their problems. With hindsight, she realized that the problems had started long before Andy had met Philip.

Thinking about it now, she understood that Andy was never as happy as she had been when they were growing up. Her twin had hidden the fact that she craved her independence. Laurie herself had never felt that she needed that kind of independence, she was content being half of a pair. Looking back, though, she had to admit that she had been painfully obnoxious about their duality. How she'd had the gall to take it upon herself to go to her father when Andy had gotten pregnant was beyond her now. Asking him for money for an abortion for her sister without consulting Andy had been absurd and, to some extent, she didn't blame Andy for leaving school and running away.

Even now it still hurt to remember the three and a half years when she and Andy had been completely estranged. During that difficult time she had finished medical school and Andy had emerged as a superstar. She felt her scar and thought about the kidney transplant that had finally brought them together. Andy had been so near death that Laurie shuddered whenever she thought about it. All of a sudden remembering the past became very painful to her. She jumped up from the bed, ran down the stairs and called out to her mother. "Ma, I'm going out for a little while. I'll be back before dinner."

Adrienne came to the kitchen door. "Where are you going?"

"I'm going downtown to see if there are any bargains in Filene's basement. I need some clothes for my vacation." Laurie bolted out the door, hopped in her car, backed it out of the driveway and headed for downtown Boston.

Philip stared out the window of his office onto

PROMISES TO KEEP

Tremont Street. Lately he hadn't been able to concentrate on his work at all. It occurred to him that his position at the law firm of Kaplan, Goffe, Belman and Shotsky was in jeopardy, but he couldn't really care. He knew it wasn't fair to his clients either, but the confrontations with Marilyn were becoming more frequent now, and it was all he could do to make himself go home at night. He understood how she felt, but he also thought that she should understand that he was as upset as she was about the situation. He had suggested adoption and even artificial insemination, but she had refused emphatically. At this point he wasn't sure if anything could please her.

He sighed and was just about to turn back to his desk when he saw a familiar figure walking down the street. That blond hair, that certain walk. His heart dropped into his stomach as he realized who he thought it was. He rushed out the door and down the stairs to the street. "Jesus Christ," he mumbled to himself, "It's her, it's actually her!" He ran after the now disappearing figure and shouted, "Hey, Andy! Stop, Andy!"

Laurie turned around and was shocked to see a conservatively dressed man flying down the street.

As he looked at her face, Philip stopped short and shook his head. "Oh no," he said softly, "I should have realized. Laurie." Slowly he walked up to her and put out his hand. "Well, Laurel, long time no see. Philip Koppel."

Laurie stared at Philip in disbelief. How could he think she would have forgotten him? "Yes, of course, Philip. It's been a very long time. How are

Wendy Susans

you?"

"Hey, how about coming with me for a drink." He took her elbow and steered her toward a small pub on the corner.

"Wait a minute," she protested. "I really don't have the time. I was just going to do some shopping, and then I have to get back to my mother's house. My daughter—"

"You have a daughter?" Philip stopped and turned to her. "How old is she? When did you get married? Please, Laurie, just one drink. I won't take up much of your time and I really would like to talk to you."

"I warn you, Philip, I don't talk very much about Andy."

"Come on, Laurie, give me a break. I just want to talk to you for a while. Please, for old times sake."

Laurie thought for a moment. Although she didn't want to go with him, she saw no way to refuse without causing a scene, so she allowed herself to be pulled into the dark, smoky bar. They sat in a booth and Philip asked her what she would like to drink. "Club soda with a twist of lime, please," she answered.

Philip called over a waiter and ordered a double scotch on the rocks and the club soda. He turned to Laurie and smiled. "Well, so how's it been going for you these past few years?"

Laurie shrugged her shoulders. "Not too badly. I'm a neonatologist at New York Hospital and I have a little four-year-old girl named Bette."

"What does your husband do?"

"I'm divorced."

"Oh," he said. "I'm married, but I don't have any children. And Andy, is she planning to have any children?"

"I have no idea. Are you practicing law now?"

"I'm a junior partner. But tell me, does Andy ever mention me at all?"

"I don't remember ever hearing her mention you. Where are you living?"

"We just bought a house in Newton." He played with the silverware and looked up. "I guess children don't fit into her lifestyle today any more than they did ten years ago when she killed my baby, huh?"

His biting remark was unexpected and bitter. Carefully measuring her words, Laurie said, "I'm sure it wasn't anything she wanted to do, but what she decided was necessary at the time. She was in no position to either have a child or to marry. She was so confused and so young." Laurie paused. "Let's face it, Philip. You really weren't any more ready than she was for the responsibility. It would have been like the blind leading the blind."

He slammed his fist on the table. "What do you know about me? I wanted to marry her. We could have made it together." He gestured toward himself. "Now look at me. You can't imagine the problems she's caused me."

"Problems? What are you talking about?" Laurie glanced around, desperately trying to think of a graceful way to extricate herself from the uncomfortable situation.

"I just have problems, that's all, and Andy is the cause of all of them."

Laurie stood up. "Look, I'm awfully sorry you have problems, but there really is nothing I can do about them. I have to get going now. My mother expects me soon."

Philip grabbed her wrist. "You tell your damn sister that she's made my life miserable and that I won't forget it!" he shouted. "That bitch hasn't heard the last of me!" Abruptly he let her go and left.

Just then the waiter brought their drinks. Shaking, Laurie picked up the check, glanced at it and threw some money on the table. Disturbed and vaguely afraid, she decided to forget about shopping. She breathed a sigh of relief as she walked out into the sunshine and turned toward the garage.

It was 6:00 A.M. and everyone was asleep in the Rabinowitz house. The morning silence was cut by the shrill ringing of the telephone, and Adrienne, groggily fumbled for the receiver. "Hello?"

"Hi! It's Andy. How're you doing?"

"Andrea! My goodness! Why are you calling here so early? Is something the matter?"

"No, nothing's the matter. Actually, I called to speak to Melissa. Is she there?"

"Of course she's here. Where would you expect her to be at this time of the morning?"

"Could you put her on then, please?"

Adrienne placed the receiver on her night table and got out of bed. She walked to Melissa's room

PROMISES TO KEEP

and knocked on the door. "Melissa, honey, Andy's on the phone and she wants to speak to you."

Melissa rolled over and picked up the phone. "Andy! Hi! I missed you yesterday. Can you believe I actually did it?"

Andy laughed. "I'm really proud of you, Lis. Hey, have you looked out the window to see what the weather is like this morning?"

"Why would I care what the weather's like? I plan to sleep all day."

"Aw, come on. Here I am stuck in Atlanta with all this disgusting sunshine. Tell me what it's like in Boston, please?"

Confused, Melissa decided to humor her sister, and looked out the window. "There's a Porsche 944 down there!" she screamed. She ran back to the phone. "Andy you're crazy and I love you. What a car! My God, it's red, my favorite color. I can't believe it!"

"Well, I decided that a 911 was too extravagant, so you'll have to make do with this. I had one of my people drive it over last night. Listen, the registration, keys, and insurance policy are in the glove compartment. Just be careful; that thing really moves."

"Oh, Andy, what can I say?"

"Just hand the phone over to Adrienne and go for a drive. I know you're dying to take a spin in it, so go already!"

A jubilant Melissa handed the phone to her mother, who was standing at the window staring at the expensive sports car. "Andy," she said, "you spoil that girl. Anything she wants, she knows she can get from you."

"It's okay. I have the money and I like doing it. Why shouldn't I give her what she wants?"

"Well, I'm glad you at least thought of her. It would have been nice to have had you here, though."

"I know. I would have loved to have been there, but I had to work. I was thinking about her the whole day. Look, I'm sorry, I have to go. I'm catching a plane in an hour. Give my love to Laurie and Bette, and tell them I'll see them soon."

"All right, Andrea. Take care of yourself now. Really, that's a very lovely car. Melissa is already dressed and out in it. I'm sure she's going to enjoy it. Good-bye now." She hung up the phone, sighed, turned around and saw Laurie standing in the doorway with her arms folded over her chest.

Laurie shook her head and smiled. "That Andy, always the grand gesture. She can't do anything on a small scale, can she? Melissa virtually flew down the stairs without touching a one. So, what do you think?"

"I'll tell you one thing, if your father was alive, he would have been furious. He disliked extravagance, and that was one of the things he complained about in Andrea. He thought she was too careless when it came to her money, and I agree."

Laurie laughed. "You know what, Ma? She can afford to be careless and extravagant. She can afford anything!"

"I know, darling. But she should understand

that we don't need expensive presents and monthly checks to love her. We do anyway."

"Oh, she knows that. She just has no time, and this makes it easy for her to show her love. Just accept it. I do. It bothered me, too, for a long time, until I realized that Andy just loves to give. How can we take that joy away from her?"

"I worry about her." Adrienne sighed. "In spite of everything, I do love her. . . ."

"I know, Ma. Really, I'm sure that she knows it too. She's just very stubborn. Come on, let's get Bette and have breakfast as long as we're up. I guess I'll be leaving for New York soon anyway." She put her arm through her mother's and they walked together to get the little girl.

July

Glistening with perspiration, Andy ran off the stage to tumultuous applause and shook her head at her stage manager. "That's enough! No more! I don't want to go out there again." She headed backstage to her dressing room. Once inside, she threw everyone out but a young, very pale girl named Janna. She collapsed into a chair and picked up a cold 7-Up. "I am so incredibly wet," she said as she gulped down the drink. "God, that place was so humid I could barely breathe. Hey, Janna, throw me a couple of towels, will you?"

Janna handed her some towels and gushed, "You were wonderful tonight, Andy, just wonderful. Can I get you anything else? Can I do anything else for you?"

"No," she said as she rubbed her hair dry. "Thanks a lot. You can go now, too."

There was a knock on the door and Janna

scrambled to answer it. "Hey, Andy, we've been invited to a bash. You feel up to it?"

Andy's first thought was to answer no, but then she remembered the empty hotel room she had to return to and she changed her mind. "Okay, sure. Just give me a few minutes to change. I'll be right with you." She wearily got up and went to change her sopping wet clothes.

The stage door was jammed with fans by the time Andy and her band members left. As soon as the crowd saw her they surged forward against the police barricades and tried to touch her. Andy and her entourage slipped into the waiting limousines and she thankfully sank back into the seat. "Whew," she sighed, "those crowds drive me crazy. I never know what they'll do. Just seeing all those people rushing at me makes me want to quit this scene."

Toby, her bass guitarist, took an envelope out of his pocket and touched her arm. "Try to relax, Andy. You've been so tight lately. Here, I have something to help you." He poured some white powder into a spoon and put it towards her nose.

Andy considered the offer for a moment. "No thanks, Toby," she said. "I don't do dope anymore. You know that." She sank deeper into the luxurious leather seats, closed her eyes and let her exhaustion take over.

The tour had been a real drag. It had become increasingly more difficult to get herself up for each of the shows, and although her reviews were excellent, she felt she wasn't really in top form. She was lonely for New York, Laurie and Bette,

PROMISES TO KEEP

but strangely not for Fred.

She sighed again. She didn't feel that she could keep up this sham of a marriage any longer. She had slept with other men during the tour, and she knew that it had gotten back to her husband. And she had to admit that Fred's constant wheeling and dealing on her behalf was getting to her. He never seemed to stop. He never seemed to give her a chance to catch her breath. She was going to have to make a decision soon, one way or another, painful as it might be. Next stop was Los Angeles. Fred was meeting her there. She opened her eyes and stared bleakly out the window. They'd have to have a showdown in L.A.

Andy was aware of a ringing far, far away. She put her pillow over her head and willed the noise to stop. It didn't, and she finally realized that it was her phone. Reluctantly, she pulled herself out of her stupor and reached for it. "Hello," she mumbled, "Who is this?"

"Jesus, Andy, aren't you up yet? It's one in the afternoon there and you're due to leave at three."

"Oh, come on, Fred, you know I'll make it. I've never missed a plane yet. What do you want?"

"Look, I've just seen the papers. The concert got great reviews but, as usual, there was criticism about your behavior."

"What behavior?"

"It seems that you were seen at a party where the drugs were flowing like water. You know that's not good public relations. We try to steer clear of that stuff. You're not a twenty-year-old punk rocker who can get away with that stuff any more. Your image is—"

"My image, Freddie?" she interrupted angrily. "Don't you care whether I was actually involved with the drugs or not? You didn't ask me that. No, because you don't care whether I was involved! You don't worry about the dope hurting me, you're just worried about P.R. Well, I'm sick of P.R. That's all I am to you. You're constantly worried about my image, whether what I do is good for the business, will it make money. God, I'm tired of it! I can't take any more of it! I'm not a commodity! You married me because you loved me, or so you've said over and over again. You know, I really have to wonder about your motives at this point. And I'm getting real tired of your so-called concern for me. Not only that, but you're depressing me. I get the feeling that I'm just a business to you and nothing more."

"That's ridiculous. I love you and you know it. I wouldn't put up with your garbage if I didn't love you."

"Don't give me that one again, either. I've heard it too many times. You like the 'garbage'! It gives you a reason to be a martyr. Good Fred and bad Andy, I'm tired of that game. But not you, you love it. Well you know what? I'm not going to play the game anymore. Good Fred will have to be good without bad Andy. Look, I don't feel like talking to you now, so I'm going to hang up—"

"Well, Andy, you gave the stud in bed with you

PROMISES TO KEEP

a good show. Now get your ass up and get dressed. You have a plane to catch." Fred slammed the receiver down.

Andy sat up in bed, fully awake. "That son of a bitch! How dare he! All right, that's it. I've had it! There's no reason for me to take this from anyone, least of all him." She got up, showered and threw her few remaining clothes into her suitcase. "God, I hate hotels," she said as she slammed the door on the empty room.

Andy alighted from her limousine amidst a flurry of activity. Hotel employees held back the crowd waiting to get a glimpse of her as she hurried through to the entrance of the Beverly Wilshire. The doorman tipped his hat and smiled, "Good afternoon, Ms. Reuben. It's a pleasure to see you again."

Andy gave him a quick smile and whisked into the lobby of the elegant hotel. Within seconds, the manager was at her side. He escorted her up the elevator to her suite, opened the door with a flourish and handed her the key. "If there is any way we can be of service to you, please don't hesitate to ask." He bowed and left the room.

She kicked off her shoes, walked over to the bar and splashed some bourbon in a glass. The plane trip had tired her and she was looking forward to relaxing before dinner. The following evening was her final concert and she would then be off to Hawaii for a real vacation. She walked into the bedroom and undressed. The king size bed looked so inviting that she pulled back the bedspread and climbed in. Contentedly, she snuggled under the soft velour of the blanket.

A short time later, Fred strode into the room and violently shook her awake. "Come on, Andy, let's go. We have a meeting in a half an hour."

"What kind of meeting?"

"A meeting with the movie people. I promised you'd be there."

She got out of bed, put on her robe and turned to face her husband. "Look, Fred, I don't care how many people you've promised. I'm sick and tired of this. I've decided that I will not be forced to do things that I don't want to do. I don't want to do movies. Not three movies, not even one movie. The deal is off. I'm doing this concert, and then I'm going to Hawaii. No more Hollywood, no more movies, ever!"

Fred walked over to her, put his hands on her shoulders and calmly said, "Andy, you know that's not fair. I've committed us, and ethically, I don't think we can get out of it. You can understand that, can't you?"

She looked at him through narrowed eyes. "You'll get out of it, no matter what. And don't you dare talk to me about ethics! Ethics has nothing to do with it. I never wanted to make movies."

"But if you don't go through with this it'll be harder to make a deal later on."

"Why don't you listen to me? I don't want a deal, not now or at any time in the future!"

"Damn you, Andy!" he screamed. "I gave my word! Don't you understand? You're going to

PROMISES TO KEEP

ruin my reputation in this town. I won't stand for this. You can't play the spoiled child now. You will do those pictures!"

Andy pulled away from his tightening grip. "No, I won't, and that's final! And don't you dare call me a child again!" She walked across the room and balled her fists. "Now listen to me for once. I've given a lot of thought to many things during these past few weeks, and I've made some important decisions. I will not be coerced into doing anything I don't want to do, not even by you. There's no reason for me to endure doing things I don't enjoy at this point. I'm sorry, but I don't think you know what's best for me anymore. I only want the music. I've always only wanted the music. Don't look at me like that, Fred, I won't be persuaded. No more movies!"

"Well, Andy," he said angrily, "you now have a choice. Either you follow through with this deal or I'm quitting. My credibility will be nil after this, and I still have some pride."

Andy felt panic rising inside her at the thought of losing Fred as her manager, and she had to sit down in a chair. She gripped the arms tightly and said, "To tell you the truth, that scares me a little, but I think maybe its for the best." She took a deep breath and continued. "You see, one of the other decisions I made was that I want a separation from you."

Fred leaned against the wall, flabbergasted. He had never thought that she would go this far. She needed him. She couldn't survive without him. Who would be there to bail her out when she got

Wendy Susans

into trouble? She was incapable of making decisions. She couldn't handle money. *She needed him, damn it!* She would find out. He would let her go through with this separation and then she'd see how much she depended on him. "Okay, Andy," he said confidently. "If that's the way you want it, we'll try it your way. As of this minute, we're separated." He picked up his attache case, hesitated and turned to her. "Definitely no more movies?" he asked one more time.

"No movies, Fred," she said softly.

He nodded slightly, turned and walked out of the suite without a backward glance.

Puzzled, Andy stared at the door he had closed behind him. She hadn't expected him to give in so easily. *I wonder what he's up to?* she thought.

Fred walked briskly down Wilshire Boulevard toward Marty Kantor's office, wondering what he would tell him. Andy's decision not to do the movies had caught him by surprise. He had promised Marty that he would deliver her for three pictures because he'd been positive that he could talk her into it. After all, she had never refused him before. Sure she complained, but she always did everything he suggested. It hurt him that she thought she didn't need him, but he wouldn't give up that easily. He had a few tricks up his sleeve to get her back. Right now, though, he had to deal with Marty. He entered a large office building, took the elevator up to the fourth floor, and walked into Marty's office.

PROMISES TO KEEP

Marty Kantor was a thin man with a head full of kinky black hair. He had a bushy mustache and a five o'clock shadow that appeared at noon. When Fred entered his office he was putting the finishing touches on his third shave of the day. He wore continental styled clothes, usually of Italian origin, and custom-made silk shirts unbuttoned to the chest. He never wore a tie, preferring instead a tangle of gold chains around his neck. Marty was a small-time agent searching for the big deal that somehow always eluded his grasp. This time, though, he knew he had it.

He'd been waiting for the time when Andy Reuben would do something for him, and now it had arrived. He had discovered Andy in Fred's dinky coffeehouse in Cambridge, and it was to him that Andy had run to when she was pregnant and needed an abortion. Marty had helped her get her first record contract, and then she had dumped him.

Knowing he couldn't get Andy to consent to a deal, Marty had called Fred and proposed a package to him. To his surprise, Fred had been very enthusiastic and had readily agreed to convince Andy, with the stipulation that Marty's name wouldn't be mentioned until after the contract was signed. Sensing that there was a problem, Marty stood up and asked, "What the hell's going on Fred? Weren't you supposed to take Andy to the studio?"

"She won't go. She doesn't want to do the pictures." Fred sank limply into a chrome chair in front of Marty's desk. "I'm sorry, old pal."

Marty stood up and poured himself a drink. "What do you mean she won't do the pictures? I busted my butt to put this thing together and now you tell me she won't do it? I thought it was definite."

Fred ran his hand through his hair. "I really don't know what's gotten into her. She's probably exhausted from the tour, and Andy doesn't think very clearly when she's tired. I'll tell you one thing, we're going to have to shelve the project for a while. Andy was quite emphatic, and there's absolutely nothing I can do about it now."

"Freddie, are you positive? You don't know how much I wanted this deal."

Freddie sighed. "Oh hell, Marty, I might as well tell you. We're separated. Not legally yet, but it might as well be. She doesn't want the commitment any more. I've resigned as her manager as of Monday."

"What? Andy Reuben without Fred Arnold? What an item!" He swirled the drink around in his glass. "Ah, yes, good old Andy, up to her old tricks. Never did think of anyone but herself, did she? Yeah, she owed me years ago, but that means zilch to her. I'll tell you, Fred, you're well rid of her. You're the genius in the relationship. She can't do diddly-squat without you."

Fred frowned. "I wouldn't be so sure, Marty. Don't underestimate her talent, its formidable. Anyway, I've really got to go. Look, I'm really sorry, Marty. See you soon. Ciao, pal." Freddie shook Marty's hand, slapped him on the back and

PROMISES TO KEEP

left the office.

Marty paced the room, fists clenched, his face red with suppressed anger. "Damn it! That bitch screwed me again. It was her fault that I lost my job at SMW Records ten years ago—the princess didn't want me around so she had me fired." This could have been the deal of a lifetime. He'd never be able to duplicate it. "Damn you, Andy Reuben! I could kill you for this!"

Laurie looked out of the window as the 747 circled in preparation for its landing at Honolulu International Airport. She gazed at the sprawl of freeways and suburbs between two mountain ranges that was Honolulu, and sighed. It had been a long trip—eleven hours in the air and an hour and a half on the ground in Los Angeles. Bette had been fine for the first five hours. The steward pinned wings on her and on her doll, and she had helped him serve drinks. But after Los Angeles she began to wilt, and now she was draped across Laurie's lap, sound asleep.

The plane taxied to a stop in front of the terminal and the passengers disembarked. A uniformed man hurried over to Laurie, stared at a piece of paper in his hand and asked, "Are you Dr. Laurel Rabinowitz?" She nodded and he said, "My name is Elvis. I'm Ms. Reuben's chauffeur and I'm to take you to the villa." He smiled and reached for Bette. "I'll bring you and your daughter to the car and then go back for the luggage." Gratefully, Laurie handed him Bette and followed him to the silver Mercedes stretch limo.

By the time the limo pulled up to the house, Bette was wide awake and taking in the beautiful scenery. When the car stopped she and Laurie jumped out and looked around. Located on the ocean side of Diamond Head, Honolulu's Gold Coast, the estate was overwhelming. It was the most exclusive area in all of Hawaii. The property was abloom with hibiscus, bougainvilla and poinsettas. Laurie plucked a petal off a hibiscus blossom and crushed it between her fingers. Its redolence was breathtaking. "Bette," she called. "Smell this."

Bette took the flower in her hand and smelled it. "Oh, mommy, that's so beautiful. Isn't Hawaii the most wonderful place you've ever been?"

Laurie nodded and turned around to look for Andy. She saw her sister running toward them over the wide expanse of green lawn, and she rushed to meet her.

"I was beginning to think you'd never get here," Andy said as they embraced. "Now I can really start enjoying this place!"

Bette threw her arms around her aunt's legs and shouted, "Oh, Andy, thank you for letting us come here! I love it!"

Andy bent down and kissed Bette on the cheek. "And I love having you here, little one." She took the little girl's hand, threw her other arm around her sister's shoulder and together the three of them walked toward the private and secluded villa. Laurie gasped when she saw the extent of the estate. The huge main house had an Italian flavor, with porticos on the first and second level. There was a private beach and a tidal pool out back and two tennis courts on the side. The servant's quarters stood next to the courts.

They entered the house and Andy showed her sister and niece to their large, airy rooms. "You unpack now and then come down for lunch. I have a few phone calls to make and then I'll meet you in the dining room." She kissed Laurie on the cheek. "God, am I glad you're here," she exclaimed as she left the room.

Laurie and Bette quickly put away their things, hurried down the magnificent staircase and entered the cavernous dining room. All Laurie could think of was Tara from *Gone With The Wind*, transplanted to Hawaii. Why her sister needed such a huge place was beyond her, but it didn't surprise her. It seemed that Andy always had to be stupendous, no matter what she did.

Lunch was a buffet set out on a sideboard. There were different types of seafood salads stuffed in avocados and a variety of exotic fruits. The two filled their plates and sat down. Laurie poured herself a glass of white wine from a carafe in the middle of the table, and Bette helped herself to some pineapple juice. They were almost finished with their lunch when Andy flew in, put about a teaspoon of salad on her plate, poured herself a glass of bourbon and sat down at the head of the table.

She took a bite of her food and put her fork down. "I might as well tell you before you read it in Liz Smith's column," she said, a note of exasperation in her voice. "Freddie and I are separated. I just got off the phone with the head of publicity at Nickelodean. The story breaks tomorrow. The ghouls just can't resist a juicy tidbit."

Shocked, Laurie scrutinized her sister's face. "How can you be so calm about it? What happened?"

"Believe me, it wasn't all of a sudden. It's been brewing for a long time. We just don't have that much to say to each other any more outside of my career, and even that has become a constant source of friction. Anyway, now that I've told you, let's not dwell on it. I want us to have a good time these two weeks, and talking about Freddie is not my idea of a good time."

Laurie wanted to continue the discussion, but one look at her sister's set jaw told her that it wouldn't be wise. She was also looking forward to a good time and was loath to do or say anything that might spoil one of her infrequent vacations.

"We'll have dessert out on the veranda, Pawn." Andy got up from the table and motioned for Laurie and Bette to follow her. Pawn, the Filipino houseboy, nodded and went to bring the fresh fruit and coffee outside.

Once outside, Bette ran in front of her aunt and asked, "Andy, you know what?"

Andy looked down and smiled. "What is it, little one?"

"I know all the words to your new song. Want to hear me?"

Laurie frowned. "Bette, have you been watching MTV again? I'm going to have that cable taken out. I told you that I don't want you watching trash."

"Hey, watch what you call trash. It could be me!"

"Oh, Andy, you know I didn't mean you. I was talking about television in general."

"Yeah, I know. You intellectuals are all alike," she said with a smile. "You have no use for us plebians." She bent down to her niece. "So tell me, Bette. How did you learn my new song?"

Bette looked sheepish. "I watched MTV," she said, avoiding her mother's eyes.

Andy and Laurie looked at each other and burst out laughing. "You see, Laur, that's what you get for exposing your daughter to a degenerate like me." Grinning, she sat down in a chair. "So, Bette, you want to sing it for me?"

"Yes, I do." The child stood in the middle of the veranda and began to sing Andy's latest hit.

Laurie sat flabbergasted as her small daughter flounced and moved provocatively, exactly the way her sister did while singing the song. The resemblance was uncanny. Bette looked like a miniature version of Andy.. Laurie didn't know why, but she felt a premonition of doom, and she shivered a little.

When Bette finished, Andy clapped her hands delightedly. "My God, Bette, you're wonderful, just wonderful! Isn't she terrific, Laur? She should come on tour with me. I can't believe it! You copied me perfectly. What a fantastic little mime you are!"

Bette glowed with the praise, and shot a quick

glance at her mother's disapproving face before saying to Andy, "I know some more of your songs, too. Want to hear them?"

Laurie stood up and scooped Bette into her arms. "I think that's enough showing off for one day. We wanted to go swimming this afternoon, didn't we?"

"You guys go without me, I have work to do," Andy replied. "I'd love to listen to you some other time, Bette. I really like the way you sing." She touched her sister's shoulder tenderly. "Hey, Laur, don't worry, she's not corrupted yet. I'll bet she doesn't even understand half the words."

"But she will," Laurie said mournfully. "It won't be long before she will." She took her daughter's hand in hers, and together they walked into the house to get their bathing suits.

The moon hung low over the water, almost touching the horizon as waves crashed gently against the narrow beach's sand. The air was heavy with the fragrance of tropical vegetation mixed with the tangy odor of the sea. From off in the distance the mournful horn of a passing ship clashed with the cheerful cacophony of the brilliantly plumed island birds. Myriad constellations, many of which Laurie had never seen before, lit up the sky. Try as she might, she couldn't begin to identify them.

Andy lay back in the sand and listened to the wind through the palm trees. It was a sultry evening and she contemplated taking a swim in the surging dark surf, but she was reluctant to move from her comfortable position. Turning to her sister sitting quietly next to her, she asked, "What are you thinking, Laur?"

"I'm thinking that I should have taken astronomy in college," she said ruefully. "This sky has me totally disoriented." She paused and sifted sand through her fingers. "You know, I could get used to this life very easily. Hawaii is so peaceful. I could almost forget that there's a real world out there, full of problems that I can't solve."

Andy nodded her head. "Yeah, I know. It seems as if life would be so easy here, doesn't it? But don't kid yourself, kid, your problems follow you wherever you go. If it isn't one thing, it's bound to be another." She sighed. "Fred called me again this afternoon when you and Bette were swimming, and I made the mistake of taking the call."

"What do you mean, 'made the mistake of taking the call?'"

"I instructed the staff to say that I'm unavailable to him."

Laurie looked at her sister closely. "I thought you seemed awfully preoccupied at dinner. What did he want?"

"What do you think he wanted? He misses me and loves me and needs me. He sounded so desperate that I almost told him to fly out here. I didn't though," she stated grimly. "I will not give in to him again. I shouldn't have married him in the first place, and I don't want him to make me feel sorry for him now that I'll stay married to him."

"Is it really all that bad, Andy? I know you love each other. What's wrong with staying married to him?"

Andy dug her toes into the sand, then answered, "Laur, you have no idea. He runs my entire life. I know he loves me, but sometimes he is so cold-blooded about the relationship. This is good for business, that's bad for business. If only he would say, that's good for Andy or that's bad for Andy, I might not mind so much."

"Oh, Andy, I'm sure that's what he means," Laurie reassured her. "Maybe I'm wrong, but it seems to me he's afraid to show you just how vulnerable he really is. Maybe this 'all for business' is his way of covering up how scared he is that you'll hurt him."

"Another case of noncommunication, is that what you're trying to say?" Andy scoffed. "Well, I'm bored with that and I don't believe in pop psychology. Look, this is the way it is. Fred is an extremely ambitious man and I am a huge part of that ambition. You'll notice that he won't be making much of an effort to find some new talent to manage. No, because the man is obsessed with me and my career, and I can't take it anymore. He never stops, he never gives me a moment to rest. I know it's selfish, but I want time for myself. I don't want to be somebody's obsession. It was flattering for a while, but now it's become tiresome. I feel—"

"Trapped." Laurie finished her sentence. "Andy, you always feel trapped. Did you ever think that maybe you trap yourself?"

Andy stood up and brushed the sand from her swimsuit. "That's exactly what Fred said before I left New York. But Laurie, let's face it, what's the difference? The fact is that I want to be free and I don't feel that I can be free when I'm married. Anyway, I spoke to my lawyer yesterday and he's working out a divorce for me. Come on now, let's go swimming. I feel like working off some of my hostilities."

"Look who's talking about pop psychology!" Laurie laughed and put her hand out for her sister to pull her up.

George threw down the newspaper in disgust. He had hoped that Andy was different, but she was the same as the rest of them. She needed Fred Arnold to keep her on the straight and narrow. Sluts, all of them were sluts. He had seen her concert and she was wonderful, as usual, but he'd never expected this. There was only one reason why she would leave her husband, and that was to fool around. If she fooled around she would be just like his wife. He hated to think that Andy Reuben was like Vera, but he feared that only Fred Arnold could keep her from turning into a slut. Vera was a slut. He had to write to Andy to tell her she was making a mistake, a very serious mistake. No, he had better write to Fred Arnold. He would understand. George desperately needed Andy Reuben to be his angel, otherwise he didn't know what he would do.

The limousine crawled between industrial warehouses down the unprepossessing street. It stopped at the end, on a rise overlooking the Pacific Ocean. The smell of fish permeated the air. They were in front of John Dominis, one of Honolulu's most extraordinary restaurants. The fashionable eatery was crowded, and Andy hesitated before getting out of the car. Having mobs of people surrounding her, closing in on her, suffocating her, was one of her biggest fears. It wasn't the fact that they asked for autographs that disturbed her; she gave her signature readily. What drove her crazy were the hands, reaching out for her, touching her, grabbing at her. They would pull at her clothes and her hair, sometimes ripping it out at the roots. They would scratch her arms and face in a futile effort to get her attention.

And the sound—Oh, God she had nightmares about the sound. It started with everyone pleading with her to notice them, and crescendoed to an indecipherable roar. It was a dichotomy to her that civilized people could become such frenzied animals in the presence of someone they purported to admire.

"Are you sure you want to go in, Laur? I don't know, I'm kind of nervous. I'm mobbed wherever I go, you know? That's why I don't go out in public much." She looked at her sister's disappointed face and took a deep breath. "Occasionally, though, I don't mind." She nodded to Elvis and he opened the door.

Almost immediately curious passersby recognized her and ran over. Within seconds, more people saw her and a large crowd formed around the limousine. Elvis tried to protect Andy, but it was impossible. Finally, he managed to get her back in the car and close the door behind her.

Andy shook her head. "Look, Laur, do you really want to eat here that badly?"

Laurie sighed. "I guess not. I'm just tired of hanging around the villa, and I heard this was a great place."

"I'll tell you what, then. You and Bette can go by yourselves, and I'll have the car pick you up later. I'm sorry, I really can't face that scene again."

"No, it's okay, there's no point in going in alone," Laurie said, reluctant to leave her sister alone.

Andy kissed her on the cheek. "I'm so sorry, Laur. I swear I'll make it up to you when we get back to New York. People there tend to be more nonchalant about seeing a famous face."

Laurie put her hand to her forehead and closed her eyes. "You know, I think I understand why you feel trapped. This sort of thing is definitely not fun. It's crazy, we can't even go out to eat if we want to. What's the use of your money if you're too famous to use it?"

"Well, if worse comes to worse, I can always buy the restaurant." Andy laughed as she patted her sister's hand. "Hey, Laurie, don't be depressed for me. I'm used to it." She turned to Bette and asked, "Are you hungry, little one?"

Bette nodded her head. "Why didn't we go into

the restaurant? I want to eat."

Andy kissed the top of her head. "It was too crowded. Didn't you see all the people?"

"Yes, and they all came up to you and touched you. I got scared."

"Well, that's why we didn't stay. I sort of got scared, too. I didn't want them to hurt us. I'll tell you what, let's stop at a pizza parlor and we'll let Elvis get out and order us a couple of pies. Is that all right with you?"

"But I wore my pretty dress and I wanted to go to a real restaurant." The girl started crying.

Laurie hugged her daughter. "I'm sorry, honey. I promise you we'll go to a nice restaurant as soon as we can. Anyway, you like pizza, don't you?"

"Yes," she sniffed.

"Okay, then," Andy said, "we'll get pizza, go back to the house, and have our own party." She explained the plan to Elvis, and twenty minutes later were on their way back to the house, with the spicy smell of pizza lifting all of their spirits.

At 3 A.M. Laurie awoke with a start. The room was chilly, and she went to the window to close it. Glancing out, she noticed Andy sitting outside near the water. Laurie pulled on a pair of pants and a sweatshirt and ran out to join her.

Andy looked up as Laurie sat down next to her. "Couldn't sleep, so I thought I'd get some fresh air."

"Oh, and you needed a bottle of bourbon along with your fresh air? Come on, what's the problem?"

"The problem?" She shook her head. "It's

PROMISES TO KEEP

always the same problem, Laur. I have everything I've always dreamed of having, and yet I feel like I have nothing. What's it all worth? I couldn't even take you and Bette to a restaurant tonight." She looked out toward the ocean. "I'm so lonely so much of the time. I can't help but wonder whether people are interested in me for myself of for my status. I can't be sure of anyone liking me for myself but you."

Laurie touched her sister's arm. "You know, Andy, I get lonely too, but I don't dwell on it. I do my work and then I go home to Bette and spend the rest of the night curled up with a good book. Don't you think that I would like a companion to share things with? You're usually too busy, and Bette is still too young." She gave a wry laugh. "And I even think about being with men too, and not just platonically. I think your problem is that you introspect too much, and that only makes you even more unhappy."

"I know. Dr. Bartis tells me that all the time, only she's not as kind as you. She calls it self-indulgence! She says I'm too narcissistic." Andy looked down and examined her fingers. "I guess that's why I'm so . . . so drawn to men. I need to know they all desire me. And I'm not all that choosy. If the body turns me on, I take it home. I don't even have to know his name. Then afterwards, I can't stand him and usually kick him out. You'd think that after eight years of analysis, I'd be able to control myself," she said in disgust. "God, I hate myself for it."

"Oh, Andy, you're smart enough to know that

loneliness doesn't disappear just because you have a warm body next to you. You have to be able to totally relate to someone." Leaning back on her elbows, Laurie explained, "You think that you're the center of the universe because everyone around tells you that you are. But you're not, and you have to stop examining yourself and thinking about yourself to realize it, because none of your so-called friends are going to tell you that. Andy, it's time to get back into the real world. You won't be happy if this goes on any longer."

Andy sighed. "I'm sure you're right, but once you're used to it, it's hard to give up. Being a god can be kind of nice, Laur. Sometimes I hate myself for fostering it, though. For instance, there's this girl named Janna. I first saw her in Philadelphia, and by Atlanta she was part of my entourage. She's eighteen years old, Laurie, eighteen years old, and she was traveling around just following me. Her whole purpose in life was to follow my tour. I can't understand it! Where were her parents? I mean, that kid would have done anything for me. Anything! She begged and begged to help me and didn't want a penny for it. All she wanted was to be around me. The whole thing turned my stomach, but I allowed it. I encouraged it. Believe me, that wasn't the first time it's happened. I left that poor kid alone in L.A. God knows what will happen to her, it's a lousy place for a kid alone. I've been thinking a lot about her, but what could I do? There's so many like her out there." She hesitated. "I guess we do get an exaggerated view of our importance in the scheme of things. . . ."

Laurie looked at Andy. Her sister's plight touched her, and she wanted to help get her life together. She decided to tell Andy about a project she had been toying with. "I don't know whether you would be interested, but I have an idea. I've been thinking about it for quite a while, but I was afraid to ask you about it."

"You shouldn't be afraid to ask me anything."

"Well, it would mean quite a commitment, and I'm not sure you would be interested in committing yourself to anything like this. Then again, you might not even have the time. . . ."

"Well, you might as well ask me; you'll never know until you try."

Laurie took a deep breath. "Okay. I know a patient who suffers from post-anoxic myoclonus. Without the drug L-5HTP, he will die, but that's an orphan drug and—"

"—and it's not profitable enough for the pharmaceutical companies to produce, since orphan drugs are for somewhat rare illnesses," Andy finished for her. "See, med school came in handy for something." She flashed a smile. "So what's this got to do with me?"

"We need to make the public aware of the problem," Laurie explained, "and we desperately need to get these drugs on the market. That's where you would come in. As a famous person, you have a tremendous audience. If you could become a spokesperson for orphan drugs . . ."

"Who's going to listen to me? What do I know?"

Wendy Susans

"What did Jerry Lewis know when he started working for muscular dystrophy? We need you, Andy. Please, just think about it."

Andy touched her sister's cheek. "Oh, Laur, you know that it's always been impossible for me to refuse you anything. What the hell, why not? When we get back to New York you can fill me in on the details and I'll see what I can do. Maybe it's about time that Andy Reuben became altruistically inclined."

Laurie smiled. "Hey, kid, have I told you lately how much I love you?"

"Not lately, but I know anyway." She gave her sister a quick hug, then picked up the bottle of bourbon and took a drink.

Laurie shook her head and winced. "Please, Andy, that's so bad for you; your kidney—"

"But this is a special occasion!" She lifted the bottle and shouted, "Hey, out there, here's to my new image! God knows I need one!"

It was a few days later, and Laurie was very disappointed. She had expected to spend a full two weeks on vacation, but suddenly Andy insisted that she had to get back.

"Mommy, don't forget to pack my hula skirt." Bette brought the colorful skirt over to the bed.

"Don't worry, honey, we'll take everything. Why don't you go see if Andy's almost ready?"

"Okay." Bette skipped happily out of the room.

Just as Laurie was closing her last suitcase, Pawn rushed into the bedroom and grabbed her arm. "Doctor, come quick, it's 'Nando! He can't

PROMISES TO KEEP

breathe!"

Laurie reached for her satchel and hurried down the hallway after Pawn. "Andy," she yelled as she passed her sister's room, "Come with me! Pawn's son is in trouble and I might need you. Bette, stay put!"

The three reached Pawn's cottage in seconds and Laurie immediately assessed the situation. The baby was turning blue, lying limply in his mother's arms.

"He was eating a cookie and he started choking!" screamed Maria, Pawn's wife.

Laurie grabbed the child, turned him upside down, and pounded his back. Unfortunately, it didn't dislodge the piece of food. "Andy, I'm afraid I have to do a tracheotomy and I'll need your help." She laid the baby on the table and opened her bag. "Hold him still. Like this." She took 'Nando's cheeks in her hand and tilted his head back. Andy moved over and held him as she was instructed.

"Laurie, please, I don't know if I can do this." The panic was evident in Andy's eyes.

"Oh yes you can!" Laurie snapped. "You have to or else he'll die!" She ripped open a package of sterile instruments and selected a scalpel. Then she felt for the space between two rings of cartilage on the trachea and she cut. At once there was a rush of air and the little boy turned pink. She inserted a tube in the incision and said, "Call an ambulance now. We have to get him to a hospital."

Pawn ran to the phone and called.

Wendy Susans

"Will he die?" asked Maria frantically.

"No, he'll be alright," answered Laurie as she taped the tube in place. "Look, he's opening his eyes."

Maria looked down and began to weep.

Laurie stared at Andy and smiled softly. "This is what I used to dream of, you and me working together to save someone's life. It felt so right."

"I hate to spoil your dream, Sis, but I almost fainted back there. I really can't take that stuff."

"You would have learned to take it, just like we all did. But oh, how dull this world would have been without the incredible Andy Reuben!" She winked at her sister and went back to tending the child.

August

The crowds gatherd on Seventh Avenue and 33rd Street, unable to get closer to Madison Square Garden because of the extensive security necessary at an Andy Reuben concert. The barricades were arranged so that only ticket holders were allowed to snake their way through to the entrance. Although there were policemen around, scalpers were having a field day selling tickets for up to five times their face value. Those people unfortunate enough not to purchase tickets before they were sold out, and too poor to meet scalped prices, were buying bootleg T-shirts from the many hawkers milling about. They stared longingly at their lucky peers.

Once inside, the ticket holders threaded their way up the escalator system to their levels, then through the doors to their respective seats. As showtime approached every seat was filled and the noise was deafening.

Backstage, the band was getting ready to go on. Noticeably missing was Andy, who remained behind in her dressing room psyching herself up for the strenuous activity that was *de rigueur* for an Andy Reuben concert. She nodded as a stagehand opened the door for her two-minute warning and looked at herself in the mirror once more. She stood up, took a gulp of bourbon, flexed her legs and walked out. Security guards took up positions on each side of her and escorted her to the wings. Her band was already on the stage and beginning the introduction to her first song, "Reckless Lies." Andy threw her head back, closed her eyes, clenched her fists and pumped her arms up and down. "Five, six, seven, eight," she chanted, then ran onstage.

The lights dimmed and the audienced roared. Slowly the spotlights came up, revealing Andy in a brightly colored layered chiffon dress. The uneven hem covered the tops of her yellow boots. She jumped forward, slamming the tambourine she held in her hand against her hip. The extravaganza had begun, and would continue for two solid hours without a break, except for Andy's frequent trips to the wings for costume changes.

The song ended and the crowd went wild, whistling and shouting her name over and over. She held up her hands and quickly lowered them to start up the band behind her. Rock music filled the Garden as Andy began to sing again.

Laurie watched her sister intently and realized that she could never really accept the fact that her twin was a rock singer. When she was performing she looked so foreign to Laurie—almost like a caricature. Listening to Andy, she thought with amusement of her mother's remark of some years back. She had asked Andy if what she was doing was any way for a grown woman to make a living, and she'd wanted to know when Andy would outgrow her antics. As she looked at her sister onstage, Laurie was sure of the answer to her mother's questions: Andy would never outgrow it.

Melissa, on the other hand, was a died-in-the-wool fan. She stood next to Laurie, totally lost in her sister's performance. Unlike Laurie, she saw Andy as a superstar first and a sister second. She had been just under eleven when Andy had left home, and had never really known her sister until Andy's kidney operation. After that, Andy had seemed to suddenly notice her younger sister, and she couldn't do enough for her.

"Well, how about it, Lis?" Laurie said, poking her sister in the ribs. "Is she as good as the last time you saw her?"

"Good? She's great! I don't know how she does it!" Melissa grinned. "But, boy, has she ever gotten thin. I wish I knew her secret."

"Hah!" Laurie scoffed. "It's no secret. She doesn't eat and she doesn't sleep. It was agony watching her in Hawaii. She's so on edge. I don't know why she won't admit how exhausted she really is."

"I don't know," Melissa said, annoyed. "She looks pretty good to me. Why are you always worrying so much about her? I'm sure she can take care of herself."

"Well, then, you don't know her very well at all. She's—"

"Shhh!" the person sitting behind the sisters whispered. "Can't you keep your mouths shut? We paid to hear Andy Reuben, not you two."

Embarrassed, Melissa and Laurie smiled at each other and turned their attention back to the stage.

Andy returned from the wings wearing tight royal blue satin pants and a multicolored shirt that shimmered in the glow of the bright spotlights. She strutted to the end of the stage and picked up the cordless microphone. "Nothing like New York people!" she said huskily. "I've been all over the United States and it feels fantastic to be back home." She pulled a stool over to center stage, climbed on it and said, "Recently, I wrote a song for someone and I would like to share it, for the first time, with you and with the special person I wrote it for. I call it 'She's The Best Part of Me'."

A screen dropped behind her and slides of Andy and Laurie growing up were projected on it. The final one would show the two of them with Bette in Hawaii.

> She's always done the things
> That she's supposed to do.
> Never felt the need to sprout wings,
> Thinks her actions through.
> The smile that adorns her face,
> Tells me she doesn't mind.

PROMISES TO KEEP

Careful to live life at an even pace,
Leaves temptation behind.

Adores me for the things I am,
And even for things that I'm not.
Doesn't question when I get into a jam,
And I get into jams quite a lot.
Though I know she can't always condone,
She'll stand by me 'til the end.
Won't allow me to cope with hurts alone.
Forever my dearest friend.
She's the best part of me,
Always has been, always will be.
She's the best part of me.
Take a look you'll clearly see.
Yeah, she's the best part of me.

I know our paths don't run parallel,
I've ruined that general plan.
Still, we find we get along awfully well,
Better than most people can.
Though I know her disappointment still
    runs deep,
She won't blame me, she won't let on.
But I wonder whether while in deep sleep,
She returns to those dreams now long gone.

Always killed me if she was in pain.
It still does, I hope it's not so.
I'm sorry my life is insane.
Maybe it's kinder if she doesn't know,
The tortures that run through my soul.
It's better if she could just see,
That she's what I need to feel whole,
Cause she's the best part of me.

She's the best part of me.
Always has been, always will be.
She's the best part of me.

> Take a look you'll clearly see.
> She's the best part of me.
> Doesn't curse, or drink or sin.
> She's the best part of me.
> She's my identical twin.

Tears stung Laurie's eyes as Andy sang the song, which was clearly a tender tribute to her. She felt a strong rush of love for her twin, a love even greater than ever before. She looked up at Andy and saw that she was gazing down at her as she sang. Their eyes met, and Laurie felt as if everything was totally right with the world. Melissa reached for her hand and clasped it tightly. When the song ended, Laurie stood up and clapped long and hard with the audience as her eyes remained locked with her twin's.

Andy pranced and cavorted on stage for a full two and a half hours. When the concert ended, she went back to her dressing room, shooed everyone out and lay exhausted on the cot provided for her. A full fifteen minutes elapsed before she could even think of letting anyone in. The security guards had been advised that Fred was not to be allowed to enter, and she could hear him arguing with them in the corridor. She closed her eyes and covered her ears, trying to shut it out. He had been calling nightly and had been coming over to the brownstone constantly. She'd finally resorted to changing all her locks since he refused to give her back the keys. All she wanted was for him to leave her alone.

Wearily, she pulled herself up and walked to the door. She opened it a crack and told the guard to let only her sisters in, then she slammed it shut before Fred could get a chance to say anything. Laurie and Melissa slipped into the room a few minutes later and walked over to hug Andy. She waved them away and croaked in a hoarse voice, "Not now. I've got to change and generally collect myself. I'm sorry, it's just that these things take an awful lot out of me." She held onto the table for support and took a deep breath. Her makeup had been washed off by sweat, and her face was completely white.

Alarmed at her sister's drained appearance, Laurie reached out for her and asked, "Andy, are you all right? You look terrible."

Andy put up her hand and gently pushed her away. "I'm okay. Really, it's normal. I'll be fine in just a minute. Come on, tell me, how was the concert? Did you enjoy it?"

Melissa smiled. "You were terrific as usual, Andy. You had the audience in the palm of your hand."

Andy looked at Laurie. "And my new song? What did you think of my new song, Laur? Did you like it?"

Laurie smiled softly. "Like it? I love it. You knew I would. Andy, really, thank you. I don't know what to say—I—"

Embarrassed, Andy turned around so she wasn't facing her sister and interrupted, "Nothing to thank me for, it'll make me tons of money." She took off her glasses and rubbed her eyes. "Hey, you two want to do me a favor? Wait outside for a bit while I change and then we'll go back to the house together in the limo." She turned to Melissa. "Is the squash player with you?"

Melissa nodded her head.

"Well, bring him along. I'm having a few people over. It's more relaxing than going out after a concert." She kissed each of her sisters and ushered them out the door.

When she emerged from the dressing room, freshly showered, the change in her appearance was breathtaking. Her hair, still damp, fell carelessly around her face. She had carefully replaced the worn off makeup, and she looked exquisite in her pleated gray linen slacks and black silk camisole. "Okay, let's go," she said as she walked briskly down the corridor.

The limousine was waiting at the stage door entrance as Andy and her group left the Garden. As soon as she reached the street, Andy walked directly over to the barricades and shook hands with the fans waiting there. She signed autographs and talked with her fans for about fifteen minutes, then waved good-bye as she entered the car.

Gratefully, Andy sank into the plush leather upholstery. She was perspiring heavily and she reached for a handkerchief to wipe her face. She couldn't understand why she was feeling so weak, and she wished that she could just go home and get into bed.

Melissa leaned forward to catch her eye. "Andy, I want you to meet Shep Greenberg." She gestured toward the man sitting next to her. Shep was six feet tall and athletic looking, with dark curly hair, a sprinkle of freckles across his nose and a very engaging smile. "Remember I told you he's the U.S. squash champion? Shep and I want to talk to you about a great investment—"

"Come on, not now," Laurie interrupted sharply. "This is no time to bother her. Why don't you be businesslike and make an appointment to see her tomorrow."

"Hey, Andy, do I have to do that? I really wanted to talk to you about it tonight. I don't know if the deal will wait."

Andy was a little dizzy and she put her head in her hands. "Please, Melissa, give me a break. I'm really bushed. I promise, I'll talk to you tomorrow. I do want to hear about your deal, but not tonight."

Melissa angrily looked at Laurie and said, "Well, if we have to I guess we'll wait, right, Shep?"

"Yeah, Missy, it's cool. We won't offer this opportunity to anyone else before your sister has a chance at it." He put his arm around Melissa's shoulders and squeezed hard.

"Oh, stuff it!" Laurie murmured under her breath.

Andy heard her and patted her leg. "It's okay," she whispered, almost inaudibly. "Stay calm."

The limousine pulled up in front of Andy's brownstone and the four passengers got out. The party was already in full swing when they entered the living room. As soon as she appeared in the doorway, the crowd of people gathered around Andy, but she pushed through them and sat down on the couch. For some reason she wasn't rebounding as quickly as she usually did after a concert and she needed to rest a moment. She turned to one of the men nearby. "How about bringing me a nice big bourbon on the rocks," she said, then she lay back, closed her eyes, and listened to the party going on around her.

As soon as the drink was brought to her she drained it and took a look at the people in the room. It was an eclectic group. Some of the men wore three piece suits, some were in casual clothes and some effected a balance between the two. The women were just as diversified. Andy recognized many original designer clothes, but then she noticed that a few were clad in jeans and T-shirts. Laurie and Melissa, sitting together across the living room, caught her eye and she smiled to herself. Melissa looked au courant in her bright new Norma Kamali outfit and Laurie, well, she looked like Laurie in a tailored Anne Klein ensemble.

Most of the other guests were from Nickelodean, but there were some others she didn't know. She looked across the room and noticed a young man who seemed vaguely familiar. She stared at him. He was gorgeous. His hair was blond and very curly, and he looked as though he would be at least six feet two inches tall standing. His body was slim and muscular, and he wore jeans that were so tight they appeared to have been molded to his body. A yellow oxford shirt rolled up at the sleeves completed the casual, but sexy look. She knew she had seen him before, but it took a few minutes until she remembered where. He was the actor who played the heartthrob on her mother's favorite soap opera. Curious as to why he was at her party, she continued staring at him. Suddenly he looked directly at her and their eyes met. Andy felt the electricity in his stare and she shivered slightly. Then she lowered her gaze. Abruptly, she got up from the couch and went to join her friend Erica Abbott, who was standing with a group of Nickelodean people by the fireplace.

Erica, a Nickelodean co-owner and a rock singer-songwriter, turned to greet her. "Andy, hey!" she exclaimed. "Are you sick or something? You're white as a sheet!"

Andy barely heard Erica as a wave of lightheadedness swept over her. She knew that if she didn't get upstairs and in bed immediately she was going to faint. "Erica," she whispered, "get Laurie for me. I think I'm going to pass out."

Erica put her arm around Andy's waist and yelled, "Laurie, Andy's in trouble!" Just then, Andy buckled.

Laurie pushed her way through the crowded room. Kneeling down by Andy, she felt for her pulse and clocked it as one hundred fifty. Alarmed, she looked up at the crowd of people encircling them. "Melissa, call an ambulance," she said to her sister, who was standing there, horrified. "Make sure it will go to New York Hospital. Quickly!" At that moment Andy's eyelids fluttered. "Shhh, Andy, just relax. It's okay, kid, we're getting an ambulance. It'll be here in a few minutes."

Andy sat up. "No, I'm fine now," she protested. "Really, I don't need an ambulance. Just help me upstairs." She tried to stand, but her legs gave out under her.

Laurie brushed her sister's hair away with her hand and kissed her forehead. "Just lie down, kiddo. You have a fever. How you got through that concert is beyond me! I think we'd better have you checked out." She took a pillow from the couch, put it under Andy's head and gently pushed her down on it. Too exhausted to protest any more, Andy lay back on the soft cushion and closed her eyes.

The ambulance pulled up at the emergency room entrance of New York Hospital, and the paramedics rushed Andy in. Laurie clung to the edge of the gurney as they ran it down the corridor and into one of the cubicles. She helped her sister onto the examining table. "Wait here a minute," she said to Andy, "I'll be right back."

At the nurse's station, she put in a call to Dr. Levatino, the head of Nephrology. He wasn't on duty, but she did manage to speak to the chief resident who promised to come down and examine Andy immediately. Then she went back to keep her sister company until the doctor came.

Within minutes, Dr. Elizabeth Dreyer entered the small room, nodded to Laurie and asked, "What seems to be the trouble here, Laurie?"

Laurie briefly outlined Andy's symptoms and past medical history while Dr. Dreyer did a preliminary examination and jotted down notes. "Exactly when did you have the kidney transplant?" she asked Andy.

"Seven years ago next month," Andy answered.

"Have you had any problems recently? Any discomfort? Difficulty urinating?"

"No, not really. As far as I know, I've been fine. I'm not feeling so great right now, but ..." she let her voice train off. "Do you see any problems?"

"Well, there's nothing concrete that I can pinpoint right now, but just to be on the safe side, I'd like to admit you and run some tests. Is that all right with you?"

"No, it's not all right. I can't take the time right now. I have some very pressing business to take care of in the next few days."

Laurie touched Andy's arm. "I think it would be prudent for you to take a few days rest anyway," she said gently. "You've been moving at an incredibly strenuous pace for too long and, quite frankly, I don't think that Hawaii vacation was any help at all. Don't make waves, Andy, do what the doctor wants."

Andy closed her eyes and sighed. "This is impossible. I really don't have the time. How long will all this take?"

Dr. Dreyer thought for a moment. "Shouldn't be more than a week. I truly think it's necessary."

"Oh, all right. Just make sure I have a private room as isolated as possible and a telephone, preferably one that doesn't go through the switchboard."

"We do have some suites that are equipped with private phones. I think we can manage to accommodate you." Dr. Dreyer motioned for one of the nurses and told her to make the necessary arrangements. Then she tucked her stethoscope into the pocket of her jacket and patted Andy on the shoulder. "Sleep well," she said as she walked out of the room. "I'll see you in the morning."

The moment she left, Andy sat up and grabbed her twin's arm. "God, Laurie, you don't think it's a kidney thing again, do you? I couldn't take that again. I mean, I really don't think I'm having any trouble at all."

Laurie squeezed her sister's hand reassuringly. "No Andy, I don't think the kidney is failing. But it can't hurt to have some tests done. Anyway, look on the bright side. It'll be a nice rest for you."

"This isn't rest. You know I hate it when doctors poke and pry. And I can never sleep when I'm in the hospital."

"Stop pouting and acting like a spoiled brat. You know this is necessary, so you might as well make the best of it."

Just then the nurse came back with some forms and handed them to Andy to fill out. "Dr. Rabinowitz, Dr. Dreyer would like to see you outside."

"What the hell does she want?" Andy muttered.

"I don't know. Fill out the papers and I'll be back in a minute."

Andy threw the forms on the floor. "I can't fill

them out. You do it. I don't want you speaking to that doctor without me there."

"Oh, Andy, take it easy. It probably isn't about you anyway. Just hold on and I'll be right back." She hurried into the hallway where she saw Dr. Dreyer sitting at the nurse's station writing in Andy's chart. "You wanted to speak to me, Elizabeth?"

"Yes, Laurie. I need some more information about your sister and I thought perhaps you could expedite things and give it to me."

"What type of information?"

Dr. Dreyer proceeded to quiz Laurie about the transplant, asking her some of the more technical aspects of Andy's illness, operation and recovery. Laurie answered her to the best of her memory and instructed her as to where she could find the information she was unable to supply. Finally she turned to go back to Andy and was surprised to see her sister standing behind her, clad only in a hospital gown. Sheepishly, Andy half-grinned. "I just wanted to make sure you weren't saying anything important behind my back."

"You jerk! Get back to that room before they arrest you for indecent exposure!" She put her arm around her sister and, laughing, they walked back to the examining room together.

Andy lay back on the pillow and wished she could get some sleep. After the full battery of tests she had undergone that morning she was utterly exhausted, but still sleep would not come. The smells and sounds of a hospital always unnerved her and the food they served didn't interest her at all. Besides feeling very sick and weak, she was scared, uncomfortable and bored. The nurses didn't treat her with the deference she was accustomed to and repeatedly refused her request for a pill to help her sleep. They insisted that the doctor hadn't left an order for a sleeping pill and that they had no authority to give it to her. She understood their problem, but she wanted them to understand hers and call Dr. Dreyer for a perscription. Her pleas fell on deaf ears, though, and Andy was positive that the nurses were taking perverse pleasure in torturing her. She sighed, squeezed her eyes closed and tried to will herself to sleep.

Just then the phone rang. She sat up and picked up the receiver. It was the front desk inquiring whether she would allow Melissa and Shep up to see her. "You can send Melissa Rabinowitz up, but not the guy," she said tersely. "Make sure he doesn't come up." She hung up the phone and lay back to wait for her sister.

Within minutes Melissa opened the door and strode into the room. "Hey, what's the idea? Shep and I have something important to discuss with you. Why wouldn't you let him up?"

"You have a lot of nerve barging into my hospital room like this demanding my attention!" Andy shouted. "What do you think I'm in this place for? They told me I have to rest and I sure don't need that egotistical jock gaping at me in my nightgown. If you have something to say, say it and then leave, but don't give me that 'important business to discuss' bit. I don't have the strength to play games with you."

Melissa was taken aback. She had never seen her sister so angry or arrogant—especially to her. She opened her mouth to speak, but couldn't get a word out.

"Well, what do you want? Come on, spit it out, I haven't got all day. I'm tired, Melissa. I want to go to sleep."

"Can't Shep come up here to tell you about it? He's much better at this than I am."

"Better at what? Come on, Melisa, what do you want?"

Melissa swallowed hard. "Half a million dollars."

Andy sat up in shock. "Half a million dollars! Are you crazy? For what?"

"Oh, Andy, come on, you can afford it. We're interested in buying a health club here in Manhattan. We found the perfect place, but we need the money to close the deal."

"First of all, that's a lot of liquid cash to anyone. And second of all, what in the world do you know about running a health club?"

"Well, I don't know too much, but Shep does. He's really so athletic and, after all, my degree is in Physical Education." She smiled and continued, "We're planning on having all kinds of racquet sports including squash. It seems there aren't any squash courts in New York City open to people who aren't members of those really exclusive clubs. We would also offer a swimming pool, saunas, whirlpools, steam rooms, masseuse—"

"Enough, I get the picture." Andy interrupted. "But that's a trendy business, Melissa. What makes you think it's going to work?"

"Oh, come on, Andy, I think we'll make it. We at least deserve a chance."

"Yeah, sure, but it's my money that you want to take a chance with. I'll tell you what: I'll think about it and get back to you." She pulled a pen and pad out from the night table and looked at her younger sister. "What's the name of the place you want to buy?"

"Big Apple Health Fare. Why?"

"You must think that I'm vacuous. Didn't it occur to you that I would check out the place before investing half a million dollars in it? Come on, Melissa, give me some credit for some brains." Andy scribbled the name on the pad. "By the way, whose name do you expect this business to be in?"

"Mine and Shep's, of course."

"Of course nothing. If I do decide to give you the money, and right now that's a big if, the business will be in your name and my name. If you want to employ Shep, fine, but he is not going to use my money to own anything."

Stunned, Melissa stared wide-eyed at Andy. "But it was his idea! I mean, he won the U.S. Squash Championship! He has a name! People will come just to see him."

"I very strongly doubt that, Melissa, but even if it's true, he is not going to be part owner of anything I put money into. I've worked too long

PROMISES TO KEEP

and hard for my money to hand it over to someone I neither know nor like. I will not even consider backing you if you don't agree to my terms. Is that clear, and do you understand?"

Subdued, Melissa nodded her head. "I'm going to have to speak to Shep about this, Andy. I'll get back to you. Meanwhile, why don't you do all those business things you have to do to make your decision."

"Yeah, sure," Andy said as she lay back on the bed. "Oh, Lis, by the way, your concern for my health is really touching." She closed her eyes and returned to her pursuit of sleep as her sister dashed out of the room.

Dr. Dreyer clasped her hands behind her back and approached Andy, who was sitting in a chair by the window reading through a sheaf of papers her lawyer had brought her. She looked up. "Well, is the verdict in?" she asked nervously.

"Your test results have come back and I have both good news and bad news for you. The good news is that you do have a kidney infection, but it's one that should be cleared up within a few days with antibiotics—"

"And the bad news?"

"The bad news is that we did find a somewhat significant decrease in kidney output as compared with your previous tests."

Andy's heart raced. "Exactly what does that mean?"

"It will certainly mean some curtailed activity for a while and a very strict adherence to your special diet. Just by looking at you I assume that you don't follow it as you should. You drink alcoholic beverages, don't you?"

"To some extent. Oh, don't give me a face. I know I'm not supposed to. Look, is this decreased output dangerous?"

"Not at the moment, but if it continues to drop I can promise you that your problems will start all over again. You are going to have to be a very, very good girl from now on."

Andy sighed. "Where have I heard that before? All right, I'll try to behave. Now, how long do I have to stay here?"

"At least another three days, until the infection is cleared up. And when you're released, you've got to continue taking your medication religiously and come back to see me once a week. I'm not kidding, Andy, this may be your last chance!"

Andy half-smiled. "Well, that's it, huh?" she said ruefully. "I suppose I can give up the fast life for a while."

"No 'while,' Andy—forever!"

"Okay, Doctor, I get the picture. I'll try my best. Really I will. Thank you." She lowered her head as Dr. Dreyer walked out of the room so the physician wouldn't see the tears that were forming in her eyes. She suddenly felt very lonely and wanted someone to talk to very badly. The problem was there was no one to talk to: Laurie was working and she didn't want to bother her; Fred would take her calling as a sign that she needed him again; and she certainly couldn't talk

PROMISES TO KEEP

to Melissa at this point. Then she realized there was someone whom she could call. She'd call Adrienne.

Adrienne gently placed the receiver back on its cradle, sat down on the kitchen chair and put her hands on the table. Andrea's phone call had upset her and she was feeling very guilty. But it was Andrea who always forced her to say the wrong thing, she thought defensively. She poured herself a cup of coffee and took a bite of her doughnut. It bothered her that she felt so close to one twin and so distant from the other. As far as she could tell she had treated them both the same when they were growing up.

Shaking her head, she said aloud, "I don't know what I did wrong." Then she picked up the phone again, dialed Laurie's number and waited while she was called to the phone.

"Hello, dear," she said when her daughter got on. "How are you?"

"Ma! What's the problem? Why are you calling me at work?"

"Andy just called me. She said that she's sick. I wanted to ask you about it."

"Didn't she tell you? I haven't seen her yet today, but she seemed to be progressing nicely when I visited her last night. Did she get all her test results back?"

"I have no idea. All she told me was that she was sick with a kidney infection and that she was divorcing Fred. Then she started telling me how unhappy she was, that she had to give up everything in life that she enjoys and that nobody cares what happens to her. She sounded so unlike herself, it worried me."

"She was feeling sorry for herself. I guess her doctor told her about the decreased kidney functon—"

"She told me that she couldn't drink anymore or carouse late into the night. So I said 'good, now you'll be more healthy.' I wasn't criticizing her, believe me Laurie. I was happy that she called and was telling me these things. She never calls me just to talk. Then she started yelling at me," Adrienne said in a frustrated voice. "She said that I never take her side, and that I shouldn't worry, she'll take care of herself. So I said 'that's what got you into this mess in the first place, obviously you can't take care of yourself.'"

"Oh no, Ma, you didn't," Laurie groaned. "Why did you have to do that!"

"What do you mean why did I have to do that? What did I do? She started yelling at me for no good reason so I told her what I thought."

"What else did you say?"

"I told her she was a stupid girl. I mean, what would happen if this kidney failed? Where did she expect to get another one? You only have one left and you need it for yourself, you're not giving it to her."

"You know you shouldn't have said that, Ma," Laurie replied in a strained voice. "It really didn't do any good and I'm sure Andy didn't appreciate it. I don't know what gets into you when you talk to her. Why can't you just listen?"

PROMISES TO KEEP

"I was listening to her, but she got nasty as usual. I didn't like her tone of voice. Besides, why is she divorcing Fred? She would never have been in this fix if she wasn't separated from him."

Laurie cringed. "Did you say that to her?"

"Yes I did, and then she hung up on me. Oh, Laurel, I know I shouldn't have said those things, but I can't help it. I only said I wanted her to be healthy and she started yelling at me."

"Ma, all she wanted was a little sympathy. Why couldn't you have given her that?"

"She didn't give me a chance. I told you, she started yelling at me. I don't want to talk to her anymore. It only upsets me and I'm getting too old for this."

"Suit yourself, Ma. It's obvious that the two of you just can't have a pleasant conversation, and I'm tired of being stuck in the middle. You gave me an earful now, and I guarantee Andy will give me another one when I see her later. Just do me a favor and leave me out of it from now on. Look, I have to get back to work now. I'll speak to you again next week. Take care. Good-bye." She nodded as she heard her mother say "I love you" and hung up the phone. This was getting ridiculous she thought as she walked briskly back to the nursery. She was always the go-between, and she couldn't take the games anymore. They were going to have to work out their differences without her from now on. With that decision made, she opened the door to the nursery, put on a hospital gown and went to check on her tiny patients.

Wendy Susans

* * *

Marilyn Koppel sat down at the breakfast table across from Philip and thought about the juicy piece of gossip she was about to impart to him. She knew that it would ruin her husband's day, but she didn't care. She wanted to ruin his day. He wasn't concerned about her feelings, so why should she worry about his? She threw the Boston Globe at her husband and sat back with a satisfied smile on her face.

Startled, Philip looked up. "What was that for?"

"Look on page 29. There's an article about your former girlfriend there."

Philip glanced at the paper and sighed. "Please, Marilyn, let's not start so early in the morning. I have enough on my mind today without you bringing this up again."

Marilyn ignored her husband and pointed to the newspaper. "You see, she's in the hospital. There's a whole long story describing her kidney problems. Gee whiz, isn't it too bad that she has such problems? Hey, I have an idea. Maybe you should go visit her. You and she can talk over your illnesses. Compare notes, so to speak."

Philip turned white with anger and pushed his breakfast plate across the table. "Damn you! You never know when to quit. Can't you ever give up? You're such a ball buster!"

She laughed cynically. "Nothing much left to bust, is there?"

Philip stood up. "I've had it! You've succeeded in lousing up another day for me. I hope that pleases you immensely."

"Oh yes, Philip, it pleases me, considering that you've succeeded in ruining my life."

"Then why don't you leave, damn it?"

Marilyn's eyes misted, and she abruptly stood and began loading dishes into the dishwasher. "I love you, and I wanted your children," she said in an unsteady voice. "Now I'll never have them. Don't you understand what that's doing to me?"

Not able to take any more, Philip picked up his briefcase, walked out of the kitchen and left his wife sobbing at the sink. He thought for the millionth time how much better his life would be if Andy Reuben didn't exist. Every time Marilyn read about her she went crazy, and the tension Andy's name evoked was destroying both of them.

The hot August sun beat down relentlessly on the city streets as Andy paid the taxi driver and hurried into the apartment building on Park Avenue. She was grateful for the blast of cold air that hit her as she opened the door to her psychiatrist's office.

Andy nodded to the receptionist and she slipped into the comfortable and familiar office of Dr. Gloria Bartis. The room was decorated in shades of brown with touches of yellow and light blue. Andy sat down in a dark brown leather wing chair and waited for Dr. Bartis. For the past eight and a half years she had been regularly seeing the doctor. She wasn't sure whether the frequent sessions had actually helped her solve any of her problems, but by now they had become a habit. And it was nice to bounce her thoughts off someone who was relatively objective about her life.

"Hello, Andy," Dr. Bartis said, smiling broadly, as she walked into the room. She was a middle-aged woman with brown hair that softly framed a lined but attractive face. She took off her cream colored linen suit jacket, sat down behind the large mahogany desk and eased her feet out of her shoes. "It's so good to see you! I assume that this visit means we will be resuming our regular weekly sessions?"

"Yeah, well, I haven't been in since I got home and I thought it might be time, you know?"

Dr. Bartis nodded her head. "Are you feeling well? Is the kidney infection cleared up yet?"

"Pretty much so. I'm still on antibiotics, and of course they said I have to swear off liquor."

"Is that a problem for you?"

"Sometimes, yeah. You know that I enjoy the high that a drink gives me. Damn, what good is it all? I don't do drugs anymore and now liquor is off-limits, too. I don't know what I'm going to do. I really do need something to help relax me."

"Are we starting that again, Andy? Why are you so tense?"

"Oh, the damn business is driving me crazy, Fred isn't around to discuss things with anymore, and my sister Melissa has turned into a money grubbing bitch."

"Hmm, we've already spoken over the phone about Freddie, so tell me about Melissa."

PROMISES TO KEEP

Andy related the whole story about Melissa, Shep and the health club. Melissa had been bothering her constantly. So much, in fact, that Andy was considering refusing her the money if only because of her incessant nagging.

"So Melissa is really pushing you to the limit, isn't she?"

"She sure is. I don't know if I was the one who created the monster by indulging her too much, but I do know that I can't take her selfishness right now. I have too many other problems."

"I don't think you should blame yourself. You felt you were being good to your sister. After all, your father died when she was young, and you tried to compensate for the fact that you couldn't be with her very much. It's very common to over-give under those circumstances, but you certainly shouldn't feel guilty about it. The question is, do you want to give her this?"

"I do and I don't. She's pushing me too hard, and even though I had planned to help her she's making it almost impossible to do so."

"How about this fellow she's living with?"

Andy lit a cigarette, took a long drag and waved her hand. "He's typical for her. He comes from Long Island and he's about as ruthlessly ambitious as they come. But, of course, my mother thinks he's a wonderful, smart Jewish boy. You know, I really find it annoying. I don't think my mother blinks an eye at the fact that Melissa is living with him." She laughed humorlessly. "Boy, what a difference from when I was sleeping with Philip. Oh, by the way, I have something really interesting to tell you."

Andy shifted in her chair and leaned forward. "When Laurie went up to Boston for Melissa's graduation she ran into Philip, or rather he ran after her. He spotted her going shopping and insisted on buying her a drink. Then when they sat down in the bar he went crazy and started blaming me for problem's he's having. Poor guy, it sounds as if he's really unhappy. He mentioned the abortion and said that I haven't heard the last of him."

"That is strange. Does it frighten you?"

"No, not really. Philip was never the violent type. I just feel badly that his life isn't going as well as he planned."

"He must be very unhappy. People who are unhappy frequently live in the past."

"That's true, I guess, but it really is weird to have something like that dredged up again."

"You never think about the abortion?"

Andy took a puff of her cigarette and shook her head. "Not really. What's done is done. Besides, I really have no desire to have a child. I mean, why do I need to have my own kid? I have a niece whom I adore and can send home when I want to, and she even looks like me. That's all I need. Having a child is not one of my priorities." She stood up and walked to the window. "Anyway, I'd be a lousy mother." Abruptly, she spun around. "Speaking of lousy mothers, mine was pretty lousy when I was in the hospital."

"What do you mean?"

"Boy, did she ever dump on me when I called to

tell her I was sick." She imitated her mother. "It's all your fault. Because of your stupidity you'll lose Laurie's kidney and, get this Doctor, *she'll* have gone through all that for nothing. She didn't care how I was, she didn't even ask. For all it mattered to her, I could have died. She didn't even offer to come down and be with me. Not that I would have let her," she amended.

"And that hurt you?"

"Yeah, it sure did! Wouldn't it have hurt you? That along with this business from Melissa, and Fred's pleadings and Nickelodean's board—did I tell you they were mad that they had to postpone a board meeting because I was sick? They wanted to actually conduct it in my hospital room! God, I feel so used. Do you know the only one, *the only one,* who was at all solicitous of me because I was sick was Laurie? Maybe too solicitous, but solicitous nonetheless. That nut kept bringing me snacks from a health food store across the street from the hospital." She made a face, laughed and then grew serious. "She visited me every chance she got, and that first night, when I was feeling really horrendous and couldn't sleep, she stayed with me all night. You know, the only time I felt safe in that cruddy place was when she was with me."

"You've really reconciled your relationship with Laurie, haven't you?"

Andy nodded solemnly. "Yeah, I suppose I have." She put out her cigarette. "God, Dr. Bartis, can you believe it? She's the only one I know in the whole world who always loves me.

Wendy Susans

And you know what? It's not because of all the money I make or can give her, not because I'm this great big star called Andy Reuben. She doesn't care anything about that." She smiled and shook her head. "I guess to her I'll always be Andy her twin sister. She loves me because she just plain does and that's such a nice feeling."

"Yes it is, isn't it? But Andy, I'd like to talk some more about your mother. You've made two disparaging remarks about her today, and I think—"

Andy looked at her watch and picked up her attache case. "Whoops, sorry, I've got to get going. I know this session was awfully short, but that board meeting was rescheduled for today and they'll have my head if I'm late. Thanks, Dr. Bartis, see you next week." She waved as she breezed out of the office.

"Andy, wait a minute! Andy!" Gloria Bartis threw up her hands in disgust. Damn! Every time she wanted to delve deeper into an unpleasant subject, Andy either refused or left. Despite Andy's long association with her, they never actually went beneath the surface. Dr. Bartis wrote a few notes in a bulging file, then stood and left her office.

The Nickelodean executive offices were located on Avenue of the Americas, near Radio City. The company had been called SMW Records until it had been bought out by Fred, Andy and four other rock stars. They'd renamed it and saved it from bankruptcy. For eight years the company had prospered, but the past year had been plagued by falling sales and diminished profits. As far as Andy knew, the board meeting that day was to be a brainstorming session in the hopes that they could stem the tide and reverse the downward slide.

Andy was late, so she ran past the secretary, hurried into her boardroom and quickly slipped into her assigned seat at the table. The meeting had already begun and the quarterly financial report was being discussed. Before looking over the papers in front of her, she scanned the board members present. Sitting directly across from her was Erica Abbott, who was her only real friend on the board. Red-haired and freckle-faced, she was a native of Iowa and had a levelheaded midwestern disposition. Although Erica was one of the foremost rock song writers in the business, and had been since the early sixties, she did not have an ego that needed to be constantly petted. Not so Ginny Paul, who was sitting next to Erica. Ginny's thick mane of black hair surrounded a small heart-shaped face that wore a perpetual frown. She had been singing professionally for twenty years, since she was fifteen years old, and her career had stagnated. Her selfishness was well-known, and she and Andy were constantly at odds about one thing or another. Next to Ginny sat Maddy Gabriel, who had recently divorced another board member, Jesse Fowler. Jesse was absent from the meeting, an increasingly common event since he was strung out on heroin much of the time and couldn't function. Maddy, a Barnard graduate whose long-legged good looks had been featured in Vogue and Harper's Bazaar, had been left with five children and a waning career. She refused to tour and her records weren't selling anymore. The last board member who was a performer was David McAllister, whose sandy-colored hair, big ears and short stature gave him an elfish appearance. David was trying to revive his salability as a performer by doing television and making personal appearances. Nickelodean had rejected his last album, and he had been very upset about it. Fred was also on the board, along with five other non-musicians.

When the accountant finished reading the report, Fred commented, "Well, it looks like we're in for a little bit of trouble here. The future doesn't look too promising if we continue to ignore what the public wants. It seems that the only reason we managed to stay in the black last quarter was because Andy's record 'Reckless Lies;' was released. None of our new people did anything spectacular and there doesn't seem to be very much interest in our other established performers."

Ginny Paul jumped up. "If you and your publicity people would do as much for us as you do for her," she said, pointing a finger at Andy, "we might be able to do something to help this damn company. I wanted to make a video of my new single but I was refused. What makes Andy worth videos and not me? Look, there better be some changes made here or I'm selling out. I have no desire to record for the Andy Reuben record

PROMISES TO KEEP

company." She sat down angrily.

Erica turned to her. "Come on, Ginny, that's not fair. Andy's style is better suited to video music. She moves well, she's attractive, and she appeals to the age group watching the videos. The rest of us haven't been able to change our music to fit the times. Quite frankly, I don't know if we can."

Maddy smiled. "Do we really want to change? Face it, Erica, it's just not our style. I'm not sure I care, either. My music may be getting older, but so am I. I just don't have that drive anymore. I have plenty of money, my children, my lifestyle and I'm very happy living out of the public eye. The only time I care to do any performing is when it's for causes I believe in."

"Well, that's you," Ginny retorted. "I won't sit back on my ass and let the world pass me by. I can't stand this company anymore. The only promotion that's done is for Andy and those new wave and punk groups. They're so piss poor musically—"

"I assume you're including me in that evaluation?" Andy glared at Ginny. "Be that as it may, the kids like my kind of music and they don't like yours, Ginny, and it's the kids who buy most of the records. Who do you think watches MTV? Certainly not your few fans!"

"The hell with MTV! We don't need it!"

"I beg your pardon, Ginny," Fred interrupted, "but that's what's happening now. I think we have to get into videos even more heavily or else we're not going to survive. We're having all our new people videotaped and we're plugging the hell out of them. All we need is one of those groups to take off. The potential is there, we just have to exploit it."

Jim Duncan, Chairman of the Board, agreed. "No question about it, that has to be our direction now. You people are still superb musicians, but you're not what the audience is buying, with the exception of Andy over there. She still goes platinum even before we ship her records out, and she still appeals to a tremendous cross section. That's exactly why we're preparing a two record set of Andy's greatest hits for early fall release."

Shocked speechless, Andy sat up and listened very closely. Her feelings about a greatest hits album were well-known. She never wanted to release one. She meticulously constructed each album so that it was an entity unto itself, a complete musical statement, so to speak. To pull pieces out of each one and then put them together randomly was to completely destroy any continuity. She strove for a distinctly different style on each album, and to mix those styles on one record would, she believed, be disconcerting to the listener.

Fred continued Jim's argument. "You've never had a greatest hits album, Andy, and we feel it's time. We all know it will be a blockbuster, just what we need."

Andy gripped the edge of the table and stood up, angrily narrowing her eyes. "My integrity means more to me than a blockbuster. You know

I like to move on. There's nothing artistically innovative about one of those albums."

"What about your new fans?" Fred countered. "Maybe they want some of your more popular older songs without buying the whole album. There's nothing wrong with that; it actually saves them money."

"Christ, you above all should know that I don't want some of that old material re-released. It was for another time in my life. Those songs can't be resurrected just like that and still be meaningful. No, I won't allow it."

Jim smiled softly, "I'm afraid there's nothing you can do about it."

"What do you mean there's nothing I can do about it?"

"If you check your contract, you'll see that the company owns all the rights to your recordings. We have the last word in the matter."

Andy felt as though the wind had been knocked out of her. "What?" she croaked. "Fred, is that true?"

"I'm afraid so, Andy."

Emotionally overwrought, Andy sat down and held her head in her hands. "My God, this is like a nightmare! Why didn't you tell me that you were considering this? Am I just some piece of meat that can be used any way you see fit? Fred, you knew I wouldn't want this."

"There was nothing I could do about it."

"You could have told me. You at least owed me that."

"It would have made no difference. The

decision was made and the album has, for the most part, already been put together." He hesitated. "I'm afraid I have some other news for you that you might not like. We're setting up a promotional campaign for the record that will entail personal appearances, TV interviews and the like. You're obligated to do that, too."

Drained, Andy didn't know whether she had strength left to fight. "You know I've just been sick and I'm supposed to take it easy! I have no stamina! Why are you doing this to me? Why are you punishing me for being the only one who makes money for this company?"

Jim Duncan answered. "Because otherwise I don't think we can save the company from bankruptcy, it's that simple. You're an owner of the company and you've got to do what you can to salvage it. You're our only real salable produce right now, and we expect this album to buy us some time. We hope that in the future we'll have more artists with your earning potential but, quite frankly, you're our only strength at this moment."

Andy closed her eyes and slumped down in her seat. She knew that she could find some way to fight this legally, but what was the point? If the company went under she would stand to lose a tremendous amount of money. It was obvious that she would have to do what they wanted. The record was bad enough, but traveling on a promotional tour was the worst. There was none of the artistic satisfaction she got during a singing tour. This type of thing was sheer torture to her—the

PROMISES TO KEEP

same interviews day after day, mouthing the same words, one night in each city, the lonely hotels, being mauled by over-enthusiastic fans. She didn't know whether she could endure it. "When will I have to go?"

"Well, we're hoping to record something a little different for the album first," Fred replied. "We'd like a new song as the first cut."

"What kind of new song?" Andy asked softly.

"We just signed a kid who we want to introduce through you," Jim said. "His name is Eric Boutelle and we're very high on him."

"So I'm supposed to do a duet with him?"

"That's right."

"Any other surprises for me?"

"Well," Fred said, "we've got to put a rush job on the album so we'd like a song we could use by next week at the latest."

Andy shook her head. "Thanks a lot. I'm surprised you didn't want it yesterday." Exhausted and feeling physically ill, she picked up the papers in front of her and pushed away from the table. "You'll have to excuse me now, I'm not feeling too well. I'll be in my office if you need me." She walked to the door and slowly left the room.

Erica looked after her friend. "That was a rotten thing to do and a rotten way to do it."

Fred pursed his lips. "I wouldn't waste any time worrying about her, Erica. She'll end up on her feet. She always does." He felt a twinge of regret that he hadn't told Andy about the record before the meeting, but pushed it aside.

Andy practically ran down the hallway to her office. It took every bit of self-control she could muster to keep herself from screaming. She desperately needed to be alone and to think things over. To her dismay, when she reached her office door, she saw Melissa and Shep waiting for her. Barely restraining her anger, she sat down behind the modern glass desk and snapped, "What do you want?"

Melissa leaned across the desk, "Look, Andy," she said in an irritated voice, "we really have to have your answer this morning. We've been waiting for almost two weeks and I don't think there's any sense in dragging this out any longer. Shep agrees to your terms, so what's the problem?"

Andy felt the rage that she had kept bottled up during the meeting explode inside her. She stood up and started pacing around the room. "The problem?" she yelled. "What problem could there be? After all, it's only half a million dollars that you're asking for, it's only a questionable deal at best, it's only that I'm not sure that the two of you won't lose my very hard earned money, and it's only that I just got out of the hospital and haven't even fully recovered! What's the problem, you say? Try that I'm sick and tired of your nagging and whining. I told you that as soon as I could I would give you an answer, but that's not good enough for you! Damn it, Melissa, you're being pushy and I don't like pushy people."

Melissa, her face white, stood up and walked

PROMISES TO KEEP

toward the door. "Come on, Shep, let's go. She obviously needs to cool down and I don't need to be insulted any more."

Shep took her arm. "Wait a minute. She hasn't told us whether she'll give us the money or not."

"Are you crazy? You mean you still think she'll give us the money?"

"Sure, why not? We need it, don't we?"

Andy smiled sardonically. Shep disgusted her and Melissa's attitude bitterly disappointed her, but according to the information she had gathered, there was an excellent possibility that the health club could be a real money-make. It was fashionable to be a health fanatic, and the location was convenient and would almost certainly be profitable with the correct management. Her lawyer had indicated that the present owners had left the busness cash poor and had over expanded. It would be a perfect setup for Melissa if only the deal didn't include Shep. As a matter of fact, she had been hoping to do something like this for Melissa after she graduated from college.

Andy stood up and walked in front of her desk. "Very good, Shep," she spat out. "You really know the bottom line, don't you. Take the insults, but get the cash." Her whole body sagged. "I'm tired of arguing. See my lawyer tomorrow." She wrote a name on a piece of paper and handed it to Melissa. "You know, Lis," she said, looking directly into her eyes, "you've turned into a poor excuse for a sister. I don't know why, but I expected more from you. Now get out," she concluded wearily.

Melissa, still white-faced, reached out to her sister. "Don't say that, Andy! Please, Andy, don't! I love you! You know I do!"

Andy pushed her arm away and said quietly, "Just get out of here. Don't you understand, I don't want you here."

Shep took Melissa's arm and began pulling her to the door. "Thank you, you won't regret it," he mumbled. As they left the room, Melissa turned to Andy, her eyes pleading for forgiveness.

Stony-faced, Andy stared back at her contemptuously. When the door closed, she dropped in her chair, tears rolling down her face. "Damn you all to hell," she whispered. "What do all of you want from me? What's the use?" She rubbed her face and looked around the office. "I've got to get out of here." Grabbing her briefcase, she fled from her office. As she approached the bank of elevators, Erica caught up with her and put her hand out to comfort her. Andy gave her a ferocious look and roughly pushed her away. When the elevator door opened, she slipped in without a backward glance.

Laurie hovered over the isolette, unwilling to leave the tiny infant who was inside. The baby girl had been born the previous night and was having trouble breathing. She weighed one pound, four ounces and Laurie was afraid she wouldn't survive. "We can't allow her to lose weight," Laurie said aloud to the nurse standing beside her. She checked the respirator the child was hooked up to. "Keep a sharp eye on her, please."

The nurse nodded. "Dr. Rabinowitz, why don't you go take a break? You've been here all night and I can see that you're exhausted. Don't worry, I'll take good care of this little sweetheart."

Laurie smiled. "I know you will, Maureen. You neo-natal nurses are the best around. I love you all." She wearily took off the green gown and put on a white hopsital jacket over her Polo shirt and cocoa brown slacks. As she left the nursery, she was surprised to see Andy staring through the plate glass window. She walked over and put her hand on her sister's shoulder. "What are you doing here? How did you manage to get up without anyone stopping you?"

Andy started, as if coming out of a deep reverie. "I asked where you were and they told me," she answered in a dull voice. "Then I took the elevator up."

"Impossible. You aren't allowed up here." Laurie frowned. "Hey, wasn't today your first day back at work?" Andy didn't answer her. She looked at her sister closely. "What's the matter? Are you okay?"

Andy continued to look into the nursery. "You really enjoy your work, don't you? Watching you, it's so obvious. That baby is awfully small. Will she live?"

"Hopefully. We have an excellent track record." Laurie hesitated. "Andy, is there something wrong?"

"Things are more sophisticated now. When we

were born, premature babies didn't have much of a chance, did they?"

"Oh, I don't know. It depended on how healthy they were to begin with. I guess we save more of the unhealthy ones now, though. Andy, come on, what's the matter?"

Andy looked at her sister wistfully. "You know, I should have finished medical school with you and become a doctor. I envy you. Your life is so much better than mine."

Shocked and scared by the way her sister was speaking, Laurie took her by the shoulders and shook her gently. "Stop it, Andy. Talk to me!"

Andy hung her head. "Oh, Laur, I can't take it any more. I have to find a way out of this life. Nothing I do ever works out right, everyone takes advantage of me. I have no life to call my own. Oh God, Laur!" Tears ran down her cheeks.

Worried and upset, Laurie led her sister to her office, sat her down, closed the door and knelt in front of her. Andy's emotional health had been of great concern to her since the breakup with Fred. She knew that the impending divorce was more difficult for Andy than she would ever admit and she wished her sister would talk to her about it.

Andy slumped in the chair and held her head in her hands. "Do you have any Percodan? I have a wicked headache."

"Percodan? I don't know Andy, that's pretty strong medication for just a headache."

"Please, Laur, I really need one."

"What's bothering you? I haven't seen you this disturbed in ages. How can I help you if you won't tell me what's wrong?"

"Just give me the pill, please!" Andy wept hysterically and Laurie was becoming frantic.

"I'll be right back." Laurie left the office and returned a few minutes later with a glass of water and a pill in a small paper cup. "Here, try this. I think it'll help."

Andy nodded her head, swallowed the pill and gulped down the water.

Laurie sat down next to her sister and took her hand. "Now, tell me what's wrong."

"Everything. I just can't seem to get a handle on anything anymore. And it's not that I'm not trying. I went to Dr. Bartis this morning and I was telling her how awful everything was and then I had to go to a Nickelodean board meeting. You know, it was supposed to be last week but I was in the hospital and they refused to have it without me. Now I know why."

"Is there some trouble with the company?"

"Well, obviously we aren't doing too well. The industry slump has hit us particularly hard for a number of reasons. You know that Maddy, Erica, Jesse, David and Ginny aren't selling, and the company hasn't really replaced them. I'm the only one who makes any money at all for us. Now all of a sudden they've decided to change direction and are picking up new groups, making videos and so on. As far as I'm concerned, that's great. Until all this pays off though, they're depending entirely on me. Five thousand jobs, Laurie, all my responsibility! Then they dropped this bomb on me. To increase profits next quarter they decided to release a two record set of my greatest hits."

"What! I thought you've always refused to do one of those?"

"I have. But apparently I have no say in the matter. Nickelodean owns all the rights to my recordings and they'll do it even without my consent. What makes it even worse is that I have to go away again."

"Again? So soon? Why?"

"I have to promote the record. You know, talk shows, interviews, personal appearances ... God, what a drag. It's going to drive me crazy. You know what happens to me when I'm on the road alone."

"But you can't do that! You're still not well. Physically it's impossible, and mentally ... didn't Fred stop them?"

"He probably initiated the whole thing. I didn't realize his urge for revenge was so strong. Anyway, impossible or not, I have to go. It's my company, too, and I guess I'm sort of as dependent on it as it is on me."

Laurie closed her eyes and shook her head. "Andy, I really don't think it's such a good idea."

Andy snapped, "What do you mean it's not a good idea? Don't you understand I have no choice?" Tears continued to flow from her eyes.

Laurie took a tissue from her drawer and gently wiped her sister's eyes. "All right, don't get upset. I'm just trying to help."

"Well, you can't help, nobody can. It's all settled, and I can't do anything about it."

PROMISES TO KEEP

"I'm just worried about you. I feel so helpless. Isn't there anything I can do for you?"

"Nothing except what you're doing right now. At least I know you care about me, and I don't get hassles from you. Not like good old Melissa."

"Melissa? How does she hassle you?"

"Don't you know? You mean she didn't tell you about it?"

"Tell me about what?"

"About her great business deal."

"Oh, right. She mentioned something about an investment the night of your concert. Is there a problem?"

"No, no problem at all. I just have to finance her to the tune of half a million dollars."

Laurie choked and put her hand to her mouth. "What? Half a million dollars? Do you mean to tell me you gave her that kind of money?"

"Gave is not exactly the right word. Badgered into giving is more like it. You just have no idea . . . She's been at me since the day after I went into the hospital. It seems that she and Shep want to start a health club in New York, and who do you think their friendly banker is?"

"Oh, Andy, why did you to it? I don't think she knows how to do anything on her own. You give her too much. It's not necessary." Laurie touched her sister's cheek tenderly. "You're such a soft touch, always have been. Nobody knows that better than I." She frowned, then asked, "How did she dare ask you for that kind of money?"

"Oh, that was easy. She just came right out and asked, and she hasn't stopped asking since.

I've gotten a call from her and that boyfriend of hers at least once, usually three or four times a day."

Laurie made a face. "I don't like him at all, Andy. He's such an opportunist."

"That's why I won't allow his name to be on any of the legal papers. He'll own that club over my dead body! Melissa had a fit about that, too."

"So why did you give her the money? You haven't answered me."

Andy sighed. "They showed up right after that damn board meeting and I just wanted to get rid of them. I threw them out of my office and told Melissa that I didn't want to see her again. I've had it. If she has to contact me for any reason, it'll be through my lawyer."

"Oh, Andy, no! I hate for something like this to happen between you two. I can't believe Melissa would do something like that. It has to be Shep's influence."

"What difference does it make? She still did it to me, and it really hurts. Laurie, I can't take much more of this." Andy's voice broke and she began sobbing anew.

Laurie put her arms around her sister and hugged her. Andy returned the embrace with a fierceness that brought tears to Laurie's eyes. She thought a moment, then said, "Andy, how about this? Come home with me for a few days. Don't tell anyone where you are and we'll take care of you—pamper you a little. You'll have no phone calls, no hassling, no nothing, just boring me and Bette. How about it kid? How does that sound?"

"I'd like that but—"

"No buts. We want you and you need us. Okay?"

Andy attempted a smile. "I don't know. I—"

"I'll tell you what. Don't even stop at home to get clothes. We'll handle it all. Okay?"

Andy hesitated. Although the offer was tempting, she was reluctant to take Laurie up on it. Over the past ten years she had gotten used to living away from her twin. If she went, she was afraid that she would fall into the old pattern of letting Laurie take over for her. That was one of the reasons that she left Fred: he had become a substitute for Laurie after she ran away from home. Now she felt that she was strong enough to stand on her own.

On the other hand, it would be nice to stay with Laurie and Bette and forget how troubled her own life was. A few days wouldn't hurt . . . she could go back to being strong after that . . . . Just a few days of blissful peace. She stood up and kissed Laurie on the cheek. "A deal. If you're sure I won't be any trouble, I'll come. And thank you, Laur, I don't know what I would do without you."

Laurie was surprised but pleased that her sister had agreed so readily to her proposal. "Wait here for a minute," she said. "I'll check the nursery and then we can leave." She hurried out, leaving Andy alone in the small office.

Andy put her hand to her forehead. "Oh, God," she thought. "I hope I'm not making a mistake."

Laurie's co-op apartment was on the 17th floor

of a high rise building on the upper east side, between 1st and 2nd Avenues. Although she had lived there for four years, she had not bothered to do much decorating. Before she'd moved in, she'd gone to a furniture store and completely furnished the entire apartment in 2 hours. Everything she put into the apartment was functional and spare, except for a few modern paintings on the walls, which had been given to her by Andy.

Laurie stood at the counter in the narrow kitchen preparing a spinach salad for dinner. She checked the frozen sourdough rolls in the oven, and ran cold water over the hard-boiled eggs. After pulling over a stool, she sliced the eggs into the salad and shook some bacon bits over it. She was more than a little upset about her sister's problems, although she loved having her at the apartment. Andy was sitting on the patterned Danish wool rug in the living room playing a game of Candyland with Bette, and she could hear them laughing and chattering.

If only there was something she could do to help her, she thought, then she laughed and shook her head. That's what had caused the rift between them in the first place.

Involuntarily, she thought back on their childhood. It had always been this way, as far back as she could remember. She continuously wanted to help Andy but was never able to. Andy had her own private anguishes and she never let Laurie intrude upon them. But she always knew, she always felt guilty. Laurie couldn't help but think that all of Andy's troubles stemmed from what had happened so long ago. She frequently wished that she could go back and right all the wrongs she had done to her sister.

The sound of giggling snapped her out of her reverie and she turned to see her sister and daughter in the doorway watching her. As always, she was struck by how alike they looked, not only in appearance, but in mannerisms.

"Mommy, we're hungry. Andy wants dinner and so do I."

Andy grinned down at her niece. "We decided that you were eating all that delectable rabbit food all by yourself. Can't we at least have a nibble?"

Laurie laughed. "I guess I was daydreaming. Here, it's all ready. Help me take it to the table." They each picked up a dish and carried it to the dining room.

They sat at the glass table and quietly attacked the salad. Andy and Laurie quickly finished their dinner, but Bette dawdled and played with the food.

"Bette, stop dreaming and eat your dinner!" Laurie said sternly. "I want to get this place cleaned up before I go back to the hospital."

"Oh, Mommy, I thought you were staying home tonight. Is Andy staying with me instead of Mrs. Barrett?"

"I certainly am, sweetie. I'll tell you what. We'll have some fun before you go to bed, maybe play some cards, watch some MTV . . ." She looked at Laurie slyly.

"Just make sure she gets to bed by seven-thirty, Andy. She has to be up early." Laurie started stacking the dishes and brought them into the kitchen to be put into the dishwasher. Then she looked at the kitchen clock. "Could you two please finish cleaning up? I want to take a shower before I leave."

"What? The great Andy Reuben cleaning up a kitchen?" Andy cried in mock horror. "Unthinkable!"

"Oh please, Andy, we can do it together. It won't be too bad," Bette pleaded, unaware that her aunt was teasing.

"Okay, Bette," Andy whispered, "I'll do it under one condition. You come out with me to get some Häagen-Daz."

Bette's eyes lit up. "Oh boy! Häagen-Daz! I love chocolate chocolate chip!"

Laurie turned around and laughed. "I heard that. Andy, you are incorrigible. You're going to spoil Bette outrageously. All that sugar—"

"Oh, come on, Laur. What better things do I have to do with my life than spoil the people I love." Andy smiled and sat back in her chair. She was feeling mellow and relaxed. Visiting Laurie wasn't turning out to be so bad after all.

Late that night, Andy put out her cigarette, immediately lit another one and paced the living room. She was still furious at Jim Duncan and the rest of the board. Why hadn't Fred stopped them? Was he so hell-bent on revenge that he would stoop to something that was so abhorrent to her? The album was bad enough, but she had no desire to write a song for someone else to sing, especially when he was supposed to ride on her

PROMISES TO KEEP

coattails to success. Feeling discouraged, she hummed a tune and scratched down some melody ideas. Restless again, she stood up, walked to the window and gazed at Queens across the East River. The twinkling lights mesmerized her and she stood watching, with her arms folded across her chest.

Laurie put her key in the lock and quietly opened the door to the apartment. As she entered the living room, she saw Andy standing at the window, deep in thought. "Andy?" she whispered. "What are you doing up at this hour?"

Startled, Andy spun around. "Laurie! I didn't hear you come in." She looked at her watch. "It's only two o'clock. That's not so late. I've got to write a new song for that album and I'm having trouble with the lyrics."

"New song? I thought the record was only going to have your old songs."

"Oh, I guess I forgot to tell you. They want one new song right away. I'm supposed to do it with one of their new artists. Their plan is to promote him quickly and I'm the vehicle they're using."

"Who is he?"

"Beats me. They told me his name, but it means nothing to me."

"Bette went to sleep with no trouble?"

"Oh yeah, no trouble at all. We had such a good time after you left. You want to hear something funny? I put on some of your clothes to go out to Häagen-Daz with her and absolutely nobody recognized me! It was the weirdest feeling!"

"Did you like it?"

Andy cocked her head to the side. "It was sort of nice . . . different. But, believe it or not, I wanted to shout 'Hey, look, at me! I'm Andy Reuben!'"

"You are strange. You always say you hate all the attention and then when you don't get it, you miss it." She looked at her sister curiously. "How in the world are you holding my jeans up?"

Andy stood up and lifted the shirt she was wearing. "I had to ruin one of your belts." The belt was wrapped around her waist and there was an obviously homemade hole punched in it. "I couldn't find scissors, so I had to use a knife. I'm sorry, but don't worry, I'll buy you a new one."

Laurie laughed. "I'm not worried, believe me."

"How's that baby you were working on today?"

"She's fine. She's the reason I went back to the hospital. I'm glad you were here so that I could do it. She seems to be responding quite well. We'll keep our fingers crossed."

"Good," Andy said enthusiastically. "Oh, guess what? Bette and I brought you a surprise." She walked into the kitchen, took a spoon from the drawer, opened the freezer and extracted a pint of ice cream. "Bette said that you liked carob, so that's what I bought. What a vile sounding flavor!"

Laurie took the carton and opened it eagerly. "Great, that's just what I'm in the mood for!" She held out the spoon. "You want a taste?"

"Are you crazy? It's all for you."

PROMISES TO KEEP

Laurie ate her ice cream slowly. "Are you all right?" she asked. "Is it okay here for you?"

"Oh, I'm fine. It's just that I feel so isolated. It's weird not having anyone know where I am."

"But that was the whole point," Laurie reminded her.

"I know," Andy said wryly. "But I'm going to have to get in touch with people sooner or later. If it's all right with you, though, I'd like to spend three or four days here before I return to the real world."

"'Real world?' This is the real world."

"I know, but it's so different from mine."

"Maybe that's part of your problem."

"Hey, no lectures. That was one of the conditions that you agreed to when I came here."

"Andy, I'm not lecturing. I just wish you were happier."

"I'm happy," Andy snapped. "Look who I am!"

"I know who you are," Laurie said softly. "And I still wish you were happier."

"Well, I'll tell you something. It's for sure I'll be happier when I finish this song. So why don't you get some sleep and I'll go back to work, okay?"

"Aren't you going to sleep?"

"I'll sleep plenty after you and Bette leave tomorrow."

Laurie sighed. "I'll tell you what: I'll sleep in the bottom bunk in Bette's room and leave my room for you in case you change your mind."

Andy nodded absentmindedly. She was already

Wendy Susans

writing, working on some lyrics. Laurie stood for a minute watching, and then walked down the hallway to her daughter's room.

A loud booming noise woke Laurie abruptly. Forgetting that she was in the lower bunk, she sat up and slammed her head on the bed above her. "Dammit! What in the world is going on out there?" She slipped on a robe, put slippers on her feet and went to see what was going on. There in the living room, with the stereo blasting away, were Andy and Bette. "What are you doing? Are you crazy? Do you know how early it is?" She walked over to the stereo and lowered the volume. She was surprised to see that Bette was already dressed and she noticed the remnants of breakfast still on the dining room table.

"Mommy, look! Andy's teaching me how to dance." Bette said excitedly. "Watch me boogie." Bette started dancing to the music.

Andy grinned wickedly. "This is some great kid you have here, Laur. She obviously comes from quality stock."

"Come on, Andy, you'll get me thrown out of here! I have neighbors, you know."

"Don't be such a fuddy-duddy. And hey, don't you believe in buying good breakfast food? We couldn't find the Captain Crunch with Crunchberries anywhere."

"Shut up, Andy, that's not funny! Now Bette will nag me to death for that junk. Hey you two, I'm serious!"

Contrite, Andy got up from the couch and

PROMISES TO KEEP

touched her sister's shoulder. "I'm sorry, Laur, I was just kidding. Look, why don't you go back to bed for a bit and I'll take care of everything here."

"No, I'm up already, it's okay. Bette, do you have everything ready?"

"Yes, Mommy. Can Andy take me down to the bus, please?"

Laurie looked at Andy. "I don't know if she wants to."

"Sure I will. No problem. Hey, Laurie come on, don't be mad at me. I'm sorry. We were just having a little fun."

"Yes, Mommy, we were just having a little fun. I loved it." Bette wrapped her arms around her mother's legs and hugged hard.

Laurie smiled at the two of them and rubbed her head. "I know you were. Of course I'm not mad. Hey, I love you two more than anything else in the world. Don't you know that? Okay, Bette, but you'll have to show Andy the bus stop. Do you remember?"

"Sure I do. I'll show her." She took Andy's hand. "Come on, we can go now."

"It's kind of early yet, isn't it, little one? Why don't we clean the table off and do the dishes first." She turned to her sister. "Go ahead, Laur, go sleep a little longer. I'll take care of everything around here."

Shaking her head, Laurie padded back to her bedroom to lie down for another half hour.

George was very upset. Mr. Arnold hadn't

Wendy Susans

answered any of his letters, and it was imperative that he get in touch with him soon. Andy Reuben was getting into trouble and he didn't know how long he could stand it. She was getting more and more like Vera every day. It was lucky that she had gotten sick. There hadn't been much in the hospital to take her away from the straight and narrow, but now she was out of the hospital and there wasn't much time. Why didn't Mr. Arnold answer his letters? He could have saved her. Now George would have to take action. His angel belonged in heaven before she fell too far.

Laurie and Bette entered the apartment together. Bette was excited about her swimming lesson at camp and had been telling her mother about it since she had picked her up at the bus stop. "You know, Mommy, I was the only one who wasn't afraid to dive for the pennies under water! Look—" she held out her hand "—I got ten pennies!"

"That's wonderful, sweetheart. I'll bet you'll learn to swim in no time at all. Why don't you show them to Andy?"

Bette ran into the living room and looked around. "Where is she mommy? She's not here."

Puzzled, Laurie walked into the room. It smelled of cigarette smoke, and there was clutter all over the place—not at all the way Laurie was used to seeing it. "Hmm, let's look in my bedroom. Maybe she's in there." The two of them walked down the hallway to the bedrooms. A trail of clothes led directly to Laurie's room. "Shh, I'll bet she's asleep in my room." Laurie opened the door a crack. Andy was fast asleep in her bed, a sheet barely covering her nude form. "Let's let her sleep, Bette. She doesn't get very much of it and it's good for her."

"Okay, Mommy, but can we have Chinese food for dinner? Andy said she wanted it, and I do, too."

"Sure, why not? Just let me call my service, then we'll go down and get some." She reached for the phone and dialed her answering service. There were several medical related messages along with calls from Fred, her mother, Alice and Erica Abbott. She thought for a moment and she decided to call only Erica back. She didn't want to be bothered by Fred or her mother and she knew that Alice just wanted to know if Andy was all right. She was curious, though, as to why Erica Abbott would call her.

Erica's secretary answered the phone and immediately put Laurie through. "Laurie, do you know where Andy is?"

"Why?"

"Look, this is really urgent. Let's not fool around here. Do you know where she is?"

"What kind of urgent?"

"Laurie, this could be life or death! We have to know if she's safe or not."

"Why wouldn't she be safe? Is there a problem?"

"I've really got to speak to Andy. If you know where she is, please, just tell me."

"Obviously if Andy has disappeared, it's

Wendy Susans

because she wants to be alone, away from you people. Even if I knew where she was, I couldn't say."

"Look, Laurie, I have no desire to play games with you. Please have Andy call me if you can get in touch with her. Tell her we have to hear from her."

"You and Nickelodean are a large part of my sister's problems. She needs time by herself and I want her to have it."

"Why don't you tell her I called and let her decide whether to call me or not. Just tell her that Erica is worried."

"If I can get in touch with her, I'll give her the message. Don't be surprised if she doesn't call you though."

"Fine, good-bye." Erica slammed down the phone so hard that it made Laurie's ears ring.

Angry at Erica's attitude, but worried about what the "problem" might be, Laurie decided to compromise. She'd give Andy Erica's message; but *after* Andy had a good meal in her. Aloud she said, "Come on, Bette, we'll get dinner, and then we'll wake Andy up."

Andy looked up from her plate. "This is definitely Chinese food that I haven't tasted before. What is it?"

"That's Buddha's Delight," Bette answered. "Do you like it?"

"Well, it's not Szechuan, but it is tasty. No meat I assume."

Laurie smiled. "What do you think?"

PROMISES TO KEEP

"I think no meat. I guess it's healthy, though. The two of you don't look any the worse for it."

"We're much healthier because of it. You should try it," Laurie coaxed with a smile.

"Come on, I'm too old to convert. I need my Big Mac fixes on occasion."

Bette looked at her aunt. "I'd like a Big Mac sometime, Andy."

"Oh, no you don't! I put my foot down there. I've worked too hard to have you poisoned like that!"

"Laurie, that's ridiculous!"

"Yes mommy, that's—"

"Stop it now! I don't want to hear another word!" Laurie turned to her sister and casually added, "By the way, Andy, Erica Abbott called me. She was looking for you."

"Erica called you? That's strange. I wonder what she wants?"

"Nickelodean must be trying to get her to do their dirty work."

"No, that's not her style. Erica's too straight for that. What did she say?"

"She said it was urgent that you call her and she told me to tell you that she was worried about you."

"Why would she be worried about me? Laurie, I have to call her. There must be something wrong."

"Oh, Andy, I thought you wanted to forget about all that for a while. You've been so relaxed, so happy. Can't she wait?"

"No, Laur, if Erica says that it's urgent, then it

must be. I'll be right back."

Andy was on the telephone for about a half hour. Laurie, anxiously listened to Andy's side of the conversation for a few minutes, then put Bette to sleep and sat down in the living room to wait for her sister. Finally Andy came and sat next to Laurie. "Well, what was so urgent?" Laurie asked.

"Nothing much, I wouldn't worry about it."

"What wouldn't you worry about?"

"Look, if I tell you about it, you'll worry. So let's forget about it."

"I'm not going to forget about it, so you might as well tell me."

Andy sighed. "Okay, it seems that there's some nut who's calling Nickelodean with threats on my life."

Laurie's hand flew to her mouth. "My God, she wasn't kidding! It was life or death! Andy, what are you going to do about it?"

"I'm not going to do anything. Like I said, the guy's a wacko. He kept calling me a fallen angel or something and said I had to stay 'good' or else I have to die."

Laurie stood up and paced in front of the couch. "You can't go out anymore. You've got to stay indoors until they find him. Damn it, Andy, how can you be so calm? Somebody wants to kill you!"

"Oh, I get weird phone calls all the time, although this guy seems to be a bit more persistant than most. I don't think there's anything to worry about."

PROMISES TO KEEP

"You don't *think* there's anything to worry about, but you can't be sure. He could be serious. Andy, please, I'm petrified!" Laurie stopped in front of her sister and stretched her hand out pleadingly.

Andy shook her head. "I knew you would react this way. Look, Nickelodean is right on top of it. They called the police and they even hired a private investigator. There are taps on the phones in case he calls back and I guarantee he'll call back—these people are compulsive. He'll be caught; they always have been before."

Laurie swallowed hard. "This sort of thing has happened before?"

"Once or twice." Andy laughed. "I seem to attract all the loonies."

"Promise me you won't go out until they catch him."

"I'm not promising any such thing, Laurie. You're being ridiculous."

"Does anyone know you're here?"

"No, I didn't tell Erica where I was. Hey, Laurie, take it easy, I'll be fine."

Laurie put her hand on her chest. "You've given me palpitations. There's no way I'll be able to sleep tonight. Thank God I don't have to go into work tomorrow so I can stay with you."

"Laurie, I don't need you to stay with me," Andy said in exasperation. "You do what you have to and let me work. I told you I've got to get this song finished."

"How can I be sure you'll be okay?"

"Of course I'll be okay. How could anyone

know I'm here?"

"Let me sleep in with you tonight, please?"

"But I'm not at all tired. I slept most of the day, and I'll probably work most of the night."

"Then I'll stay up with you."

"Don't get me annoyed, Laurie! I'll be fine. You go to sleep when you have to and leave me alone."

Laurie stood in front of her sister and gazed at her in anguish. "Don't you understand, Andy? I don't want to lose you. I love you too much. I'd go crazy if anything ever happened to you."

"Just stop it now! You won't lose me and nothing is going to happen to me."

Laurie hugged her sister and whispered, "Do you promise?"

"I promise. Now stop bothering me."

Laurie put her hand to her forehead. "Why didn't you tell me you've gotten threats before?"

"What for? I mean, it's the nature of the game. All celebrities have strange people bothering them. After awhile you learn to ignore it."

"But you have to admit that sometimes these crazy people do . . . do things."

"Yes, and for every one of those, there are a thousand who don't. Laurie, I won't live my life in fear. It's not worth it."

Just then the telephone rang. Laurie got up to answer it and Andy returned to her music. After a few minutes, Laurie came back into the room and flopped down on the couch. "That was ma. She really is something. She started yelling at me because no one knows where you are. Apparently she's had her share of calls about you also."

PROMISES TO KEEP

"Poor Adrienne, that's just what she needs."

"You better not tell her about the threats. She would be frantic."

Andy's face grew dark. "I don't know whether she would be frantic or not. She expects things like that from me, I think. Always has. She doesn't much approve of my life anyway."

"Ma may not approve of your life, but she loves you and wouldn't want anything to happen to you."

Andy raised her eyebrows. "Maybe. I'm not so sure about that. Not that she would want anything to happen to me, but that she loves me..."

"Where would you ever get an idea like that? Of course she loves you! How could you even think that?"

"What's the use of even discussing it?" Andy took a deep breath. "It has no relevance in the scheme of things."

Laurie walked over to her sister. "Andy, if that's the way you feel, then it's my fault. I—"

"Don't!" Andy interrupted sharply. "Look Laur, forget I said anything, okay? It's irrelevant. Come on, I have to do some work now. I'm in trouble if I don't get this done. Why don't you go about your business and leave me to mine?"

"Andy, I can't stop worrying...."

"Laur, I said leave me alone! I've got to get this work done!"

Hurt, Laurie looked sadly at her sister, then turned away. She sat down on the couch and quietly watched her sister compose her music.

Wendy Susans

* * *

George sat in the hotel room and brooded. He hadn't been able to talk to either Fred Arnold or Andy Reuben, and he was very upset. He had tried to explain to the people at the record company that Andy was evil and had to die, but they wouldn't put him through to her. They'd tried to find out who he was, but he'd been too smart for them. He hadn't told them anything.

He opened his suitcase and took out the rifle. Soon, he thought, he'd find her, then—

There was a knock on the door. "This is the police. Open up!"

Frantically, George looked for an escape, but there was none.

"Open up or we'll break down the door!"

George looked sadly at the picture of Andy Reuben on the night table beside him. "I tried, I tried to keep you an angel. You had to be bad. Oh, Vera, why did you do it to me?" He put the rifle in his mouth and pulled the trigger.

Laurie was sprawled on the couch in an old T-shirt and cut-off jeans, her head in Andy's lap. She reached for the popcorn and said, "God, it's been years since I've watched this soap. I think the last time I saw it Joanna was married to Phil. What ever happened to him?"

Andy shrugged her shoulders. "Beats me. The only soap I occasionally catch now is 'Another Time.' Alice watches it every day religiously. You want to hear something funny? I gave her a VCR for her birthday last year and she got so

PROMISES TO KEEP

excited. I asked her why she liked it so much and she said that now she would never miss her soap. Reminded me of Adrienne. She never missed any of them. Remember? She'd put the TV on at noon and wouldn't turn it off until they were all over."

"I know, she's still the same way. She talks about the characters as if they were real people. I'll tell you a secret, I used to watch them with her after you left home. They took my mind off my troubles."

Andy laughed. "After seeing their troubles ours seem so paltry."

Laurie sat up and stared at her twin. "Not yours! I swear, a soap opera writer could have a field day with your problems. What are you going to do if they don't catch this nut?"

Andy set her lips. "Laurie, I told you I wouldn't leave this apartment until I hear from the police. What more do you want from me?"

"I want you to be more careful. Please, Andy, you have to hire a bodyguard—" The telephone rang and Laurie stood to answer it. Andy heard her sister shriek, "Fred! A rifle? He's dead? You're sure?"

Andy grabbed the phone from Laurie. "Fred, what's going on? Who's dead?" She listened while Fred told her the story. Laurie collapsed on the couch. Andy turned to make sure her sister was all right and then spoke again. "Yes, I know. Okay, I'll be back home soon. I'll see you later." She hung up, walked to the couch and sat next to Laurie. "Well, it's over, and it was for real." Laurie clenched Andy's hand tightly, as though she'd never let her go. "Sometimes you're right, Laur," Andy continued. "I guess I took this one too lightly. Hey, take it easy. Stop crying. It's all right now."

Laurie sat up and wiped her eyes. "Tell me what happened."

"This guy, George Sloane I think Fred said his name was, had been in and out of mental institutions for the past five years. He had a thing about women, especially those who didn't meet his high ideals. Apparently he put women on a pedestal and inevitably they disappointed him. Then he'd become enraged and felt they had to be killed. He almost murdered his wife because he thought that she was betraying him.

"He obviously fixated on me and from the notes he kept it seems that he viewed my separation from Fred as a betrayal. He figured that I had to be punished. Whew, what a weirdo!" Andy nervously ran her fingers through her hair. "They traced his phone calls to a hotel and when the police came he shot himself."

Laurie felt sick to her stomach. "You see, I told you it was dangerous for you. Hire a bodyguard! You need protection!"

"No, Laur. I couldn't live with a bodyguard following me all the time. The chances of another nut trying the same thing are miniscule. Anyway, I have got to go home now. I've been away too long as it is and I have an awful lot of work I can't put off anymore."

"Andy, just stay another day or so. You'll be dumped on the minute you leave, and you can do

PROMISES TO KEEP

with some more rest."

"I'm okay now, Laur, and I do have to get back. I have responsibilities, you know. Besides, I've disrupted your routine enough. It's not fair to you." She got up from the couch and went to the bedroom to get ready to leave.

Sadly, Laurie followed her. "But I've loved having you here. Won't you at least wait until Bette comes home?"

"No, I'm sorry I can't. Tell her I'll see her soon, though."

"But she'll be so disappointed. She was looking forward to seeing you tonight."

"I can't help it, Laurie. It's time for me to get back." She changed into the suit she had worn to the board meeting just a couple of days before and turned around.

Laurie looked at her sister. Once more she was Andy Reuben the superstar, not just plain old Andy, her twin sister. Laurie felt an overwhelming sadness, as if she had lost something precious all over again. She followed Andy into the living room and watched her pick up her music.

Andy gave her sister a quick kiss and headed for the door. "I'll call you later, Laur, as soon as I get some things straightened out. Hey, kid, thanks. I had a wonderful time. You're the best sister in the world." She left the apartment, took the elevator down and hailed a cab to take her home.

Fred stood at the window of the brownstone

nursing his glass of Johnnie Walker Black. The events of the past few hours had shocked him, and at that moment his only desire was to see Andy safely home. He was hoping that the incident would bring her to her senses and make her realize just how much she needed him. He certainly needed her. It had never occurred to him that he could miss anyone as badly as he had missed Andy. The hell of having her so near him and not being able to touch her kept him awake in the middle of the night. No woman could compare to her.

He remembered his relief at hearing her voice when he'd called Laurie's apartment. Up until that point everyone had feared she had been abducted. What had gotten into her? It had been foolish of her to have disappeared without even telling Alice where she was. He assumed that her vanishing act had had something to do with what had occurred at the board meeting, and even he had to admit that it had been done badly. He should have explained why the greatest hits album was necessary before the meeting.

Actually, he had tried to see her, but she hadn't allowed him into her hospital room. If she had, he knew he could have made her understand the urgency of the situation. Andy was a pro, she did what had to be done even though at times she protested vehemently. After all, she would never have been the superstar she was without some sacrifices.

Noise outside distracted him and he looked out the bay window. Andy's cab was sitting at the curb, completely surrounded by media people. He ran out, pushed them out of the way and opened the taxi door. Grabbing Andy by the hand, he shoved his way past the reporters and cameras, pulled her into the house, slammed the door, scooped her up in his arms and held her close to him. "Oh God, baby! You scared me half to death. I thought for sure that guy had killed you."

"Don't be silly Fred," she said as she struggled out of his arms. "You're letting your imagination run away with you. Where's Alice?"

"I reassured her that you were alive and well, then I gave her Nickelodean's box seats to tonight's Mets-Cubs game. I think she was planning to take her nephews with her."

Andy frowned and looked around the hallway for her mail. Seeing the stack of letters on the hall table, she picked it up and took it into the living room. She sat herself in her favorite wing chair by the fireplace and began leafing through the letters. Fred followed her and knelt beside the chair.

"Andy, baby, look at me. Please. Can't you understand how worried I was? I still love you and want you. Please, please reconsider this divorce."

Andy looked at him sympathetically. "Fred, there's no reason to reconsider. Things haven't changed since my decision. I still want my freedom and I have no desire to be married to you or to anyone else. Why can't you face that, and then maybe we can go on from there? Actually, I'm not sure that I can ever forgive you for what you allowed to happen to me at that board meeting."

"Me? I didn't do anything. The decision came from higher up and there was no way that we could get around it according to your contract."

"That was part of the problem, Fred. Those contracts of yours certainly didn't do their job of protecting me. All along you kept telling me how much I needed your protection, otherwise I'd be taken advantage of. It seems to me that you let things be written into my contracts that never should have been there. Quite frankly, I feel violated, and it's a lousy feeling. I don't think I can ever trust you again with my business dealings. I'd really prefer to take care of them myself. At least then I'll have only myself to blame for any mistakes." She picked up a letter opener and slit open one of the envelopes.

Fred stood up and clenched his fists. This conversation was not going the way he thought it would. He'd thought that she would come in, fall into his arms and he could take her up to bed where they belonged. He wasn't prepared for a strong Andy, and he wasn't sure how to handle her. "That would be unfortunate," he said evenly. "You don't have any business sense, and if a problem arises you'll lose control. You always used Laurie as your buffer when you didn't want to face a decision, and then you used me. Let's face it, Andy, you can never take care of yourself without making a mess of it . . . ." He let his voice trail off as he realized with dismay that he had made a fatal mistake. In treating the new Andy like the old, he had lost whatever chance he might have had to regain her love.

Andy stood up, the mail spilling out of her lap onto the thick rug. "Stop it, Fred!" she shouted. "I don't have to hear this from you anymore! I know what I am, believe it or not, and I don't need you to remind me of my weaknesses. How about talking about your weaknesses for a change." She stopped, took off her glasses and rubbed her eyes. "Look, I think you'd better go. We just can't seem to hold a civil conversation and I'm really not up to this right now." She walked away from the chair toward the kitchen. Fred followed her and tried to put his arms around her. With great hostility, she pushed him away. "Don't you understand that until you stop playing my lord and master we can never have any kind of relationship?"

"I can't help it. It's a habit, it's been my job for so many years. I worry about you—"

"Well, don't worry so much. You've got to learn that I'm going to handle my own life from now on. Face it, Fred, the separation is permanent." She paused. "But I would like to be friends."

"Oh, Andy, I still love you," Freddie whispered. "I miss you—"

"Stop it! I don't want to feel sorry for you, and I'm sure you don't want me to. I'll tell you what. Let's call a truce now and try relating to each other again. How does that sound?" She put out her hand to him.

Fred took it in his. "You're right, I don't want

Wendy Susans

you to feel sorry for me. I have more pride than that. All right, truce."

Andy withdrew her hand from his and sighed. "Hey, Fred, I'm kind of tired, and I think I'd better rest now."

Fred nodded. "That's a polite way of telling me you want me out of here, right? Fine. I know you need your rest, and I have to get down to the office anyway. Call me if there's anything you need. I'll see you later." He gave her a half-wave and left the room.

As soon as he left, Andy climbed the two flights to her bedroom, threw her clothes off and crawled into bed. Tasha, who was sleeping on the rug next to the bed, jumped up and rubbed against her. Andy took the cat in her arms, snuggled under the goose down quilt that shielded them against the chill of the central air conditioning and tried to drift off to sleep. Fred's outburst had unnerved her, but her response to it delighted her. It was about time that she was able to stand up to Fred's haranguing. *I guess I really am getting stronger,* she thought sleepily. Or at least her mind was, she amended. She hated to admit it, but she'd wanted him. Their lovemaking used to be so good. . . . She closed her eyes and fell asleep dreaming of the intimacy and excitement of making love.

September

Andy strode into the rehearsal studio at Nickelodean. It was her first meeting with Eric Boutelle and she was late. She had never done a duet before and she was not delighted with the prospect. He'd better be good, she thought bitterly, she didn't want to waste her time with an amateur.

In the recording studio, Andy was a compulsive perfectionist. She supervised the mixing on all her recordings and no imperfection ever passed her by. Each of her recordings had to be as flawless as possible, and she was afraid that singing a duet with someone would make that aspect more difficult to control.

"Well, here goes nothing," she said to herself as she opened the door. The room was empty and Andy felt a surge of irritation rise within her. Just as she turned to leave, the door opened and

Eric Boutelle walked in. Andy looked up into the most vivid blue eyes she had ever seen. The man was magnificent, with broad shoulders, powerful arms, a slim waist and long, long legs. His jeans were old and worn and so was his blue oxford button down shirt. Andy looked down and was amused to see that there was a penny in the slit of each loafer. She suddenly realized who Eric Boutelle was. He was the actor who had been at the party after her concert.

"It's a good thing you showed up," he drawled. "I was just going to leave. Well, are you ready to work?"

Shocked and somewhat annoyed at his tone, Andy opened her attache case, took out the music and threw it on the piano bench. "Here, do you know how to read music?"

"Pretty well." He placed the music in front of him, sat down at the piano and started to play.

Andy watched him as he played her song. He was even more gorgeous than she remembered. With his smooth cheeks and Grecian nose, he reminded her of a young Adonis. A strong urge to place her lips on his full, sensuous mouth swept over her, and she closed her eyes for a second. He was so young—in his early twenties at the most. Did she dare?

Eric looked up. "Hey, this is pretty good. I think I'll like singing it. Do you want to try to run through it together?"

Andy sat down next to him. "Sure, let's go."

They started the song, with Andy playing the piano. Every so often she would stop and correct

PROMISES TO KEEP

Eric's phrasing. Finally, they reached the end of the song. She turned to him. "That wasn't as bad as I thought it would be."

Stung, Eric retorted, "Hey, if you have any doubts, count me out. I don't need this. It's your record company that wants me, not the other way around."

"Oh? You may be a pretty boy on a soap opera, but selling records is a whole different ball game."

"I guarantee that this pretty boy will sell a lot of records."

Andy laughed. "How little you know. You can't guarantee anything. Without the publicity and expertise we can give you, you'll sell nothing."

Eric gazed at the remarkably beautiful face so close to his. From the moment he had first seen her at her party, he had been inexplicably drawn to her, and now he longed to take her in his arms and make her want him as much as he wanted her. He looked into her eyes. "Don't underestimate my expertise," he warned. "My reputation speaks for itself."

Andy looked back at him. It was all she could do to keep from touching his curly blond hair. "Reputations can be created by publicity departments," she murmured. "I've always been more interested in action than reputation." She moved closer to him until their legs were touching.

They stared into each other's eyes for a few moments. Eric reached over and stroked her cheek gently, then drew her lips to his. Andy responded with overwhelming passion and then

Wendy Susans

buried her face in his chest. "Come home with me," she whispered breathlessly. "I need you to come home with me." She stood up and led the bemused Eric out of the studio.

Eric lay stretched out nude on Andy's bed while she took a business call. He lazily ran his finger down her spine and thought about the turn of events. When they'd left the rehearsal studio, they'd taken her car to her house and immediately went up to her bedroom. It didn't look anything the way he'd thought it would. He had expected a very tailored room, but instead it was a soft, sunny, feminine room in shades of white, green and yellow. White frilly curtains framed the bay window and a plush white carpet covered the floor. The flowered fabric wallpaper matched the bedspread and the two easy chairs. In the window alcove was a delicate antique desk and chair. Cut flowers in bowls were on every table, giving off a wonderful fragrance. When Andy had pulled off the bedspread, he'd noticed that the sheets were pale yellow satin.

And what a time they had in that luxurious bed! She was incredible; nothing like the girls he was used to. She knew tricks that he never could have imagined—warm, sensuous tricks that gave him new found respect for the word "woman." "Hey, come on, get off the phone," he whispered. She shot him a withering look and continued her conversation for a few minutes longer.

When Andy hung up the phone, she turned around and warned, "Don't you ever do that again. I don't like being interrupted when I'm doing business."

Eric didn't particularly care for the put-down, but he swallowed the retort that came to his lips. Instead, he pulled her down beside him and kissed her. She pressed her body close and moved seductively against him. Desire swelled within him and he gently caressed her. This time the lovemaking was even more satisfying, and Andy held him for a long time afterward. Finally, she gently moved her body out from under his, reached for her cigarettes and lit one. "How old are you?" she asked.

Half-asleep, he mumbled, "Why do you want to know?"

"Just curious."

Eric turned over on his back and lifted himself up on one elbow. He looked down at Andy and smiled. "Afraid of corrupting a minor?"

"Well, did I?"

"No such luck. I'm twenty-five. And you? How old are you?"

"Let's just say, older."

"Is that a problem?"

"Not at all. Is it a problem for you?"

"Not that I've noticed." He leaned down and kissed her breast.

Andy thought for a moment, then looked at Eric.

"Is something wrong?" he asked.

She stroked his chest. "How would you like to come with me to the Limelight tonight? I arranged a benefit party there and I'd like you to come along."

"I'd love to go to the Limelight with you tonight, Andy Reuben." Eric grinned and kissed her ear.

"Good," she said as she got out of bed. "I'll pick you up at eleven. Just put your address on the night table when you leave. I have to go now." She quickly got into her clothes and left Eric alone in her bed.

He sat up and touched the place on the bed where Andy had been just moments before. It was still warm. "This is going to be an interesting relationship," he said out loud. "An extremely interesting relationship."

The red Porsche roared around the corner of West 20th Street and screeched to a stop. "Damn it, Shep, why must you drive like a maniac? You're going to ruin this car yet! Anyway, I don't like parking it in the street. Can't we find a lot somewhere?"

"I'm not parking where those car jockeys will take it for a joyride. We'll put on the security system and it'll be safe." He took off his seat belt and opened the door.

Melissa looked at her watch. "It's nine-thirty. Laurie said the party starts at ten. Should we go in?"

"I don't know. I've never been here before. It looks pretty weird though."

They were standing in front of an old large church that looked very dark. There was no one outside, and for a minute they thought perhaps

PROMISES TO KEEP

they had the wrong night. A glance at the invitation Laurie had procured for them reassured her that the benefit party for orphan drugs was, indeed, that evening, and at the renovated church, which was now a club—the Limelight.

Melissa and Shep walked around the building and looked for the entrance, but couldn't find it. Melissa fought to keep her impatience in check. She'd come to New York to become a part of the high life that was Andy's everyday existence, but it seemed as though she was frustrated at every turn. First of all, the apartment she and Shep were sharing was in Rego Park. When he'd told her he lived in New York City, she'd assumed he meant Manhattan. Rego Park was in Queens, across the river from the New York City she knew—the New York City of Andy and Laurie. The neighborhood she was now living in was an ordinary, middle-class community, with none of the excitement that she craved.

Secondly, and most upsetting to Melissa, was her estrangement from Andy. She knew now that she hadn't handled the situation well. She shouldn't have been so persistent when Andy was in the hospital. But Shep had been on her back day and night about the health club, and she'd been afraid he would leave her. She'd never imagined that Andy would get violent. After all, it was a good investment.

To top things off, Laurie was angry at her also. She'd accused Melissa of being insensitive and immature. As usual, Laurie had sided with Andy against her.

Melissa sighed as she looked up at the imposing church. She wished that, just once, one of her sisters could see her side of a situation. She knew, though, that no matter what, it was up to her to make the first move with Andy. If they were ever to be friends again, she was going to have to apologize for her behavior and show Andy that she really was not a "poor excuse for a sister." She was hoping that tonight she would have a chance to do just that.

Shep tugged at her arm. "There's Laurie," he said. "Maybe she knows what's going on."

Melissa ran over to her sister. "Thank goodness, you're here," she said. "Do you know how to get into this place?"

By now there was a crowd milling in front of the Limelight. Laurie, Melissa and Shep pushed their way through to an unobtrusive entrance Laurie pointed out. She knocked on the door. A gentleman put his head out and said, "We're not open."

Laurie held out a piece of paper to him and said, "My name is Dr. Laurel Rabinowitz. I'm on your list. May I come in?"

"We're not set up yet."

She pulled the door open. "My sister, Andy Reuben, assured me that we could come in early. You wouldn't want to disappoint her, would you?"

Immediately the man stepped aside and allowed the three in. "I'm sorry, Doctor. I didn't realize who you were."

They entered the former Church of the Holy

PROMISES TO KEEP

Communion. Although the one hundred and thirty seven year old church had been deconsecrated years before, the decor was still ecclesiastical. They walked through the white marble entrance hall to a small wood-panelled room with upholstered seating. The large stained glass windows were brilliantly lit from behind. Melissa looked around in amazement. "Have you ever been here before, Laurie?"

"Yes," Laurie answered. "I came with Fred and Andy to a party for some hot shot celebrity."

"Wow!" gasped Melissa. "Who was there?"

"Probably the same people who'll be here tonight. Andy knows them all."

Shep stood up. "I'm going to get a drink," he said. "Can I get you girls anything?"

Laurie looked at him for a moment. "This *woman* will have a white wine spritzer with a twist of lime, thank you."

"And I'll have a Bloody Mary, Shep." Melissa stared as she saw a notorious gossip columnist talking to a famous actor. "Oh my God, Laurie! Is that who I think it is?"

"Probably. Come on, Melissa, close your mouth. You'll look ridiculous all night if you can't control yourself. Andy would find this very childish. She hates gaping ninnies."

Quickly Melissa closed her mouth. "When will Andy be here, Laurie? I'd like to talk to her."

"Don't expect her for quite awhile and don't expect to be able to talk to her here. The minute she walks in, she'll be surrounded by people who won't leave her alone until she leaves. And if she's

Wendy Susans

true to form, that won't be very long." She accepted her drink as Shep returned from the bar.

"Come on, Missy, let's dance." Shep pulled Melissa up and started through the bar to the nave where the dance floor was located. Melissa turned to Laurie, but her sister smiled and waved at her to go.

The doors had been opened, and the guests were pouring in. High energy rock music echoed through the nave as the gathering crowd danced and cavorted under the flickering lights and laser beams. At intervals, smoke was blown into the room and fake snow fell from the ceiling. Melissa and Shep recognized many celebrities dancing next to them and after a while, exhausted, they climbed up on one of the catwalks that surrounded the dance floor, and watched as the throng below them moved to the loud, rhythmic beat.

Suddenly, there was a commotion near the entrance to the nave. Melissa leaned over the railing to get a better look, and then it dawned upon her that her sister had finally arrived. She watched as Andy walked through the crowd. Anxious to speak to her, Melissa raced down the steps, leaving Shep alone.

It was impossible to walk on the main level. Melissa could see Andy, but she couldn't get through to her. She watched in awe as her sister held court next to the altar. Andy was wearing a black velvet tunic, artfully draped at the hip and tied with a black silk charmeuse bow. Her black silk charmeuse slacks were pleated and ankle

PROMISES TO KEEP

length. Andy was the epitome of everything Melissa wanted to be. She took her attention off her sister and became aware of a familiar looking man standing next to Andy.

"Oh my God!" Melissa sputterred. "It's Chad!" She saw Andy turn and give him a slow, sexy smile. The way they looked at each other made Melissa weak in the knees. She knew at once that this was Andy's latest lover. Aggressively she elbowed her way up to her sister and reached out to her.

"What are you doing here?" Andy said icily.

"Laurie invited me."

Andy raised her eyebrows. "Without my permission? I told you, Melissa, I don't want to see you. If you had to come, you could have had the decency to stay out of my sight."

Melissa drew back, hurt and humiliated at being scolded in public. "Andy, please," she whispered. "I have to talk to you. You can't imagine how sorry I am. Don't do this to me."

Andy sighed. The discord between them had bothered her also. She knew that for her own peace of mind, she had to resolve the situation. "I can't talk to you now. How about lunch some time next week?"

"Monday?"

Andy thought for a moment. "Fine, I'll make room on my calender. Two o'clock at Elaine's, and don't bring Shep!"

"Oh, thank you, Andy," Melissa gushed, relieved. "Definitely! Two sharp! Without Shep." She backed away from Andy, then turned and ran.

Andy turned back to Eric. "Wait here a minute. I'll be right back." She walked out of the room quickly, avoiding the people who wanted to speak to her, and went directly into the side room next to the bar where she had seen Laurie.

Laurie was nursing another white wine spritzer when Andy came up to her. She was enjoying herself immensely just watching the people and their antics, but she knew that she was going to have to leave soon. Bette's baby-sitter tonight was a high school student, and she had to be home by one o'clock. She was pleased to see her twin coming across the room toward her.

"That was cute of you, Laurie," Andy said wryly.

"Cute? What was cute?" Laurie asked innocently.

"You know what I'm talking about. I know you invited Melissa just so I could see her."

Laurie held up her hands. "Guilty as charged! I take full responsibility. Do you think I could let the animosity between you two continue much longer? Come on, admit it, you haven't been happy about it."

"You know that," Andy admitted. "Well, you'll be happy to know that I consented to lunch with her on Monday."

Laurie stood up and smoothed her skirt. "Good. That's what I was waiting for. Now I can leave."

"Leave? I just got here. It's still early."

"But I've been here for almost three hours and

PROMISES TO KEEP

I'm getting a little bored."

Andy shook her head. "Only you could get bored at the Limelight!" She hugged Laurie. "Yeah, yeah, I understand. We just don't have the same tastes. Look, why don't you take the limo. I won't need it for a while."

Laurie's eyes lit up. She hadn't been looking forward to hailing a cab so late at night. "That's the best offer I've had all evening! Thanks." She picked up her purse, kissed Andy on the cheek and whispered, "That guy you came in with is gorgeous! I assume that he's already fallen madly and passionately in love with you!" She laughed as her sister grabbed a matchbook and threw it at her.

"Of course!" Andy grinned. "How could he not!" She watched her sister leave the room and then went to join Eric on the dance floor.

It was 5 A.M., and they had been making love continuously almost from the moment they had arrived back at her house. Andy ran her fingers across Eric's chest as he kissed her tenderly on the lips. He caressed her breasts as he whispered, "Andy, you're so warm. I want you again so much."

Smiling, she pushed him down on the bed and climbed on top of him. Slowly at first, and then more quickly, she moved until she felt him quivering beneath her. He pulled her down so she lay on top of him, and they kissed passionately and clung to each other tightly as they climaxed together.

Wendy Susans

"You are utterly unbelievable," he said as he held her close, and his breathing steadied. She started to move away from him. "Mmm, don't. I want to stay in you the rest of the night."

Andy stretched out her legs and buried her face in his neck. "Sounds good to me," she murmured drowsily. Warm and content, they both closed their eyes and fell into deep sleep.

Laurie awoke abruptly as Bette jumped into bed with her, but she had a difficult time opening her eyes. It felt as though she had just gotten into bed, and she certainly didn't want to get up so soon.

"Mommy, tell me about last night. You promised. Was it fun?"

Groggily, Laurie sat up and looked at her daughter. More and more Bette reminded her of a young Andy. Bette's fascination with the fast life and her exuberant personality was so much like her sister's, but Laurie felt that if she was able to temper the wildness, Bette might have the best of both worlds. "Let me get up and make some coffee," she said. "And then we can talk."

Bette hopped off the bed and ran into the kitchen. "I'll get out the things for you!" she yelled as Laurie got up to start her day.

Over their poached eggs and whole wheat toast, Laurie described the party to her daughter. "It was very dark when I got in, and then there's a big room with lots of lights above the dance floor."

"Was there a lot of music?"

"Yes, and it was very loud and booming. Much too loud for me."

"Not for me," Bette said, her eyes shining. "Did you see Andy?"

"Yes, of course. She came later."

"Did she look pretty?"

"Andy always looks pretty. She looked especially pretty last night, though. I'm sure you would have liked what she was wearing, as a matter of fact, you probably would have liked to have been there."

"I'll go there someday," Bette stated confidently. "I know I will."

"I'm sure you will," Laurie murmured ruefully. "Come, you'd better get ready for school."

Bette jumped up and kissed her mother. "Mommy, did you like the party?"

"Not really, Bette. You know I don't like that kind of music, and it's a very strange place. But luckily, everyone at the party enjoyed themselves and we got lots of money to help sick people. That's the important thing."

Bette nodded her head, but it was evident from her expression that she had her doubts.

Melissa had been sitting in Elaine's for a half an hour by the time her sister arrived. Andy sat down and ordered a mushroom omelet and a diet coke. "I'm in a hurry, Melissa. I have to get back to the Hit Factory. Eric and I are recording today. We've been working around the clock trying to get this song put together." She looked at her watch and lit a cigarette. "Damn, I shouldn't have said I'd meet you. My schedule is really tight."

"I'm glad you came, Andy," Melissa put in hurriedly, trying to distract her sister. "I want to fix things between us. I didn't mean to make you angry and I was very upset when you wouldn't return my phone calls. It terrified me when I read about that guy who wanted to kill you."

"Well, I'm fine. I was too busy these past few weeks to return any calls. Besides, I really wasn't thrilled with the way you nagged me about the money, and I definitely don't care for your boyfriend. Keep him away from me and everything will be fine."

"I promise you that we'll make money for you. I know we will."

Andy nodded. "Just see that you do. I wouldn't want to throw away that much cash."

"The grand opening's in a few weeks and we'd very much like you to come. The restaurant won't be open yet, but the health club will. We've sent out invitations to a lot of celebrities. Thank you for letting us use your name."

"Yeah, well, my lawyers told me that it would be good publicity, and the chances for success would be that much greater if I'm publically involved. But I won't be able to come to the opening," she averred. "I'm making the rounds of the talk shows starting next week and I'll be away for a little while. I'll come when I get back."

Melissa's face fell. "I really wanted you at the opening. I was looking forward to having you there, sort of for moral support, you know? Hey, maybe Chad could come?"

"His name is Eric Boutelle, and I'm afraid he won't be able to be there either. He's coming along with me. He's on vacation from the soap for a week."

"Gosh, Andy, he's really a knockout! What a body!" She leaned forward. "Are you sleeping with him?"

"Melissa!" Andy said, exasperated. "That's none of your business! You have no right to ask me that kind of thing!"

Melissa sat back and smiled. "Okay, so you are. I don't care. I wouldn't mind getting into bed with him myself."

"That's enough! I don't want to hear that kind of talk from my baby sister!" Andy looked at the omelet that had been set in front of her with distaste. "Is there anything else on your mind?"

"No, I only wanted to tell you that I was sorry for the way I acted. I know I didn't show it, but I really was worried about you when you were in the hospital and I didn't mean to bother you like that. It's just that Shep was so impatient—"

"I figured that. Melissa, you simply cannot allow someone to dominate you like that. You're in the catbird seat—he needs you more than you need him."

"I wish that were true . . . ."

"I'm positive it is. Look, Lis, I know his type very well. Stop letting him push you around."

Melissa sighed. "We'll see. Right now he's good for the club."

"No, I'm good for the club. We can hire a dozen

of his type."

"Hey," Melissa replied angrily, "you should mind your own business too! It just so happens I'm in love with him. I told you, I don't want to lose him."

Andy put out her cigarette, put on her sunglasses and stood up. "You won't lose him. I guarantee it. Look, I'm sorry Melissa, I have to go. I only had ten minutes for lunch anyway. I'll speak to you when I get back."

"But Andy, you didn't even touch your lunch—"

"You eat it, Lis," she said as she threw money on the table. "I'm not hungry."

Melissa watched Andy leave the restaurant, shrugged her shoulders, took the mushroom omelet and began to eat.

Philip unlocked the door to the split-level house and walked directly into the first floor den. As was becoming increasingly common, Marilyn was sitting in front of the television with a vodka on the rocks beside her. He went to the window and pulled the drapes open. "How the hell can you sit here in the dark all day? It's so beautiful outside."

"What do you care what I do all day?" she snapped.

"Please, Marilyn, don't start the minute I get in. Let's wait an hour or so." He walked to the bar and fixed himself a drink.

Marilyn held out her glass to him. "Freshen mine, will you?"

PROMISES TO KEEP

"Don't you think you've had enough?" He held up the bottle of vodka. "This was almost full this morning. You're turning into a goddamn drunk."

"Shut up," she said as she got up to fill the glass herself. "Guess who's going to be on 'Live at Five' today?"

"How the hell should I know and why the hell should I care?"

"Oh, you'll care all right. It's your old girlfriend, Andy Reuben."

Philip glanced at the TV. "Andy's going to be on TV here? Why?" He sat down and took a sip of his drink.

"Oh, so now you're interested? Still have the hots for her, huh?"

Wearily, Philip looked at his wife. Life at home had become impossible. Marilyn was drinking more and more, the house looked like a pigpen and she had lost all interest in her appearance. It had been months since they had made love. He'd begged her to get out and find a job just to keep her busy and to get her mind off their problems, but she refused. He'd bought the house thinking that it would make her happy, but she missed her in-town friends and didn't want to make any new ones.

He turned his attention to the television as he heard Andy being introduced. She was sitting next to a young man. "Who's that guy sitting next to her?" Philip asked Marilyn.

"Eric Boutelle. He plays Chad on 'Another Time.' A real heartthrob. Apparently they've recorded a song together. Well, does she look like you remember her?"

Philip was amazed at Andy's appearance. She looked nothing like the girl he had been in love with so many years before. Although he had seen pictures of her, up until now he had consciously avoided seeing her on television or in her movie, and nothing had prepared him for the fragile look of the rock star named Andy Reuben. "My God!" he exclaimed. "She looks younger than she did ten years ago!" He was amazed that he still felt the tightness that he always used to feel when he looked at her.

Marilyn watched his face as he stared at the television set. She saw the longing in his eyes and she took a long swallow of her drink. Suddenly, she took the glass and threw it at the screen. "Idiot!" she screamed. "Do you think she even remembers you? You were just one in a long list. Look at you! You still wish you were in bed with her! Goddamn it to hell!" She started weeping uncontrollably.

"Oh, Marilyn, can't you leave well enough alone? She wasn't Andy Reuben then, she was Andrea Rabinowitz. That girl doesn't exist any more. All I feel when I look at her is a longing for a time when life was less complicated. Can't you understand that?"

"All I understand is that for the first time in a long time you're showing an interest in something. You still love her, I can tell."

He sighed and tried to put his hand on Marilyn's arm. "I love *you*. Why can't you believe that?"

She pulled away. "I'll never have a child with

you. She could have. Don't tell me you don't regret that!"

Philip stood up and walked across the room. "All right!" he yelled as he turned back to her. "Yes, damn it! I do! I do regret that! I always have!"

"Well, don't blame me!" Marilyn yelled. "So I didn't want a baby right after we got married! So I wanted to live a bit, travel, make some money, buy a house. How the hell was I to know you were going to get the goddamn mumps?"

"But if we'd had a child right away—"

"Don't lay the guilt on me, Philip. It's you who can't have the kid, not me. Maybe I should find myself a young stud who's really a man."

"Always getting down to the nitty gritty, aren't you, Marilyn? Now we play dirty, don't we? I'm supposed to yell obscenities at you and you'll answer them with more obscenities. What happens if I refuse to play your little game? I've had it," he declared. "I can't live like this anymore. Go, find yourself another man. It would be a relief. This time I'm really going to leave you, no more threats."

"Can the bull. You won't leave me, you never do. You need me as your scapegoat. Who will you blame for all your inadequacies if you leave me? I'm your catharsis." She picked up a glass and poured herself another drink.

Philip looked at her with disgust. "I'll leave, don't you doubt it. But it'll be in my own good time."

Marilyn laughed. "I won't hold my breath."

October

Andy downshifted into third as she rounded the curve, and took pleasure in the smoothness of her rented Ferrari. She smelled the salt air, felt the wind blow through her hair and turned up the volume on the stereo. The exhilaration of the drive combined with the relief that the promotional tour was almost over made her feel totally relaxed. She was heading for a private party in Malibu given by some Nickelodean people, and she expected to have a very good time.

Eric had left for New York a week into the tour. He'd had to get back to the soap, and she had been alone ever since. This party was her first social venture since she'd left New York, and she was looking forward to it. As she approached the shingled New England style beach house, she could hear loud music and laughter. She parked the car and entered the house. Most of the people were acquaintances, and they greeted her enthusiastically. Andy went to the bar and ordered a Perrier and lime. She hadn't had any alcohol since her latest kidney trouble, and she was trying very hard to follow her doctor's orders. Drink in hand, she stepped out the door to the deck overlooking the ocean. On virtually every table there was a dish overflowing with cocaine that everyone was constantly dipping into. Andy lamented the fact that she couldn't partake, and walked out to the beach. She joined a group of studio musicians who were sitting on the sand talking. They made a place for her and started discussing the rise on the charts of her duet with Eric. "The Love We Share" was released just after she left Boston, and the following week it had hit number one. It was a monster. She lay back and enjoyed the conversation and the night air. Suddenly she felt a hand on her shoulder. Startled, she looked up and saw Marty Kantor kneeling next to her.

"Hi, Andy. We haven't seen each other in a long time, have we?"

"That's certainly true, Marty," she said pleasantly, hiding her disgust.

"I saw you on the 'Tonight' show yesterday. You really gave Johnny a run for his money."

"Yeah, well, it's all in a day's work. You just have to be quick on your feet."

"You sure didn't let him get away with anything. You gave as good as you got."

"Thank you. I'll take that as a compliment."

"I was hoping to get to see you while you were in L.A. I called Nickelodean but they said you weren't making any appointments this trip."

"That's right, I'll be in and out. I'm leaving in the morning for New York."

"I'm glad that we met here, then. Why don't we take a walk?"

"Look Marty, I'm kind of tired right now. I'm not in the mood for rehashing old times."

"Oh, come on, Andy, just a few minutes. I really would like to talk to you."

"Well then, talk. I just don't want to move."

"I can't talk here," he whispered. "I need to see you alone."

"Look, Marty, anything you have to say to me will have to be said here. I'm not moving."

Marty frowned and said, "I was very impressed with the movie you did."

"Thank you."

"I was wondering why you decided not to do any more?"

Andy looked at him, puzzled. "How did you know I refused to do any more movies?"

"Word gets around in this town. You know, you really are a natural. You should think of coming back here."

She shook her head vehemently. "Uh-uh. It's not for me. I like singing and songwriting. I don't like acting."

"How about if we could get you an original musical to write?"

"Didn't you hear me, Marty? I said I don't like doing movies." She moved away from him and started to get up.

Roughly, he pulled her down again. "Fred promised me that you would do those movies. You owe me!"

Furious now, Andy hissed, "Who the hell was Fred to promise you anything? I knew there was something fishy about that deal! Get your hands off me, dammit! I'd never do a movie for you!" She pushed him away and ran across the sand to the house.

Following her, he yelled, "You owe me Andy, God damn you! I was the one who took you in when you showed up in New York penniless, and I was the one who got SMW to give you a contract. You owe me!"

"I owe you nothing! You were a no-talent when I knew you then, and you're a no-talent now! Stay out of my life, you leech! You make me sick to my stomach!"

The party was silent as Andy made her way into the house. Marty looked around at the accusing faces and stomped off down the beach. "Fucking bitch!" he screamed. "Deadbeat! You owe me, and I intend to collect on my marker, one way or another!"

Immediately people surrounded Andy, sympathizing with her, fawning over her. She shoved her way through the house. Once out front, she jumped into the Ferrari, shifted into reverse, then peeled away. At breakneck speed, she flew down the highway back to her hotel. "Leave me alone, all of you!" she yelled into the night. "Leave me alone!"

PROMISES TO KEEP

* * *

Fred sat at his desk trying to work out the company's six month projection for its new division. Nickelodean was now committed to a video production group, and it was his job to formulate a solid plan for its implementation and growth. The idea was not only to produce music videos, but to create a line of full-length tapes for retail sale.

Work had been his only comfort since his last confrontation with Andy. Sometimes he would spend twenty-four hours at the office, taking time out only for a nap or two on his couch. He desired no other woman—his memories of Andy were still too fresh—and the only thing he was interested in was saving Nickelodean. He wouldn't let it go under.

He looked up as Andy burst into his office. He hadn't realized that she was back in New York yet, and he was surprised to see her.

"How dare you, how dare you?" Andy screeched. "You know I never wanted to have anything to do with him again!"

"Slow down. What are you talking about?"

"Marty Kantor, that's what I'm talking about. You had no right to make a deal with him."

"Why not? He put together the best package. Besides, he's an old friend of mine."

Andy slammed her fist down on the desk. "You know I loathe him. He's a slimy bastard who preys on people's weaknesses. You knew I wouldn't like it, that's why you never mentioned it."

"I never mentioned it because it wasn't important. Besides, what difference does it make? You didn't do the movies anyway."

"He buttonholed me at a party last night and said some very vile things. We put on quite a show."

"So what makes this different from any other time you're away? You always manage to get your name in the paper with some messy sort of gossip." He tossed a copy of the New York Post across his desk.

Andy picked it up and read a sensational version of what had happened the night before. She ripped it in two and threw it on the floor. "You are a louse, Fred Arnold! I won't have you in my life anymore! Just stay away from me! I'm going to warn Jim that you are not to be a part of any decisions concerning my career. Right now I'm having my lawyers review my contracts with an eye toward revising them. And once that's completed, I won't ever have to deal with you again. I'll find out everything, so don't let me hear that you've made any more plans for me. You stick to your end of the business, and I'll stick to mine. I intend to produce my own records from now on."

He leaned back in his chair. "As far as I'm concerned, you're not the future of this company anyway. We're pushing the new groups now. They're the ones that appeal to the kids."

Andy laughed. "You can push those groups all the way to China, but they'll never have the class of an Erica Abbott, a David McAllister *or* an

PROMISES TO KEEP

Andy Reuben. It would take a hundred of those groups to make what we've made of this company, and even then, they'll only be flashes in the pan. And you know what? You're the one who ends up losing. At least we still have our integrity. I feel sorry for you," she said, hands on her hips. "What do you have left besides your lust for money?"

"At least I don't lust after my youth," Fred stated in a nasty tone. "What's the matter Andy, afraid you're getting old? Does screwing someone six years younger than you soothe your ego?"

She shook her head in disgust. "How stupid and how typical. It's okay for a man, but not for a woman, right? Men are showing their sexual prowess, but women are longing for their youth." She glared at him with a superior look. "This is a new world and you just don't belong in it. Remember, mister, you are not to be a part of my life anymore. I just want to be rid of you and your plans for me." She turned, strode down the hall, stepped into an elevator and went down to the waiting taxi. She had an appointment with Dr. Bartis and she was late.

Andy lit another cigarette and continued speaking. "You see, Doctor, the problem is that I'm afraid Fred is right. I just don't have that hunger anymore. Day by day it's becoming more of a business and less of a joy. I think that's one of the reasons I love to be with Eric so much. He's relatively new to it all, and I love watching his excitement. It comes too easily for me now. He's still pushing to make it."

Dr. Bartis nodded her head. "I understand exactly what you mean. Life has become too predictable for you, hasn't it? Eric adds a newness to it all again."

"But that's not the only reason I enjoy being with him. He's very mature. He understands a lot of the things I go through. And of course—" Andy smiled—"he's very good in bed. I had forgotten how good it can be."

"Do you want to sustain the image you've created? I get the feeling that you're tired of it all."

"Not exactly. It's just that I worry that I'm beginning to look a little foolish up there on stage, strutting around and mouthing sexual innuendoes. I'd like to just concentrate on my music, from now on."

"Do you worry that you won't be accepted if you do that?"

"Probably, my image you know . . . ." She laughed.

"How about working to change that image? Do you think perhaps it's time?"

"I guess so. I've been thinking about it for a while. We'll see what happens. Right now I still have a number one song on the charts, so I can't be slipping too badly. I'm not finished yet. I think I still have a few good years in me."

"How was the promotional tour? Was it as bad as you thought it would be?"

"Let's put it this way, I'm really glad to be home."

"Did you see your mother when you were in Boston?"

"Yeah, she came out to dinner with Eric and me. Of course, she was very impressed with him. She's an 'Another Time' freak—been watching it since it first came on television." She shook her head. "God, she's incredible. She kept asking me how Fred was. 'Such a nice man' she constantly told Eric. She's so transparent. Eric and I kept looking at each other, and it really was hard not to laugh. She definitely is not happy about the divorce. It only reinforces her feelings about me and my life-style."

"Did she feel that way when Laurie got divorced?"

"That's an interesting question," Andy said reflectively, adjusting her glasses on her nose. "I'm not sure. I know she wasn't thrilled, but she seemed to sympathize a lot more with her. She didn't blame Laurie, but she certainly blamed me. She wanted to know what I did to make him leave."

"You think your mother is harder on you than she is on Laurie?"

"It's not only that, she expects these things to happen to me. Laurie is always right and I'm always wrong."

"How do you feel about that?"

She shrugged her shoulders. "I don't care. I'm used to it, been conditioned to it for a long, long time. Thank God I don't have that much contact with her, otherwise she might drive me batty."

Dr. Bartis looked at her watch. "Unfortunately

your time is up today. I would like to continue this train of thought, though. Let's keep it for our next session."

Andy stood up. "Yeah, I'll see you then. I'm off to Melissa's health club now. It's about time I visited my newest investment. Besides, I could use a little toning up."

Dr. Bartis laughed. "Maybe I should go, too. The cellulite is creeping up on me."

"Oh, come on, there's not an ounce of fat on you! But go anyway. I'll make sure to tell Melissa to expect you. She'll leave a pass at the door." She waved her hand and left.

In addition to the restaurant on the ground floor, the Big Apple Health Fare contained five floors of sport and exercise rooms. There was a bubble over the roof under which two clay tennis courts were laid out. The heated swimming pool, whirlpool baths, saunas, steam and massage rooms were located on the fifth floor. Below that were the squash, racketball and handball courts. Under that were the gyms and weight rooms. Around the perimeter of the floor was an artificial surface track. The second floor contained aerobic exercise rooms and personal lockers for each of the members. The reception desk, store and administration offices took up the rest of the ground floor.

The woman at the reception desk looked up as Andy approached her. She stared for a moment and then stuttered. "You're Andy Reuben!"

Andy smiled. "Could you tell me where Melissa

Rabinowitz is?"

"Uh, she's conducting an aerobics class."

"Where?"

"Up on the second floor. Would you like to join them?"

Andy thought for a moment. "Sure, why not? Can I borrow a leotard?"

"You can go over to our store and get one."

Andy walked over to the shop, picked out a leotard, tights and sneakers and went upstairs to change. Then she found the room that Melissa's class was in and watched for a few minutes. Her sister was in front of the class and Andy was amazed at how gorgeous she looked. She had developed into a very attractive woman with a slim, muscular body and an expressive face. The only thing left from her childhood was the waist-length mane of straight brown hair, which she now had in a long braid. She was no longer the young girl Andy remembered.

Melissa had always been the baby. She'd been petted and pampered by the whole family. Her parents were never as strict with Melissa as they were with her and Laurie. Melissa was allowed to eat what she wanted, wear what she wanted and study when she wanted to. She was "the athletic one." Andy and Laurie were "the smart ones." The odd thing was that Andy had never resented Melissa. She spoiled her as much, if not more, than anyone else. She was sorry that she had missed those adolescent years when Melissa was maturing. It was one of the few regrets she had from those early times after she left Boston, and she had been trying to make up for her neglect ever since.

Andy joined the back line and tried to keep up, but her sister was too fast for her. Finally, the class ended and the people started to leave the room.

"You are all welcome to use the rest of our facilities with our compliments, and I hope that you will all be back as members next time."

Andy listened to the group as they exited and was pleased to hear their very favorable comments from them. A few recognized her, and soon she had a ring of people around her asking for an autograph. Curious as to what was going on, Melissa walked to the back of the room to see what the commotion was about.

"Andy!" she cried, "you came!"

Andy looked up from the middle of the crowd and smiled at Melissa. "Of course I came, I said I would." She pushed her way to her sister. "Come on," she said, "let's go some place quiet."

Melissa grabbed her arm and walked her down the steps to her office. She picked up a sweatsuit from the chair and put it on. "I see you found our shop," she said, pointing to the leotard Andy was wearing.

Andy looked down at herself. "Yeah, I was surprised they had one to fit me there. Usually everything off the rack is too big for me."

"Well, we cater to everyone, even impossibly skinny people like you!"

"Hey, don't call me skinny, I'm just fashionably slim."

PROMISES TO KEEP

"Call it what you want, you're still skinny. You need to come here regularly. We'll give you a great body."

Andy looked at her sister admiringly. "You know, you're looking pretty good yourself. I guess this place agrees with you."

"Yup, I'm really happy here. The crowds we're getting are fantastic." She smiled. "Andy, I don't know what to say. I have you to thank for all this."

"Please, I just gave the money, you're the one who's putting it all together. By the way, where is Shep? Shouldn't he be here?"

"Oh, he isn't here right now. He's out doing some public relations."

"What kind of public relations? He's supposed to be helping you run the place. That's what he's being paid for."

"It's okay. I don't mind doing it myself."

"Well, I mind. Tell him to stop running all over town and spend some time here."

"What do you mean?"

"Look, Melissa, I know he doesn't grace this place with his presence that much. I'm sorry, I just don't want him freeloading off me."

"Andy, that's not true. He's very important—"

"Yeah, I know, squash and all that, but I think that you're handling the whole operation and it's too much for you."

Melissa sighed. "I enjoy it. I've never felt so happy. I'm finally getting my own special kind of success, just like you and Laurie each have."

Andy nodded. "I know, Lis, and I can see that

Wendy Susans

you're doing a good job, but you're letting him take advantage of you. Don't ever let a man take advantage of you."

"Don't worry, I can take care of myself. Shep loves me and I love him. We're planning to get married eventually."

Andy stood up, obviously uspet. "Don't do that! Okay, you're sleeping with him, okay you're living with him, but just don't marry him!" She took a deep breath and put her hand to her forehead. "Enough about that. Why don't you show me around this place."

Relieved to change the subject, Melissa nodded her head. "Okay, let's go." They started with the top floor and worked their way down. Andy was impressed with everything she saw—the racquet courts, the weight rooms, the large heated pool, the saunas, steam rooms, massage rooms and finally, the restaurant.

"We just opened the restaurant Monday," Melissa said proudly. "Want to have lunch?"

"No, I'm afraid not. I've got to leave. I'm meeting Eric."

"Did he tell you that he's been working out here?"

"Yes he did. He says the equipment here is first rate. Oh, by the way, my shrink may be coming by. I told her you would leave a pass at the door. Gloria Bartis, okay? Look, I've got to run now. Hey, keep in touch." She kissed her sister on the cheek and went to change.

Laurie sat at her desk and rereard the letter

that she held in her hand. She would have to call Andy to tell her that the publicity she was giving orphan drugs was paying off. They now had drug companies willing to bear the cost of development for some drugs. She put down the letter from the latest pharmaceutical company pledging to "adopt" a drug. Every time they got a response like this it meant that a few more people would be helped. Suddenly her beeper went off. She picked up the telephone and dialed the nurse's station. There was an emergency in the neo-natal critical care unit. She ran down the hallway, quickly put on a gown and rushed into the nursery. A group of nurses stood around the isolette of one of the twin boys born prematurely that morning. Laurie pushed them away and looked down at the infant.

"He's in severe respiratory distress," one of the nurses informed her. "The respirator doesn't seem to be doing the job anymore."

Laurie nodded and placed her stethescope on the tiny chest. "His lungs are filled with fluid. We've got to try to empty them. Let's go! Syringe." Piercing the skin with a needle, she withdrew about 10 cc.'s of fluid and listened again. "Not enough! Come on, let's move it!" Desperately she worked on the infant, trying to relieve the congestion, but it was evident that the baby was getting weaker and weaker. Finally, he gave out. The team tried to get the heart beating again, but the efforts were futile and at last they had to give up. Laurie looked at the baby and uncharacteristically uttered, "Damn! I thought we could save him. I wanted to save him!" She looked up. "How is the other one?"

"He's holding his own very nicely. No problems yet."

"Well, keep an eye on him. Call me if there's any irregularity at all. Anything! I will not lose both of them!" She took off the gown and, disgusted, threw it into the wastebasket. She dreaded having to tell the mother that one of her babies had died. "God, I hate doing this," she muttered as she walked down the corridor.

Eric sprawled on the couch in Andy's studio, leaned over and put out his cigarette. "I don't know why you're so upset Andy," he said. "It's not really any of your business."

"You tell me that Shep wants you to introduce him to one of the women on the show and I shouldn't be upset? He's living with my sister!"

"I shouldn't have mentioned it."

"He's making a fool out of Melissa and I won't stand for it!" She stood up and paced back and forth in front of the piano. "I'm going to tell her."

"Oh, no you aren't! That would be worse! You know better than that. Leave it alone! She's a big girl, she'll take care of herself."

"I'm sure he's fooling around at the health club, too. The vibes are coming through loud and clear."

"Stop it, Andy! It's their business!"

"Who are you to tell me that? I decide what's my business and what isn't. I am part owner of that club, you know," she informed him, eyes flashing.

"This has nothing to do with the club, it has to do with other people's personal lives. Don't butt in!"

She pointed her finger at him. "No, *you* don't butt in. This is my family and my business." She picked up the cordless phone and dialed the health club. "May I speak to Shep Greenburg, please? Well, would you have him call Andy Reuben at Nickelodean Records, please? That's right. Make sure he gets that message. I'll be expecting his call. Thank you." She slammed down the receiver and spun around. "He's not there again. Look, I'm going to my office now. I'll see you later."

Eric shrugged his shoulders. "Suit yourself, but you're making a big mistake."

"No I'm not. That guy is taking advantage of my sister and I will not allow it." She walked out of the room and angrily slammed the door behind her.

Shep nervously waited in the Nickelodean reception area for Andy to see him. He had returned her call and she had insisted that he come to see her immediately. No matter how hard he had tried, he couldn't convince her to postpone the meeting. He'd briefly considered not showing up, but ultimately decided to go. It wouldn't be smart to cross her, he had too much to lose and he had worked too hard to get where he was now. All his life he had wanted to be somebody, now he had the chance and he didn't want to blow it. Even though he wasn't an owner of the club, he expected to marry Melissa soon, and then he would have it all.

Unless Andy messed it up. He didn't know why she had called him in and he was more than a little worried. Who the hell does she think she is? he thought sullenly.

The receptionist broke into his thoughts. "Ms. Reuben will see you now," she said. He walked down the corridor and stepped into her office.

"Sit down, Shep, I'll be with you in a moment." She finished writing some notes and looked up. "Melissa tells me that you've been doing some public relations work for the club. Exactly what does that entail?"

Shep stared at her. "Well, I'm writing ads—"

"No, I mean the work that keeps you away from the club most of the time."

"I'm, uh, well, going around to radio stations and that sort of stuff."

"What sort of stuff?"

He scratched his head. "What do you mean?"

"I mean that there really is no reason for you to be doing public relations work on club time. You have an office, why don't you use it? Most of the things you have to do can be done there. I don't want you leaving Melissa to run the place herself, although I must say she'd doing an exceptional job."

"Yeah, she is, isn't she?" he said eagerly.

She glared at him. "Right now I'm more interested in your contribution. What are we paying you for? I thought that you were supposed to have squash exhibitions? I under-

PROMISES TO KEEP

stand they were cancelled. Why?"

"I wasn't feeling well that day. My old thigh injury was acting up."

"The hell with your thigh injury! You reschedule your exhibitions immediately or else I'll cancel your contract. I won't have you pulling stunts like this. I want that club to be credible, and your actions are not professional." Andy flipped a lock of blond hair out of her eyes and leaned back in her chair.

"I fully intended to reschedule the matches. You don't have to remind me of that." Shep glared at her.

"I also want to remind you that you have a nine to five job. Make sure you stay at the club during those hours," she said, emphasizing her remark with a tapping finger.

"Look, sometimes I have to be there at night."

"Fine, eight hours a day, no less. Make sure you're there, I'll be checking." She turned back to her work. "I'm busy now. Why don't you go back and help Melissa. I'll bet she's forgotten what you look like."

Shep opened his mouth as if to say something, but didn't. He got up from the chair and walked to the door.

Andy picked her head up. "Oh, by the way, Shep, leave the girls alone. It's not good business."

Shep quickly walked out without a backward glance. That damned broad, he thought. She thinks she knows everything. Nevertheless, he hurried out of the building and headed back to the health club.

Laurie opened the door to her apartment, wheeled the shopping cart into the kitchen and started putting the groceries away. When she was finished, she carefully folded the paper bags and stored them in the broom closet. Then she took out her teapot and brewed herself some camomile tea. Feeling hungry, she sat down at the dining room table, opened a box of water biscuits, spread some brie cheese on a cracker and ate it slowly, savoring each bite.

She was lonely. Bette was sleeping over a friend's house that night, and she was aware of how empty the apartment was without her daughter. The death of the infant that day had affected her more than she wanted to admit, and she desperately wanted to be with someone she cared about. Wondering what Andy was doing for dinner, she kicked off her shoes, padded in her stocking feet to the phone and dialed. "Hello, Alice? Is Andy there? Oh, do you know when she'll be back? I see. Well, would you please tell her I called? Thanks." Slowly, she put the phone down. Maybe Melissa was home, she thought. She dialed her younger sister's number and let it ring for a long time. "Nobody home," she muttered to herself. "Well then, I might as well go back to the hospital. I should check on that little boy anyway." She picked up her jacket, turned out the lights and locked the door behind her.

The neo-natal critical care unit was dimly lit,

PROMISES TO KEEP

and when Laurie walked in, Rosemary Bellon, the head nurse looked up, surprised. "Dr. Rabinowitz, what are you doing here? You're off tonight, aren't you?"

"Yes, but I wanted to check on the little Gebby baby. How is he doing?"

"Just fine, Doctor. Come see for yourself."

They walked over to the isolette in the corner. The infant was lying on his back, under lights. His eyes were covered with cotton and gauze and his small chest rose up and down rapidly. Laurie looked at the latest test results on him, then placed her stethescope on him and listened. She nodded approvingly. "Strong as an ox," she said. "He's definitely a fighter. His color is getting better, too. I have a feeling he's going to make it. I felt so badly this morning when his brother died. You know, this little fellow will probably miss his twin terribly for the rest of his life. He's always going to feel incomplete." She paused. "His mother was very upset when I told her. She couldn't accept it. I guess I can't blame her. She insisted on being brought to the nursery to see him, and then she wouldn't leave this little guy's side. It was very difficult for me to convince her that he's stable." She ran her hand across the baby's face and looked up. "Oh, by the way, we have a name for him now: Joshua. Please put it on the card."

Ms. Bellon smiled. "Joshua it is," she said, and wrote it on the card taped to the front of the isolette. She stroked the baby's tiny arm and murmured, "You're the sweetest little thing,

Joshua. We all love you."

Laurie patted Joshua's foot. "I'll see you tomorrow, kiddo," she said. "Keep up the good work." She looked up and noticed a tall, handsome bearded man staring at her. Puzzled, she stared back at him then went to the door. " Can I help you?"

"Don't I know you from somewhere?" he asked.

Annoyed at his obvious line, Laurie answered, "No, I don't think so."

"Yes, I'm sure of it." He snapped his fingers. "Of course, Laurel Rabinowitz. Don't you recognize me? No, you wouldn't. I didn't have a beard in med school." He put out his hand. "Adam Ezra."

"Adam! My God, I don't believe it! I never would have recognized you! What are you doing here?"

"Well, I've been working for the National Institute of Health in Bethesda for the past six, almost seven, years and now I'm moving to New York. I'm opening my own oncological practice here and I'm going to be affiliated with New York Hospital and Memorial-Sloan Kettering."

"What are you doing on this floor?"

"Believe it or not, I'm visiting that little fellow over there. He's my nephew."

"You mean Joshua Gebby?"

"That's the one. How's he doing?"

"He's stable. Would you like to meet him?"

"I sure would. I just came from my sister's room. She's pretty torn up about Daniel."

PROMISES TO KEEP

"Daniel?"

"Joshua's brother."

Laurie's whole body appeared to slump. "Oh, of course. We were very sorry to lose him, but his lungs were just too undeveloped."

"So I understand. But you say Josh will definitely be all right?"

"Come on, Adam, you know better than to try to pin me down like that. He's holding his own and he's improving, but he weights only 731 grams and it will be awhile before he's out of the woods. Come on, let's visit with him." She offered him a gown and he put it on.

The two doctors went back to the isolette and stared at Joshua. Adam closed his eyes and shook his head. "He's so little, I can't get used to it."

Laurie smiled. "He'll grow. They always do, and obviously your family carries genes for height." She looked up at the six foot tall doctor. "Seen enough now? We should leave him to the nurses."

"Yes, I guess we should." He hesitated. "Uh, would you like to come out and have a drink with me?"

Laurie thought for a moment. "Yes, as a matter of fact, I would. We can catch up on each other's lives since school."

"I'm sorry, but I don't know anyplace around here. I just got in from Washington and I don't know my way around yet."

"Well, there's a pub right across the street from the hospital. It's nice, and they don't rush us. They're used to doctors relaxing there."

"Fine. Are you finished here?"

"Uh-huh. I just came back to see your nephew. I'm not on tonight."

"Thank you," he said simply. "I appreciate it."

"Just doing my job. Besides, I really am rooting for that little fellow. Let's go. I'd love to sit down."

They'd settled in a booth and ordered their drinks before they spoke again. Adam smiled. "So, how has life been treating you since Harvard?"

"Moderately well, I guess. I've been down here at New York Hospital since graduation, and now I'm head of the neo-natal critical care unit."

"Do you have a private practice also?"

"No, the hospital keeps me busy enough."

"I didn't want to go into private practice either, but I'm ready for a change now, and when I was offered a partnership with Dr. Nelson..."

"Dr. Miles Nelson? He's doing marvelous work in cancer research. That's quite a plum."

"Yeah, well, I just couldn't refuse. Besides, I got a grant at Sloan-Kettering and I'll be doing some research myself."

"That's very exciting. I used to think I might go into research, but I realized I'm too people oriented. I like the immediate satisfaction of helping individuals."

Adam nodded. "I like that feeling, too. That's why I left the Institute. I felt that I was missing that human contact." He took a sip of his drink. "So tell me, do you see your sister Andy very often?"

"Sure. She lives here in the city. We get together a lot."

"Do you remember? She was my cadavar partner in Human Anatomy I. She always made me do all the work." He smiled. "Said it made her nauseous. I remember when she left medical school. You were pretty shook up about it."

"I was, wasn't I? Well, it all turned out for the best. Andy definitely was not cut out for medicine." She laughed.

Adam shook his head in agreement. "From what I could see, she never seemed to enjoy med school much. But she sure was smart. She would copy my notes the night before a practical and the next day she would ace the exam." He paused. "Believe it or not, I like her music."

"So do I, although I must admit I fought it at first."

Adam relaxed against the back of the booth. "So tell me, are you married?"

"I was. I'm divorced now. I have a four-and-a-half-year-old daughter named Bette. How about you?"

"No, I've never married. Too involved with my work, I guess. My hours in research are so irregular no woman will hang around long enough to find out if I'm worth it."

"Well, New York is certainly the place for a brilliant young doctor in search of a social life. You'll be fighting off the women before you know it," Laurie said teasingly.

"Not me. I don't meet people all that easily."

"I know the feeling," Laurie said, looking down

and turning her wineglass in her hands. "It's funny. I used to think that Andy and I were exactly alike in every way." She looked up. "Now I realize how different we are. She can walk into a party where she knows absolutely no one and right away be the center of attention and love it. I usually stand on the side and watch what's going on. That is, if I decide to go to the party at all! Somehow I usually prefer to stay at home and read."

Adam studied Laurie for a moment. Her candor charmed him, and her appearance pleased him even more. Her hair was shorter now than it had been in medical school, but somehow it suited her better. Her face was softer, less tense, and he felt as if he could drown in her deep blue eyes. Her casual, loose fitting clothes hid what was surely a most attractive body, and he longed to take her slim expressive hands in his. He nodded and said, "Me, too, although I must admit, I do get lonesome at times."

"So do I." She hesitated. "You know, I haven't talked to anyone like this for a long time."

"Neither have I." He held her eyes with his. "Let's not lose contact with each other again."

"No, let's not."

Adam looked at his watch. "Oh no! I was supposed to call my brother-in-law after I saw the baby. I really do have to get going. Do you live near here? Can I walk you home? Or at least get you a taxi?"

"Actually, I live just two blocks from the hospital, but it's not necessary for you to go out

PROMISES TO KEEP

of your way."

"No, it's okay, I'd like to walk with you. I'm subletting a place near Memorial, so it's not too much out of my way."

"All right. I'm sure your brother-in-law is anxious to speak to you. You tell him that he has a terrific son and that we're optimistic about his chances."

"Thank God he's holding his own. I don't know if my sister would be able to take it if anything happened to him."

"Let's not borrow trouble. We'll take it day by day. Right now, we have every reason to be extremely hopeful. Come, let's get going."

Adam picked up the check, paid, and they left. He walked with her to her apartment building and then insisted on going up with her. At the door, he waited until she got in and put the lights on, and then said, "You wouldn't be free for dinner tomorrow night, would you?"

"Well, I have to be at the hospital until about seven, but after that I'm not busy. I have an idea. Why don't you come here and I'll make dinner for you? That way I don't have to get a babysitter for Bette."

"I'd like that. I'll be at the hospital, too, so we can come back here together." He smiled down at her.

"That's fine. I had a wonderful time tonight, Adam. Thank you. I'll see you tomorrow."

"Yes, till then," Adam said, and he left.

Laurie took off her jacket and walked into the living room. She went over to the stereo, put on a record and sat down on the couch.

She'd felt so comfortable with him. Adam was much more sensitive than she remembered him to be. She was attracted to him, and it was such a good feeling. It had been a long time since a man had interested her. Putting her head back, she listened to the music and began to plan the next night's dinner.

October was always an unpredictable month in New York City. The weather was likely to be warm and muggy, and what little fall foliage there was, was more a bother than a delight to pedestrians slogging their way through the wet, dirty leaves. But this October night was one that songs are written about: clear, crisp and cool. Shep and Melissa were walking down 67th Street after parking the Porsche in an underground garage. It was Laurie and Andy's 31st birthday and they were going to dinner at Andy's house to celebrate.

"I told you, Melissa, I don't want to come here. Your sister Andy bugs the hell out of me," Shep muttered petulantly as they climbed the steps to the brownstone.

Melissa rang the door bell and turned around to Shep. "Shut up already! I want to celebrate my sisters' birthday with them and I want you with me. Laurie is bringing a friend of hers, and Eric will be there, too. You can take it for one night."

"We're leaving early. I don't give a damn what excuse you give, but we're leaving."

Just then, the door opened and Alice led the

couple into the living room. Andy stood up from where she was sitting on the couch with Eric, and kissed her sister.

"Happy birthday, Andy." Melissa's eyes widened at her sister's outfit. Andy was dressed like a man. She had on a black and white striped short-sleeved shirt with crisp white satin pants. Under the shirt collar was a wide black tie with white polka dots, tied loosely. On her feet were black patterned socks and black and white wing shoes. A black and white polka dot handkerchief hung out of the shirt's breast pocket. She looked surprisingly sexy.

Andy laughed at her sister and struck a pose that accentuated the wideness of the shirtsleeves. "You like? I borrowed Eric's shirt. I thought it would make a great look."

Eric nodded approvingly. "It looks better on her than on me," he said as he put his arms lovingly around her waist.

Melissa laughed and said, "I don't know about that, you might fill it out better, Eric! Oh, by the way, Andy, we have those exercise routines ready to go. When can I use the studio to tape them?"

"Why don't you give me a call Monday morning and I'll have it all set up. If it's okay with you, I'll dub in some appropriate music. Oh, and I've arranged for Nickelodean to distribute it. There's quite a market for this sort of thing and we're going into commercial videotapes anyway. Up until now, we've only made promos."

Melissa nodded. "I saw a video of Eric's on cable the other day. It was great."

Eric smiled at Andy. "You mean 'Leave It Alone', right? Your sister produced it. We've finished up the whole album now with Andy as my producer. That song is on it."

The doorbell rang and they heard Alice answer it. Laurie and Adam came into the room and Laurie immediately walked over to hug Andy. "Happy birthday, old lady," she teased.

"Who are you calling an old lady?" Andy turned to the group. "I'll have you know that this is my older sister."

"Only by five minutes, sweetie."

Fascinated, Adam watched the two of them— Andy in her avant-garde outfit, and Laurie in her purple and gray plaid skirt, V-neck crocheted top and mauve wool oversweater pushed up at the wrists. For two women who were nearly identical twins, they looked startlingly different. Much more so now than when he'd known them in school.

Andy smiled and looked at Adam. "Come on, Laur, introduce this handsome gentleman to us all."

"Well, I'll introduce him to Eric, Melissa and Shep, but he's an old friend of yours."

"An old friend? I really don't remember ever meeting—"

"I'm insulted," Adam cut in, smiling. "We shared some intimate anatomical moments at one time."

Andy's eyes widened and she swallowed hard. "Are you sure?"

"Oh yes, very sure," Adam replied with a smug

PROMISES TO KEEP

smile and a glint in his eye. "How could I forget something like that? It was many a night we stayed together."

Andy looked pleadingly at Laurie, who was obviously enjoying the exchange.

"Oh, come on, Adam," Laurie said. "You're embarrassing my poor sister. Andy, don't you remember Adam Ezra?"

"Adam Ezra. I'm sorry, but you'll have to give me some more clues."

Adam sighed dramatically. "How soon we forget the important things in life. Human Anatomy I and Nicodemus?"

"Oh no! Adam Ezra, of course! My cadaver partner in med school! We called our cadaver Nicodemus! But you didn't have a beard then, and you wore glasses."

"And you didn't wear glasses then, but I still recognize you. I'm hurt."

Andy put her head in her hands. "My sordid past is coming back to haunt me. Spare me, please!"

Shocked, Eric exclaimed, "What are you two talking about? You went to medical school, Andy?"

"Not often, but she was enrolled," Adam quipped.

"Andy! I didn't know you cut classes," Melissa remarked. "Ma used to go wild whenever I cut classes. She always told me how studious the two of you were."

"Oh no, Melissa, I was a very good girl in college. I never cut classes in college. Ask Laurie.

But med school, now that was another story. I hated med school! Lord knows I should never have gone."

"Then why did you go?" Adam asked.

"That's a long, sad story," Andy drawled, "and I don't feel like going into it now." She looked at Laurie. "At least we have one eminent physician in the family, and that's all that counts. Let's all go into the dining room now, okay? Alice is waiting for us." She held back for Laurie so they could walk together. "So he's the interesting man you wanted me to meet. How in the world did you two get together again? He's awfully good-looking now."

Laurie blushed. "He is, isn't he? He just moved here from Washington D.C. I really do like him. We've been seeing quite a bit of each other these past couple of weeks. His nephew is a patient of mine."

Andy put her arm around her sister. "I'm so happy for you, Laur. I've been kind of worried about you lately. You've seemed so lonely."

"I was, but not anymore. Adam and I are very simpatico."

They entered the large dining room with its Oriental motif. The room had Queen Anne pedestal tables, a chinoiserie cabinet and a Persian rug. Japanese silkscreens covered the walls. There were two armchairs upholstered in striped silk and four unmatched side chairs around the dining table. The table was covered with a pale pink linen cloth and a bowl of fresh cut flowers decorated the center. The dishes and stemware were ringed in twenty-four carat gold and intialed "A.R." Ornate place settings of sterling completed the very elegant table.

Everyone sat down, and Andy rang for Alice to begin serving the birthday dinner. "Eric, would you please pour the wine?" Andy asked as she drew the standing ice bucket close to him. She turned to her guests. "It's a Montrachet Grand Cru. Really a magnificent wine. I hope you enjoy it. Sorry I can't partake." She looked at Laurie with a rueful smile.

Eric poured the wine and held up his glass. "A toast to the most beautiful birthday women in the world—may we have many more celebrations together!"

"I'll drink to that!" Adam exclaimed as he took a sip of his wine. "Hey, this is wonderful! So smooth! I've never tasted anything quite like it."

"And you probably rarely will," Andy bragged. "There are only about twenty six hundred cases produced annually. I have a fan in Paris who sends me a case each year."

Just then, Alice brought in the first course, prosciutto and melon, and the convivial group laughed and chatted their way through the meal until the main course was served.

As Andy cut into the steak Diane and watched Laurie serve herself some spinach souffle, she commented, "I keep telling you, sis, you may wind up being the healthiest of us all, but you sure are missing out on the finer things in life."

"That's quite all right, Andy. I really don't miss meat in the least." Laurie smiled and reached for the bowl of wild rice.

"My mother can't stand the fact that Laurie is a veggie," Melissa said to Adam. "She keeps saying that it's her fault, that Laurie didn't like her cooking when she was growing up."

"She knows that's not true," Laurie protested. "I became a vegetarian when I was in medical school and I saw how badly cholesterol clogs the arteries. I decided that I never wanted that to happen to my body."

"Please, Laurie, no preaching in my house," Andy begged in mock displeasure. "We're supposed to be enjoying ourselves. Why don't you eat what you like and leave the rest of us to wallow in our weaknesses!"

After the meal, Eric turned to Adam, "Hey, I want to hear some more about this medical school thing. I can't believe that Andy Reuben went to Harvard Medical School."

Andy laughed. "No, Eric, Andy Reuben did not go to medical school. Andrea Rabinowitz did. She also went to Radcliffe and graduated Phi Beta Kappa at nineteen."

Adam smiled. "Andy, do you remember when we first got the cadavar and Marc Furman dressed it up in a bowtie and jockstrap? I thought you were going to faint when you saw it."

"Boy, do I remember!" Andy said with a chuckle. "I thought that was disgusting—sacreligious or something. I felt so sorry for that poor man lying there on the table, and there was no way I wanted to cut into him."

Laurie shook her head. "You never did get over

that feeling. You could never look clinically at the cadavar, it was always a person to you. That's dangerous."

Andy sighed. "I wondered about his life and his family and why he was there instead of in a grave like he should have been. It was a devastating experience for me. You just can't imagine . . . I don't even like to remember it. I think that was the class I cut the most."

"I think I would cut that class, too," Melissa agreed. "Just the thought of putting my hands into a human body turns my stomach."

"Wait a minute," Adam protested. "Human Anatomy is one of the most important classes a medical student takes. We learn an incredible amount of information about the human body, and we lose our fear of cutting into it."

"I never did," Andy disagreed.

"But you never wanted to be a doctor!" Laurie interjected. "You've told me that often enough."

"Lucky for mankind I never did become one!" Andy laughed. "What are you specializing in, Adam?"

"Oncology."

Eric looked at Andy. "What's that?"

"He works with cancer patients," she answered.

Adam nodded. "That's right. I'm also doing research in chemotherapy. We're trying to find drugs that have a minimal amount of side effects and maximum potency. So many times patients die as a result of complications due to side effects from the drugs rather than the cancer itself."

"Cancer certainly is a terrible disease," Andy remarked as she proceeded to light a cigarette.

Laurie grabbed it away from her. "Andy, that isn't funny! Sometimes you are just too much to handle!"

"I pride myself on that," she quipped, looking impishly at Eric. "Oh, by the way, I have a special birthday present for you, Laurie. I'm setting up a free Central Park concert for the spring. Probably some time in May. It'll be televised live on cable and all the proceeds for that and the souvenirs will go to the orphan drug thing." She smiled expectantly at Laurie.

"That's great, Andy! Thanks, we need the publicity."

"And the money!" Andy added.

"That's for sure!" Laurie grinned at her sister.

There was a brief moment of silence while everyone digested the news, then suddenly Shep stood up. "Come on, Melissa, we have to get going. I have an exhibition match at the club tomorrow and I need my rest."

"Oh, Shep, we could stay just a little longer. We haven't even had coffee and cake yet."

"Let him go, Melissa," Andy said. "We'll get you home."

Melissa looked at Shep and sighed. "No, that's okay. I'll leave with him. I have to get over to the club early tomorrow anyway." She stood up and walked out of the dining room with Shep. At the door she turned around and looked back forlornly at her sisters. "Will I see you guys soon?"

Andy nodded. "Sure, Lis. You're going to call

me Monday about the taping session, right? You take care now, and I'll speak to you then."

"I'll be at the club sometime next week," Laurie reassured her. "I'm bringing Adam over. He says that he can use some exercise."

Melissa's face brightened. "Great, I'll see you then. Happy birthday, you two. I love you both," she said simply, and then she left.

"What was that all about?" Laurie asked Andy.

"I guess Shep just doesn't enjoy our company," she answered innocently.

"Come on, Andy, what did you do to him? He avoided you all evening, and he barely said a word."

"Let's just say we've come to an understanding. We both want to keep Melissa happy."

"Okay, I can see that I won't get a straight answer from you now, but I do want to know what happened."

"In due time, dear sister, just don't be impatient." She stood up. "Follow me, Alice will serve coffee in the living room."

Adam and Laurie walked back to her apartment after the dinner party ended. Laurie was silent as she unlocked the door. Abruptly, she turned to Adam. "Would you like to come in for a while?" she asked hesitantly.

"Yes, I'd like that very much."

They walked into the living room and Mrs. Barrett stood up. "Mrs. Barrett, this is Dr. Adam Ezra. Adam, I'd like you to meet Bette's sitter."

Wendy Susans

"Pleased to meet you, Dr. Ezra."

"Was Bette all right tonight," Laurie inquired.

"Oh, yes, Dr. Rabinowitz, she was fine." Mrs. Barrett gathered up her knitting and walked to the door.

"Will you be able to come in on Sunday? I have to be at the hospital for a few hours."

"Oh, I'm sorry, I can't. I'm visiting my daughter on Sunday. They're picking me up and taking me to their house in Scarsdale."

"I hope I can get Alice to come over here . . ."

"Laurie? How about if I stayed with her?" Adam asked. "I'm free the whole weekend, and I think it would be fun."

"Are you sure, Adam? She can be quite a handful sometimes."

"If she wouldn't mind, then I wouldn't."

"Oh, I guarantee that she won't mind, but—"

"No buts about it. It's settled."

Laurie laughed. "Well, if you're sure . . ." She turned to Mrs. Barrett. "Have a good time on Sunday."

"Thank you doctor. Good-bye." Laurie watched as she walked to her apartment across the hall, then she closed the door.

Nervously, Laurie walked across the room. "Would you like something to drink?"

"No thank you." Adam ambled to the stereo and looked at her albums.

"How about some music?" she suggested, following him.

He pulled out a copy of Vivaldi's "Four Seasons" and said, "This is my favorite, why don't we listen to it?"

Laurie took it from him and put it on the turntable. Adam sat down in a chair, put his head back and closed his eyes.

"Well, what did you think of Andy?" Laurie asked, as she fiddled with the stereo controls.

Adam sat up and thought for a moment. "She looks somewhat different, of course. I think she's much too thin, but underneath it all, she's really the same old Andy, isn't she?"

Laurie sat down on the arm of Adam's chair. "I guess she is to some extent, although she's certainly mellowed with age."

"So have we all. You aren't the same driven girl I remember, either. You were so single-minded in school. Had to get those A's. Had to be number one in the class."

"Oh Adam, I was proving something then. Andy had left and I doubted myself so much. I had to prove to myself that I could succeed without her. And I was so lonely . . . ."

"You never socialized at all. Always by yourself—"

"All I wanted was for Andy to come home. But I'll tell you something. It made me strong. I knew then that I could do whatever I wanted to do. When I finally came to New York to find Andy, I didn't need her in the same way that I did before. I wanted to be with her and talk with her and be friends with her, but I didn't need her to survive anymore. It's made a great difference in my life."

"It made you a much healthier person I would imagine." He leaned forward. "Would you tell me why Andy went to medical school when it's so obvious that she never had any desire to be a doctor?"

Laurie sighed. "It was my fault. I wouldn't listen to her. She really wanted to go into music, but I had this grand dream of us both being doctors, and in those days, she would do anything to make me happy. Anything, even if it meant giving up her own dreams."

"What happened to change that?"

"She met a guy, and he gave her a life independent of me for the first time." She shook her head in amazement. "How I resented him! God, you wouldn't believe the fights that went on between Andy and me about him! He convinced her to do her own thing, and finally she couldn't take it anymore so she just left."

"I understand a lot more now about your actions then. We were all so puzzled about the two of you." He turned, looked directly into her deep blue eyes and took her hand. "I was always in awe of you. You seemed so untouchable. I wanted so much to ask you out, but I was so shy."

Laurie's eyes widened. "I never realized that! I didn't think anyone liked me."

"I liked you, I liked you very much. But it seemed to me—to us—that you didn't want any one near you."

Her heart raced as she saw the desire in his eyes. Suddenly she wasn't afraid any more. "I want someone now," she whispered as she sat down in his lap and buried her head in his chest.

PROMISES TO KEEP

Adam put his finger under her chin and lifted her face to him. He kissed her tenderly. "I think I'm in love with you."

"Oh, Adam, I need you with me so much. You make me feel so safe and comfortable."

"Laurie," he whispered, holding her close, "I want to make love to you tonight."

"Yes," she murmured. "I want that, too. I want that so very much." She led him to her bedroom and closed the door. Adam pulled her to him and kissed her passionately. Laurie kissed him back ardently, then suddenly, unexpectedly, she moved away.

"What's the matter?" Adam inched closer and lifted her chin with one finger.

"I'm frightened. I haven't been with a man in so long, not since my divorce. I don't want it to change things between us." She covered her face with her hands.

He took her hands away. "Laurie, it can only change things for the better. We need each other."

"But what if you don't like me?"

"How could I not like you?"

She looked away. "I don't know very much about pleasing a man."

"You please me very much." He turned so that she was facing him again, then gently drew her down on the bed. As he caressed her face with one hand, he began to remove her sweater with the other. "Laurie," he whispered, "you feel so good. You're so soft. See, you're pleasing me already." He guided her hand to him, then kissed her shoulders and breasts. His touch sent shivers through her body. She wanted to touch him and hold him close to her for a long time. Slowly and softly, he made love to her. The roughness of his beard against her skin aroused her in a way that she had never been aroused before. She responded to his caresses passionately and her hands moved over his body as if they had a mind of their own.

Everything about him excited her—his sensitivity, his instinctive knowledge of what would please her, his masculinity. It was the most exquisite thing she had ever experienced.

"How could you ever think you wouldn't please me?" he tenderly asked her as he looked into her eyes. "You're the most wonderful thing that's ever happened to me."

"Oh, Adam, I love you. I've never felt like this before. It's never been so good. Don't ever leave me, please."

"I'll never leave you Laurie, I promise." Holding each other tightly, they fell into a deep, satisfied sleep.

Eric sat in the buttery soft leather chair in Andy's upstairs den, the room that held all of the awards and memorabilia of her career. The walls were covered with plaques and platinum records. The mantel held her Oscar and some of her Grammys, and the rest were haphazardly distributed on bookshelves. Record album covers and pictures taken with other famous people hung around the room, as did copies of Billboard, Variety, Rolling Stone, People Magazine, Time,

Newsweek, Cosmospolitan, Ms., and others featuring her on their covers. It was a very impressive room filled with momentoes of all types, the kind of room he had always dreamed of for himself. Eric wanted success so badly he could taste it.

When he had left Tulsa for Northwestern University, he had done so without looking back. When the opportunity to take a major part in a soap opera presented itself, he'd left the university during his junior year. Now he was ready to move on again.

When Nickelodean approached his agent with the idea of recording some of the songs he had sung on "Another Time," he'd jumped at the chance. He'd figured that a hit record would give him the exposure he needed to make it really big. And when Nickelodean told him that he would be recording with Andy Reuben, he couldn't believe it. She was the biggest! A hit with her would insure his success.

His plans hadn't included falling in love with her, though, and fall in love he had. She was the most exciting, glamorous woman he had ever encountered. It didn't matter to him that she was six years older—women who were self-assured and successful had always appealed to him. The problem was that he wasn't sure about her feelings for him. He knew that she found him attractive and satisfying in bed, but was there any more? He didn't like to commit himself to a woman until she committed herself to him, and yet . . . Eric sighed, leaned back in the chair and closed his eyes.

Andy awoke with a start and realized that Eric wasn't next to her in bed. She slipped into her robe and picked up Tasha, then left the room to look for him. A light under the door in the room next to hers caught her eye and she went in. There she saw Eric, so deep in thought that she hated to interrupt him. "What are you doing here?" she asked him quietly.

Eric turned around, startled. "I didn't hear you come in. I was just looking at all these things." He lifted his arm and made a sweeping motion with his hand. "Why do you keep them all hidden away like this?"

Andy shrugged her shoulders. "I don't know. It seemed like the right thing to do. I used to put the records in my office, but after a while it got silly. This seemed like the perfect compromise. I like keeping these things, but it's not necessary to have them on view all the time."

"I would if I had them."

She laughed. "Wait a few years, and then we'll see." She knelt next to him and put down the cat. "Eric, let me tell you something. I know what I am. I know that I'm famous, a great big star and very good at my work. It's not necessary to proclaim it. Believe it or not, I rarely come in here."

"It's like a museum," Eric commented with a bemused smile.

"That's right. That's exactly what it is, but I don't get off on it. I prefer to concentrate on what I'm doing next, not what I did before."

"You've done so much though. I never

realized—"

"Stop it, you're making me feel like an old lady," she said with a laugh.

"I didn't mean it that way. I'm just so envious of you."

"Don't be. I'm nobody that special."

"Oh, yes you are. You're incredible." He hesitated. "I love you, Andy."

She expelled a deep breath. "Is it me you love, or all this?"

"I think both. It's kind of heady breathing the rarified air around you."

"Eric, please don't do this. I'm a living, breathing human being. These things are not me, they're not even extensions of me. They're just things, and more and more I realize that they're not that important. It's nice to be recognized, especially when you're judged by your peers, but it's not everything." She touched his arm. "I'll tell you a secret. With all of this, I still feel that there's something missing in my life. When I first started, I thought that fame and money were all I wanted. Now I know that no matter what, the people in my life are more important. Take this dinner tonight, for example. I loved having my sisters here with me. I need them very much. My family makes what I do worthwhile. Can you understand that?"

"Not really," Eric said honestly, shaking his tousled head. "I couldn't wait to leave Tulsa. I was such a misfit there."

Andy laughed. "Oh, Eric, people like us all feel like misfits. That's why we try so hard. That's why we're so driven. We want to prove ourselves to the world. And for what?" she asked rhetorically. "We want the human contact, the acceptance, the love. We just don't think we're good enough and we need this stuff to perhaps reassure ourselves that we are. Someday Tulsa may seem very appealing.

"Take me, for instance," she continued. "I found it very difficult being an identical twin. All I wanted was to be away from Laurie, and now I love being with her so much. I don't know what I'd do without her."

"I want all this so badly," Eric said, looking younger and more vulnerable than usual.

"You'll have it. I would place bets on that. You're very good. But don't fool yourself; it's not the only thing in life."

"It's what I want now." He covered his face. "This is terrible. It must sound as if I'm using you to get what I want, but—"

"You don't have to explain to me, Eric. I understand. You're not taking anything that I don't want to give. After all, I'm sort of using you too. You're handsome, charming, people's heads turn when we go out together. I like you as an ornament as much as you like me for the doors I can open for you. Besides, you're very good in bed and I really enjoy that." She touched his cheek tenderly. "But we're more than just that to each other now, aren't we? We're also good friends."

"Yes, I guess we are. And I do love you, you know."

"I know. I wouldn't have it any other way."

PROMISES TO KEEP

She smiled seductively. "Come back to bed," she whispered in his ear. "I get lonely without you there."

Eric turned her face to his and kissed her. "You're a very special lady and I'm very lucky to have you in my life." They sat that way for a few minutes more and then, hand in hand, they walked back to Andy's bed. Eric gazed into her eyes, lifted her in his strong arms and gently placed her on the silk sheets. "I have never wanted a woman as much as I want you," he murmured softly in her ear, breathing in her sweet, intoxicating fragrance.

She shivered with desire and drew him close to her. His nearness was dizzying and she felt as if she had been propelled into a world in which only the two of them existed. The electricity between them was palpable, and the highly-charged momentum carried them to heights of passion neither of them had ever experienced.

"I love you, Andy," Eric said as, exhausted, he lay his head back on the soft down pillow. Slowly, his eyes closed. Within minutes he was fast asleep.

Andy lifted herself up on one elbow and looked at her sleeping lover in the shimmering moonlight. She tenderly caressed his damp curls and placed her lips softly on his. Eric had touched her in a way she didn't know she could be touched. She felt her defenses slipping away and she was afraid. He was all she had ever dreamed of in a man. He was strong yet sensitive, brash yet caring, confident without being arrogant. They shared so many interests that she felt as if he was her male counterpart, as if they were destined for one another.

"I do love you," she whispered to the unaware Eric as she molded her body to his. "God help me, I do love you."

Laurie awoke and looked at the clock on her night table. It was only six in the morning. Then realizing it was Saturday, she settled back and snuggled into Adam. *Adam.* "Adam," she whispered. "Get up! You have to leave!"

Adam opened his eyes and turned to her, just as he caught a movement at the door. "If you're worried about your daughter, Laurie, I'm afraid it's too late. She's over there."

Laurie sat up and covered herself. "Bette! What do you want?" she snapped angrily.

Bette cringed. "Nothing, Mommy. I just wanted to come into bed with you."

"You can't now. Get out of here," she scolded, angry at herself, not her daughter. "Now! Go have breakfast. I'll be up soon."

Adam put his hand on her shoulder. "Don't do this, Laurie. It's all right. Come over here," he said to Bette," patting the mattress next to him.

Bette looked at her mother, but Laurie was silent. Bette slowly walked over to the bed and climbed on. "Did you stay here all night?" she asked.

"Yes, I did."

"Why?"

"Because your mommy and I wanted to be

together."

"Do you love my mommy?"

"Yes, I do. Very much."

"Mommy?"

Laurie turned over and opened her eyes. "What, Bette?"

"Do you love Adam?"

"Yes, I do."

Bette started jumping up and down on the bed. "Goody! Then we're going to get married. You'll be my daddy! I'll have a daddy!" She flung her arms around Adam and hugged him.

Adam peered over Bette's head. He could see that Laurie was very upset about this situation. He knew that she was mortified to have Bette find him there. "Hey, honey, how about starting breakfast so that your mother and I can get dressed."

Bette scrambled down from the bed. "I'll make the orange juice, I know how. And I'll make the coffee, too."

"Don't make the coffee, please," Laurie admonished. "Just get everything out. I'll start the pot."

Bette nodded her head and ran out of the room.

"Oh, Adam," Laurie groaned, "how could I have been so stupid? You shouldn't have stayed."

Adam took her in his arms, and wouldn't let her push him away. "Don't be like this, Laurie. There's nothing wrong with Bette seeing two people who love each other in bed. It's the most natural thing in the world."

She put her hand to her forehead. "This has

never happened before. I don't want to confuse her."

"What's confusing about it?"

"She's never mentioned anything before about having a daddy. You can't imagine how upsetting that is to me."

"Doesn't she ever see her father?"

"No, she never saw him. He left the country before she was born and he died a couple of years ago in a car accident."

"Did he know he had a daughter?" Adam asked softly.

"He knew he had a child. I'm not sure he knew it was a girl."

"Would you like to tell me about it?"

"I don't know if I can." Laurie gently removed his arm and leaned back on a pillow. "It's so painful."

"I'd like to know about it. I think it's important."

"Which version do you want to hear? The one I've told everyone, or the truth?"

"What do you think?" he asked with a wry smile.

"I've never told this to anyone before. It hurts too much." She took a deep breath. "Okay, here goes. Ed Chancellor was part of the team that worked on Andy when they transplanted one of my kidneys to her. I assume you read about that. I had just come to New York, and after so many years of longing to see her again, I found her dying of uremic poisoning. It was incredibly emotional for me. You can't imagine what seeing her like that did to me. I was a wreck.

"Chance was there all the time, comforting me, giving me the strength to argue with Andy about taking my kidney—she refused at first, and that didn't help any. It was horrendous, a nightmare. He courted me, and I thought he was in love with me. A few months after Andy left the hospital, we were married. Immediately after we got married, though, I realized that he wasn't in love with me, but with Andy. He expected me to be just like her in every way. Of course I wasn't, nor did I ever want to be, and the marriage deteriorated quickly. He began sleeping with other women and then one night . . ." She paused and tears welled up in her eyes.

"One night he called me Andy while we were making love. It was bad enough when I knew he was thinking it, but when he said it out loud . . . I couldn't stand it anymore, so I decided to divorce him. I realized that I never really loved him, he was just there at a difficult time. When he found out I was pregnant, he wanted me to get an abortion. But I wouldn't, so here I am."

"And you never had any contact with him about Bette before he died?"

"None at all."

"Whew, that's some story. I'm so sorry, Laurie, you deserved better." Laurie put her arms around Adam's neck. He held her close and he could feel the tears run down her face. "Laurie, don't cry," he whispered. "I love you. I won't leave you and Bette. You can be sure of me."

"I want to believe you, Adam, but it's so hard

for me."

"Well then, we'll work on it until you're sure. I want you to trust me, but I know it will take time."

"I do trust you, it's just that—"

Just then, Bette came into the room. "Come on, I'm hungry and you're not even dressed yet."

Laurie held out her arms to her daughter. "Come give me a hug and then I'll get dressed."

Bette jumped up on the bed and pushed in between Adam and Laurie. The three hugged each other tightly.

"Since we're all off today, what do you say to a trip to the Bronx Zoo?" Adam asked.

"I love the Children's Zoo! Can we take Adam there?"

"Yes, of course, Bette. We'll pack a lunch and picnic there. Come on, now, let us get dressed."

Bette jumped off the bed and went back to the kitchen.

"I'll go home after breakfast, change my clothes and then come back to pick you up."

"Are you sure you'll come back? You aren't tired of us?" She laughed nervously.

Adam shook his head. "I'll never be tired of you. I feel like my life is just beginning now." He kissed her with passion and reluctantly let her go. "We can't keep Bette waiting. After all, we have the whole day ahead of us."

"I'm so happy," Laurie whispered. "I've never known such happiness."

November

"What the hell kind of crazy place are you taking me to?" Eric looked around Delancy Street. The whole scene was completely foreign to him. The street led over the Williamsburg Bridge and was clogged with traffic. The stores were crowded one next to the other and hordes of people streamed in and out of them. Eric glanced down one of the side streets—they were virtually impassable. Carts filled with merchandise spilled over into the roadway and he could hear the haggling between the cart owners and the customers. He couldn't believe that he was still in New York City.

"You'll see," Andy said. "I'm taking you for some good Jewish cooking." She took his hand and led him into Ratner's Restaurant. The minute they were inside, some people standing on line at the bakery turned around. "There's Andy Reuben!" one of the women whispered.

"Look, there's Chad!" another yelled. A crowd formed around the couple and they were busy for quite a while signing autographs on napkins and stray pieces of paper.

Finally Andy grabbed Eric's hand. "Enough! We came here to eat, let's go." They spoke to a waiter who led them to a table in one of the far corners of the restaurant.

"God, I hate it when I'm called Chad," Eric complained after they sat down. "It's as if that's my only identity. Believe it or not, when I went home to Tulsa last Christmas, my mother introduced me to people as Chad."

Andy laughed. "At least she recognizes what you do. My mother still calls me Andrea Rabinowitz. I've never received a piece of mail from her addressed to Andy Reuben, and *that's* a really weird feeling. Not only that, but I haven't ever heard her acknowledge that she's proud of me and what I've accomplished. Anyway, you won't be Chad Stevens much longer. When does yesterday's taping air?"

"I guess in about two weeks. It felt really strange saying good-bye and taking off for Oregon as Chad, knowing that I'll never be back as Eric."

"Why didn't they kill him off?"

"I guess they're hoping that I'll come back."

"But you won't. This move is too important to your career. You've got to keep moving forward. Your album will be out within the month and I predict a blockbuster. Is the tour all set up?"

"Uh-huh. I'll be away until February." Eric

reached across the table and briefly touched her cheek. "I never would have had the courage to do this without you."

"Don't say that!" she said sharply. "You have to do what you believe in. You have to make moves that other people warn you against because you're the only one who knows what's best for yourself. I never would have made it if I had listened to other people."

"Even Fred?"

She sighed. "In the early days of my career, Fred just reinforced what I felt was right for me. When our opinions started to diverge, I followed my own instincts."

"Was that why you split up?"

"Partially. He not only wanted to run my career, he wanted to run the rest of my life, too. That was impossible for me to take. By that time, things were pretty involved though, and getting rid of him as a business manager and producer wasn't a simple matter."

"You mean that in order to stop him from being involved in your career, you had to divorce him?"

"That's about it."

They became aware of someone standing next to the table and looked up. The waiter looked down at them. "Would you like to order now?"

"No," Andy answered. "We'll be ready in a few minutes. Please come back."

They picked up the menus and Eric started laughing. "Is this in English?"

"What do you mean?"

"What the hell is kasha varnishkes? I think I

know what borscht is—"

"The way you say it, it sounds like gibberish."

"Hey, come on, I'm just a poor Okie. What do you want from me?"

"Why don't we make it simple and have blintzes and sour cream? I think you'd like cheese, potato and cherry, okay?"

"Anything you say. I'm not very fussy."

The waiter returned and they placed their order. Their blintzes arrived and Eric cautiously tasted one.

"Put some sour cream on it," Andy suggested. "That's part of the mystique."

He dipped it in sour cream. "Hey, these are pretty good," he said as he took another mouthful.

"Of course they are. If nothing else, we Jews know how to eat well!"

He looked at her plate. "If you aren't going to finish yours, I'll take them."

She pushed it towards him. "Be my guest. We also love to watch our men eat well." She looked at her watch and gasped. "Oh my God, I'm due at Francesco's in an hour and I have to change."

"Francesco? The photographer? Why?"

"My sisters and I are having a portrait done for my mother."

"Sounds nice. Can I come watch?"

"I don't think so. Francesco is kind of weird. He thinks of himself as an 'artiste', and doesn't let anyone into his sessions. I'll see you later."

"I think I'll hit Bloomingdale's."

Andy smiled. "You do more shopping than I

PROMISES TO KEEP

do, and I bet you have more clothes." She touched his knee under the table. "But you do look so sexy in them," she said teasingly.

They looked at each other with subdued mirth as the waiter brought the check and presented it to Eric. He snatched it, stood up and bowed. "My treat, young lady," he said as he put his hand out to her. She took it and rose.

"As long as you're feeling so generous," she joked, "why don't you bring me a present from Bloomie's. I love the place." She kissed him on the cheek and dashed off to find a cab.

Fred picked up a towel and wiped the sweat off his face. He'd been working out in the weight room at the Big Apple Health Fare for about an hour. He considered going to the pool to cool off, but decided to have something to eat first. He put on his sweat suit and went down the elevator to the restaurant. On his way, he saw Melissa and called out to her. "Hey, Melissa, what are you doing now?"

"I thought I'd grab some lunch. You, too?"

"Sure, why not?" They went into the restaurant and sat down.

"This place is terrific," Fred said. "I've been working out for two weeks now and I feet great."

"What's the matter? You feeling your age?" Melissa teased.

"Hey, what do you mean? I'm not so old. I just want to keep in shape, that's all." They both ordered salads and fruit juice.

Their food arrived a few minutes later, and

after a few bites. Melissa looked up at Freddie. "Is the divorce final yet?" she asked tentatively.

"Didn't Andy tell you?"

"No, she never speaks about it, and I wouldn't ask her, but I'm curious."

He looked away for a moment, then turned back to her. "Yes, the divorce is final. I went to Haiti a couple of weeks ago. I figured I might as well get it over with. She's so goddam pigheaded."

"That she is. Once she makes up her mind about something, that's it."

"She won't ever compromise either. I'd always want to discuss things with her, but she doesn't discuss. She never believed that I knew what was best for her."

"That's not fair!" Melissa snapped. "Have you ever tried to look at it from her point of view? Maybe she felt that you were the one who would never discuss things. Laurie said you made all the decisions and then told her about them. Of course she couldn't take that. Andy always wants to feel as if she's in control of her own life. I think you should have given her a chance for some input."

"I don't know, perhaps you're right." He sighed. "I suppose I should have done a lot of things differently."

Melissa looked at him. "She's working on a new record now, isn't she?"

"Yeah, and she's producing it herself. She didn't even want me near it. That's her new hobby—producing. She produced Eric Boutelle's record, too. Just like her to pick someone she can dominate."

"Oh, I don't think she dominates Eric. He seems pretty strong-willed himself."

"Yeah, but he's using her to get what he wants."

"I don't agree, Fred. I hate to say this to you, but they have a very nice relationship—really close."

"I'll bet. I know all about Andy and her 'close' relationships. You forget that I spent years dealing with her many Erics. She'll tire of him soon."

"You're wrong Fred. Andy's different now—much softer, calmer. She and Eric complement each other very well. I don't think he really needs Andy to make it. He was pretty popular on that soap opera, and he has a nice voice."

"Nice voices are all over the place." Freddie picked up a lettuce leaf and started ripping it apart. "Nickelodean has a dozen people who can sing rings around him, but he's getting the bucks. She's appropriated money for him that should have gone elsewhere. You can't imagine how much his new video cost—more than Andy's latest, for Christ's sake, and she makes our most expensive ones."

"Maybe you should spend more. The video is great. I hear the album is, too."

"It's okay. He'll make money for us, but Andy really is hell-bent on making him a superstar."

"So what? Nickelodean needs that, doesn't it? Why shouldn't she promote him? Hey, Fred, don't let your jealousy get in the way of your good business sense."

Fred laughed. "Always the practical one, aren't you? But I guess you're right. Why should I care what Andy does as long as it helps Nickelodean?"

"But you do care, don't you?"

"Of course I care. Andy and I went through a lot together, don't you forget that."

"I know, and I always liked you so much. I still do, but I think it's better for both of you this way. You fought too much about everything."

"Hey, let's not talk about Andy anymore. I'm tired of it."

Melissa looked at the clock. "Well, I have to go anyway. Andy, Laurie and I are having a portrait photograph done for my mother. It was Andy's idea, but I'm kind of excited about it. We're going to Francesco's studio, no less. Do you know him?"

Fred nodded. "He's done almost all of Andy's album covers." He smiled. "He loves photographing her, says the camera makes love to her. He's a little tempermental, but he's the best there is. You'll enjoy it."

Melissa signed the check, and she and Fred left the restaurant together.

"I'm going up to take a swim now, see you later, Melissa."

Melissa kissed him on the cheek and patted his shoulder. "Take care, Fred, and don't worry, everything will work out fine."

"Hey, it's fine now, Melissa baby. Look at my almost beautiful body. A little more pectoral muscle and I'm in the running for Mr. America."

PROMISES TO KEEP

Melissa laughed. "I'll vote for you any time! Have fun." She waved good-bye and walked back to her office.

Andy sat on her bed with her legs pulled up to her chest. Eric was at her desk making a list of the hotels he was staying at on his tour, and she watched him with mixed emotions. Although she had admitted to herself that she loved him, she still hadn't told him. Try as she might, she couldn't get their age difference out of her mind. Eric insisted that it didn't matter, but she didn't know if that was entirely true. He was so young, so vulnerable to women. She wondered how long he would find her attractive. Feeling weepy, she buried her face in Tasha's fur.

Eric looked up at her. "I wish you were going with me, Andy."

"I can't," she said brusquely. "I have too much work here, and besides, this is your tour, not mine. You need to do it alone."

Alarmed at her tone of voice, he got up and lay down next to her. "I'll miss you."

"No you don't. There'll be plenty of groupies ready to take my place."

Angrily, Eric sat up. "What the hell are you talking about? Do you think I only want you for the sex?"

Andy shrugged her shoulders. "You'll get very lonesome in those hotel rooms. A willing body does keep you company."

"Hey, I thought we had some sort of commitment here. Do you mean it wouldn't bother you if

I screw other women?"

Andy sighed. "Just don't tell me. What's the difference if I don't know?"

"The difference is that I'm in love with you. I've never been interested in casual sex, I guess it's my Baptist upbringing." He picked up some clothes and threw them in his suitcase.

"So don't sleep with other people. I'm just suggesting that it might be there, and you might want to take advantage of it." Andy lay down on the bed and turned away from him.

Eric stormed to the other side of the bed and lifted her onto the floor. "I don't believe you! Don't you think I've had plenty of opportunities here in New York? Are you saying that I mean so little to you that you expect that sort of thing from me? Do you want someone else?"

She pushed him away and walked to the window. "No," she said softly. "I'm happy right now, but who knows what tomorrow might bring? At twenty-five I would expect that to be your attitude, too."

"Hey, lady, I don't like being jacked around. If that's the way you feel, then I'm leaving." He grabbed his suitcase and strode out of the room. As he violently pulled the door open, he stopped short, turned and said, "I can't believe that we're having this conversation the day before I'm leaving for three months. You're unbelievable!"

Andy heard him running down the stairs, and realizing that she couldn't bear to lose him, followed after him. "Eric, don't go!" she yelled, "I'm sorry. I don't want you to leave this way."

PROMISES TO KEEP

He paused and yelled back at her, "The hell with you, Andy Reuben! I don't need you and your hang-ups."

She rushed down the steps and stood in front of him. "But I need you. So much. Don't you realize how much I'm going to miss you?"

"Actually I don't. I figure that you can't wait to get rid of me so that you can start having fun again." He tried to push past her.

"But I don't have fun when you're not with me," she whimpered as she held him back. "I just don't want to force you to make promises you can't keep."

"Don't you dare project your attitudes on me. I don't want or need anybody else but you. Damn it, I love you, and that's a hell of a lot more than you've ever said about your feelings for me."

Andy put her arms around his waist and her head on his chest. "Oh, Eric," she said softly. "I'm so in love with you. Sometimes I feel as though I'm going to burst for loving you."

Eric hugged her with all his might. "My God, Andy, you don't know how long I've been waiting for you to say that. Why couldn't you tell me that before?"

She rained kisses all over his face. "I didn't think we needed the words. Come upstairs and I'll show you how much I love you." She took him by the hand but Eric pulled away and shook his head.

"Andy, sex isn't the only way to show me that you love me. I want your trust, too. What good is having a relationship if there's no trust?"

"Trust takes a long time to develop, and even then it doesn't mean much in the scheme of things." She sat down on the steps. "What's the point of it, anyway? We all have to look out for ourselves to survive in this world. It's only human nature. No matter how much you love someone, when the chips are down you're going to protect yourself."

"You mean you've never known anyone who didn't disappoint you?"

"No. I've had love relationships, I've had business relationships and I've had family relationships. In one way or another I've always been disappointed. I understand now that in order not to be hurt, I can't expect people to always do what I hope they'll do. It doesn't mean that I don't love these people, it just means that I've learned to be cautious."

He sat down next to her. "You mean if you don't expect too much, you won't get hurt?"

"Not only that, but sometimes you're pleasantly surprised, and you get more than you expected. Like with you. I never hoped to have such a beautiful relationship when we first started. But I still live day to day with it. If you love me, that's the way you'll have to take me."

"You make it pretty hard for a guy, don't you? Now I have to show you that I'm worth trusting."

She put her fingers to his lips. "Shh. No more. We love each other, we'll miss each other, let's make this night one that will last us for three months."

PROMISES TO KEEP

Eric stood up, pulled her to her feet, lifted her into his arms and pressed his lips to hers. "We'll make this a night that will last us forever," he whispered as he carried her to her bedroom.

Andy sat in the Nickelodean studio trying to convince Erica Abbott and David McAllister to record a song she had just written for them.

"It's an interesting idea, Andy. I just don't know if we can pull it off," David said apprehensively.

"Come on, David, where's your sense of adventure? I think you and Erica will sound terrific together."

Erica raised her eyebrows. "I've never done anything like this before. It certainly will be a different experience."

"Here, listen." Andy sat down at the piano and started playing the melody. "I have it all worked out—arranged, orchestrated, everything. Come on, try it. It can't hurt."

David and Erica looked at each other and smiled. When Andy first came to them with the idea, they had both immediately said no. It sounded absurd; they were two singers—two stars—with completely different styles and completely different audiences. Andy had just laughed and said, "But that's all the more reason to do this. It's fresh and it's new, and you'll each gain new fans. Besides, let's face it, neither of you are exactly storming the charts right now. Both your careers need a shot in the arm and maybe, just maybe, I can help you."

Wendy Susans

Now, listening to her enthusiasm, and liking the song very much, Erica said, "Okay, I'll try it. Sing it with me, David."

Andy began the tune again, and Erica and David joined in. Their voices blended in perfect harmony, and as the song ended, Erica and David turned to each other.

"It has possibilities," David said. "What do you think, Erica?"

"I like it. I'm willing to do it if you are."

David smiled. "The hell with it. Okay, Andy, you win."

"You know, guys, this was just an impulse on my part," Andy said. "I was fooling around with some material for myself when this song just popped into my head. It's not right for me, but I knew right away it would be perfect for you two."

Erica sat down next to her at the piano. "I guess you're bound and determined to save us all, aren't you?"

Andy laughed. "Something like that." Just then the phone rang. Andy picked it up. "Yes? This is Andy." She listened for a minute. "What!" she screamed. "Oh my God! Are you alright Alice? I'll be right there!" She slammed the phone down and stood up. "Can you believe it? My house is on fire! I have to get home!" She rushed out of the studio, down the elevator and hailed a cab.

The taxi pulled up a block away from her house. "Sorry, we can't get down this street," the driver said, "the firetrucks are blocking it."

Andy threw some money at him, got out and

looked up the street. Then she started walking, as if in a trance, towards the chaotic scene before her. Crowds of onlookers filled the street, but she pushed through them, ignoring their cries of "It's Andy Reuben," and the pieces of paper they thrust in front of her. She roughly elbowed away the reporters who were preventing her from getting to her beloved house. Cameras from all the networks were trained on her as she finally reached the steps, but she was too distraught to notice them. She did see the firemen moving equipment in and out of the brownstone and the firetrucks and police cars in front. Alice was standing outside crying, Tasha in her arms. "Oh, Andy, I'm so glad you're here. I smelled smoke and I looked in the pantry and there was a fire! I picked up Tasha, ran out of the house and pulled the fire alarm. Then I called you."

Andy walked up to the fire chief. "I'm Andy Reuben," she said. "I own the house. How bad is it?"

"Well, ma'am, we have it completely out now. It shot up the back of the house but I'm not sure how much damage there actually was."

"Can I go in and take a look?"

"I guess so. As I said, it's completely out. I'll go in with you."

The front door was open and they went in. Andy felt physically sick at the sight of her home. "Oh no!" she cried. "My beautiful house!" She stepped into the living room and picked up the Degas painting that was lying on the water soaked floor, half out of its frame. She tenderly clasped it to her bosom as tears fell from her eyes. Then she looked around at the rest of the room. All the furniture was dripping wet and there was a large hole smashed in the wall leading to the dining room. She went in and shook her head sorrowfully at the ruin. An acrid smell of smoke hung over the whole place. They carefully walked into the kitchen, which had been badly gutted by the fire. She looked up. There was a hole in the ceiling and she could look into her music studio, which was blackened also. "My music! My work! Oh, my God! All that work down the drain!" She held her head in her hands. "Can I go upstairs? I want to see if I can salvage any of my music."

"It's not really safe at this time, Ms. Reuben."

"When will it be safe? I have to get up there!"

"We'll be sending inspectors over this afternoon to see what started the fire. We'll let you know within a few days."

"What do you think started it?"

"We can't really tell yet, but I'm pretty sure it was electrical."

"What about rebuilding?"

"I don't know. You'll have to wait until the inspectors finish their job. Why don't we walk around back and see what it looks like there."

Mutely she followed him out of the house and into the backyard. Andy looked up and saw that the fire had reached the third floor bedrooms. Fortunately, her bedroom and den were not in line with the kitchen. It was Fred's old room that had taken the brunt of the fire. She looked at the charred house, tears streaming down her face.

Laurie paced up and down nervously as Alice and Andy sat together on the couch in her living room. Alice was recounting her story of the fire to Laurie. "It was horrible! Flames were shooting out of the pantry. I couldn't even get to my room. My clothes, my pictures . . ."

"I wasn't allowed back there yet, maybe some things will be salvageable," Andy said soothingly.

"Exactly what happened?" Laurie asked. "Do they know how it started?"

"Probably it was old wiring. Maybe a short in the walls. They're not sure yet."

"Do you think someone could have set it deliberately?"

"Oh, Laurie, don't be silly," she said angrily. "The firemen didn't say anything about arson."

"I don't know, Andy, it's possible, isn't it?"

"Let's wait for the report before we speculate. Right now I have more immediate concerns, like where I'm going to stay. I was thinking of going to a hotel, but I really don't want to do that."

"You know you're always welcome to stay here."

"I know, Laur, and thank you, but I really can't. I need a place for myself. Besides, with Alice staying here you don't have the room."

"I'd love to have you," Laurie assured her. "I'd make room."

"No, I'll find someplace else." She snapped her fingers. "You know what? I'll stay at Eric's apartment! He's on tour and I have the key right here." She held up a key chain. "I'll call him right now and see if it's all right."

Just then, Adam walked in the front door of the apartment. "Andy! You're here! I was just coming by to find out if Laurie knew anything about the fire."

"What? How do you know about it?"

"Look." He showed them the bold headline on the front page of the New York Post. "HOUSE BURNS, ANDY WEEPS." There was a picture of Andy in the backyard crying.

Andy grabbed the paper from him, quickly scanned the short article then crumpled the paper in her hands. "They have my address here! You don't know how hard I've worked to keep my address out of the press! This is unbelievable!" She threw the paper across the room in disgust.

"Oh God, no, Andy!" cried Laurie. "What are you going to do? Now you'll have every kook in the city camping on your doorstep."

Andy sat down with her head in her hands. "I can't think right now. I don't know what I'll do."

"I know what you'll do. You can't live there anymore. You'll move."

"What's the big deal?" Adam asked. "Why are you so upset, Laurie?"

"Don't you understand? She's in danger if the whole world knows where she lives. She's had one close call already."

"Stop it, Laurie," Andy snapped. "It's not that bad. I'm going to call Eric now." She took out the piece of paper in her wallet with Eric's itinerary on it, then he went to the phone and dialed his hotel. After explaining the situation, she spoke for a few more minutes, then hung up and turned around. "It's okay with him. I'll be staying there. He wanted to come back here, but I told him it wasn't necessary. If you don't mind, I think I'll go right now and settle in."

"Do you want me to come with you?" Laurie asked.

"No, I'm tired." Andy pushed up her glasses and rubbed her eyes. "I just want to get over there and lie down. I'll speak to you later. Take care, Alice." She kissed her sister, picked up Tasha and her things and slowly walked out the door.

"I'm worried about her," Laurie stated to Adam. "She shouldn't be alone. I don't care what she says, I'm going with her." She grabbed her jacket and ran after her sister. When she got into the hall she saw Andy waiting for the elevator, the damaged Degas cradled in her arms. Laurie quietly went up to her, put her arms around her waist and her head on her shoulder. "I think I'll go with you anyway, just to make sure you get settled in okay."

"Laurel, I don't need a mother now."

"No, but you do need a friend," she said as she wiped a smudge of soot off her sister's cheek.

Andy slumped down against Laurie. "That I

do," she whispered. "That I do." The elevator door opened and, together, they walked in.

Melissa picked up the newspaper that was left on the receptionist's desk and casually glanced at the headline. Shocked, she realized that it was about her sister. "A fire in Andy's house?" She opened the paper and read the small article, then she went down to Shep's office. "Look at this! There was a fire at Andy's house!"

Shep looked at the picture and shrugged. "It doesn't look too bad. What's the big deal?"

"Not too bad? It looks terrible to me. I'll bet she went over to Laurie's." She reached for his phone.

"Why bother? If she wanted you to know, she would have called you. Obviously she couldn't care less if you know."

"That's not true! It's probably been very hectic for her. She'll get around to calling me. I know Andy."

"By the time she gets around to calling you, the whole world will have read about it in the newspaper," Shep said callously.

She hung up the telephone. "What the hell are you trying to do?"

"I'm not trying to do anything, it's just a fact."

"You know, Shep, I'm really tired of your attitude towards Andy. We wouldn't be here if it wasn't for her. I know she's hard sometimes, but that's why she's so successful."

"Hard isn't the word, she's a bitch!"

Melissa leaned over the desk and slapped his

face. "Don't you ever say anything like that about her to me again. Ever!" She turned and left the office, slamming the door behind her.

"Goddamn it! The whole house should have burned down, with her in it," Shep snarled. "I'm so sick of that witch." He picked up his pencil and went back to his crossword puzzle.

The L.A. Times was folded on Marty's desk when he stepped into his office. He put down his coffee and picked it up, intending to turn immediately to the entertainment section. A picture on the front page made him stop short. What the hell was Andy's picture doing there, he wondered. He looked closely and read the article about the fire. "Heh, her precious house," he said out loud with a malicious chuckle. As he looked at the paper an idea slowly formed in his mind. A trip to New York within the next couple of months sounded like a good idea. A very good idea.

Philip rushed into the kitchen and sat down at the table. He was surprised to see Marilyn calmly buttering a piece of toast. It wasn't very often that she had breakfast with him anymore. She poured him a cup of coffee and said, "Look at the newspaper."

"What for? I'm late as it is."

"There's something that might interest you on the front page."

"I'll read it at the office. Right now I want to get going."

She picked up the paper and shoved it in his face. "Read it now!" she snapped.

He saw Andy Reuben's picture and immediately threw it down. "Dammit! I'm not interested in what happens to her. Can't you understand that she means nothing to me?"

"I know you. Now you'll go to the office and read it. You just don't want me to know you care."

"I don't care, and I can't take much more of this! You are totally obsessed with her. Don't think I don't know that you read everything that's written about her. I've seen the magazines and trashy newspapers under the bed. You're a sick woman and the sooner you get help the better. Your craziness is driving me away, can't you see that? I can't believe that she's screwing up my life like this again."

"Look at her address. She certainly does live in a swanky neighborhood, doesn't she?"

He looked at it. "Why the hell should I care where she lives?"

"Maybe you'll want to visit her someday. Maybe she'd like to see you? You know, old time's sake and all?"

"I very strongly doubt that. Jeez, Marilyn, you've done it again. You've killed another day for me. You can be happy now."

Marilyn smiled at him. "How many nice days do you think I've had knowing that you wish I was someone else?"

PROMISES TO KEEP

Philip shook his head, picked up his briefcase and left the house. He had to find some way out of this living hell.

December

LaGuardia Airport was very crowded and there was a long delay before take-off. Andy, Laurie, Melissa and Bette sat in the Nickelodean Lear jet waiting for their turn on the runway. The Francesco portrait had been ready earlier than expected and Andy had decided that they should make a surprise trip to Boston to present it to their mother in person. It was no coincidence that Eric was performing in the area that very night. Convincing Melissa to come had been no problem, but Laurie had had to rearrange her schedule and cancel a dinner date with Adam to accommodate Andy's desires. Although Laurie had been reluctant to upset her routine, in the end she'd acquiesced because she knew how much it meant to her twin.

Life these days for Laurie was very sweet. She had fallen completely and passionately in love with Adam, and it was a heavenly feeling. He stayed at her apartment most weekends, providing her with a domesticity she hadn't realized she longed for. It was wonderful having an intelligent companion to talk to, and a tender lover to go to bed with. She was beginning to think of spending the rest of her life with him, and she knew that he felt the same way about her. Bette was happy also. She thought of Adam as the daddy she had never had. He played with her, read to her and even disciplined her. Laurie approved of the way he handled her daughter, and delegated some of the parenting to him with as much relief as pleasure.

Melissa, on the other hand, was having some problems. Although the health club was successful beyond her expectations and she was excited about her new video, her personal life had taken a turn for the worse. Shep was spending more and more time away from her—sometimes not coming back to the apartment all night. When she'd asked him where he'd been, he'd tell her he had spent the night at his parents, and was irritated that she asked. The trip to Boston was a welcome reprieve—even if only for a day or so. And it would be so nice to see her mother. She was surprised at how much she missed her.

Finally the jet took off and they were airborne. Within an hour they had landed at Boston's Logan Airport and were in the terminal. They loaded their bags in the waiting limousine and headed toward Brookline.

"I've never been in an airplane that has

couches," Bette said. "I loved that airplane. It was so much fun."

Andy hugged her niece. "Well, you'll be going home in it tomorrow, so you'll have fun then, too, little one."

"I wonder if Ma will like the picture?" Melissa wondered out loud. "It is sort of different from the usual one."

"Please, Melissa, remember what Francesco said," Laurie admonished mockingly. "It is not a picture, it is a portrait!"

"Well, excuse me! It looks like a picture to me."

"A hell of an expensive picture," Andy remarked wryly.

The limousine pulled up to the Rabinowitz house, and the four got out. Bette ran up to the door and rang the bell. When the door opened she yelled, "Look who's here, Grandma! It's all of us! All together!"

Adrienne took a step backward and dropped the dish towel she was wiping her hands on. "My goodness, what are you doing here? I didn't expect you."

"Of course not," Andy smiled. "We wanted to surprise you."

Melissa arrived at the door carrying a large package. "Let's go, you guys. This is bulky. Let me get it into the house."

Adrienne moved away. "What in the world?"

Melissa took her mother's arm. "Come on, Ma, we want you to open it now. It's your Chanukah gift."

"But it's not Chanukah yet."

"That's okay," Laurie said. "Andy wanted to come up today and she convinced us that we wanted to come also, so we decided it might as well be Chanukah for us."

They went into the living room, where Adrienne opened the package. The hand-colored portrait was breathtaking, soft and pastel with an ethereal quality. Andy and Laurie were standing on either side of Melissa. Andy was wearing a pink and gray geometrically patterned mohair sweater with pink camel's hair pleated slacks. Her boots were also pink and her hair fell wildly around her face. As was her style, Laurie was neat as a pin in pale blue wool slacks and matching cashmere sweater. Melissa was all in lavender, wearing sweat pants, vest, and striped rugby shirt. Andy and Laurie looked remarkably alike once more. There was the same wistful look in their eyes and gentleness around their mouths. It was as if they'd been photographed at some long ago time when their lives had been less divergent, less disparate. Tears came to Adrienne's eyes. "My twins and my baby," she whispered. "I see them again."

"Ma, why are you crying?" Melissa asked. "We thought you would love it. You know, it was Andy's idea."

"Oh, I do love it. I do. Thank you so much, Andrea. I couldn't ask for a better present." She hugged Andy tightly and put out her arms to her other daughters. Finally, she pulled away. "You all must be hungry. I'll make some dinner for you. First I have to go down to the butcher. What should I buy?"

"Oh no! We want to take you out to dinner," Melissa protested.

"Not tonight. I haven't cooked a meal for so many people in I don't know how long. We can go out to dinner tomorrow night."

Andy shook her head. "I'm afraid we're leaving tomorrow. The three of us have to get back to work."

"You're staying only one night?" Adrienne's face fell. "I thought maybe you would stay for a few days."

"Not this time, Ma," Laurie said, as she put her arm around Adrienne. "Look, why don't you come back to New York with us? There's plenty of room on the plane. We took a Nickelodean company jet."

"Oh please, Grandma, come back with us."

"No, no, I really can't now," Adrienne protested. "Besides where would I stay? Andrea, how is the house coming along?"

"Slowly, I'm afraid. There's quite a bit more work to be done than I originally thought. There was some structural damage from the water, and since it was an electrical fire, I'm having the whole place rewired."

"That fire was a terrible tragedy. Your house was so beautiful. I was very worried when Laurel called to tell me about it. I didn't even know where you were."

"I'm okay, Adrienne. No need to worry about me. I should be back home within the month."

"Thank goodness no one was hurt." She turned

to the rest of the group. "Well, what should I get?"

"How about a london broil?" Melissa said. "I haven't had a decent slice of london broil since I left here."

"Make hamburgers, Grandma. I love your hamburgers!" Bette yelled.

Laurie shook her head. "Bette, that's junk and we don't eat junk."

Andy put her arm around her niece. "Oh, leave her alone! I'd eat a hamburger too."

Melissa sighed. "That's fine with me."

Laurie shrugged her shoulders. "If you people want to poison yourselves, go right ahead. I'll have a cheese omelet and a salad, thank you. Bette, do you really want a hamburger?"

Bette looked at her mother sheepishly. "Yes, Mommy."

Laurie sighed. "Well, I guess it's okay this once. But we won't make a habit of it."

Relieved, Adrienne said, "Come on, Bette, let's go to the butcher. You girls put your things away."

"Oh, I won't be sleeping here tonight," Andy said tersely. "I'm staying in town."

"Why?" Adrienne asked. "I thought we'd all be together for once."

"I would rather stay there. I'll come back out here tomorrow to see you and to pick everyone up."

"Well, I should have expected it from you. It never changes. Come on, Bette, let's go get the meat." Adrienne took Bette's hand and walked out.

As soon as she left, Melissa turned to Andy. "Why aren't you staying here? What is it with you? Do you enjoying disappointing Ma? You could have pleased her just this once."

Andy lit a cigarette and sat down on the couch. "I thought the portrait pleased her. She doesn't need me here."

"It would have been nice though. What's so much better about a hotel?"

"Eric's here," Laurie said softly. "Andy is surprising him."

"Oh, I see. I was wondering why you were so hot to visit Ma just now. It wasn't her at all, was it?"

"It was a little bit her, and a lot Eric. Come on, Lis, what's the difference where I sleep. I made Adrienne happy with the present and I am eating dinner here."

"Well, well! What a favor the great one does us!"

Laurie angrily gave Melissa a shove. "Shut up, Melissa! You have no right to say something like that to her! She's entitled to go see Eric if that's what she wants to do. It's none of your business."

"That's right, Melissa, it's none of your business," Andy said harshly.

"Okay, okay, let's forget it. You sleep where you want to. What the hell difference does it make anyway?"

"Just what is that supposed to mean?"

"It means that we never expect you to be at family gatherings anyway, so why should this time be any different?"

Andy stood up. "You keep this up and I'll skip dinner, too."

Laurie touched her sister's shoulder gently. "You don't want to do that, Andy. Ma would be too disappointed and so would Bette. Just stick to your original plan and leave after dinner. Please? For me?"

Andy looked into her twin's eyes for a long time. She thought of the arduous dinner that lay ahead and looked at Laurie's pleading face. "Okay," she whispered almost inaudibly. "I'll stay." She sat back down on the couch and snuffed out her cigarette.

Andy looked at her watch, put down her coffee cup and stood up. "I'm afraid I have to get going now. I guess I'll call a cab." She walked into the kitchen to make her phone call.

"Where is she going so soon? She can't sit around and talk to us for a while?" Adrienne looked at Laurie and Melissa quizzically.

"She's going to see Eric Boutelle's concert. He's at B.U. tonight," Melissa said.

"Oh," said Adrienne. "And why all the secrecy? As if I didn't know he's her latest lover. I read the magazines, too, you know. It's the only way I find anything out about her. My daughter wouldn't tell me anything."

"It's her life," Laurie said softly.

"Yes, I know it's her life. You tell me that often enough. And your life, my dear? Is that only your business also?"

"What do you mean?"

"Bette, do me a favor. Will you go upstairs and get grandma's sweater? I'm a little chilly."

Bette stood up. "Yes, Grandma. Where is it?"

"On my bed, dear. That's a good girl." Bette left the room and Adrienne continued. "Bette tells me that you have a new friend, Laurel."

Laurie's face reddened a little. "What else did she tell you?"

"She said that he is in there in the morning sometimes when she gets up, and that he is sort of her daddy. How come you haven't told me about him?"

Andy walked back into the room. "Maybe she wants to keep her private life private, Adrienne. Can you possibly understand that?"

"I'm her mother. I have a right to know. Besides, it's not smart to do this kind of thing in front of the baby."

"What kind of thing? I'm not doing anything wrong, and don't you dare try to make me feel guilty! Bette has never been so happy."

"You're setting a very bad example, Laurel. I thought you, of all my daughters, were above that."

"Hey, I resent that, Ma!" Melissa shouted angrily. "What makes Laurie superior to Andy and me?"

"Andrea's life-style is an old story, and I've told you how I feel about what you're doing with Shep. But Laurie—"

"I think this conversation has gone far enough, Adrienne." Andy sat down and lit a cigarette. "If you want to have any contact at all with any of us, you better quit now."

"What do you mean, quit? I'm your mother. I'm allowed to have my opinion. I don't understand any of this."

"That's the problem," Laurie retorted. "You don't understand. We do what we feel comfortable with. We're old enough to make our own decisions and if we're wrong we have to take the consequences. I appreciate your concern about Bette, but I think I'm doing a fine job with her. I'll handle it, believe me." Laurie stood up. "I think I'll go into the den now and see what's on TV. I'll see you tomorrow, Andy. Have a good time." She kissed her twin on the cheek and walked out.

The cab outside honked its horn and Andy warned, "Damn it, Adrienne, don't badger her anymore! I'm warning you, she won't take it and neither will I!" She picked up her jacket and bag and ran out.

Adrienne shook her head. "I'm very upset with the three of you, Melissa. I don't know what I've done wrong. Two of my girls are divorced, and you won't even get married."

"I guess you were just a very bad mother, right?" Melissa flashed her mother a smile and flipped her hair behind her shoulder. "Seriously, Ma, it's different out there now. We're more independent than you can ever imagine. There is no 'right thing' anymore. We live our lives as best we can, doing the things we feel are best for us."

"And what about responsibilities? Or is that a

dirty word?" Adrienne asked sarcastically.

"We're as responsible as anyone else. Probably more. We just feel responsible to ourselves first."

"But Laurel has a daughter. She should know better."

"I'm going to say something to you that you probably never believed you would hear from me. Leave Laurie alone! She's had it very rough, and she deserves a little happiness. If you so much as say one more thing to her about Adam, I'll never set foot in this house again! And that's a promise!"

Adrienne opened her mouth to say something, but then stopped. Her daughters had never rallied around each other this way. Obviously Andy and Melissa both felt very strongly about Laurie's involvement with this man. She decided to drop the subject for a while. "Well, I won't say anymore, but don't think I approve. If she wants to sleep with him she should marry him."

"You're a broken record, Ma. I've heard that one a million times. By now I just turn you off."

"Turn me off. Click, she turns me off like a radio. Well, honey, you keep turning off and see what good it does you. I'm going to watch TV with Laurie and Bette now. I'll tell you though, I'm not very happy."

Just then Bette came into the dining room. "I can't find your sweater anywhere, Grandma. I looked everyplace, even under the bed."

Adrienne waved her hand. "That's all right dear, I'm not cold any more." She got up and went into the other room.

Wendy Susans

* * *

Andy stood in the shadows backstage watching Eric. She loved the look he projected in his tight black jeans and formfitting lime green muscle shirt. Damp blond curls fell across his forehead and his powerful, fluid hips swayed to the rhythm of his music. The performance was electrifying. She waited for the applause to die down and the introduction for "The Love We Share," to start. Then she slipped onto the darkened platform at the back of the stage, whispered to the drummer, who then relayed the message to Eric's backup singer who stood aside as Andy walked up to the microphone. The crowd went wild and Eric turned to see why. When he saw Andy, he rushed to her and lifted her off the platform in a giant hug. Then he took her hand and led her to the front of the stage. They looked at each other and then they sang:

> The love we share is not like any other.
> Time spent loving you just seems to fly.
> A week, a day, an hour or a minute,
> When I'm with you they pass so quickly by.
>
> We can't be sure if what's now is forever,
> We can't predict, we don't know what will be.
> But when I'm in your arms so close beside you,
> The world consists of only you and me.
>
> The love we share is endless,
> Like a circle round and smooth.
> It flies, it swoops, it swallows us.
> It's a love we'll never lose.

PROMISES TO KEEP

And even when I'm far away,
Your soul's entwined with mine.
'Cause the love we share is precious,
It defies the sands of time.

So engulf me with your burning passion,
I'll never allow you to go.
We'll spend all our time in each other's arms,
And the love we share will flourish and grow.

The love we share is endless,
Like a circle round and smooth.
It flies, it swoops, it swallows us.
It's a love we'll never lose.

And even when I'm far away,
Your soul's entwined with mine.
'Cause the love we share is precious,
It defies the sands of time.

They had never sung the song so beautifully and passionately before, and the audience was on its feet screaming before they finished. Afterward, Andy left the stage and Eric went on with his show. Every once in a while he glanced over at her as if to make sure she was still there. Finally he performed his last encore and ran off the stage. He wrapped his arms around Andy and literally pulled her to his dressing room. "Oh, Andy, it's so good to see you! What a great surprise! Why did you come? Did you see the whole show? How was I?"

"Hey, slow down." She laughed and nuzzled his neck. "I couldn't stand not seeing you for one day more, and your show was just terrific."

"But I've only been gone a few weeks—"

"I know that, but I missed you so much. Can you understand that?"

"Can I understand that? You don't know how much I can understand that. You were right. The road is not great."

"Even with all the college women you've been meeting?" she teased.

"What do I want with college women? I have you waiting for me at home."

"Oh yes, I've been waiting. But I couldn't wait any longer, so here I am."

Eric started to pull off his sweaty shirt. "Just let me change and we'll go right back to my hotel room."

"You read my mind. I'm ready to have you right here and now," she said as she ran her hands down his chest.

He pulled her towards him and kissed her. "Soon baby," he whispered. "So soon." He dressed quickly and they rushed back to the hotel.

Eric lit Andy's cigarette, gave it to her and lay back on the pillow. "You have no idea how much I've missed you. I can't believe you're actually here."

Andy lay her head on his shoulder. "I've missed you, too, Eric. I've had such lousy luck since you left. I've wanted you so much. The fire was such a trauma for me." Her tears fell on his chest. "I can't write in your apartment. I need my own studio."

"Poor baby." He kissed her head. "You'll be

back there soon, won't you?"

"Yeah, but the newspapers printed my address and it'll never be quite the same."

Eric frowned. "I know, and I don't like it. I was thinking maybe you should sell and move someplace else."

"Never! Nobody is pushing me out of my own home. I think they'll probably forget in time. I'll just have to wait it out."

"I'm not so sure of that. You're big news, and there are nuts out there who feed upon people like you. They might come to your house."

"So what? Nobody can get in. What can happen? I'm more protected than you think. My security system is quite extensive."

"I know that, but I still don't feel that you're safe now, and it scares me. I sometimes have this dream that you're lying on the ground and I can't pick you up."

"Well, the first time you saw me I passed out," she reminded him with a grin. "Maybe that's what you're dreaming about. But that won't happen again. I go to the doctor every two weeks and the kidney hasn't gotten any worse."

"No, it's not that. It's more than just a fainting spell."

"Hey, come on, you're depressing me. I don't want to talk about this right now." She held him close. "I won't see you for such a long time, and we still have all night." She moved closer to him, kissed his neck and caressed him. "Make love with me again. Mmm, oh Eric, I can't get enough of you."

Eric closed his eyes and pushed the fears out of his mind. "I can't lose you, Andy," he whispered. "I won't lose you." He pulled her on top of him and kissed her passionately.

Andy sat back in the large comfortable chair and sighed. "I just can't stand this, Dr. Bartis. The reconstruction of the house is driving me crazy. It breaks my heart to look at it. The only thing I've salvaged are my gold and platinum records and my awards, and even they smell like smoke. My cars were untouched, but everything else—" She brushed away a tear. "It's all irreplacable. The insurance money means nothing to me, so much of it was priceless. I'm working on refurnishing and acquiring more artwork but—" She put her head in her hands and shook it.

"It must be a lot of work for you. How are you finding the time to do everything?"

"Well, actually I can't. I'm not doing much songwriting because I can't work anywhere but at home, so I've had to put my record on hold for the time being. The house is all- consuming."

"When do you think it will be finished?"

"Most of the actual construction is finished. The electricians are rewiring right now. Hopefully, I should be back there by the middle of January."

"So it's not much longer. Tell me, how did the Boston trip go? Did your mother like the portrait?"

"I guess so. She was oohing and ahhing that we looked like she remembered us from years ago.

Oh, I have something really interesting to tell you," Andy added. "She had Laurie on the hot seat this time. Bette told her about Adam and she had a fit. According to her, now we are all disappointments—morally, that is. She managed to get Bette to tell her about Adam, and then boy, did she zing it to Laurie! It was not a pretty sight."

"What happened?"

"Well, Melissa and I protected her. Laurie is very vulnerable, you know, especially about things like this. She never could take it when Adrienne scolded her. Although I must admit, she took care of herself very well. Adam must be very important to her."

"And how is Eric?"

Andy smiled. "Dr. Bartis, I feel like a lovesick teenager when it comes to him. I'm so crazy about him that I can't see straight. I think about him day and night—I can't sleep. This tour of his is absolute torture for me. I physically ache from missing him. Would you believe that last night I called him at four in the morning? And he was happy to hear from me yet! I'll tell you, this is a new experience for me. I'm actually faithful to him, and I haven't been faithful to one man since Philip. I just wish I could forget about the age thing."

"What do you mean?"

"I don't know. I'm still bothered by the fact that he's twenty-five. I'm six years older than him! I know it's silly, but I guess I'm somewhat insecure about that. I'm afraid that someday he'll realize what an old lady I am."

Dr. Bartis laughed. "Andy, you'll never be an old lady."

She closed her eyes. "I don't like having these fears. I'm scared that I'm going to try to make him prove how much he loves me one time too many and he'll get disgusted with me."

"Do you want to marry him?"

"No, I don't ever want to get married again. I don't like being married, you know that. Marriage still doesn't fit in with my lifestyle."

"Children still don't fit in either?"

"No, no way. There's no room in my life for children. I think I'm too selfish. I could never put a child's concern ahead of mine. I see Laurie doing that all the time, and I really admire her for it. I would make a very bad mother, I think. Probably ruin the kid for life. Sometimes I think of what would have happened if Philip had caught me the night before I had the abortion. I don't think I was strong enough to resist him then. I probably would have gone back to Boston and married him. That would have effectively been the end of me. There's no question that by now I would have been a dissatisfied housewife with nothing else—no music career, no medical career and too late to do either. Nobody would have been happy then, not Philip, not Laurie, not my parents and least of all me!" Andy took a cigarette out of her pocketbook and lit it.

"Oh, by the way, I'll be playing mommy toward the end of January for about ten days. Laurie is going to a medical convention at the

University of Southern California and I said that Bette could stay with me. Alice will really be caring for her, but she'll be staying at the house."

"How do you feel about that?" Dr. Bartis probed.

"Well, I offered to do it. It was Laurie who was hesitant at first. She said that she was thinking of me, but I'll bet she was worried more about how Bette would react to my crazy way of life."

"But she agreed, didn't she?"

"After I assured her that I would love it."

"Are you sure you really will love it? After all, it will create a certain lack of privacy for you, won't it?"

"I don't mind. Bette and I get along very well. She's a cool kid. Actually, I'm looking foward to it, and it'll be great for Laurie. Adam is going, too, so they'll get a chance to be alone together for the first time. It feels good to be able to help for once."

Dr. Bartis looked at her watch. "Didn't you tell me you had an appointment at two? It's one forty-five now. Do you want to leave?"

Andy jumped up. "Oh, right! David McAllister and Erica Abbott are recording today, and I promised I'd be there." She put on her blue fox coat. "I'll see you next week, same time, same place." Then she was off and running.

Andy leaned back in her chair and closed her eyes. She was in her office, impatiently waiting for a phone call from her accountant who had called while she'd been in the studio with David and Erica. He had left a message that she should wait in her office until he called her back. She was curious as to what was so important. The telephone rang and she picked it up. "Michael, hello. I'm fine. What seems to be the trouble? The health club? What type of problem at the health club? What? You've got to be kidding. How could it be losing that much money? I know we started a little slow, but that was to be expected. I thought that by now we would at least be close to being in the black." She listened momentarily. "No, no way. The membership is almost filled to capacity, and the place is constantly jammed. Yes, I know, but the payroll is reasonable and so is the overhead. What is going on?" She was quiet for a moment. "Does this make any sense to you? Look, what's the story on the cash flow? And the balance sheets?" She shook her head.

"Do you have all the cancelled checks? Well get them. I want to see everything. I'm very disturbed about this, Michael. I didn't go into this to lose that kind of money." She slammed down the phone angrily. "What is happening over there?" She stood up and started pacing across the room. Then she sat down again, picked up the telephone and called Melissa at the club. "Hi, Lis, what's new?"

"Nothing much, I'm pretty busy here. I was going to call you later. Did you notice that my videotape is in the top ten this week?"

"I sure did. That makes two of us. My album is back at number one in Billboard. I guess both greatest hits albums and exercise tapes make good Christmas gift items. Hey, by the way, how are things doing at the club?"

"Fantastic! We couldn't be doing better. I've sold an incredible number of gift memberships for the holidays and the place is swinging from opening to closing. Even the restaurant is doing well. We're getting a lot of business from the office lunch crowd from Monday to Friday."

"That's just great, Melissa. Keep up the good work. I'll be down sometime this week for an exercise class."

"Make sure you do come. It's been awhile since you were here last. Got to keep the old bod in shape."

Andy laughed. "It'll take some doing to get this old bod in shape. Hey, I'll see you soon. Bye." She put down the receiver carefully and pursed her lips. There was no way the club could be losing that kind of money with the kind of business they were doing. If Shep was fooling around with her money, he was going to be very sorry. No one messed around with Andy Reuben and got away with it.

January

Andy looked at the clock and groaned. It was no hour for a civilized person to get up, she thought. Why did Laurie have to take such an early flight? Laurie was leaving for L.A. that morning and she was bringing Bette over before she went to the airport.

Andy had been back in her house for a week, and as far as she was concerned, it wasn't a moment too soon. She was able to write again, and her life was finally getting back to normal. Talking to Eric on the phone the night before had made her very lonely, but it would only be three weeks until he returned to New York, and she knew that those weeks would pass by quickly. As she got up, she heard the doorbell ring and she quickly put on a robe. Then she opened her bedroom door and called down. "Alice! Send them right up."

Laurie and Bette climbed the three flights to Andy's bedroom and walked in. Bette immediately ran over to her aunt and hugged her. "I'm staying with you for ten whole days, Andy. We're going to have so much fun!"

"Yes, you'll have so much fun." Laurie smiled. "But right now Alice is going to take you over to school."

Bette's face fell. "But I want to go to the airport with you. I don't want to go to school."

"No, honey, I'm taking a cab to the airport and I think it would be better if you went to school today." She stroked her daughter's hair. "I'm going to miss you sweetheart. You be a very good girl and don't give your aunt too much trouble."

Andy laughed. "I hope I don't give Bette too much trouble! Seriously though, we'll have a fabulous time. I don't want you to worry about a thing."

"I'm not worried. After all, Alice is here to help and she's so good with Bette." She turned to her daughter. "I hope you don't mind that I won't be here for your birthday. I'll call you, and I promise that I'll bring you a special present from California, okay?"

"What about my birthday party?" Bette asked anxiously.

"Don't you remember? We'll have it when I get back. I've already booked the date at Serendipity. Now you have to get going or else you'll be late for school."

Alice walked into the room with Bette's coat. "The cab is waiting, honey."

PROMISES TO KEEP

Bette put her coat on and ran to her mother. Laurie bent down and picked her up. She held her tightly and whispered, "I love you, sweetheart, and I'm going to miss you very much. Save all your pictures and projects for me to see when I get home."

"I'll make you a special one every day to tell you what my most favorite thing we did was."

"That's a wonderful idea! Now get going." She kissed her and held her close for a long time. Then she gave her to Alice, and the two of them hurried down the stairs.

Andy looked at her sister. There were tears in her eyes. "I've never left her like this before," Laurie said, her voice cracking. "I feel so depressed."

Andy put her arms around Laurie. "Come on, she'll be fine. Alice and I will take great care of her, don't worry." She snapped her fingers. "Hey, I'm going to drive you to the airport. Hang on one second and I'll make a phone call to cancel my morning appointments."

Laurie touched her sister's arm. "No, that's not necessary. I'll be fine. I'll take a cab."

"No way! Which car do you want to go in? We can use either the Mercedes, the Porsche, the Excaliber or the Jaguar. I'm afraid the Ferrari is in for service."

Laurie shook her head. "You're such a nut! What in the world do you need so many cars for? I don't even have one, and I get along just fine. Really, Andy, I don't want to put you out any more than I already have. I—"

"Okay," Andy interrupted. "I'll make the decision then. We'll take the Jag; I haven't driven that one in a while." Ignoring Laurie's protests, she made her phone call and got dressed. Then she picked up the keys to the car and they went downstairs.

"I can't get over how beautiful the house looks. You've really modernized it quite a bit."

"Yeah, well, I figured why not take advantage of a bad situation? Look—" she pointed to the ceiling "—I've even had sprinklers installed throughout the house. I refuse to go through that kind of horror again. Hey, you have some time. Do you want to take a quick look around?"

"I'd love to."

They went into the living room and Laurie immediately noticed the large ornate grand piano that dominated the room. Andy strolled over to it and played some scales. "It's an old Bechstein, from Germany. Beautiful, but impossible to keep tuned. And look at this." She took Laurie's hand and led her over to a painting.

"Andy, a Klee! I love it! We used to go crazy over his pictures when we were in college. Where did you ever get it?"

Andy laughed delightedly and pulled her sister in front of another canvas.

Laurie sucked in her breath. "Chagall! I can't believe this! It's beautiful!"

"Just wait until you see what's coming. Some of them are being reframed and they haven't arrived yet. My Degas is also being restored." She looked at Laurie with a glint in her eye. "I

PROMISES TO KEEP

have a surprise for you, too. It should be here by the time you get back from California."

"Oh, Andy, you shouldn't have! But I'm sure I'll love it anyway." She kissed her sister on the cheek and walked to the kitchen. Her eyes widened as she peered in. "My God, this is fabulous!"

The whole kitchen had been renovated and Andy had spared no expense in making it the most complete gourmet kitchen possible. Every conceivable appliance was there—from a large microwave oven to a professional mixing machine. There was a double sink, an eight burner chef's stove and a thirty cubic inch refrigerator. This was Alice's domain, and Andy wanted only the best for her beloved housekeeper.

"Alice's pretty excited about this. She's chafing for a big dinner party so that she can try everything out." Andy grinned at Laurie. "Maybe we can make it an engagement party?"

Laurie blushed. "Don't rush things," she said. "He hasn't even asked me yet." She looked at her watch and said regretfully, "Andy, I think we'd better get going. I really can't miss that plane."

Andy nodded. "I guess it's time. I'll show you around the upstairs when you get home. Guess what? I've put a Jacuzzi in my bathroom!"

"How hedonistic can you get!" Laurie smiled at her sister's obvious pleasure.

"Oh, no," Andy said seriously, "it's a necessity. I need it to help me relax from the ordeals I have to go through."

"Of course, a necessity. My dear sister, you are

too much." She hugged Andy and together they walked back to the foyer.

Laurie's bag was at the foot of the stairs and Andy picked it up. "Whew! What do you have in this thing? It weighs a ton!"

Laurie shrugged her shoulders. "Books, papers, journals and a few clothes."

"A few clothes? If it was me it would be all clothes!"

Laurie laughed and took her sister's arm. "Oh, I'm going to miss you. What would I ever do without you?"

"Hah! You won't miss me much, not with Adam joining you tomorrow."

Laurie blushed again. "It'll be wonderful having him out there with me. Oh, did I tell you that we'll be going up to San Francisco to see his parents?"

"No! Hey, it really is serious then, isn't it?"

"I think so."

Andy opened the door that led to her garage, and they went in. She had the Excaliber and the Jaguar there. The others were in a private garage a few blocks away. She put the suitcase in the trunk of the Jaguar and they climbed in the car. She punched the numbers to a security combination on a console next to the car telephone. The garage door opened and they headed east.

About forty minutes later, Andy turned off into the airport. "I'll drop you off in front of the terminal, okay? I really don't feel like bucking the crowds inside."

Laurie nodded. "Of course it's okay. You know

how much I hate it when people mob you. I'm always afraid that it'll get out of hand." She touched her sister's shoulder. "You know, Andy, I still wish you would consider getting a bodyguard. I worry about you all the time."

Andy laughed. "Don't be ridiculous. I can't have someone constantly traipsing around after me. You know I like spontaneity. A bodyguard would cramp my style something fierce."

"All the same, I wish you would think about it."

Andy brushed off her concern with a wave of her hand and changed the subject. "So, you're finally going to Tinseltown. I hope you plan to take advantage of the nightlife. It's pretty decent."

"Andy, I'm not going out there for the tinsel. Besides, I don't take advantage of New York nightlife, and I'm sure that it's much better."

"In some ways, but L.A. is a pretty swinging town. Get Adam to take you down to Sunset Strip. It really is weird there."

"The convention has made plans for us. I suppose we'll do most of those activities."

Andy rolled her eyes. "Yeah, they've probably got Wayne Newton to entertain!"

"And what's wrong with Wayne Newton, tell me? Isn't he America's favorite?" They both groaned and laughed.

"At least do the town in San Francisco. That's a fabulous city."

"I'm sorry, Andy, I'll be dining at Adam's parent's house and then I'm flying home the next morning. I don't want to stay away too long. I'll miss Bette too much."

"Well, I'm going to miss you," Andy said as they pulled up to the terminal.

"Do you really mean that? Why would you miss me?"

Andy smoothed Laurie's jacket collar tenderly. "Because I love you, you dunce. You're such an important part of my life, such a wonderfully special part. I guess it's my twin mentality coming through."

Laurie looked at her sister with tears in her eyes. "Twin mentality? I never thought I would hear you say that. I can only imagine how much you must have resented me. I should have—"

"Oh Laur, stop," Andy interrupted. "That's silly. You know that it's been years since I thought of that. What happened way back then is just a distant memory." She smiled. "You are truly my very best friend, now and for always."

Laurie reached over to hug Andy. "And you are truly mine. I love you, Andy, so much." They held each other for a few moments until Laurie broke away. "Hey, we better cut this mutual admiration short. I have a plane to catch."

Andy pulled the trunk lever and Laurie got out of the car. She took her bag from the trunk and leaned in the car window.

"Have a wonderful trip," Andy said. "And don't worry about a thing. I'll see you in about ten days."

"I'll call every night, right before Bette's bedtime. I hope I'll get to speak to you too."

PROMISES TO KEEP

"I'm sure you will. I've become a real homebody lately. Now good-bye. And have yourself a ball!"

Laurie headed toward the terminal, turned and waved good-bye once more, then disappeared into the crowd. Andy looked after her sister feeling strangely weepy. "Hey, what's the matter with me? It's only ten days." She wiped her eyes and started back to the city.

Andy lay in bed hugging her pillow, thinking of Eric. She felt his absence all the more acutely because of Laurie's departure that morning. She couldn't understand what was wrong with her. Usually she liked being by herself. Now all of a sudden she couldn't stand it. She smiled to herself, thinking that she must be getting old. But it was only a few weeks until Eric was back with her. She was toying with the idea of asking him to move in with her, but she wasn't sure if he would. He was very much his own man and she knew he wouldn't want to feel kept. But she just wanted him with her. She couldn't even think of being with anyone else. Did he still feel the same way? Maybe he'd fallen victim to those preying females on tour . . . stop it, she chided herself. Just then her private phone rang. She picked it up. "Hello?"

"Hi, baby."

"Eric, oh Eric! I can't believe it! I was just thinking about you."

"Were you thinking wonderful things?"

"Of course I was thinking wonderful things. I

only think wonderful things about you."

"I hope you don't mind that I'm calling you at this hour."

"Mind? Why would I mind? If you only knew how glad I am that you called. I'm so lonely for you."

"Andy, I love you so much. You know, seeing you in Boston just made it harder to be without you. These past weeks have been hell for me."

"I know, for me, too. Even though we speak to each other all the time, it's not enough. I want you here next to me right now."

"Are you in bed?"

"Yes."

"So am I. Close your eyes now and I'll close mine. Now I'm next to you."

"Mmm, yes. I can feel you next to me. Do you feel me next to you?"

"No, it's not enough damn it! I want to kiss you all over. I want to really touch you and make you moan with pleasure. Oh, baby, I need you so badly."

"And I need you. I've never needed a man so much. Never wanted a man so much. Eric, when you come home I want you with me all the time."

"I will be with you, I promise. I'll never leave you, not ever. You're my strength."

"And you are mine." She began to weep bitterly.

"Honey, why are you crying? Please, Andy, don't. I don't want to do this to you. I'll be home soon. It'll be before you know it. These next weeks will fly by."

PROMISES TO KEEP

She tried to compose herself. "No, they won't, but I guess I'll have to wait. There's no way I can come to you now."

"I know, Bette needs you there. Hey, we can take it, can't we? As long as we know we'll see each other soon? Now you try to sleep, and I'll call you again tomorrow night."

"I'll be waiting. Eric? I love you."

"I adore you. Good-bye, babe, I'll speak to you tomorrow."

"Yes. Good-bye Eric." She hung up the phone and buried her face in the pillow.

Adam opened his eyes as he felt Laurie stirring beside him. "What's the matter?" he mumbled as he reached for her. "Don't go away."

Laurie sat up, kissed him and said, "I have to call Bette now. I promised. Today's her fifth birthday, you know." She picked up the phone and asked the operator to connect her. Adam put his arms around her and started kissing her neck. "Adam! Stop it! I feel decadent enough already. Imagine, spending the entire afternoon in bed with you!"

"Mmm, wasn't it wonderful?"

"That's besides the point . . . Oh, hello Alice, are they there?"

"They just got home, Laurie. Here's Bette."

"Mommy?"

"Happy birthday, sweetheart! How was your day?"

"Oh, Mommy, I had the best time. This afternoon Andy took me to see how she made a record.

Then we went to Windows for dinner, and I had lamp chops."

"Windows? What's that?"

"The restaurant name was Windows." She paused. "Oh, Andy says it's Windows On the World. I saw New York City from very high up."

Laurie laughed. "I'm glad you had such a good time. I wish I was with you."

"Guess what, Mommy? Andy bought me a computer with games and pictures and music for my birthday. I'm even going to go to school to learn how to play it."

"That was wonderful of Andy! I'm sure you're going to enjoy that very much. I hope you thanked her. Now you better get ready for bed, it sounds as if you had a very busy day. I'll speak to you tomorrow. I love you to bits, and happy birthday again."

"Okay, Mommy. I love you too. I can't wait til you come home. I miss you."

"I miss you, too, sweetheart. Good night, Bette. Put Andy on the phone now."

Andy took the phone from her niece. "Hi there, sis, how's it going?"

"Well, I delivered my paper this morning—"

Adam leaned over and shouted into the phone, "She was a real hit!"

Laurie made a face at him and pushed him away. "No, but it really went well," she said.

Andy laughed. "It sounds as if the paper wasn't the only thing that went well."

Laurie blushed. "Come on, stop it, Andy. You're embarrassing me. By the way, that's a great present you got for Bette. Will it spoil things if I say I approve?"

"Oh my God! I did something right for once! This has to be a memorable occasion! Maybe I should mark it down on my calendar."

"You idiot! It sounded as if she enjoyed the dinner too. Thank you for giving her such a special day. I won't tell her how heartless I think she was eating that poor little lamb."

"Don't you dare lay that guilt trip on her! I won't let you!"

"Don't worry, I'm reconciled to my daughter's passion for meat. She just won't ever have it in my house!"

"Hey, when are you going up to San Francisco?"

"I guess we're leaving in a couple of days. Then I'll be home. I really do miss you guys, you know."

"Well, we certainly do miss you. Do you want me to pick you up at the airport?"

"No, I'll take a cab home, drop my things off, and then pick Bette up. But I'll be speaking to you before then anyway."

"I know. Bette waits for your calls every night. I never saw such utter devotion."

"Believe me, the feeling is mutual. Look, I'm going to go now."

"What's the matter? You have better things to do?" Andy inquired mockingly.

"Andy, I'm warning you . . . look, I'll speak to you tomorrow. Good-bye."

"Good-bye, Laur, have fun. And don't do anything I wouldn't do."

"That's impossible, you'd do anything! Bye, sis, all my love." She hung up the phone and turned to Adam. "Andy certainly is showing Bette a good time. I don't know if I'll ever get her back down to earth."

"You really are lucky that Andy loves Bette so much."

Laurie nodded. "I've always known how much she loved her, but quite frankly, I'm amazed at how much she actually seems to enjoy having Bette there with her."

"You see how people can surprise you?" Adam reached over and kissed Laurie. "For instance, you constantly surprise me."

"Me? How do I surprise you?"

"I don't know, you give the appearance of being such an aloof person, but you're as warm and passionate a woman as I could ever hope to find."

"You think I'm passionate? My ex-husband would have disputed that."

"Well, he didn't know you as well as I do."

Laurie snuggled deeper into his arms. "Tell me more."

Adam smiled. "You're intelligent, efficient, loving, beautiful . . . let me see, what other adjectives can I use?"

"Enough! I'm getting a swelled head. I can't be as wonderful as all that."

"Oh, but you are. And now that I've found you, I'll never let you go."

"Promise?"

"I'll do more than just promise." He stood up

on the bed. "Laurel Rabinowitz, would you do me the honor of marrying me?"

"Oh, Adam, do you mean it?" She grabbed his hand and pulled him back down to her.

"I never meant anything more in my whole life."

"When?"

"Anytime you say. As soon as we get home, tomorrow . . ."

"Not tomorrow. I want my family with me."

"Okay, how's this? We'll tell my parents when we get to San Francisco, and we'll make plans then. I know they'll want to be there too. I think it would make them happy if we were married in a synagogue."

"That's fine with me. You know, Bette's father wasn't Jewish, and I haven't introduced her to religion at all yet. I think this would be a good time to start."

"Laurie?" Adam said tentatively. "I've been thinking. What would you say if I wanted to adopt Bette?"

Laurie looked at him lovingly. "Do you really want to? It really is a tremendous responsibility. One that I would never ask you to assume."

"It's the kind of responsibility I like. I'm really quite the fatherly type." He smiled at her. "Anyway, I figure that she's part of the package, and I want to be her daddy as much as I want to be your husband. Besides, let's face it, how would Bette feel if her brother or sister had a different last name?"

Laurie lowered her eyes. "Hey, aren't we

rushing things a little bit?"

"You do want more children, don't you?" he asked anxiously. "It wouldn't interfere with your work, would it?"

She hugged him. "Of course I want to have your child. Adam, Bette's going to be so happy. She wants a real family so badly. I never realized how much until I saw the way she is with you." She smiled. "Don't ever think that having a baby would interfere with my life, it would only add to it. And no, it wouldn't interfere with my work either. Bette never did."

He lay down and pulled her next to him. "What did I ever do to deserve all this? God, how perfect life is."

"Oh yes," Laurie whispered as she felt his hands caress her once again. "Life is so perfect."

Andy flew out of the elevator and ran down the corridor. She was late for a marketing meeting because she had taken Bette to school. Now she had to stop off at her office for some pertinent papers. Opening the doors, she was shocked to see Marty Kantor sitting on the couch next to the window.

"What are you doing here? How did you get in?" she said angrily.

"Simple, I was visiting your ex-husband and I waited until your secretary left her desk. Then I just came in."

"Well now you're going to get out! Either you leave now or I'm going to call security." She put her hand on the phone and he immediately put his

PROMISES TO KEEP

hand over hers.

"You don't want to do that."

"Don't I?" She pushed his hand away and lifted the receiver.

Marty smiled. "Why don't you listen to what I have to say first?"

She started dialing.

Marty reached into his jacket pocket and pulled out some pictures. He lay them down on the desk in front of Andy. She glanced down. Her eyes widened and she put down the phone.

"My, my, my," she exclaimed. "I had forgotten about these. I'm amazed that you still have them."

"Of course I still have them. I was just waiting for the right time to use them."

Andy picked up the photographs and flipped through them. "I look so young! Jesus, is that actually my body?"

"It's your body all right. Kind of kinky, aren't they?"

"Oh, I don't know about that. You know, Marty, you were about as lousy a photographer as you were a lover. God, are these pictures terrible!"

"I'm sure there are a couple of magazines that won't think so. I'm sure they would pay me well for them."

"So?"

"Come on, Andy, don't tell me you don't care if they're published. I must have a soft spot in my heart. I thought I would give you the opportunity to outbid the magazines."

Andy laughed. "You really are some kind of a jerk to think that I'd pay anything for this garbage. Go peddle them. See if I care."

Shocked, Marty said, "You mean you won't buy them?"

"Of course not. You do exactly what you want with them."

Angrily, Marty snatched them from her hand. "Oh, you just wait and see what I do with them. When I'm finished, you'll be the laughingstock of the industry."

Andy looked at him through narrowed eyes and slammed her fist on the desk. "That's what you think, buster. Nobody plays these kinds of games with me and gets away with it. You've crossed me one too many times. Sell those pictures, Marty, but it will be the last money you'll ever make! When I get through with you, you'll wish you had never heard of Andy Reuben! Now get out of here and take your trash with you!"

"What are you talking about?"

"This is it for you. As soon as you leave this office, I'm making some phone calls. You'd better start thinking of going to work for your father in the garment district because you'll never work in the entertainment industry again!"

"You bitch, you couldn't do that. You don't have the power you think you have."

"Oh don't I? Just wait and see. Go, Marty, make your lousy few thousand, but you've just made the biggest mistake of your life."

"We'll see who made the mistake. You'll never get away with this!" Marty clenched his fists. "I won't allow you to ruin me!"

"You can't stop me. You should have stayed out of my way. Now get out of here, you slimy bastard."

Philip finished packing his suitcase and went over to the desk to sort through his papers. The argument he had had with Marilyn that morning had been the last straw. Not a day went by without her harping on his relationship with Andy. He couldn't take it any more. No matter how he would plead with his wife to stop it, she continued to torment him. He had to rid his life of both of them and leaving Marilyn was a start.

Suddenly the door burst open. "What the hell do you think you're doing?" Marilyn demanded.

"What does it look like I'm doing?"

"You can't leave me. I won't let you."

"What can you do? I've had enough! I'm moving out now. Maybe then I can get some peace."

"Peace? You want peace? What about me? My life is a living hell. You owe me something."

"Owe you something? What the hell do I owe you? Morning, noon and night you're screaming at me about some figment of your imagination."

"You'll never convince me that it's all in my mind. You still love her. I know it."

"I'm not going to try to convince you of anything anymore. I'm tired, Marilyn. I just want to be left alone."

"Left alone to do what? Dream of Andy Reuben and the wonderful life you could have had with her?"

Suddenly Philip, his head pounding, turned to her and screamed, "Yes damn it! I did dream of her! I dreamed of her gentleness, and the beautiful, warm love we had. I dreamed of how it was when we were together. I dreamed of all our plans! But she killed all my dreams when she killed my baby. She was the murderer and I received the life sentence." He picked up the suitcase, pushed Marilyn aside and left.

Marilyn fell back on the bed and wept. He'd really gone. What was she going to do? She loved him. How could she prove it to him? How could she make their lives right again?

Andy paced up and down her living room. She paused and lit still another cigarette. "Are you sure?"

Michael Smith, Andy's accountant, nodded his head. "There is no question that there's been some monkey business. You were absolutely correct."

"What happened?"

"As far as I can figure out, there have been extraneous checks written on the business, probably personal, most of them to cash."

"And they're all signed by Melissa Rabinowitz?"

Michael nodded again. "One of them is for five thousand dollars."

"Let me take a look." She took the cancelled checks and studied them closely. "You wait here," she said as she walked into the kitchen.

PROMISES TO KEEP

She picked up the phone and dialed the health club. "Melissa, hello. Look, I want you over at my house immediately. Well, I'm sorry, you'll have to cancel your class, this can't wait. Yes, right now." She hung up the phone and went back to where Michael was sitting. "Melissa will be here shortly and then we'll get to the bottom of this."

Within twenty minutes the doorbell rang and Andy ran to answer it. She took Melissa by the arm and steered her into the living room. "Is this your signature?" she asked as she shoved checks into her hand.

Puzzled by her sister's sense of urgency, Melissa looked down at the checks. "It sort of looks like my handwriting, but I never wrote these checks. I swear it, Andy! I don't know anything about them!"

"How about these?" She handed her another pile.

Melissa shook her head. "We don't deal with Chemical Bank, why would I write checks to them?" She read some of the others: Paul Stuart, Empress Travel, Church's Shoes, Feron's... Suddenly she knew who had written the checks. Shep did all of his racket shopping at Feron's and his clothing came from Paul Stuart. With as sinking feeling, she knew that he was embezzling money from her business. "Oh Andy, I didn't know... oh God, Andy, I'm sorry... I'm so sorry...." Tears ran down her cheeks as she gazed at the checks in her hands.

Michael excused himself, went to the phone, and returned to the room within a few moments.

"All right, here it is. I just called Chemical Bank. Apparently these checks were written in payment for a car loan—a new Corvette."

"A Corvette? Who bought a Corvette? I don't understand."

"I have a feeling that you'll understand all too soon," Andy murmured sympathetically as she put her arm around her younger sister. "Now, how did he get the checks?"

Melissa looked up abruptly. "How do you know that it's Shep?"

"I suspected it when Michael first told me that the club was losing a tremendous amount of money."

"Losing money? Not according to my figures? I thought we were doing really well!"

"You are doing well, honey, but no business can withstand these kinds of games and survive."

Melissa started sobbing. "Oh no! Will I lose the club? I just can't lose it, Andy! Please, help me! What can I do?"

"First of all, you're going to speak to Shep. Where is he?"

"He's home, his thigh was bothering him this morning."

"That's perfect. Come on, I'll drive you there. You can pick up your things while you're at it."

"But where will I go? I don't have anyplace to go."

"That's no problem. You can stay here for the time being."

Melissa's shoulders sagged. "Oh, Andy, why? I loved him so much. . . ."

PROMISES TO KEEP

"He's not worth it, Melissa. You have to cut the ties now. I'm going to see that he's put in prison for this."

"Oh no, Andy! Please! I'll pay you back every penny."

"I don't want your money. I want him punished. Don't think we're not going to prosecute."

"Please, for my sake—"

"No, Melissa. I won't let him get away with this. You better tell him to get a good lawyer. Come on, let's go." Andy took Melissa's hand. They got into the Mercedes and headed toward Rego Park. About a half hour later, Andy stopped in front of the apartment house and turned to her sister. "Are you sure you're okay? Do you want me to come up?"

"No, I can handle it myself. You wait down here."

"He won't hurt you, will he?"

Melissa smiled grimly. "How can he hurt me? I have a black belt in karate. Nobody messes with Melissa Rabinowitz."

"You're right, I forgot. Hey, I'm sure you can handle yourself. Now go to it!"

Melissa got out of the car and entered the building. She was too impatient to wait for the elevator so she walked up the stairs to the second floor. Quietly she unlocked the door. Shep was sitting in the living room watching a videotape of his squash match. Melissa strode over to him and pushed him off the chair. "You bastard! How dare you steal from me!" She started smacking his face.

"Hey! What the hell are you doing? Stop it! Hey, Missy! Have you gone crazy?" He pushed her away and stood up.

"Why did you do it? Why?"

"Do what? I don't know what you're talking about."

"You know very well what I'm talking about. I'm talking about the thousands of dollars you appropriated from the health club. I'm talking about clothes and shoes and vacations and a new Corvette. Where are you keeping it, Shep? Is the car at your parents' house in Woodmere?"

"What car?" he said weakly. "I don't know anything about a car."

"Don't lie to me! We know all about it."

"We? Who's we?"

"Andy, the accountant and me. You must think that we're stupid. What made you think that you could get away with it?" She walked briskly into the bedroom and started packing.

Shep followed her. "Don't you want to hear what I have to say?"

"What could you say that would make any difference? What lies could you make up? You're in serious trouble, my friend. Andy is going to prosecute. I tried to convince her not to, but she insisted, and she's probably right. She said that you'd better get yourself a good lawyer."

Visibly frightened, Shep tried to grab Melissa. She pushed him away so violently that he fell back and knocked over a lamp. "Please, Melissa! Missy, I love you, you know that. Let's discuss this—"

"There is no discussing. You're finished!" She slammed shut her suitcase and briskly walked out the door.

Shep raised his fist and slammed it into the wall, punching a hole. He had to stop Andy from going to the police. He got dressed and ran out of the apartment.

Laurie turned the key to her apartment and walked in. She looked around and smiled. It was good to be back home. She missed Adam already, but he would be back in a few days. It had been so long since he had been back to San Francisco that he'd wanted to visit for a while longer with his parents. She put her hand to her eyes and decided that she had to take her contact lenses out before she did anything else. They had been bothering her since Los Angeles. That damn smog . . . .

She went into the bathroom, took out her lenses, and put her glasses on. Then she went to call Andy. She couldn't wait to see her, she had so much to say. Alice answered the phone and went to get Andy. "Hi, kid, I'm home," Laurie said. "Are you busy? I'd like to come over and talk a bit before I pick Bette up at school."

"No problem. I'm not doing much right now, and I really do want to see you. How was San Francisco?"

"It was wonderful!"

"Wonderful? You sound euphoric."

"I am. Adam and I are getting married!"

"Married! When?"

"I'm not sure yet. We have arrangements to make. It'll be very soon though."

Wendy Susans

"Are you sure that's what you want?" Andy asked carefully.

"Yes. This time it's right. I'm positive of it."

"Fantastic! Laur, that's great! I'm so happy for you! We'll have to have a celebration tonight then. You'll stay for dinner, okay? Oh, by the way, Melissa's moved in here with me."

"What happened?"

"It's a long, gruesome story. I'll tell you all about it when you get here."

"Is everything all right?"

"Not really, but she's our sister and she'll survive."

"Is she there now?"

"Yes."

"Good. I'll be right over. You can fill me in."

"Okay, we'll both be waiting. Bye. See you soon."

Laurie picked up her coat, locked her door and headed for her sister's house. The wind whipped through her as she turned the corner onto 67th Street. She shivered and lifted her hood over her head. As she climbed the steps to the brownstone, she glanced up at the big bay window and saw Andy looking through the drapes. She smiled and waved, then she saw Andy disappear. Just as she reached the door, she heard someone behind her call, "Andy!" Instinctively she turned around. A woman stood at the bottom of the steps. Laurie's eyes widened with terror as she saw her pull a gun out of her coat pocket.

"I'm doing this for Philip!" the woman yelled, "Now he'll finally be free of you."

PROMISES TO KEEP

Laurie put her hand out as if to stop her and opened her mouth to speak, but before she had a chance, the gun went off. A searing pain ripped through her and she crumbled to the ground just as the door behind her opened. The last thing she saw was her twin's horrified face.

Andy caught Laurie before she hit the steps. Blood was spurting out of her sister's abdomen and she covered the wound with her hands, but still the blood poured out. Her whole body shook as she frantically screamed, "Somebody! Help! Melissa! Alice! Help her! Oh my God, Laurie! Laurel!"

Melissa ran out and saw an hysterical Andy holding Laurie. She glanced towards the street and saw an obviously confused woman standing with a gun. Before she had a chance to think, she leaped down the steps and violently grabbed her. The gun clattered to the pavement as Marilyn Koppel stared in shock at what she had done. "But I wanted to kill Andy Reuben," she said simply. "I thought she was Andy Reuben. She looked like Andy Reuben. You're Andy Reuben, and she looks like you." She shook her head and stared laughing hysterically. "Now he'll never be all mine. . . ."

Seconds later, Alice ran out and knelt beside Andy. She pushed her hands away and firmly pressed a large towel over the wound. The towel became blood soaked immediately. "I've called the police," she said gently. "They'll be right here."

Andy desperately clung to her sister, rocked

her back and forth, and wept. "Please, Laurie, please don't die! I can't stand it. Please, Laurie, hang on a little longer. Please!"

She lifted her tear-streaked face to Alice. "She wanted to kill *me,* that woman wanted to kill me. Oh, Laurie," she whispered as she put her cheek next to her sister's. "My poor sweet Laurie, why did she have to hurt you?"

An ambulance pulled up to the curb with two police cars right behind it. Quickly, they moved Laurie onto a stretcher and immediately began working on her. They hurried her into the ambulance with Andy following closely. "Take her to New York Hospital! She's a doctor there!" She climbed into the back with Laurie and the ambulance sped away.

Two policemen ran toward Melissa and grabbed the woman. They handcuffed her and read her her rights while Melissa, tears running down her face, watched. Marilyn gave no resistance as the policemen roughly shoved her into the car.

"Is that the gun?" an officer from the second car asked, looking down at the sidewalk.

Melissa nodded.

"What happened?"

Melissa held her head in her hands. "I don't know," she whispered. "That woman shot my sister. I don't understand."

"We'll catch up with you at the hospital. We'll need to question you. Now you go be with your sister."

As the first police car sped off, Alice ran over to

Melissa and held her tightly. "What a tragedy!" she cried as she stroked Melissa's hair. "What a terrible, terrible tragedy!"

Melissa ran into the Emergency room of New York Hospital, looked around and finally went up to the desk. "Could you tell me if Laurel Rabinowitz was brought here?"

Before the nurse at the station could answer, Andy ran over and put her arms around her. "Oh my God, Melissa! She's lost so much blood! They can't stop the bleeding!"

"Where is she?"

Andy pointed, her hand shaking. "Back there. They won't let me in."

Melissa stared at her grief stricken sister. Blood covered the entire front of her shirt and pants. Her hands were also streaked with red. For the first time, Melissa realized that it was possible that Laurie might die. "Sit down over here. Andy, please, sit down with me." She led her to a bench and gently sat her down.

Almost immediately Andy jumped up again when she saw a doctor leave the examining room Laurie was in. The doctor strode up to them and said, "We're taking her upstairs to the operating room. She's hemorrhaging from somewhere inside her abdomen and we've got to try to stop it."

Andy clung to the doctor. "But she will be all right, won't she? You'll stop the bleeding, and she'll be all right?"

"We'll do what we can. Right now she's in very

critical condition. We're transfusing her, but the loss of blood is extensive, and she's still bleeding."

"Oh, please!" Andy cried. "Please! Don't let her die!"

"I promise you we will do everything we can. Dr. Malone himself will operate. Your sister is much loved in this hospital."

"Oh yes, she's much loved. She—" Andy looked up. "Oh my God! Bette! I forgot about Bette! Melissa, what about Bette?"

"Don't worry. Alice is picking her up at school and bringing her back to Laurie's apartment."

Andy closed her eyes. "That poor baby. What are we going to tell her?"

"Shh, Andy, don't worry. We'll handle it."

Just then, Laurie was wheeled out of the examining room. Tubes seemed connected to every part of her body, and she was unconscious. Andy rushed to her side and grabbed her hand. It was cold. The nurse tried to take her away, but Andy hung on until they reached the elevator. "Let me go with her, please! I have to be with her. She needs me."

"No, dear, I'm sorry but we can't let you. She's going straight into the OR. You wait here, and the doctor will be down as soon as they're finished."

Reluctantly Andy let go and allowed Melissa to lead her away. "I spoke to the nurse at the desk. She said we could use the office over there to wait in. It will be more private."

Andy nodded and Melissa led her into the

PROMISES TO KEEP

room. When they got in, Andy turned to her sister and grabbed her sleeve. "Melissa, you've got to believe me. It never occurred to me that this could happen. Never! If it had, I would have—I should have—" She broke down and wept.

"Shh, Andy, I know that. Of course I know that." Melissa put her arms around her sister. They stood holding each other silently until there was a knock on the door. A policeman opened it and walked in.

"I'm sorry to have to come in now, but we have to ask you some questions."

"Do you have to do it now?" Melissa asked. "Can't it wait awhile?"

"I'm sorry, it can't." He walked out again and reentered with two other policemen. "I'm Sergeant Perry. Did either of you actually see the shooting?"

"I did," Andy whispered. "The gun went off just as I opened the door."

"Did you recognize the person who fired the gun?"

"No! I never saw her before. She shouted that she wanted to kill me? She, damn it—she mistook my sister for me. We're twins—we're—identical—" She shook her head as tears welled up in her eyes.

The sergeant consulted his notebook. "Her name is Marilyn Koppel. She seemed to know you very well, Miss Reuben. Said you killed her husband's baby. Does that mean anything to you?"

Andy's eyes widened. "Koppel? Koppel? Philip Koppel . . . Oh my God! Philip Koppel!" She collapsed onto a chair and began sobbing uncontrollably.

Melissa looked at her sister in confusion. "What do you mean? Who is—? Philip, is that the guy you were going out with before you left Boston?"

Andy nodded, still crying.

"What baby? Andy, what baby?"

Her whole body shaking, Andy replied, "An abortion. Eleven years ago. When I left . . . it was Philip's child. They never told you about it."

"But why would his wife—"

"She said she was trying to get her husband back," the policeman interrupted. "Actually, she was not too coherent. She was brought over to Bellevue for observation. We've called her husband in Boston and he's coming down."

Melissa looked at her sister. Andy was doubled over as if in terrible pain, and she was moaning. "Look, I don't think you should ask anymore questions. My sister is in no shape to answer them right now."

Sympathetically, the policeman agreed. "We'll speak with you tomorrow. Take care of her. Should we call a doctor?"

"No, I'll take care of her. Thank you." She knelt next to Andy and held her tightly. "Come on, Andy, you can't blame yourself. The woman is obviously crazy. Andy, please!"

"No, Melissa, it's all my fault. Laurie is up there because of me. I can't stand it. How can I

PROMISES TO KEEP

live with myself? How can I ever forgive myself for doing this to her? What if she dies? God, I hate myself. I make myself sick."

"Stop it!" Melissa said sharply. "This is no time for self-pity. Laurie needs you to be strong. Pull yourself together, *now!*" She shook Andy hard.

Andy nodded. "Yes . . . I have to be strong for Laurie's sake. I . . . can't—Melissa, you have to help me. What should I do?"

Melissa gently took her hand. "First of all, I think you should go home and change."

"No!" Andy said fiercely. "I won't leave her!"

Melissa looked at her sister with compassion. "Okay, then, maybe they'll give you something to change into here."

"No! I don't want to change." Andy looked down at her shirt and touched it.

Melissa started to say something else, then changed her mind. "Okay, let's call Ma then. I don't want her to find out from anyone else."

"Yes," Andy whispered. "Call Ma. You do it, I can't. My God, she's going to hate me for this!"

"Hate you?"

"I did it. If it wasn't for me—"

"Andy, you can't think that way. Just wait here. I'm going to ask whether I can use this phone." She went out of the room, and when she returned she picked up the phone, asked for an outside line and dialed Adrienne's number. "Hello, Ma?" she said tentatively.

"Melissa, I was going to call you tonight. How are you?"

"Ma, I have something upsetting to tell you...."

"What? What's the matter?"

"There's been an accident. Laurie's been hurt."

"How could Laurie be hurt? An airplane crash? Melissa! I didn't hear!"

"No ma, she was home—" She looked at Andy, who sat with her hands over her head. She hesitated before she spoke again. "Laurie was, uh, shot."

"Shot? What do you mean shot? With a gun? What are you talking about? Who shot her? Melissa! How badly is she hurt?"

"She's being operated on now. We're at New York Hospital. She's lost a lot of blood." Melissa broke down and started crying.

"I'm coming right down," Adrienne told her, her voice breaking. "Where is Andrea? Is Andrea there? Is she all right?"

"Andy is right here, Ma. She's—she's very broken up."

"What happened? How did this happen?"

"You come down, Ma. We'll tell you the whole story when you get here. Hurry!"

"Hurry? Is she, is she, oh God, Melissa, is she dying?"

Melissa wiped her eyes. "She's being operated on right now, Ma. They're trying to stop the bleeding."

"I'm coming. Dear God, my baby!" She hung up the phone.

Melissa turned to Andy. "Ma is coming."

Andy shivered. "She's dying, Melissa. I know

she's dying. I can feel it."

"Come on, Andy, you don't feel any such thing! You never believed in that identical twin crap before. Don't start now!"

"I've always believed in it. I just never admitted it." She put her hand out to her sister. "Help me, Melissa. Help me. If you don't, I won't be able to make it."

Melissa knelt beside her sister and took her in her arms. They clung to each other as desperately as Laurie was clinging to her life.

Adam and his mother placed the groceries in the trunk. "Mom, that would be perfect," he said as he got into the car. "If you come to New York a few days early, you can get to know Bette too. She's the cutest five year old—so smart, just like her mother. You'll see." He started the car and turned on the radio just as the all news station finished the weather report. "Boy!" Adam exclaimed. "It'll be hard to get used to New York weather again. It's so cold this time of year. But I can't wait to get back to Laurie." They chattered away with the radio in the background until the hour's top story caused him to stop the car abruptly.

"In New York, a case of mistaken identity leaves a famous rock star unharmed and her twin sister close to death. Andy Reuben apparently was the target of a female assassin today, but the woman allegedly fired her gun at Dr. Laurel Rabinowitz, Ms. Reuben's identical twin sister. At last word, Dr. Rabinowitz was in critical condition, in surgery at New York Hospital.

"Andy Reuben, the country's most popular female rock star, is up for seven Grammys next month. Her sister is a prominent neonatologist at New York Hospital. More on this tragic story as details become available."

Adam paled. "Laurie?" He looked at his mother. "Laurie?" he repeated, still uncomprehending. His mother got out of the car, went over to the driver's side, pushed him over and drove the short distance home.

Once home, Adam called New York Hospital and was told that Laurie was still in surgery. Then he packed his things and rushed to the airport to take the next available flight out.

Eric lay down on the bed in his hotel room, exhausted. He had been rehearsing and doing sound checks all morning, and had made a personal appearance at a record store in the early afternoon. There were only another 10 days until he saw Andy. He sighed, put the earphones to his Walkman on and tried to find a station to his liking. As he went through the stations, a news story made him stop. "Andy? Laurie?" he said aloud. "No! Andy! I have to go to Andy!" He stood up, made the necessary phone calls to cancel his concert, then headed to the airport to catch a plane for New York.

Adrienne ran down the hallway of the hospital, her pocketbook flapping against her leg. It was almost exactly four hours since Melissa had called. She ran up to the Emergency Room desk. "My daughter, Laurel Rabinowitz, where is she?"

The nurse looked at her sympathetically. "She's still in the OR." She touched Adrienne's hand. "Your other daughters are in that room over there. Why don't you go to them."

Adrienne nodded and rushed off. She opened the door and saw Andy and Melissa silently huddled together.

Melissa jumped up and ran to her mother. "Ma! You're finally here! Thank God!"

As she hugged her youngest daughter, Adrienne could not help but stare at Andy. She looked frail, beaten—there was absolutely no life to her at all. She was horrified to see all the blood now dried to a dark brown stain that covered her.

Andy looked up slowly. "Oh, Mommy," she sobbed, her whole body trembling. "I'm so sorry . . . I—It should have been me! I wish to God it was me!"

Adrienne went over to her. "What are you talking about?" She started weeping. "Tell me! What happened?"

Andy gazed up at her. She began to speak hesitantly, tears flowing down her cheeks. "It was, uh, Philip Koppel's wife. Philip Koppel's wife shot Laurie. She meant to shoot me."

"Philip Koppel? I don't understand. Why?"

"I don't know. She—she mistook Laurie for me." Andy shook her head in anguish and put her hand through her hair. "Laurie was coming by to see me . . . She thought Laurie was me—"

"The woman is obviously insane," Melissa interrupted. "She said she wanted to kill Andy to get Philip back."

"She wanted to kill Andy to get Philip back?" Adrienne repeated. "What do you have to do with Philip Koppel now?"

"Nothing! I haven't seen him in eleven years! I don't know! I think it had something to do with the abortion . . . ."

Melissa nodded. "That freaked out woman said that Andy killed Philip's child. We're not really sure of the whole story."

Suddenly Andy could stand it no more. She went over to the wall and slammed it with her fist. "Goddamn it!" she screamed. "What's taking them so long? Oh God, why? She was so happy. Happier than she's ever been. She and Adam were—"

The doctor stode into the room. "Well, we've stopped the bleeding for now. Dr. Malone did a brilliant job. But she has extensive internal damage. Her liver—" he paused. "I'm afraid she's still in extremely critical condition. We have her in intensive care right now."

"Can we see her?" Adrienne asked.

"I don't think that would be wise. She's barely conscious."

Andy grabbed the doctor's arm. "Please, doctor, I have to see her! You have to let me be with her! She needs me. She wants me to be with her, I know she does!"

The doctor hesitated. "I don't know."

"Please, I'm begging you. It's so important to me, to her! I know it would help her!"

PROMISES TO KEEP

He sighed. "I guess it would be all right. But not for too long. She's very weak."

"I just want to sit there with her. I promise, I won't disturb her."

"All right. Come with me." He looked at her and stopped. "We've got to get you changed first. It wouldn't do for her to see you looking like that."

Andy looked down at herself and nodded. "I guess you're right. Okay, I'll change, but please take me to her now." The doctor led her out of the room and up the elevator to intensive care. He offered her a scrub suit and directed her to the bathroom, where she changed and washed. She pulled the string tight at her waist so that the oversized pants didn't fall and then she went into the ICU.

Laurie was lying with her eyes closed. Tubes and wires were attached everywhere and she was incredibly pale. Andy sat down in the chair next to her and took her hand. She was so cold and her hand felt lifeless. "I'm here, Laurie," she whispered into her sister's ear as she kissed her cheek. "You'll be okay now."

Laurie opened her eyes and stared at her twin. "Andy," she murmured. "I was wishing you were here with me. And you knew. Of course you knew." She squeezed Andy's hand weakly. "What happened?"

Andy pushed back Laurie's hair lovingly. "Shh, kid. Don't talk. You're in the hospital, you'll be all right."

"Are you all right?"

Wendy Susans

Andy swallowed a sob. "Yes, Laurie, I'm fine. Don't worry about me. For once, worry about yourself first. Really, everything is going to be fine. Just rest now. I'm here."

Laurie's eyes closed and Andy sat holding onto her hand. A nurse approached and told her it was time to leave, but Andy shook her head furiously and refused to let go of her sister's hand. Finally the nurse gave up and sat at the other end of the room.

"Andy, are you still there?"

"Yes, Laurie. I won't leave you, don't worry."

"I'm scared Andy. Don't go away. I'm scared and I'm so cold."

Andy took a blanket from the next bed and gently tucked it around her sister. "There, is that better?" she asked tenderly as she took her hand again.

Laurie nodded and closed her eyes. She drifted in and out of consciousness and each time she woke she said, "Andy, are you still there?" Andy adamantly refused to allow anyone to take her from her sister's side, and after a while they gave up trying.

She had been there for over an hour, when Laurie's eyelids fluttered once again. "Andy, I'm so scared. I'm going to die. I know I'm going to die. Help me. Please take care of Bette for me."

"No! Don't say that! The doctors stopped the bleeding. You're just weak from the operation." Tears streamed down Andy's face.

Laurie started to cry, too. "Oh Andy, I love you so much. I can't begin to tell you what you mean

PROMISES TO KEEP

to me. I couldn't stand it if you weren't with me. It's not so hard now that you're here. Please, just promise me that you'll take care of Bette."

Andy brought Laurie's hand up to her lips and kissed it. Then she held it next to her tearstained cheek. "I love you, Laur, more than you could ever imagine. You're everything to me. Anything you want, I'll promise you anything, I'll do anything. Just get better. Please! I'll make this up to you, I swear, I'll find some way to make this up to you." Her voice cracked with emotion. "I wish it had been me. It should have been me instead of you."

"No, Andy. Don't. Don't talk that way. Don't blame yourself. Please tell me you don't blame yourself." Laurie tried to lift her head, but was unable to.

"Don't. Please, don't get upset," Andy pleaded. "Save your strength." She clutched Laurie's hand tightly with both her hands. "Here, take my strength. I want you to feel it flowing out of me into you. Take it all! You're going to be all right! Laurie, you are going to live!"

Laurie attempted a smile. "Yes . . . I feel it . . . I'm trying . . . Oh, I want to live so badly," she whispered. "I have so much to live for, I have so much—" Her eyes opened wide and locked with her twin's. Then they closed, as though she were slipping somewhere far away.

"Laurie?" Andy leaned over and shook her sister's shoulders. "Laurie? Are you all right? Laurie? *Laurie!*"

Monitors started buzzing and nurses and

Wendy Susans

doctors rushed in and pushed Andy aside. Andy stood there for a moment, her fist shoved in her mouth, and then she shrieked, "Laurie! You can't die. No! Laurie! You can't die! Laurie, don't leave me!"

Finally one of the nurses grabbed her and pulled her away. "You must move, you're in the way." She placed her across from the bed, and went back to Laurie. Then, just as suddenly as it began, the frantic motion around the bed ceased. Andy knew the fight was over, and her sister had lost.

The doctors and nurses slowly started to unhook the equipment from Laurie, many of them weeping. Andy watched in shock as they pulled the sheet over her sister's head. "Don't do that!" she screamed as she ran over to the bed. "I have to be able to see her!"

One of the nurses came over to her and gently put her arm around her shoulder. "Please, you really must leave now."

Andy flung her hand out, hitting the nurse on the cheek. "No! I won't leave her! I promised her I would stay. You get out of here!" She grabbed a chair and pulled it next to the bed. Then she sat down, tenderly took the sheet off her sister's face and held her hand. "I'm here, Laur," she whispered. "I promised you I would stay. I'll never leave you. I'll always be with you."

Dr. Malone walked over to the bed and tried to take Andy's hand from Laurie's. Andy hung on frantically and hissed at him. "Leave us alone! I want to be alone with my sister."

PROMISES TO KEEP

He looked at her sympathetically. "We all loved Laurie, but now we have to . . . to take her away."

"No!" Andy said fiercely. "You can't take her away from me. I won't let you. I have to stay with her. She needs me."

Dr. Malone closed his eyes then motioned to one of the nurses. "Is there anyone outside who might be able to talk to her?"

The nurse nodded. "Her sister and mother are here."

"Have they been told?"

"Yes, just now. They're right outside."

He walked briskly out of the ICU to where Melissa and Adrienne sat crying hysterically. "I'm Jim Malone," he said softly. "I operated on Laurie. I'm so sorry. We all loved her very much. It's a terrible loss. She was a beautiful, kind, gentle person and an excellent physician."

"What happened?" Adrienne cried. "I thought the bleeding was stopped."

"Yes, we did manage to stop the bleeding, but she had already lost so much blood, and the liver damage was so extensive. It was amazing that she survived the operation at all, and a miracle that she regained consciousness for a while."

"My baby! My Laurel, you were so good. Always so good. Why?" Adrienne wept uncontrollably.

"Where's Andy?" Melissa asked through her tears. "I want Andy! Is she still in there?"

"I'm afraid we have a problem with Andy. She refused to leave Laurie's side. She seems to be in shock. I came out here to see if one of you—"

"I don't want to see her!" Adrienne screamed. "Keep her away from me! I don't want to look at her."

"Ma, please!" Melissa cried, shocked. "What are you saying? Don't do this to her! She needs us. She must be heartbroken!"

"Heartbroken? She's heartbroken?" Adrienne said through clenched teeth. "That selfish person is heartbroken? May God strike her down!"

Melissa's lips went white and she turned to Dr. Malone. "I'll go in and talk to her. Maybe I can help."

Dr. Malone led Melissa into the ICU. She saw Andy sitting beside Laurie on the bed, her face next to her twin's. She walked closer and heard Andy talking softly, lovingly to her dead sister. "Remember, Laurie? Remember when we were little girls? You would always watch what I put on in the morning and then you would put on the same thing? We loved to look alike then. We loved to do everything together when we were little." Her voice broke.

"You made up the best games. I loved to play with you. Nobody was as much fun as you. I wanted only you. We never needed anybody else, did we? Oh, and you were always so smart! Remember? You always loved school so much. What would I have done without you in school? I needed you so much. I always needed you so much . . . even when I ran away, it was only because I was afraid of needing you so much . . . I still need you . . . I—oh God, I'm sorry Laurie. I'm sorry I hurt you so badly. If only I could make it up to you . . . if only—" Her voice cracked and she hugged Laurie tightly.

Melissa moved next to Andy and put her hand on her back. "Andy, please. Come out with me. The doctors have to take care of Laurie."

Andy picked her head up and stared blankly at Melissa. "No. I'll take care of Laurie. I owe it to her. She gave me so much, and I never gave her enough."

"No, Andy, that's not true. Don't even think that. You always made Laurie happy. There was no one in the world she would rather be with than you. You were the person who gave her more than anyone else did, more than anyone else ever could."

"But I killed her!" Andy wept bitterly. "Look at her lying there! That's what I gave her!"

Tears streamed down Melissa's cheeks. "No! She was killed by a crazy person. You couldn't have controlled that."

"Oh God, Melissa. She was cold, and she was scared. I tried to make her live, but I couldn't!"

"No, Andy . . . ." Melissa covered her eyes and bowed her head.

Andy's whole body shook as she sobbed. "Why wasn't it me? It should have been me. That woman wanted to kill me, Melissa. I wish to God she had."

"But she didn't! Now you have to be as strong as possible. You can't bring her back, but you can make her proud of you."

"But I love her so much. You have no idea how

much I love her. You don't understand. Nobody does. I can't live without her, Melissa. I don't want to!"

"It will be very hard for all of us, but we have to make it. Laurie was special, and now we have to make sure that we keep her memory special."

"Memory? What are you, crazy? Do you think I could ever forget her? Look at me. Look at my face! I see her face in the mirror every day." She put her head back down on the bed. "Oh, Laurie, what did I do to you? I can't bear it, Melissa. She's gone forever and I can't bear it."

"We have to think of Bette now. She needs you to be strong. She'll need you with her."

Andy looked up. "Bette! What have I done to Bette? Melissa, no! I can't handle that right now. You have to take care of Bette. I'm sorry, Lis. You'll have to take care of . . . everything. Call Fred . . . tell him what happened . . . he'll help."

"He knows, Andy. He's downstairs." She hesitated and swallowed hard. "Andy? We have to think about—we have to make, uh, arrangements."

"Arrangements?" Andy clutched her hands to her breast. She remembered Laurie using the word "arrangements" just a few hours before, in reference to her wedding plans. "Oh God, arrangements! I can't—I—ask Freddie. Ask him to make all the arrangements. I can't, I can't. What am I going to do? I can't live without her."

Melissa held Andy tightly. "You will live! You will do it for Laurie's sake."

Andy nodded. "I . . . will . . . do it . . . for

PROMISES TO KEEP

Laurie's sake." She paused. "Two plots. Tell Freddie. Get two plots next to each other. One for Laurie and one for me. Make sure they're close together. Right next to each other."

Melissa let out a sob. "I'll tell him. I'll make sure. Now you come out with me."

Andy closed her eyes and turned back to Laurie. She smoothed her twin's hair and touched her cheek lovingly. "Good night, sister. I love you more than life itself. We'll be together again soon. I promise." She kissed Laurie and held on to her for a few minutes, then, dazed, she allowed Melissa to lead her toward the door.

Before they were able to leave the room, Adrienne burst in. She ran over to the bed where Laurie lay and fell on the body. "No! Oh no, my baby. My poor baby. Why? Why did this have to happen to you? You were so sweet, so good. You didn't deserve this!" Suddenly she stood up and turned to face Melissa and Andy. "How can you stand there like that? What are you looking at? What do you see? I'll tell you what you see." She walked over to Andy and calmly said to her, "You see a mother in mourning. A mother who will never take another breath without remembering her dead daughter. And why is she dead? I'll tell you why." She pointed her finger at Andy. "She's dead because of you! You killed her! You and your decadent life! You and your lack of morals! You and your selfishness! You didn't have to pay for your sins." Adrienne pointed toward the bed. "She paid for them for you!"

Melissa raised her hand and slapped her

mother's face. "Stop it!" she screamed at the top of her lungs. "Stop it, do you hear me! Don't do this to her! Stop it!"

Andy stood trembling as her mother spoke. Tears fell down her cheeks onto the floor. "I'm sorry, Mommy," she whispered. "So sorry."

"Sorry? You're sorry? What good is sorry? All your filthy money and stinking fame can't do anything for Laurie now. Oh, how I wish it was you lying there instead of her!"

Andy let out a moan, then turned from her mother and ran. She ran out of the ICU, searching wildly for a way out. She ran down the stairs and out of the hospital. A crowd of reporters stood on the front steps waiting. Strobes flashed as she blindly ran through them. She covered her face with her hands, and screamed, "You vultures! Damn you! Leave me alone! Get away from me! I can't take any more!" She ran and ran until finally she reached her house.

Melissa went after her, but Andy was too fast. She tried to run faster, but Andy was like the wind, weaving through cars and people. Melissa followed her to her house and just as she got there, a cab pulled up. Fred threw some money at the driver and rushed up to Melissa. "I saw her run out of the hospital and I figured she would come here," he said.

They both climbed the steps and saw that the thick stained glass window next to the door was broken. The door was ajar and there was a trail of blood staining the otherwise clean, shiny floor. Melissa grabbed Fred's arm. "She smashed the glass with her hand to get in!" They glanced into the living room and saw shattered liquor bottles near the bar. The trail of blood led up the stairs. They followed it to her den on the third floor.

Andy was shouting and screaming in an anguished voice behind the door. They heard sounds of glass breaking and metal being thrown against the walls. Fred tried the door, but it was locked from the inside. "Andy!" she shouted. "Let me in! Andy! Please, open up!"

"Get out of here!" she shrieked. "Stay away! I don't want you here! I don't want anyone here! Goddamn you, stay out!" She smashed more things in her frenzy and then it became eerily quiet in the room.

"Andy? Andy, it's Melissa. I just want to help you. Please open the door. Let me be with you." She pushed the door, but Andy's shouts made her stop.

"Don't you dare come in here! I'm warning you. Get out of my house! Leave me alone! Oh God, leave me alone!" She threw a heavy object at the door and screamed. "Get away from here! I just want to be alone! I'm warning you, don't you dare try to come in here!"

Melissa looked at Fred. "I can break it down," she whispered. "Should I break it down?"

"I don't know what to do," he answered. "I don't know if it would upset her even more. But if she's hurting herself . . . maybe we should."

Suddenly, they heard someone run into the house. "Andy, are you here? Baby, are you here?"

Freddie called down. "Eric! We're up here.

She's locked herself in the den."

Eric ran up the stairs and threw himself at the door. He slammed himself into it twice more until it gave way, then he walked in and looked around the room. It was in shambles. All the awards, records, pictures and memorabilia were completely destroyed. Andy was in a corner of the room holding an open bottle of scotch, shivering. He ran over to her and put his arms around her. She looked up at him with vacant eyes. "I killed Laurie."

"Hush, baby, hush. You didn't kill anyone." He kissed the top of her head. "My poor Andy. I'm here now. Everything is going to be all right."

Andy pushed him away. "No!" she screamed. "It will never be all right again. The best part of me is gone. Gone forever. And nothing will ever bring her back."

Eric grabbed her wrist and turned it up towards him. Blood was still oozing from the deep cuts. He turned to Melissa. "Get me something to put on this. We've got to stop this bleeding."

She pulled her hand away. "No. Let it bleed. It has to bleed. Let it all flow away."

Eric ignored her and pressed the gauze that Melissa brought him tightly on Andy's wrist. She fought him violently, but finally, exhausted, she allowed him to tie the gauze around her wrist. "I just want to be with her again," she explained weeping. "I'm so lonely without her. Just let me go to her. Oh Laurie, Laurie, why did you leave me here alone? You know how lonely I am without you." She crouched on the floor, her arms wrapped around herself, rocking to and fro, huddled in a ball of misery.

The small room at Riverside Chapel was crowded. People milled around speaking softly. Melissa and Adrienne sat on a couch next to the casket. Bette was in Melissa's lap. Her arms were wrapped around her aunt's waist and her head was resting on her breast. Adam sat next to them, both hands clutching the arms of the chair. Two of the many doctors present from New York Hospital walked up to him and murmured their condolences. Erica Abbott, Ginny Paul, David McAllister and Maddy Gabrielle sat with some Nickelodean executives on the other side of the room. Mrs. Barrett and Alice stood near the door next to a group of nurses from the neonatal critical care unit. Fred walked in and went over to Adrienne and Melissa. They looked up as he spoke to them. "Uh, Adrienne, Melissa. Andy is in a room with Eric and her psychiatrist. We'll bring her in here as soon as everyone is moved into the chapel."

"How is she?" Adrienne asked in a broken voice. She'd too late realized the cruel blow she had dealt her suffering daughter, and she wanted to try to undo the damage she knew she had done.

Fred sighed. "Well, right now she's a bit sedated. Don't worry, we'll take care of her."

A man came in and asked all except the family to please step into the chapel. The mourners left, leaving only Adrienne, Melissa and Bette. Andy entered the room with Fred on one side of her holding her arm and Eric on the other side holding her waist. Dr. Bartis followed close behind. Andy's face, completely devoid of color, was sunk almost to her chest. Her black suit hung limply on her body. It was obvious that the emotional strain was too much for her to bear. Dr. Bartis whispered a few words into her ear. Andy nodded slowly and looked up. Her eyes met her mother's. Tears formed in both their eyes, and Adrienne moved as if to go to her daughter.

At that precise moment the rabbi came in and they all turned towards him. Rabbi Melchior stood in front of the little group and explained the procedure. One of the chapel staff pinned a small piece of black ribbon on each of the family members and had them repeat the prayer of mourning. Then he slashed the ribbons. "Follow me into the chapel now," he said.

Adrienne, Bette, Melissa and Andy sat down in the front row. Fred, Eric and Dr. Bartis sat directly behind. The Rabbi intoned the prayers for the dead and then began his eulogy. "We have here the saddest of deaths. Laurel Rabinowitz was a young woman with as bright a future as could be found. It is natural for us to wonder why God in his infinite wisdom would cut short such a life. It is natural for us to be angry at the sheer waste of it all. There is no purpose, we say. It is all so arbitrary. Could it have been a mistake? Does the Almighty make mistakes? Perhaps so, perhaps everything does not go according to plan in His Universe. But one death, however tragic and untimely, must be looked upon within the whole scheme of things. What can we learn from it? What can we do to make it more than just a meaningless occurance?

"Laurel Rabinowitz lived an exemplary life. She was a devoted daughter to her mother, Adrienne, a loving mother to Bette, and a caring sister to Andrea and Melissa. She was always there when they needed her, even if it meant putting aside her own needs.

"As head of the Neonatal Critical Care Unit at New York Hospital she saved countless numbers of babies who otherwise might never have survived to lead fruitful and productive lives. I was told of infants that she literally willed to live, each a miracle of life, a miracle born of her skill and dedication.

"All of these: her family in whose memory she'll always live and the future generation of children whose lives would not have been had it not been for her, are her legacy. They are a testament of faith. Faith that the human race will survive. Faith that mankind, however imperfect, is basically good. We needed Laurel Rabinowitz to remind us of that. We needed her to remind us of the many people who, quietly and without fanfare, help to rectify God's mistakes. We can find hope and comfort in her life, however short, because she exemplifies all of the best that mankind has to offer. Let us now stand for the benediction."

Eric reached forward and helped a weeping Andy to stand. He kept his hand on her arm throughout the prayer. The rabbi finished and people filed out to their cars. Bette looked at Andy hesitantly, then took a few tentative steps toward her. Andy bent down. "Come here, little one," she said, her voice breaking with emotion. "Let me hold you."

Bette started sobbing and ran into Andy's waiting arms. "I want Mommy, Andy. Why did she have to die? I can't be happy ever again without Mommy."

"Oh no, Bette. Don't say that. Your mommy wants you to be happy. If nothing else, I know that. Please, Bette, don't cry like that. I'm here."

"Will you be with me?"

"Yes, I'll be with you. I promise. Go to Grandma now. We have to go." She stood up, took Bette's hand and gave it to Adrienne. Adrienne reached for Andy, but Andy would not acknowledge her.

Adrienne watched helplessly as her daughter left the chapel.

The cars pulled up to the section at Wellwood Cemetery on Long Island where Fred had bought the adjoining plots. Everyone except Alice and Bette got out. The mourners stepped up to the grave with the mound of earth next to it and watched as the casket was brought over and lowered into the grave. Rabbi Melchior began his prayers and the crowd bowed their heads as they listened to the sorrowful words.

When the prayers were finished, the rabbi asked one of the grave diggers for a shovel. He picked up some dirt and threw it onto the casket. It landed with a hollow thud. Andy began to tremble and she clutched Eric's jacket. The rabbi handed the shovel to Adam who took a deep breath and threw another shovelful into the grave. Suddenly Andy broke away and rushed towards the grave screaming, "No! No! Stop it! Please! No more! Don't do this to her!" She reached the edge and would have thrown herself in it if Fred hadn't grabbed her and pulled her back.

"Let me go! Let me go! Laurie! Laurie, please! I only want to be with you! Damn it! Let me go! She wants me with her, she needs me!" She struggled violently as Eric ran over to help hold her. Fred and Eric pulled her away toward the limousine. She thrashed and hit at them, screaming all the while. A photographer who'd been waiting nearby ran up as soon as he heard the commotion. He stood in front of Fred and Eric as they tried to get Andy away from the grave and his strobe went off in her face. With all the strength she could muster, she broke away from the two men and ran toward the photographer.

"You leech! You lousy, stinking leeches!" She shoved him, grabbed his camera and smashed it against a headstone. "I can't take it any more!" she shrieked as she turned toward the mourners and opened her arms wide. "Oh God, I can't take it any more! Kill me too! Please! Someone kill me! Let me die so I can be with Laurie!" Dr. Bartis ran up to her, took out a syringe and injected a sedative into her. Almost immediately, her legs buckled and the doctor held on to her tightly.

"Quickly," she said. "Carry her to the car."

Adrienne pushed through the crowd and tried to get to her daughter, but she was too late. All she saw was Andy's anguished face looking out the rear window as the limousine sped away. Adrienne ran after it, arms out, until it disappeared from her sight.

Adrienne and Melissa sat in the kitchen of Laurie's apartment drinking a cup of tea. Melissa had just put Bette to bed and, mercifully, she had fallen right to sleep. "That poor little baby." Adrienne sighed. "She's so bewildered. She just can't understand what happened."

Melissa nodded. "It's hard for me to understand too. God, Ma, I'm so exhausted. I have no strength left. I've never felt so drained."

Adrienne held her head in her hands. "Oh, Melissa, did you see Andy's face? Did you see the pain in it? She needed me and I failed her. How can I live with myself now? I should never have spoken to her that way at the hospital. I don't know what came over me. Haven't you been able to find out anything about her?"

Melissa shook her head. "Nobody is at her house, and I couldn't get a hold of Fred, Eric or Dr. Bartis." She closed her eyes. "I can't get that scene at the cemetery out of my mind. I never saw anyone so tortured."

"It was all my fault. If only I hadn't spoken so cruelly to her. I should have tried to comfort her. After all, I'm her mother, too."

"You're right, you shouldn't have said those

things to her, but I don't think that was what caused that breakdown. I don't believe she was able to cope with the torments in her own mind. I sincerely believe that she doesn't want to live any more. Oh God, Ma, I don't know what's going to happen to her now."

Tears rolled down Adrienne's cheeks. "I just wish I could help her." She bowed her head. "My poor Laurel, my darling Laurel. What will we do without you?"

The doorbell rang and Melissa jumped to answer it. Fred walked in and immediately took her in his arms. Melissa buried her head in his shoulder and started crying. He ran his hand through his hair. "Is there something to drink in this place? I really could use a drink now."

"I'm sure there's something. She has a bar in the living room." They walked into the room and Fred took a bottle of scotch from the shelf.

"Pour me a little of that, too," Adrienne said as she entered the room. "Fred, please, how is Andy?"

Fred collapsed into a chair and took a gulp of his drink. "She's in pretty bad shape, Adrienne. Dr. Bartis thought it would be best if she was admitted to a clinic. We had a very rough time with her. I've never seen anyone fight sedation the way she did."

Adrienne went to the closet and took her coat out. "I want to see her. I have to talk to her," she cried.

"There's no way you'd be able to talk to her tonight. When I left the clinic she finally seemed to be sleeping. She was so exhausted that I doubt she'll wake up any time soon. I just came here to tell you what happened. I'm on my way home now."

"You don't think it would be possible just to see her anyway?"

"No. Absolutely not. Dr. Bartis told me to tell you to come by her office tomorrow morning at ten. She'd like to speak with you then."

Adrienne nodded and returned her coat to the closet. She finished her drink and stood up. "Well, I think I'm going to lie down now. I'm tired, so very tired. Good night, Fred." She put her hand on her forehead and slowly walked out of the room.

"Is she all right?" Fred asked.

"It's been pure hell for her. Laurie's death has just about destroyed her, and the guilt she's feeling about her outburst—"

"Outburst? What outburst?"

"Right after Laurie died she told Andy she wished that it was her lying there dead instead of Laurie," Melissa said, rubbing her neck. "She said that Laurie was dead because of Andy."

Fred closed his eyes and shook his head. "Damn! That piled on top of Andy's own guilt must have been the last straw. No wonder she's so freaked out."

"That's what my mother is afraid of. She thinks she pushed Andy over the edge."

"I wonder if Dr. Bartis knows what happened? She should know."

"I think that's what Ma wants to talk to her

PROMISES TO KEEP

about." Melissa closed her eyes and tears slipped down her face. "I can't believe Laurie's dead. Now Andy's in a psychiatric hospital . . . I feel like I've lost both of them and I don't know what to do. It's like a nightmare that I can't wake up from."

"I wish I could say something that would help. I wish I could do something. Melissa, I'm sorry. This whole thing has tired me out. I have to go home and get some sleep."

Melissa kissed him. "You're such a nice man. I don't know what we would have done without you."

"You know how much I care. Call me if you need me, anytime, night or day." He gave Melissa one last hug and left.

Melissa looked around the living room in despair, turned off the lights and lay down on the couch to try to sleep.

Adrienne sat nervously in the office waiting for Dr. Bartis to come in. She had not been aware that Andy had been seeing a psychiatrist regularly until Melissa had informed her that Andy had been in analysis for the past nine years. She wondered what Dr. Bartis would have to say to her about her daughter and how she herself would react to meeting with the psychiatrist.

The doctor entered the room, immediately walked over to Adrienne and held out her hand. She gently smiled and said, "I'm so very happy to meet you Mrs. Rabinowitz, and so sorry about Laurie."

Adrienne shook her hand and said quietly, "I'm having trouble accepting it. It's so senseless."

"Yes it is. I've spoken to the doctors over at Bellevue and I was told that Marilyn Koppel will probably be judged incompetent and unable to stand trial. She's a very sick woman."

"Does that mean that she'll get away with murdering my daughter?"

"No. Absolutely not. She is going to be institutionized and my feeling is that she will never be released."

Adrienne nodded. "Tell me about Andrea. How is she?"

Dr. Bartis sighed. "I've just come from her room. Right now, she doesn't want to face reality. It's much too painful for her. The human mind is a miraculous thing. We tend to be able to block out what we don't want to remember."

"Is that what Andy is doing?"

"Basically, yes. The problem is that what happened is impossible for her to ignore, and her violent reaction is the only way she has of fighting back at the horror of it all. You know that she truly feels that a part of her is dead and she's not too sure that the rest of her is worth saving. She's totally unable to cope with her sense of loss. She feels that she has no right to be alive when Laurie isn't. I must make her understand that Laurie's death is separate from her life—that she can have a meaningful existance without her. The fact that they were identical twins makes my task all the more difficult."

"But she will be all right, won't she?"

"I certainly hope so. Much of it is up to Andy herself. She has to want to be all right. She has to make an effort to face reality."

Adrienne began to cry. "This was all my fault, doctor. I pushed her to this—"

"Why do you say that?"

"I—I told her that I wished she had been killed instead of Laurel. Doctor, I didn't mean that. May God forgive me for saying that. I didn't know what I was saying, I was so distraught. I told her that she killed Laurel."

"You didn't say anything that Andy didn't feel herself," Dr. Bartis said gently. "Her guilt is overwhelming, it has taken over all rational thought. No, Mrs. Rabinowitz, you can't take responsibility for what has happened to Andy. You spoke in the midst of tremendous grief. What you said was the product of your sorrow at losing your daughter. You wanted to hurt as you were hurting. Andy just happened to be the target."

"But I shouldn't have said it. She's my daughter."

"You just lashed out at the most convenient person. Please, try not to dwell on it. It is not productive. We have to concern ourselves now with helping Andy to get well. I wanted to speak to you today to reassure you that Andy is a strong person and I believe we will be able to help her adjust to her loss. I also want to tell you that it probably will take some time and patience on all our parts." She sighed. "I'm very fond of your daughter."

"Believe me, Doctor, I love her dearly. I may

not have told her often enough, but I do love her. The only thing I ask for in life right now is that she get well again. Tell me, can I see her?"

"She's still not quite lucid. She badly needs some rest. I'm afraid we've had to restrain her arms. She's very restless and at this point we're concerned that she might hurt herself."

"What do you mean 'restrain?'"

"We have her hands tied down loosely with gauze strips. It might be upsetting for you to see her like that."

"Can't I just go into her room and see her for a moment?"

"If you insist."

They took the elevator to the eleventh floor and walked to Andy's room. The doctor opened the door and Adrienne stepped in. Andy was lying on her back with her arms tied at the wrists to the bed's guard rails. Her tangled hair was fanned out on the pillow, framing her pale, anguished face. Adrienne's heart ached as she looked at her daughter. "Are you sure she's not in pain?" she whispered as Andy tossed and moaned.

"No, she's not in any physical pain," Dr. Bartis reassured her. "She's not even aware that we're here. Her reality is internal now—it's more pleasant for her to live in her thoughts because she can shape them the way she wants to. The real world is a nightmare."

Adrienne was visibly shaken. "What does that mean for her future?"

"We will eventually try to bring her out of it, but I must warn you that the prognosis is uncertain."

"Can I help in any way? I need to help her get better."

Dr. Bartis smiled and nodded her head. "If you can help in any way, I will be sure to contact you."

Adrienne stared at Andy. She looked so innocent, so vulnerable. She walked over to the bed and bent down. Lovingly, she pushed the perspiration-drenched hair off her daughter's forehead and kissed her. "I love you, sweetheart," she whispered. "Mommy loves you."

Dr. Bartis stepped behind Adrienne and put her hand on her shoulder. "We'll let her rest now. I promise you that I will let you see her again as soon as she is up to it."

Adrienne nodded. "Thank you, Doctor," she said as she turned away from the bed and reluctantly left the room. "Thank you for helping both of us."

Andy roused herself a few hours later. Her strangely active mind began replaying scenes of her life. Her first day of school . . . the dual birthday parties . . . snuggling in bed together, pleased they were twins . . . their Radcliffe graduation party, where even their Uncle Morris couldn't tell them apart . . . then, *"Oh No! Please! Not a gun!"*

She struggled against the recollection, but still it stuck with her. She thrashed in the bed. "No, not Laurie! She doesn't deserve—it's a mistake! It's all a mistake!" But she knew. The truth had overtaken her and the intensity of her pain overwhelmed her. She felt as if she were suffocating. Laurie was dead, gone forever and there was nothing in the world she could do about it.

Nothing in *this* world . . . but in her panic it occurred to her that *her* world was one place that she could have Laurie alive. She could be with her, laugh with her, love her. And she was sure it was what Laurie wanted, too. Yes, she reasoned, that was the only way out of this nightmare.

Though her mind was still hazy, she was lucid enough to firmly resolve to herself not to allow anyone or anything from the outside world to intrude on them. The world within her mind was enough for her.

February

Melissa sat at her desk sorting through the mounds of paperwork that had piled up in the past few days, but Laurie was still too vivid in her mind for her to concentrate on what she was doing. The loss was devastating. Laurie was her confidante, her mentor, her beloved older sister. She was close to her in a way that she had never been with Andy. It had been so much easier to pick up the phone and call Laurie when she had a problem. Not that Andy wasn't interested, she just never had the time.

It was torture to Melissa that just when Laurie was beginning to have the happiness she deserved, she was struck down so cruelly. Adam had told Melissa of his plan to adopt Bette after he and Laurie were married, and it tore her apart to hear the grief in his voice. She and Adrienne were having trouble with Bette now. The little girl refused to go to school. She spent her days sitting in the living room holding the picture of the three sisters and asking mournfully, "Where's Andy? Why doesn't she want to see me? She said she'd be with me."

Melissa had consoled her and explained that Andy would be with her if she could, but that she was very sick right now. Bette had wanted to know if Andy was going to die, too. Both Melissa and her mother were worried, and not sure of how to handle the situation. Adrienne had even spoken to Dr. Bartis about the child. Melissa was relieved when the psychiatrist suggested that Bette be brought in to see her.

There was a light tap on the door. "Come in," Melissa said. Shep walked in. "What do you want? I thought you weren't supposed to be here any more."

"I came back to get my things. Robin told me you were here."

"So? Why do you want to see me?"

"I want to ask you something. Do you think Andy is still going to prosecute?"

"Prosecute?" she repeated incredulously. "I'm sure you're the last thing on her mind right now."

"Yeah, but do you think she ever will?"

"Why don't you get the hell out of here? You're not worth it! I strongly doubt that she'll ever want to bother with the likes of you again."

"Are you sure?"

She held her head in her hands. "Oh, get out! Just get out of here!" She heard him leave her office as she folded her arms on the desk and lay anymore."

her head down on them. Great sobs wracked her body as she finally let herself lose control. Her life was in pieces and she wasn't sure if the pieces would ever fit together again. Laurie was dead; Andy was lying, unreachable, in a mental hospital; her mother was inconsolable; her niece was so depressed that she couldn't function; Shep had betrayed her, and there was imminent danger of her losing the health club because of him. She heaved a tremendous sigh and lifted her tear-streaked face from her arms. She needed someone, someone she could lean on, who would give her the strength to carry on. She thought of Fred. He had said that she could call him anytime, night or day. Melissa looked up his private number at Nickelodean and dialed.

"Hello? Fred, is that you? It's Melissa . . . I was wondering if maybe you'd like to go to dinner tonight with me. It's no trouble? Yes, yes, I'll see you there . . . at 7:30. Thanks, Fred. No. I'll be all right 'til then. Bye." She hung up the phone slowly, wiped her eyes with a tissue and thought for a moment. Then she picked up the phone again, dialed Kenneth's Beauty Salon and, using Andy's name to get preferential treatment, made an appointment for that afternoon with Kenneth. With a fierce look on her face, she grabbed her credit cards and flew out the door to Bloomingdale's. "The hell with everything," she said with renewed purpose. "I can still have a future. I will not live in the past."

Fred was sitting at the bar in the restaurant

nursing his second Johnny Walker Black when Melissa arrived. He looked up and almost didn't recognize her. She had cut her hair very short and very fashionably, and she had it streaked with blond. He smiled with pleasure at the woman he saw in front of him. Up until now, he had only thought of her as Andy's baby sister, but this was an entirely different Melissa—sophisticated, finely tailored, beautiful. She was wearing a periwinkle blue jacket with matching full skirt and a white silk blouse. She looked feminine, grown up. He jumped off the stool and kissed her on the cheek. "You are smashing!" he exclaimed.

Pleased, Melissa lowered her eyes. "Thank you," she said shyly. "I decided it was about time I bought myself some new things. Life's too short—" She caught her breath and bit her lip.

Fred whispered, "I know it's hard, Melissa, it's going to take time." He held her close to him as they made their way to the dining room.

The maitre d' greeted them. "Mr. Arnold, your table is ready." He led them to the table, seated them and handed them menus. "Would you care for a cocktail?"

"Thanks, I already have one," Fred said, tapping the glass he had brought from the bar. "Melissa?"

"Some white wine, please," she said. The maitre d' nodded and left.

"Have you seen Andy?" asked Freddie.

Melissa shook her head. "I tried, but she went wild. Oh, Fred, I can't bear to see her like that. I keep remembering how competent she was, how together, and now I'm scared that she won't pull out of this. I love her, but there's nothing I can do to help her. It's a horrible feeling." A tear slid down her cheek. "Her psychiatrist told us that she wants no part of reality. She's living entirely in the past. Apparently she just lies in her bed totally oblivious to whatever is going on around her. The doctor says that it's impossible to get through to her. She won't talk, she won't eat . . . She's letting her pain kill her."

"I know. I spoke to Dr. Bartis last week. She's very concerned."

"So am I. The thought of her like this—" She closed her eyes briefly. "Ma's nearly out of her mind with worry, and Bette is sure she'll never see her again. You know, I never realized how much that baby loves Andy. I guess I never realized a lot of things."

"At this point there's nothing you can do," Fred said gently. "You just have to trust Dr. Bartis. She understands Andy very well. I've had quite a bit of contact with her over the years and I think she's very competent."

"Why did you have contact with her?" Melissa asked curiously.

Fred sighed. "Well, you know our relationship was a very stormy one. Sometimes when I was half out of my mind with fear that I would lose her, I would go see Dr. Bartis. Unfortunately, I never listened to her advice."

"What do you mean?"

"I've made some serious mistakes these past years, and I'm just beginning to understand them." He hesitated for a moment. "Andy never really wanted to marry me. I forced her into it."

"Forced her into it? How?"

"I threatened her. I said that if she didn't marry me, I wouldn't be her manager."

"Why was that a threat?"

"Melissa, you really don't know your sister very well. You think of her as some sort of all-powerful woman with the strength of a Diana. A lot of her bravado is just a facade. She's probably the most insecure and fragile person I know."

"I'm beginning to see that. I guess when I was younger she was sort of a goddess to me."

"She was to me, too. I loved her so much I couldn't think straight. Anyway, you asked why my not managing her was a threat. You see, all her life, Andy's needed someone to depend on. Of course, at first it was Laurie, but eventually she wanted more freedom than that relationship could afford her. But her desire for freedom didn't lessen her need to depend on someone, and eventually she began to lean on me. It would have been much too frightening for her to go it alone."

"But what happened? Why did she stop needing you?"

"I guess I held on to her too tightly. I knew that she didn't love me as much as I loved her, and I wanted her so much. I pushed her and pushed her into things she never wanted to do. She's so talented, Melissa, head and shoulders above the others in this crazy business. She can do it all and do it well." He laughed deprecatingly. "It's funny, I thought that I was making her need me more and more, but what I actually was doing was teaching her that she could handle anything—even things she didn't like. She became so confident that eventually she realized that she could stand alone. She keeps saying that I used her, but in a way she used me, too. She used me to get a feeling of self-worth that she never had before."

"Do you still love her?"

Fred thought for a minute. "Do I still love her? Yes, I do. But not in that desperate way I used to. She's a dear friend to me. I'll always care deeply about Andy, but I'm ready to move on to a new chapter in my life. I knew that when I spoke to Eric today. For the first time I could look at him without seeing them together in bed. I actually wanted to help him help Andy. Dr. Bartis said he can see her tomorrow."

"I hope he can help her, too. She needs something real to hang on to, and some reason to look forward to the future." Melissa shook her head and put her hand to her forehead. "I guess I've sort of taken Andy for granted. I can't believe I was so insensitive when I first came down to New York. I was so used to getting what I wanted when I wanted it from her, that I didn't think of what I might be doing to her."

Fred smiled. "Well, she wasn't too thrilled with you right then, but she chalked it up to your infatuation with Shep. She didn't refuse you though, did she? She loves you very much, Melissa."

"I know, and I betrayed that love. Shep put the health club in such jeopardy, and I'm not sure I'll be able to save it."

"It's worth saving. You're an excellent manager, and it would be a shame to see it go under." He paused. "After you called, I spoke to Michael and I think I have a solution. Since Andy is unable to help you right now, and I know she would if she could, I'm going to cover the losses."

"You can't! I mean, I won't let you! It's not your problem."

"Well then, I'll make it my problem. Don't refuse me this Melissa, please. I want very much to help you."

Melissa looked at him for a long time. His eyes told her how much this gesture meant to him. "Okay," she said softly. "But only as a loan. I want to pay you back with interest." She took Fred's hand. "You're such a good person, and I appreciate this very much. Thank you. Andy was very lucky to have you all those years."

"I was lucky to have her," Fred said firmly. "She gave me as much as I gave her. She's quite a lady and I hope to God she pulls out of this." He paused. "A loan then, but we'll see about the interest. You're not a risk, Melissa. Why don't you meet me at Michael's tomorrow and we'll get things settled? Now, no more business or talk of Andy. Let's just concentrate on having a good time for the rest of the evening."

Melissa smiled. "Yes, let's," she said. "I think we both deserve the distraction."

Eric and Dr. Bartis walked out of her office together. He had been calling her every day, but ever since the time that Melissa had come to the hospital and Andy had become so agitated, Dr. Bartis had not allowed any one to see her. At this point though, the psychiatrist was willing to try anything. It was impossible to get through to Andy. No amount of gentle coaxing on her part would bring her patient out of her psychotic state. She opened the door to Andy's room and motioned for him to follow her. The private nurse looked up. "It's all right, Nancy," Dr. Bartis said. "He's with me."

Eric tentatively went over to the bed and peered down at Andy. He was sobered by her appearance. Intravenous lines dangled above her head, and she was curled up in a fetal position in one corner of the bed. She was gaunt, her hair was unkempt and a flowered hospital gown covered her slight frame. She showed no sign of consciousness.

"Andy, you have a visitor," Dr. Bartis said softly. She leaned over and touched the motionless woman on the shoulder. Andy started shuddering violently. The whole bed shook and moved away from the wall. Eric looked panic-stricken, and Dr. Bartis gently explained to him that touching Andy made her aware of an outside world that she didn't want to admit existed. She motioned him closer. "Talk to her. Tell her what you feel. If she responds at all, touch her." She moved back and he took her place beside Andy.

Slowly, hesitantly, Eric began speaking to Andy. He told her about his tour, how much he had missed her, then, in a shaky voice, began to tell her of their times together. He put his hand on her shoulder. Andy cringed and tried to inch away, never opening her eyes.

Something was distracting her. A voice. A deep voice. A nice voice. She wanted to get to that voice but it was so far away. She looked up the long black tunnel that led to the kind, tender voice and started climbing. It was so hard that she had to stop and rest. Then the loving voice drew her on again. She reached back for Laurie, but couldn't find her. Frantically, she searched until the awful reality of it hit her. Laurie was dead. Her twin was dead. Tears filled her eyes.

"Andy, please . . . Dr. Bartis! She's crying!"

Dr. Bartis, her heart pounding, quickly moved over to the bed. "Eric!" She said with excitment. "Hold her. Make her aware of you!"

He picked up Andy's featherlight body and crushed her to his bosom. "Oh, my sweet Andy. Please look at me. I love you, baby. Couldn't you look at me?"

Someone was holding her. It felt so good, so comforting. Someone was making her feel better. She wanted to be held like this forever. A name appeared in the haze of her mind. "Eric," she whimpered. "Hold me, Eric. Laurie is dead."

It was two weeks later, and Dr. Bartis was pleased with Andy's progress. She had begun to take some nourishment and was occasionally getting out of bed to sit by the window. Eric was there frequently, and it was obvious that the love between them was stronger than ever. Right now,

PROMISES TO KEEP

however, Dr. Bartis was bringing Andy a visitor she knew would be unwelcome. She paused outside Andy's room, knocked and walked in.

Andy was lying on her bed with her eyes closed. "I thought we had our session for today. I'm tired, I can't talk anymore." She turned toward the wall, away from the doctor.

"Andy, Melissa is here."

Andy looked at Dr. Bartis sharply. "Didn't you tell her that I wasn't having visitors?"

"She knows that, but she has something important that she would like to show you."

"I'm not interested."

"It concerns Laurie."

Andy put her hand over her eyes. "I don't think I'm up to speaking about her right now."

"I'm afraid this can't be put off any longer. I think I'm going to insist that you see her."

"You're going to insist? So it is a therapy session! Do you get time and a half for overtime?"

Dr. Bartis smiled. "Now that's the Andy Reuben that I remember. I'm calling her in now."

"Do what you want. You're the doctor." She turned back toward the wall.

Melissa came in timidly, carring a large manila envelope. She moved over to the bed and touched her sister's back. "Andy? Hi, how are you feeling?"

"Okay," she said, expressionlessly.

"Hey, Andy, how about turning around? Please? Let me see you?"

Slowly, Andy turned over and looked at

Melissa. "What happened to your hair?" she asked.

"I had it cut. Do you like it?" Andy stared at Melissa for a long time but didn't answer. Melissa touched her sister's hand lightly. "Andy?" she said gently.

"What do you want, Melissa?" Andy whispered. "Why did you come here?"

"Well, I have some things here that I have to talk to you about."

"What things?"

"Well, we went to the reading of Laurie's will yesterday—"

Andy got out of bed, walked over to the window and put her cheek against it. "Why would that concern me?"

"Uh, she left me her apartment. I think I'm going to keep it. It's very nice."

"I know how nice it is. I helped her find it."

Melissa sighed. "She left almost everything else to Bette."

"So? Didn't you expect that? Melissa, please! Why are you coming to me with this?" She put her hands over her head and her whole body trembled. "Leave me alone! A will! Don't tell me about wills! Oh God, I just want Laurie, that's all, and you come in here and tell me about her will! I can't take it Melissa, please!"

Melissa took a deep breath and looked over at Dr. Bartis, who nodded. She continued. "There is something else. Something that very much concerns you. You were named as Bette's guardian."

PROMISES TO KEEP

"What? Me? Bette's guardian? How could she have done that? How can I take care of her? How could she have done this to me?" Andy sat down in a chair and began to cry. "Laurie." She wept. "Laurie. Why did you complicate things like this? Aren't things bad enough as it is?"

"Andy? Ma's talking about taking her back to Boston with her. She's thinking about asking for custody."

Andy nodded. "Maybe that would be for the best."

"Ma wants to see you very much. She really needs to speak with you. I think it would be a good idea."

Andy's face twisted. "Never! I don't ever want to see that woman again! She hates me!"

Dr. Bartis interrupted. "Andy, I told you that your mother was sorry she said those things to you. She didn't mean them. Why don't you give her a chance to talk to you."

"What do you know about it? She's always hated me! She said what was on her mind. It was true all right. She wishes I was dead."

"Oh no, Andy," said Melissa softly. "She cries about you every night. Please, don't say that."

"Get out of here!" Andy screamed. "Leave me alone. I don't want to hear about any of this." She turned back to the window.

"I'll leave, but I have a letter for you that was in with the will. Laurie addressed it to you."

Andy didn't say anything, she just stared out the window.

Melissa put the letter on the night table. "I'm

sorry, Andy. I didn't mean to upset you. You know I love you very much. Good-bye." She ran from the door as the tears began to fall from her eyes.

Dr. Bartis put her hand on Andy's shoulder. She pulled away. "Leave me alone! I don't want to see you any more. I just don't want to think anymore!" She put her head down in her lap and covered it with her hands. The doctor stood there for few minutes more and then quietly left.

As soon as the door closed, Andy rushed over to the night table and grabbed the letter. She clutched it to her breast and moaned, then she ripped it open and sat down on the bed to read it.

"Mr. Dearest Andy,
  Of course I don't for one moment think that you will ever have to read this, but just in case, I want to explain a few things to you. Knowing you as well as I do, I know exactly what you are thinking right now. You are angry at me, aren't you? And yes, I understand that you are not only thinking about the fact that I have awarded guardianship of Bette to you. You are also angry that I have left you. But I know you, better than you know yourself. You're strong, you're a survivor, and that's why I want Bette to be with you. She's going to need you so very much. She will need you to love her and to care for her. Only you know how much that little girl means to me. I am entrusting you with her life. Treat it as you would a precious flower whose petals are easily crushed. She loves you, and she wants so much to be like you, but she has a lot of me in her too. I've often thought that someday she will embody the very best of both of us. It will be up to you to see

PROMISES TO KEEP

that she fulfills that awesome potential. I want you to promise me that you will put aside the despair you are feeling right now, I want you to promise me that you will go back to work and continue to make beautiful music. I want you to promise me that you will use your considerable resources to help people who are unable to help themselves (as I know your kind heart is so capable of doing), and most of all, I want you to promise me that you will show Bette all the love that I know you feel for her. No, Andy, I'm not asking too much of you. You've always thought too little of yourself. I know that you can accomplish all this and more. Don't worry, you won't let me down. You never have before. I love you with all my heart and soul forever and always.

Your Laurie

P.S. Now remember kid, you have promises to keep."

Andy put her hand to her forehead and wept copiously. "Laurie, Laurie, I love you with all my heart and soul forever and always. You have too much faith in me though. I'm not all you think I am . . . but I'll try, I'll try for your sake . . . and for Bette's." She clenched her fists. "I want to take care of Bette! I love her! Laurie, I love that baby so much! I'll be damned if she's going to go to Boston with Ma! She belongs here with me! She and I will make quite a team, just like you and I used to make, Laur."

She reread the letter, tears obscuring some of the words. "I'll try, Laurie, I'll try," she vowed out loud. "For all our sakes." She thought for a moment then reached for the telephone and dialed. "Eric? It's Andy. Are you coming to see me today? Well, before you come could you go over to my house? Uh-huh. Ask Alice to find a book called *Twelve Poets*. Yes, that's right. It's on the shelf in the library. Would you please bring it with you? Thanks, I'll see you later then. I love you, too. Good-bye."

She hung up the phone and redialed. "May I please speak to Dr. Bartis? I think she'll speak to me, this is Andy Reuben. Doctor? I need you to help me get well enough to get out of here as quickly as possible. What do I have to do? What? With my mother? I—I don't know if I can. I'm scared of—" She paused for a moment. "Oh, all right, even that. Anything. I just have to get better. What? Yes, I'm all right. Laurie's helped me to realize what I have to do. Uh-huh, I know that it might take some time, but I have promises to keep doctor, so many promises to keep."

Andy sat quietly in Dr. Bartis's office at the hospital waiting for her mother to arrive. She was not happy about this therapy session her psychiatrist had set up with Adrienne, but the doctor had insisted that it was necessary for her recovery. "I'm tired," she said softly. "Please, let me go back to my room."

"Andy, if you want to get out of the hospital we can't postpone this."

Andy looked up. "Maybe she isn't coming. Maybe she doesn't want to see me as much as I don't want to see her."

"That's not the case at all. I told you how anxious she is to see you. She calls me every day to find out how you are. She's been very worried about you."

"Yeah, sure." Andy put her hands on the huge mahogany desk and leaned forward. "I'm afraid to see her, doctor," she whispered. "Really afraid."

"I know honey, but—"

There was a knock on the door and Adrienne walked in. "The secretary said I should just come in. Am I late?"

"No, not at all," Dr. Bartis said. "Please sit down."

Adrienne sat, clutching a brown paper bag. She was stunned when she turned to Andy. Although Dr. Bartis had told her that Andy wasn't sleeping or eating well, she was unprepared for what she saw. Her daughter looked totally unlike her usual flamboyant self. Her emaciated frame seemed lost in the large gray sweatshirt and baggy jeans she wore. Wrinkles had formed around her sad, puffy eyes and there were dark circles underneath them. She looked excruciatingly tired—as though she hadn't had any real sleep since Laurie's death. No make up adorned her face, and her permanent was beginning to grow out. Adrienne was horrified to see that her hair was flecked with gray. She longed to reach out and touch her, but instead said, "I made some chicken for Bette last night, just the way you used to like it." She held the bag out. "Here, I brought you two pieces."

Andy looked up. "No thank you," she said

dully. "I'm not hungry." She lit a cigarette and slumped in her chair.

"I was very proud of you last night," Adrienne began tentatively.

"Proud of me? What for?"

"Those record awards? The ones on television? You know. You won some and Eric made such a nice speech for you. He also won one. You didn't watch?"

Andy bowed her head. "No."

"But Andy, you love the awards. Why didn't you—"

"Look, I wasn't interested! It's that simple!"

Dr. Bartis cut in. "Andy feels that she is just about ready to leave the hospital. However, I feel that it is very important that you and she have some sessions together with me before she is released." She smiled. "If you don't mind Mrs. Rabinowitz, I would like you to tell me the first thing that comes into your head when I say some words. Remember, I want the very first thing."

Adrienne nodded. "All right."

"Dog."

"Cat."

"Very good. Red."

"Blue."

"House."

"Boston."

"Children."

"Laurel, Andrea and Melissa. Is that all right?"

"That was just fine. Melissa."

"Baby."

PROMISES TO KEEP

"Laurel."

"Good."

"Andrea."

Adrienne's face paled. She hesitated, looked over at Andy, who was intently watching her, and said nothing.

Dr. Bartis repeated. "Andrea."

"Please, doctor, I don't want to hurt her again." She clasped her hands to her throat.

"Andrea!" Dr. Bartis said harshly. "Say it, Mrs. Rabinowitz, the first thing that comes into your head." Andy leaned forward. Adrienne bowed her head. The doctor repeated, "Andrea!"

"Trouble," Adrienne whispered.

"What? I didn't hear you."

Adrienne looked up. "Trouble, I said trouble."

Andy shook her head. "See, Doctor," she said ruefully. "I told you."

Adrienne looked pleadingly at the doctor. "It's not that I don't love her. I do, very much. It's just that she was always a very difficult child."

"What do you mean?"

"Well, she was very small when she was born, and sickly. She had very bad lung problems. We were so worried about her, I couldn't sleep for worrying about her. Laurel came home with me, but we had to leave Andrea in the hospital. It was —it was a very hard time for me. I was young, and so overwhelmed. Ben had to work and I had no one to stay with Laurel, so I couldn't go to the hospital to see Andrea as much as I wanted to. Ben would leave his store sometimes and go over, but I had a baby at home and I couldn't get out."

"That made you feel guilty, didn't it?"

Adrienne nodded. "You see, she was so tiny and so sick, and I was so afraid that she wouldn't live. I used to get phone calls in the middle of the night asking me for permission to do this or that to her." Tears rolled down her cheeks. "My mother told me to think of the one that was home. She said—" Adrienne smiled in remembrance. "—this was one of my mother's favorite expressions, only she said it in Yiddish. 'What will be will be.' But I thought about Andrea all the time. I never expected her to come home."

"And when she did?"

Adrienne took a deep breath. "She was not an easy infant. She didn't know night from day. She cried all the time and she didn't seem to want me to touch her. I could never comfort her, never. I couldn't spend any time at all with Laurel, because Andrea took up so much of my time."

"And you resented that?"

Adrienne thought for a moment. "I guess I did. God help me, I guess I did. Laurel was always so good. I loved taking care of her. She smiled at me whenever I came to her. Andrea didn't smile very much. But they were both my children, Doctor. Why should I have resented one of them?"

"It's very normal," Dr. Bartis said gently. "Andy was an intruder at that point, so to speak. You were able to develop a bond with Laurie, but you weren't given the opportunity with Andy. It's a classic misconception that the minute a child is born, a mother automatically feels devotion towards it. A loving relationship takes time and a certain amount of nuturing. Touching and holding are crucial in the beginning. The fact that Andy was in the hospital for so long, and in those days even when you went to visit her it was forbidden for you to go near her, did not enable you to feel the love you thought you should have felt for her. Also, our minds are very protective. You didn't think that she would live. To love her would have meant that you would have felt more grief had she died."

"But I did love her!"

"Of course you loved her. It's just that, as you said, you found her to be a very difficult child."

Andy stood up, walked to the window and lit another cigarette.

"Andy please, come back here and sit down. It is vitally important for you to hear this."

"I can hear everything from over here."

Dr. Bartis sighed, then turned back to Adrienne. "Tell me about when the girls were growing up."

Adrienne looked over at Andy then back to the doctor. "They were so smart," she said eagerly. "Andrea was talking when she was only six months old! She said perfect whole sentences before she was a year old. I remember Ben would recite poems to the two of them and Andrea could memorize them and say them right back to him." She smiled. "She and Laurel would jabber away to each other in their own language—they were just adorable. Everybody said so. I used to dress them exactly alike, and whenever I would take them out for a walk, people would tell me how beautiful they were and how lucky I was."

"Did you think you were lucky?"

"Oh, I loved having twins."

"And as they got older?"

Adrienne shrugged. "There were no special problems. They just grew up."

"You said before that Andy was a very difficult child."

"Well, she was very impetuous. She never thought before she did things. I hardly ever remember having to punish Laurel, but it seemed to me that I was always punishing Andrea for one thing or another."

Dr. Bartis looked toward the window. "Do you remember that, Andy?"

She turned around. "Oh I remember that all right."

"Andy, please sit down over here," Dr. Bartis instructed her in a voice that brooked no argument. "I want you to join us. Right now!" Reluctantly Andy sat down again. "Look at me, Andy. Come on, right at me! Tell me the first thing that comes into your mind when you think of your mother."

"I don't feel like playing that stupid game."

"Let's go, Andy. The first thing! Now!"

Andy looked at Dr. Bartis, her eyes flaming. "The first thing?" she hissed. "Okay. The first thing I think of when I think of my mother is 'wrong'! She was always wrong!"

Adrienne's eyes widened. "Wrong? What do you mean wrong. Wrong about what?"

Andy waved her hand. "Never mind. I don't

want to talk about it."

Dr. Bartis leaned forward and took Andy's arm. "Andy! No more evasions! You have to talk about it!"

"No I don't! Laurie and I made a pact a long time ago—"

"A pact!" Dr. Bartis said. "Well then, the time has come for you to break that pact."

"I can't. It's not that important—"

"Yes it is. It is extremely important, Andy! Please! Open up for once!"

Andy looked at Dr. Bartis and then at her mother. She thought for a moment, then spoke directly at Adrienne. "Why were you always punishing me?"

Adrienne sighed. "I punished you because you kept getting into trouble."

"You were sure that it was me who always got into trouble, weren't you?"

"Of course it was you. You never lied. You always admitted it when you did something wrong."

"Laurie never told you that it was me?"

Adrienne thought back. "I don't remember. Maybe sometimes she did."

"And you always believed her?"

"You never denied it!"

"Come on, Andy," Dr. Bartis said impatiently. "What are you getting at?"

"What am I getting at? I'll tell you what I'm getting at." She turned to her mother. "You were always so hard on us. You expected so much of us. We were so little—why were you so hard on us?" She leaned across the desk toward Dr. Bartis. "Laurie could never stand being yelled at. Any time she was yelled at she got hysterical. I mean, her whole body shook for hours afterward. We always did things for each other and I thought I'd do this for her. You see, I didn't care. It was better for me to be yelled at than for me to see Laurie unhappy. I could never stand to see Laurie unhappy." She turned back to Adrienne.

"Do you remember the time the kitchen caught on fire? Remember punishing me for that one? What actually happened was that you were busy taking care of Melissa, as usual, and Laurie wanted lunch. She heated some oil and threw some french fries into the pan. Believe me, it wasn't my idea. Laurie had those kinds of ideas. I remember it as if it were yesterday. The oil splattered and the curtains caught fire. Laurie froze. I told her to leave before you could see her and when you got to the kitchen you found me, alone, trying to put the fire out. You punished me by not allowing me to take the guitar lessons I wanted so badly. You said that the money you saved by not giving me the lessons would pay you back for the damage I caused in the kitchen."

"But that's not fair! How could I have known that you didn't do it?" Adrienne argued.

"But that wasn't the only time. I took the blame more times than I can remember. You know, after awhile, whenever anything happened, you automatically assumed that it was my fault. But it wasn't the punishments that bothered me. That was all right, I was doing that for Laurie.

What bothered me were the times Laurie pretended to be me and you never knew!"

"What do you mean I never knew? I could always tell you apart."

Andy laughed raucously. "Boy, Laurie would laugh too if she were here. You could only tell us apart when we wanted you to. It was so easy for her to put on an Andy face to make you think she was me!"

"I don't believe you! That's a lie!"

"A lie. I can prove it to you. How do you think I learned how to play the guitar? Laurie let me take the lessons instead of her. You never knew!" Andy looked at her mother, the pain in her face obvious. "How could you not know? I could never understand. Was I really that unimportant! *How could you not know?*"

Adrienne held her head in her hands.

Suddenly Andy started weeping. "Oh no! No! Laurie! What did I do! Forgive me, Laur. God, why did I do this? We had a pact. I betrayed you . . . there's no point to it now, no reason . . ." She turned to Dr. Bartis. "You made me hurt Laurie again! Why couldn't you leave things as they were?"

The doctor put her arm around Andy. "Because it isn't necessary for you to protect Laurie anymore. Your anger at your mother for not recognizing you when you wanted her to so desperately must be resolved before you are able to become a fully functioning, productive adult again."

Adrienne's hand shook as she touched Andy's shoulder. "You loved Laurie so much that you let me punish you unnecessarily without so much as a word of protest?"

"Yes," said Andy softly. "I loved her that much and more. I'd do anything for her."

"But then why did you leave? It all but destroyed her."

"I can't believe you didn't see. What were you, blind? We were literally suffociating each other. By that time though, it was Laurie who was protecting me. But she tried to protect me from everything—from you and daddy, from the professors in med school, even from myself. I wanted so badly to just be me. My relationship with—" She put her hand to her forehead, "—with Philip, made me realize that it was possible for me to be an independent person, that it was time to break away. For both our sakes, I had to do something. The fact that I got pregnant just made it easier to run away. Now I know that running didn't solve anything. It was only when I realized that I could succeed in something Laurie couldn't do that I overcame my terrible dependence. Dr. Bartis helped me to see that. And that's what allowed us to become so close again."

Adrienne stared ahead as if in shock. "Dear Lord," she cried. "I was so cruel to you. How could I have been so cruel?"

"Oh yes, you were cruel. You never really cared about me! I knew that. If you cared you would have wondered why Laurie was always good and I was always bad." She stood up and pointed her finger angrily at her mother. "You didn't even know who I was! How could you love me if you didn't know who I was? You never took the time to find out. Don't you think I know that you hate me? Didn't you make it abundantly clear in the hospital?"

"I didn't mean those things! I was distraught."

"Those words were the first honest ones you've ever said to me."

Adrienne got up, stood in front of her daughter and reached out to her. "No! Don't say that! I love you, Andy! I've always . . ."

Andy pulled away. "I never felt loved by you!" she said in an anguished voice. "You've always extolled Laurie's virtues and made apologies for my weaknesses!"

Adrienne sank back down in her chair. "How can I make it up to you?" she said softly. "Please, let me make it up to you!"

"You can't, and if you think I'm going to let you have Bette, you're sadly mistaken. I won't allow her to vegetate in Boston with you."

"But you can't take care of her!" Adrienne said shocked. "You can barely take care of yourself now. She needs a stable home, especially now. You haven't seen her. She's only a baby and she's so depressed. She—"

"She needs me!" Andy interrupted sharply. "Laurie wanted her to be with me! I want her to be with me. You'll never have her, damn it! I won't let you!"

"Andy," Dr. Bartis cut in sharply, "you know that this type of anger is not at all productive. You did what you did when you were a child for your own reasons. Your mother never forced you to be Laurie's protector. You could have allowed her to take any punishment she deserved. It was your choice and yours alone! Don't blame your mother."

"But she was supposed to know. Why didn't she know? She's my mother. I wanted her to think that I was a good girl too. I wanted her to like me . . . to love me. I always dreamed that she would know. I wanted her to know so badly."

Adrienne stood up and went over to Andy. "I'm sorry, Andrea. What more can I say? If I could do the years over, I would. Right now I want you to know that I do love you. I always have and I always will."

Andy's whole body sagged. "I guess I sort of do know that, somewhere in the back of my mind. You'll just have to be patient with me. I'm trying to work things out, I'm really trying to learn how to deal with all this. It's just so hard. I don't know what I'm going to do without Laurie. I'm so lonely for her. I feel so empty without her . . . ."

"But Bette—"

Andy stiffened. "I don't mean that I can't take care of Bette. I can function perfectly well. You'll see. I'll be out of here soon, then you'll see."

"Andrea, I want you to get out of here more than anything in the world." Adrienne hesitated. "I'll tell you what. I'm going to wait. I'll stay in New York for a little while longer. If things work out as you think they will, I won't ask for custody. You know, Bette loves you very much.

She wants to be with you as much as you seem to want to be with her."

Andy sighed with relief. "Things will work out. I promise you they will. And I always keep my promises." She turned to Dr. Bartis. "Are we finished doctor? Please? I don't think I can take anymore. I feel so wrung out and tired. Please?"

"Yes," Dr. Bartis said. "You've had enough for today."

Andy looked at her mother, then she reached over and took the paper bag from the floor. "I guess I am sort of hungry." She started for the door, stopped abruptly and turned around. "Uh, Ma," she said shyly, "Want to keep me company? I don't much care for eating alone." Adrienne smiled, walked over to Andy, and took her outstretched hand.

Dr. Bartis wiped a tear from her eye as she watched the mother and daughter walk out of her office together.

March

The wind whipped noisily through the air, pushing the dull, white clouds rapidly across the leaden, gray skies. An icy rain was falling, and it seemed as though Jack Frost refused to relax his iron grip on the winter-weary city. It had been a hard winter, with a tremendous amount of snow and ice, and Andy felt that the arduous season was a mirror of her own inner turmoil. Her mind repeated over and over again a phrase from a Grateful Dead song, "What a long, hard trip it's been." But the trip was not over yet. Although she had progressed a great deal, she knew that she still had a way to go. But Dr. Bartis had said she was functioning well enough to return to the outside world, and let it go at that.

The taxi pulled up in front of the brownstone. Eric paid the driver and helped Andy out. She shivered slightly and pulled her jacket tightly around herself. As they moved towards the steps, Andy glanced at the ground and spotted a bit of color. She knelt down and brushed the snow from the tiny, purple bud peeking through the earth. "Oh look Eric!" she cried. "A crocus!"

He knelt beside her and protectively put his around around her shoulder. She pressed against him lovingly. "It's true," she said softly. "Life does go on."

Eric smiled sadly, and lifted her to her feet again. "It's cold, Andy, let's go."

She hesitated at the foot of the steps and looked at the spot where Laurie had fallen. Eric clutched her tighter. "Don't think about it, baby," he whispered. "Come on, let's get inside."

She nodded and they climbed up. As soon as they reached the door, Alice, with Tasha in her arms, opened it. She ran to Andy, who grabbed the cat and held her to her bosom. "Oh Tasha, I missed you so much," she whispered as she buried her face in the warm, silky fur.

"I'm so glad you're home, Andy," Alice cried. "It's been so empty here without you."

Andy smiled. "Believe me, it's good to be here." The three walked in and Andy handed the cat to Eric, took off her jacket and went into the living room. Taking Tasha in her arms again, she sat down on the couch and leaned her head back. "It does feel good to be back home," she said with a sigh. "I just wish there weren't so many things on my mind."

"Well, you just sit there and relax," Alice said. "I'll go and fix you a nice cup of tea." She hurried off to the kitchen before Andy could protest.

Eric sat down on the couch next to Andy and took her hand in his. "I've missed you, babe. I've missed being able to be with you whenever I wanted to and being able to talk things over with you."

"I guess my problems have sort of overshadowed your life. I'm sorry."

"There's nothing for you to be sorry about. Your problems are mine now, and I want to be there for you. I guess these past few months have changed my outlook somewhat."

"What do you mean?" she asked cautiously, looking into his deep blue eyes.

"When I thought that you were lost to me forever, I decided that life without love is not worth living. You can't imagine how desolate I was without you. Quite frankly, my reaction surprised me. I always thought of myself as being very selfish—I kind of only wanted to look out for numero uno, you know?"

Andy nodded. "Oh, I know very well," she said with a wry smile.

"I thought that my career was the most important thing in my life," he continued. "I didn't want anything to interfere with my climb to the top. Don't get me wrong, I still want to be a star, but somehow, it's just a little less vital now. Loving you has taken an edge off my ruthlessness. I honestly think that I could be content with a steady job and you."

She touched his cheek. "My sweet Eric," she said. "I love you so. I really don't think I could have made it back this far if it wasn't for you and your support. You were my strength when I had none of my own to fall back on, and I cherish you for that. I couldn't live without you."

He took her in his arms and held her close. "Andy," he whispered fiercely, then he leaned down and kissed her. Their lips met tenderly yet passionately.

The lovers looked so right, so at peace, that the scene caused Alice to pause, smiling, in the doorway, with the tea tray in her hands. Clearing her throat, she stepped in and set the tray down on the table in front of them. "Here's the tea. I baked a nice cinnamon coffee cake this morning and it's still warm." She cut two large slices and put them in front of Eric and Andy. "I insist, Andy. Don't you dare leave a crumb on that plate!" She put her hands over her ears and walked out to the sound of Andy's protestations.

Andy took a sip of her tea and looked at Eric. "As soon as I've rested a bit, I'm going over to Laurie's—" She closed her eyes "—I mean Melissa's apartment, to see Bette. I'm not sure whether I should bring her back here immediately, though."

"Don't worry about that until you see her, then you can make your decision. How does your mother feel about it?"

"She thinks I should wait awhile until I get myself settled. But Melissa tells me that Bette is very unhappy. I was thinking that she might feel better if I take her home with me right away and show her that I love her and that I want her with me."

PROMISES TO KEEP

"Just go see her," Eric urged. "I'm sure it will all fall into place."

She looked at her watch. "Didn't you have a rehearsal this afternoon?"

"Yeah, I do. Getting the lead in *Ruddigore* for the Shakespeare Festival was the best thing that could have happened for us. It'll keep me home all summer with you." He smiled happily.

"Well, then, you'd better get going, it's getting late."

He stood up and brushed the coffee cake crumbs off his pants. "I suppose I should go," he said, "but only if you don't mind. I can cancel if you do."

"No, I don't mind. You'll stay here with me tonight though, right? I don't want to be alone tonight."

"I wouldn't be anywhere else. I'll stay here as long as you want me." He gazed at her for a long time. "I'll see you later, baby. You take care of yourself now."

"I will, don't worry. I love you."

"I love you, too. And it's so good to have you home. I won't be long." He kissed her and left the room.

Alice came back from the kitchen with a piece of paper in her hand. "There were some phone calls for you. I made a list." She held it out to her. "Most of them were business calls, but there were a few personal ones. Adam Ezra called, and he wanted to know when you were getting home. He asked me to have you call him if it was at all possible. He seemed quite anxious to speak to you."

Andy reached for the list. "I'll call him right back." She heaved a heartfelt sigh. "What all this must have done to him."

She glanced at the number and picked up the phone. "Hello, Adam? This is Andy. Yes, I'm home. Now? Well I guess it'll have to be now then. Sure, I'll see you soon. Good-bye." She put down the phone and closed her eyes. The meeting wouldn't be easy.

The doorbell rang and Andy awoke with a start. She hadn't been aware she'd dozed off.

Alice answered the door and led Adam into the living room. He walked over to Andy and sat down next to her. She was shocked by his appearance. He was haggard and pale. Her heart went out to him and she touched his hand lightly. "Hey, Adam, how're you doing?" she asked softly.

"Fair. Somewhat better than I was before. How about you?"

"Just about the same. What's going on?"

"I just came to say good-bye. I'm leaving New York tomorrow."

"Leaving? For good? Where are you going?"

"I'm going back to San Francisco. My father wants to retire soon, and he said that he would like it very much if I would take over his practice."

"Does he do cancer work too?"

"No, he's a family practitioner, but I think I could help him a lot."

"But you had such a bright future here—"

He shook his head. "There's no furture for me

PROMISES TO KEEP

in New York without Laurie. I can't bear to be in that hospital knowing that she'll never be there again. There are just too many memories here for me."

Andy's eyes filled with tears. "Well, I know that whatever you do, you'll be brilliant at it. Have a good life, Adam."

"I'll try, but I don't think I can ever forget her."

Unable to speak, Andy looked at him, pain evident in her face.

"I guess that's all I wanted to say to you," Adam sighed. "You understand that I had to come here before I went home. I hope I didn't disturb you."

"No, Adam, you didn't disturb me at all. I'm very glad you came. Please, call me whenever you want to. I'd like to hear how you're doing."

"I will," he said. "The same goes for you." He kissed her on the cheek and exited the room, leaving Andy alone to think sadly of what might have been.

Andy stood by the door of Laurie's apartment for a moment. The thought of going in unnerved her and she closed her eyes as she rang the doorbell. Almost immediately Melissa opened the door. The two sisters hugged and Melissa took Andy by the hand to lead her inside. Adrienne jumped up from the couch and rushed forward to greet her daughter. "Andy! Oh sweetheart! We've been waiting for you. I was starting to get worried. How do you feel?"

"All right, I guess. Is Bette here?"

"No," Melissa said. "Ma thought that it might be better if we talked without her here for awhile. She's over at her friend's house."

"Is she okay? Does she know I'm coming?"

"No, we didn't tell her. Don't worry, I'll go get her soon."

Andy looked around the apartment. "The place looks different."

Melissa nodded apologetically. "Well, I had to get all my things out of Shep's apartment. It's just that there's a lot of my stuff lying around, that's all."

Andy took a deep breath and walked over to the window. "You know, I remember when we found this place. Laurie was so happy. It was perfect, right near the hospital." She smiled. "She was afraid she couldn't afford to buy it, so I told her I'd give her the money. Of course she refused to take it until I agreed that it would just be a loan. That nut! Every month she insisted on paying me. Like clockwork, on the first, there was her check. She used to get so angry at me when I told her I really didn't want her money. But you know Laurie, always one to carefully discharge her obligations. . . ." She put her hand to her forehead and rubbed it.

Melissa and Adrienne looked at each other. They watched as Andy walked around the apartment caressing things. Melissa went over to her. "Hey, are you okay?"

"Yeah, I'm fine. It's just that being here is a little difficult for me, you know?"

PROMISES TO KEEP

Adrienne sighed. "Have you heard anything about your lawsuit?" she asked tentatively.

Andy looked up. "I heard this morning. The judge refused to issue a restraining order."

"You mean those pictures are definitely going to be published?"

"Yeah, they're going to be published." She shook her head grimly. "Swank Magazine will be showing Andy Reuben in the raw in their June issue. Marty Kantor may have won the round, but I'll win the fight. He's through in this business—I've made sure of it."

"I can't believe they're allowed to invade your privacy like this!"

"Well, Ma, I'm in the public domain. Whatever I do or did belongs to everyone."

"But what about your feelings? Haven't you gone through enough lately?"

"No one cares about me personally. This means bucks, and that's all that counts."

Adrienne shook her head. "That's incredible! I hate the thought of—"

"Just don't look and don't listen. I'm sure it'll all blow over very quickly." She turned to her sister and changed the subject. "Melissa, Fred tells me you and he have been having dinner together quite frequently."

Melissa blushed. "Do you mind?"

"Why should I mind? He's a good man. Enjoy yourself."

"He has some marvelous ideas for the health club," Melissa said enthusiastically.

"Of course he does. Fred loves a challenge.

Listen to him, he'll make you rich. By the way, speaking of business, I'm retiring."

"What? What do you mean?" Adrienne asked.

"I'm not going to be singing anymore. No more records, no more tours, just one more concert. I won't give up my music entirely, though," she continued, "I'll be producing records for various Nickelodean artists and I'll stay a part owner and be on the Board of Directors. That's a lot of work in itself. Probably I'll still write some songs...."

"Won't you miss it?" Melissa asked.

"Quite frankly, I've been thinking about this move for awhile. I really don't like touring and I feel strongly that it's about time for me to change direction. Laurie's death just speeded things up a bit. Besides, Bette needs me here, not running all over the world."

Adrienne touched her shoulder. "Are you sure? This is a big decision and it's still so soon. I hope you won't regret it later on."

"No, I won't regret it. It's the best thing for Bette and me."

Melissa looked at Andy curiously. "What's this last concert?"

"Don't you remember? It's Laurie's birthday present, the concert in Central Park for orphan drugs. I cancelled the cable telecast, but the concert itself is still scheduled for the end of May. I'm going to begin preparing for it right away, you know, rehearsing, staging and the like."

"So soon?" Adrienne said anxiously. "Can you handle it?"

"I don't know, but I sure as hell am going to do

my best. After all, it's my swan song. I want to leave them begging for more."

"I suppose you'll have enough to keep you busy, but will you really be happy?" Adrienne asked gently.

"Happy?" Andy whispered. "Happy? I can't think in terms of happiness now. Let's just say I'm going to try to be content. The fact of the matter is that I just don't want to sing again. I don't have the heart for it."

"I understand, Andrea. Really I do. And I'm sure Bette will be pleased with your decision. She talks about you constantly."

"Does she ever talk about Laurie?"

Adrienne nodded. "Yes, she does. Frequently now. Those sessions she's had with Dr. Bartis have helped immeasurably."

"Good. I was worried. Dr. Bartis told me that she was very depressed when she first came in."

"She still cries at night, but I think she's beginning to accept it and deal with it about as well as a five-year-old can."

"I want to see her. Please, Melissa, can you get her now?"

"Sure. I know she's going to be overjoyed to see you here." She left the apartment.

Adrienne walked over to her daughter and hugged her. "I'm glad she's going to be with you."

"Really?" Andy asked, pleased. "Are you really and truly glad?"

Adrienne smiled. "That's what you used to say when you were a little girl and I would tell you I was happy about something you did. Yes, Andy, I'm really and truly glad. I'm glad you're healthy again, I'm glad Bette will be with you, and I'm glad that you're working out your plans for the future. But most of all, I'm glad that we can be close now. You don't know how long I've wanted to be able to feel close to you. I just never knew how."

Andy walked over to the picture of the three sisters on the bookcase and touched it lightly. "You know, I'm finally realizing that I'm as worthy a person as Laurie was. Dr. Bartis is teaching me that I wasn't the 'bad twin' who always disappointed everyone."

Adrienne went over to her daughter. "And she made me realize that I helped foster those feelings. Believe it or not, I've always been proud of you, Andy. You're the one who most reminds me of myself when I was young. I guess that's why I was so hard on you. Although we'll always miss Laurie, at least now we have each other."

"Oh, Mom, you can't imagine how much that means to me. I'm sorry, I know this has been hard on you."

"It's been hard on both of us, but I want you to remember that you're as dear to my heart as anybody could ever be." They both wept and clung to each other. I'm going home," Adrienne said softly as she pulled away.

"But you'll come back for my concert, won't you?"

"I wouldn't miss it for the world." She turned to the door as Melissa walked it with Bette.

PROMISES TO KEEP

The child stood there for a moment and looked at Andy. Her face lit up with joy as she stopped and stared with disbelief at her aunt. "Andy! Andy! You came!" she cried. "You really came!"

Andy put out her arms and Bette ran into them. "Of course, little one, my precious little one. And I'll never, ever leave you again. I promise." She wept bitterly as she held tightly onto Laurie's legacy.

May

New York City is at it's best in the late spring. The sweetly scented air, the twittering birds and the yellow-green budded trees adorned the streets like an Easter bonnet. Central Park was customarily filled with children, joggers, frisbee players, bicyclists and picnickers escaping the concrete pavements of the workaday city. Today though, hordes of people were singlemindedly moving toward Sheep Meadow, the large open space in the middle of the park. Today was the Final Concert, and the free concert had attracted a record number of Andy Reuben fans from far and wide. A huge stage with two Diamond Vision screens on either side of it was set up at one end of the meadow. Rock music was loudly playing through the large speakers situated at strategic points throughout the field, and the fans sat quietly drinking wine and smoking grass, waiting for the arrival of their beloved Andy. As crewmen finished setting up the instruments, sound men checked out the system and security people took their places.

Andy sat in front of the mirror in her dressing room behind the stage. Her makeup woman was just putting the finishing touches on her still haggard face, and a hairdresser worked on her hair. She had let her perm grow out and had cut her hair short. She was dressed in white linen slacks and a white cotton pullover with soft white kid boots. "How many people are out there, Fred?"

Fred walked over to her. "I don't know. Maybe a half million."

"Are you sure you arranged enough security?"

"I certainly hope so. There are supposed to be around a thousand New York City policemen out there, plus our own men. I would guess that we have about thirteen hundred people keeping an eye on things. Come on now, Andy, take it easy. Don't worry. There'll be bodyguards all around the perimeter of the stage. Nobody will get past them."

Andy put her head in her hands. "Fred, I'm so nervous about this whole thing. It's not just the potential danger of it either. I don't know what it will feel like singing in front of an audience again. It's very hard to get myself up for this."

Fred put his arm around her. "Just let it happen. You don't have to put on a wild show. All they want you to do is sing. Once you get out there, you'll handle it fine."

PROMISES TO KEEP

"I'm not so sure. Did you see Eric out there?"

"Yes. He's with the rest of the band. He's pretty worried about you. He's a nice guy, you know?"

She touched his hand. "I love him Fred. I—"

One of the stage hands poked his head in the door. "Five minutes, Ms. Reuben."

Andy stood up. "Well Fred, this is it. Remember the first time?"

"At that dinky club in the village? How could I forget? You were incredible then, and you'll be incredible this evening. There's never been anyone like you in this business, and there never will be again. You'll be missed, Andy Reuben!"

"Well, I'll probably miss it all, too, but this really is best for me." As she hugged him, she looked up and noticed that his eyes were moist. "Hey," she whispered. "Thank you for putting up with me all these years."

Fred smiled. "It was my pleasure, ma'am. Come on now, let's go." They walked out of the room toward the stage. Fred kissed Andy and said, "I'll see you afterwards. I'll be sitting over with Melissa, Adrienne and Bette. Hey, stop shaking. You're going to be just great!"

She smiled weakly. "Easy for you to say." She took a deep breath and ran up on stage.

A tremendous roar swelled up from the crowd. Andy looked out at the vast sea of faces and briefly turned to look at the band. Eric was standing with her backup singers, and the fact that he was right behind her calmed her a little. She caught his eye and then turned back to the crowd. The band played the intro to "I Sure Do Miss The East" and she picked up her guitar and went right into the song. The audience clapped and screamed every time she mentioned New York City. When she finished she walked to the front of the stage and peered out. "Wow!" she exclaimed. "This is pretty impressive! Did you all meet here by accident or was it planned?" There was loud laughter from the audience. She laughed also, then sat down at the piano and began to sing "You Were My First."

Standing under a tree, far back in the crowd, Philip Koppel watched the Diamond Vision screen as Andy gave her final performance. A flood of memories rushed into his head: *I was your first. I truly was. I'm sorry, Andy, so sorry for what I've done to you.* He took one last look at her face, then left the park and hailed a cab. "Take me down to Bellevue, please," he said as he leaned back and closed his eyes.

Andy's presence filled the meadow as she sang all of her biggest hits. Uncharacteristically, there was very little banter, just an evening of pure music. To the audience's delight, she and Eric sang "The Love We Share," and they rewarded them with deafening applause. The crowd urged her on, but after over three hours of singing, her voice was hoarse, and she held her hands up to try to quiet the audience. She stood there until there was minimal noise.

"As you all probably know, this is my last concert." A loud *"No"* swelled up. She raised her arms again and waited.

PROMISES TO KEEP

"I am donating all the proceeds from the sale of souvenirs tonight to a cause that I've been committed to for a while. The money will be used to fund a foundation for orphan drug research. Our hope is that, from now on, anyone who needs a lifesaving drug, however rare, will find it available. This cause was very important to my sister, and in her memory I am creating the Laurel Debra Rabinowitz Foundation. It will sponsor research dedicated to the needs of the few."

She lowered her head, wiped her eyes and turned around for a few moments. When she had composed herself, she reached back for the book that Eric held in his hand. She turned to the marked page and said, "The last few months have been very difficult for me. I felt as if I were in a deep pit with no possible means of escape. A phrase in a letter that was given to me brought to mind a poem that I had read many years ago. This poem, written by Robert Frost, gave me the strength to look towards a future I didn't think I had. I'd appreciate it if you'd indulge me and allow me to read it to you now. It's called, 'Stopping By The Woods On A Snowy Evening.'" She read through the poem, and when she reached the last stanza her voice softened perceptibly.

> The woods are lovely, dark and deep.
> But I have promises to keep.
> And miles to go before I sleep,
> And miles to go before I sleep.

"I, too, have promises to keep," she said softly. "And miles to go before I sleep. Thank you all for joining me here tonight. Good-bye, everyone." She bent down and picked up some of the items people in the audience had thrown on stage for her, and then, as the stage darkened, she waved, turned and walked slowly off.

Eric caught her as she stumbled off the platform. Adrienne and Bette stood on one side, and Melissa and Fred on the other. They encircled her and hurried her back to the dressing room, ignoring the crush of reporters and photographers. Eric sat her down in a chair and knelt beside her. "You're something else, baby," he murmured tenderly. "All that worrying was for nothing. It was great!"

She half-smiled at him. "Yeah," she said softly. "I think it was." Then she looked at the stuffed Snoopy doll in her arms and held it out to Bette. "Here, little one. Look what someone threw on stage for you."

Bette reached for it and climbed up into Andy's lap. "Andy, I'm hungry," she said. "I want something to eat."

"Good. Just wait a little bit until I get changed and we'll all go out to dinner."

"No, I can't wait. I want a hot dog from one of those men out there."

"Bette!" Andy said sternly. "That's junk and you know we don't eat junk!"

Melissa reached out and took her mother's arm. They looked at each other and smiled. "See, Ma," she whispered, "I told you. They're going to be fine. They're going to be just fine!"

BE SWEPT AWAY ON A TIDE OF PASSION BY LEISURE'S THRILLING HISTORICAL ROMANCES!

2332-6	**STILL GROW THE STARS**	$3.95 US, $4.50 Can
2328-8	**LOVESTORM**	$3.95 US, $4.95 Can
2322-9	**SECRET SPLENDOR**	$3.95 US, $4.50 Can
2311-3	**HARVEST OF DESIRE**	$3.95 US, $4.50 Can
2308-3	**RELUCTANT RAPTURE**	$3.95 US, $4.95 Can
2299-0	**NORTHWARD THE HEART**	$3.95 US, $4.95 Can
2290-7	**RAVEN McCORD**	$3.95 US, $4.50 Can
2280-x	**MOSCOW MISTS**	$3.95 US, $4.50 Can
2266-4	**THE SEVENTH SISTER**	$3.95 US, $4.95 Can
2258-3	**THE CAPTAIN'S LADIES**	$3.75 US, $4.50 Can
2255-9	**RECKLESS HEART**	$3.95 US, $4.95 Can
2216-8	**THE HEART OF THE ROSE**	$3.95 US, $4.95 Can
2205-2	**LEGACY OF HONOR**	$3.95 US, $4.95 Can
2194-3	**THORN OF LOVE**	$3.95 US, $4.95 Can
2184-6	**EMERALD DESIRE**	$3.75 US, $4.50 Can
2173-0	**TENDER FURY**	$3.75 US, $4.50 Can
2141-2	**THE PASSION STONE**	$3.50
2094-7	**DESIRE ON THE DUNES**	$3.50 US, $3.95 Can
2024-6	**FORBIDDEN LOVE**	$3.95

FOR THE FINEST IN CONTEMPORARY WOMEN'S FICTION, FOLLOW LEISURE'S LEAD

2310-5	**PATTERNS**	$3.95 US, $4.50 Can
2304-0	**VENTURES**	$3.50 US, $3.95 Can
2291-5	**GIVERS AND TAKERS**	$3.25 US, $3.75 Can
2279-6	**MARGUERITE TANNER**	3.50 US, 3.95 Can
2268-0	**OPTIONS**	$3.75 US, $4.50 Can
2257-5	**TO LOVE A STRANGER**	$3.75 US, $4.50 Can
2250-8	**FRAGMENTS**	$3.25
2249-4	**THE LOVING SEASON**	$3.50
2230-3	**A PROMISE BROKEN**	$3.25
2227-3	**THE HEART FORGIVES**	$3.75 US, $4.50 Can
2217-6	**THE GLITTER GAME**	$3.75 US, $4.50 Can
2207-9	**PARTINGS**	$3.50 US, $4.25 Can
2196-x	**THE LOVE ARENA**	$3.75 US, $4.50 Can
2155-2	**TOMORROW AND FOREVER**	$2.75
2143-9	**AMERICAN BEAUTY**	$3.50 US, $3.95 Can

Make the Most of Your Leisure Time with
LEISURE BOOKS

Please send me the following titles:

Quantity	Book Number	Price
_____	_____	_____
_____	_____	_____
_____	_____	_____
_____	_____	_____
_____	_____	_____

If out of stock on any of the above titles, please send me the alternate title(s) listed below:

_____	_____	_____
_____	_____	_____
_____	_____	_____

Postage & Handling _____

Total Enclosed $_____

☐ Please send me a free catalog.

NAME_____
(please print)

ADDRESS_____

CITY _____ STATE _____ ZIP_____

Please include $1.00 shipping and handling for the first book ordered and 25¢ for each book thereafter in the same order. All orders are shipped within approximately 4 weeks via postal service book rate. PAYMENT MUST ACCOMPANY ALL ORDERS.*

*Canadian orders must be paid in US dollars payable through a New York banking facility.

Mail coupon to: **Dorchester Publishing Co., Inc.
6 East 39 Street, Suite 900
New York, NY 10016
Att: ORDER DEPT.**